Dragony Rising

By

Michael Stephen Daigle

Copyright © 2022 by Michael Stephen Daigle
ISBN: 978-1-944653-23-1
Publisher: Imzadi Publishing LLC
www.imzadipublishing.com

Cover Art designed for Imzadi Publishing by Anita Dugan-Moore of Cyber-Bytz, www.cyber-bytz.com.

If you would like permission to use material from this book for any reason other than for review purposes, please contact the publisher at: imzadipublishing@outlook.com.

ACKNOWLEDGMENTS

For Terry, Max, Emily, Elana, and Aedan.

A special thanks to the Imzadi Publishing family without whom Frank Nagler would still be stuck in my computer: Janice Grove, Anita Dugan-Moore, and Katherine Tate.

Many thanks to the members of the Phillipsburg, N.J. writer's group and the Greater Lehigh Valley (Pa.) writer's group who patiently listened to many sections of this story and offered thoughtful insight.

This book, and the Frank Nagler series, is dedicated to lifelong friend Virginia Justard, whose support and love all those years ago helped bring Frank Nagler to life, and who passed away in 2019.

TABLE OF CONTENTS

FREE PREVIEW - THE RED HAND

CHAPTER ONE

The yellow kitchen chair

The kitchen chair caught Detective Frank Nagler's attention.

There was something impossible about it, standing as it was untouched.

Downtown Ironton *had* blown up, after all.

And a kitchen chair untouched on the roof of the old theater made no sense to him, but there it was, even as a sizable chunk of downtown Ironton smoldered. Buildings cracked open and collapsed. Stinging smoke and dust rose like a war had started.

Nagler's cop job was to make sense of the unexplained, yet with one foot on the guardrail of the highway above downtown, brow wrinkled as he puzzled at the notion that of all that stretched out before him, of everything he could see or imagine through the sunlight dappled haze – a burning, smoking, dismembered two-block section of downtown Ironton; and beyond that, a hundred hard-hatted searchers, waving and shouting words lost in the growling destructive discord, a brief sparkle of red and blue light flashing off the cracked windows and dusty air; and finally beyond it all, a huddled crowd of onlookers, witnesses to their world collapsing – of all that disorder, he was confounded by the sight of single, undamaged metal kitchen chair with yellow upholstery standing upright on the roof of the old theater a half-block way.

Ironton had been rocked at 5:15 that morning when a section of Warren Street was geysered into the air, stopped, suspended, then collapsed into the rising flames in a shower of broken wooden walls, bricks, windowsills, bed frames and refrigerators and diner counter tops. The time had been recorded by the decorative, antique clock two blocks away whose cracked glass face shielded stopped hands.

1

The ground shook for more than a mile in all directions, and the rumble had roused Nagler from his bed.

"What was that?" Lauren Fox asked shaking her head.

Nagler replied. "Earthquake?" He pulled back a window shade and said, "Jesus, look."

The sky was a dusty, burning red; beyond the fire the eastern hills glowed orange from the sunrise.

Just as Lauren joined Nagler at the window both their phones squawked out the alert: "Explosion and fire. Warren and Blackwell."

"Damn," she said, reaching for the pants and sweater she had tossed to the floor the night before. "Call me later," she yelled over a shoulder as she hopped and tripped into her pants, stumbled into her shoes, and pulled the sweater over her bare back.

"Be safe," he called back as the kitchen door slammed.

He yanked the blinds fully open and absorbed the darkening sky filling with flame-tinged smoke.

Warren and Blackwell, he thought. The center of town. Who died? He wanted to believe it was an accident, but he was too long an investigator to pretend that things happened for no reason.

****

Which is what led him to climb to the highest point near downtown, the new bridge that crossed the river a few hundred feet away, to gain some perspective on the blast scene: What he guessed was an explosive natural gas leak had destroyed that block of Warren Street and the flying debris had damaged neighboring buildings filled with businesses and apartments. Walls between structures had caved in after the explosion and fire. *But what caused the leak?*

The air was so still he could hear the shouts of searchers, the grinding of engines and the thud of debris being dumped in metal truck hoppers.

But there was that single kitchen chair.

"That seems odd," he mused. "Is that even possible?"

"What's odd?" a voice to his left asked.

"That you'd find me here, for one thing," Nagler said to reporter Jimmy Dawson. "Aren't you required to be down there, at the scene, bugging the hell out of someone else? I'm not even supposed to be here."

Dawson lowered his smart phone that he had been using to record video of the scene. "That's why I knew you'd be here. When did you ever follow the rules? Actually, I saw you sneaking around the barriers and figured you'd find the best vantage point."

Nagler waved his hand toward the scene. "So, what have you heard?"

Dawson slipped the phone into a pocket. "Same as you. Guesses. Natural gas, old buildings."

"Look at all the damage, though. That make sense?"

Dawson smiled and shrugged. *Frank's been off the front lines for six months and still understands more than the cops on the beat.* "Makes sense till it doesn't," he muttered.

"What do you think about *that*?" Nagler asked, pointing to the kitchen chair. "How is that even possible? *That* chair, on *that* roof? Not crushed, a perfect four-point landing? Okay, the blast and the fire hollowed out the buildings, but the gas lines would have entered below street level. Even if you filled one of those restaurant cellars with gas, that's what twenty-by ten? Twenty-by-ten what, cubed? Squared? I've been down there. They're damp and moldy, but maybe that doesn't matter..." He glanced again at the chair on the theater roof. "How much force *would* it take to blow a chair a half a block in the air from inside a building?"

Dawson laughed. "I don't know."

"Who would?"

"I know some army explosives experts at Picatinny. Could ask them."

3

Nagler smiled. "You know, Dawson, that sounds like a really good idea. Why don't you do that? Tell me what they say." Sourly, "After I'm reinstated."

Dawson blew out a long breath. "You need to get back to work, Frank. This place *needs* you back to work."

Nagler rolled his head on his shoulders, closed his eyes, and sighed. "I've got one more meeting with the chief, Jimmy. But then I read something, hear something, and I recall their faces and the shots and the screaming. Then I sit in Leonard's and look at the plaques hung over the door..." He squeezed his face shut and glanced at Dawson. "And then I wonder if I want to come back." His voice was as hollow as a bender the day after. "But then I see this..." he nodded to the destruction, "...and I think this is all I know."

Jimmy Dawson looked at the ground and then at Nagler. "Hey, look..."

"No, Jimmy, don't." Nagler stared again at the kitchen chair and coughed. "Now if the blast did not launch the chair into the air where it did a somersault and landed on its feet, why is it there?" He raised his eyebrows and twisted his lips into an odd grimace.

"Got it, Frank." He, too, stared at the chair. "Maybe they wanted a front row seat to the fireworks."

****

Nagler decided that standing at the corner of Blackwell and Warren was like cowering in the bottom of a metal drum while steel balls were tossed in. Motors rumbled and ravenous shovels shrieked. The pounded ground rocked in explosive waves that shivered up his legs while the sound bounced between the aching walls of what remained of the broken buildings, which vibrated like a pitchfork and threw the untuned screech into the trembling air until three blasts of an air horn would bring cries of "Silence!" and "Quiet!!" and the air stood still awaiting again that scratch underground, or a whisper of "help."

He waved at Fire Chief Damien Green, who was standing a couple piles of debris away; Green waved back and yelled through his face shield something Nagler guessed was, "Be careful," and swept his left arm in a vague circle in what Nagler thought was a suggested route across the mess.

Nagler signaled back and moved slowly to his right, his bad left ankle screaming back every time something he stepped on shifted or broke. He would pause, grit his teeth, and reach out a stretched hand to some object for balance. Of all the things that should have healed in the months he was first out on leave and then academy duty he thought it would have been his ankle.

Finally at Green's side, the men shook hands.

The fire chief's face was smoke stained below the outline of his mask. His eyes were pained, pupils collapsed in the center of his brown eyes and surrounded by angry wrinkles the result of a few hours of squinting.

"You back?" Green asked Nagler. He leaned toward Nagler to avoid shouting while searchers on the pile strained to hear any sound..

"Maybe a couple weeks. One more test to see if I'm emotionally stable after watching three of my friends being murdered in public." Nagler coughed out some smoke. "The shrink will say I'm not ready, and the chief will say, well, let him do desk duty for six more months, and I might say, put me back in the field or retire me. I keep walking around the answer."

Nagler considered his reply. He had run out of ways to answer differently the same question.

"Will they retire you?" Green's shocked response.

Nagler sighed. "Not likely. But you know, chief, there's a moment when part of me doesn't give a shit. I think I could walk away tomorrow and take one of three or four offers to head up security at a corporation. God, I'd make three times as much, workdays, holidays off, vacations, and not get shot at."

Green chuckled, his first light mood in hours. "Sounds ideal. If you go, demand they have a fire safety officer on site and I'm your man."

Behind them, a siren blast sounded an all-clear and the grinding and thumping rose again.

Nagler smiled. Green was a good chief, a good man, brave as hell. Nagler recalled how Green had, against all protocol, led a crew into a warehouse fire a few years back when a firefighter got trapped. Lot of finger wagging. But Green said, "We saved her." That's all that mattered.

Nagler nodded toward the debris. "Whatdya think?" He winked. "Unofficially."

Green wiped his mouth and hid a grin.

"Probably gas, a leak.," Green said, voice rising. "We won't know till we get there. Odd … two years ago?" He shrugged, "The gas company … new mains, all new junctions, water heaters and furnaces. Ten blocks. You remember that. Traffic was fucked up all summer."

Nagler nodded. Yeah, way worse than usual.

"Big improvement," Green said. "We had calls about gas smells for years. That mostly ended after the repairs." Green leaned in and placed one hand as a shield on the side of his mouth. "But anything can happen. Pipe gets whacked, someone shifts a water heater … you know, a guy with a wrench thinks he's a plumber … But fill an enclosed space with natural gas, and all it takes is a light switch." Green shook his head. "There's restaurants here – Barry's, right in the middle – a refrigerator kicks on … and you can blow the front off a building."

Nagler hadn't thought. Jesus, Barry's. "Anyone…?"

"Victims?" Green yelled. The noise level dropped. "Not sure." He lowered his voice. "Too early. Still extinguishing hot spots. Haven't found anyone. Shop owners are checking on their employees and social services is trying to find landlords and who lived in the apartments. Another odd thing? Just sold, this whole block from Blackwell to Bassett, and the attached buildings on Blackwell to the theater. Said it might have been the biggest real estate deal in the history of the city. I heard a billion."

"I remember that. You're right. Big, big deal. So probably not arson for profit?"

The tension and weariness of the long night finally landed on Green's shoulders. "Damn it, Frank. Why spend all that money to buy it, just to burn it down? Insurance? Never get all your money back. Makes no sense. On another day, under different circumstances I'd maybe ask who's got something to gain by all this destruction. But today…" He shook his head. "Today, I've got to find out who is buried under that pile of shit."

An airhorn blast announced an all-clear and several loud but unclear shouts echoed down the street. Green's radio garbled out a call. "Frank, gotta go. I'll fill you in later. Unofficially." He turned, then stopped. "Unless the deal went south."

Nagler scanned the chaotic, hazy scene as responders hand crawled over smoking, steaming rubble and pulled away boards and shovels full of brick and dirt and stepped back as a hot spot flared and doused the flames.

He turned back to Blackwell Street, filled with cops in black riot gear, helmeted, faceless, ready for action. Ready for war, more like it, he thought. That response puzzled him. Why aren't they knocking on doors, seeking witnesses? Yeah, it might be an accident. But until the fire marshal declares that finding, our job it to search for clues, facts. He laughed softly. "Right, our job."

He turned when he heard his name called.

"Frank. Hey, Frank."

It was Barry, the diner owner. He was covered with dust. They embraced.

"You're okay?" Nagler asked.

Barry's eyes were red and clenched with worry.

"I can't find Tony," he blurted out. "Can't find him. He was opening up early… his phone don't ring." He ran a hand through his wet, dirty hair. "Fuck, Franky. His wife. He's got two kids…"

Nagler grabbed Barry's shoulders

"Hey, Barry, Hey, man. Slow down. What about the restaurant."

Barry shook his head. "Restaurant's insured, man. Who gives a shit?"

7

"No. I mean. Is there a back way in, off the alley, maybe? Isn't that how you get deliveries? I've been coming there for what thirty years, and I've never seen you get a delivery, so it makes me wonder what it is that you exactly serve…"

Barry breathed deeply and chuckled. "You don't really want to know, Frank."

The mood broke and Barry focused on Nagler's question.

"You know, maybe Tony came in and smelled the gas, and took off before it blowed up. He's a goofy guy, can't sing, but he ain't stupid."

"Good," Nagler said, nodding. "Look, I just talked to the fire chief and so far they haven't found anyone in the wreckage."

Nagler looked past Barry's shoulder and saw an officer he knew.

"Maria," he called out. "Lieutenant Ramirez."

Ramirez slumped and shook her head, and then smiled. She walked over to Nagler and patted his cheek twice, while biting her lower lip.

"Jesus, Frank, good you see you, but you're not…"

"I'm not," he replied with a slight grin. "You never saw me."

Ramirez raised her eyebrows and smiled. "Alright. Okay. Saw who?"

"So, look," Nagler said. "This is Barry, from the diner. You know Barry, right?

Barry nodded. "Four egg omelet, chorizo, pepper jack and about ten shakes of hot sauce. Hey, Lieutenant."

"Hey, Barry. Could use that about now. Can I get it to go?" They all smiled. "Sorry about your place. You okay?" Ramirez glanced at the debris. "A mess."

"He's looking for Tony, his cook," Nagler said.

"Sergeant Hanrahan's heading that up. At the library. It's outside the hot zone." She slapped her hands on her hips. She was smiling. "Damn it, Frank, how'd you get inside the perimeter?"

Nagler ignored the question and waved a hand in the air and shrugged. He, too, was smiling. "Great. So, look, Barry, you find Tony's wife, check with her. I'll go to the library. Call me. You got my number right?" Ramirez started to interrupt; Nagler held up one hand. "Wait a minute. Call Maria, instead. I'm not actually official."

"Right," Barry said, "I forgot. Thanks, Frank, Lieutenant." And then he walked away, placing a call.

"You gotta get out of here, Frank. If command sees you, they'll..."

"I know, they'll bust me. But know what, until just this minute I didn't give a shit. I might have even come down here so they could see me and bust me."

Ramirez placed a gloved hand on Nagler's chest. "Frank, we need you back. Don't think like that. Clear your head, compadre." She patted his cheek twice again, and then walked away.

Nagler watched as Ramirez called out, "Hey. Gather up," and then issued commands to the officers.

He slipped behind a fire truck at Warren and Blackwell, making his way around the hot zone to the library, just to see Hanrahan.

Clusters of onlookers huddled at the curbs, couples tightly embracing, pulling children to their hips, women sobbing into the shoulders of other women; this, he thought, more than sirens and shouted orders, the crashing, and the roar of fire, this is what needs attention.

This is what we do, he thought. What *I* do. Ironton, N.J. Police Detective Frank Nagler. That's who I've been for so long. It's tattooed on my skin. I wear it to work each morning, take it off at night and put it back on the next day. Who would I be without that?

CHAPTER TWO

Not enough dead people

Lauren Fox forced her way through the half-opened door into the lobby of a bank she had commandeered on Blackwell, a block away from the explosion site. Hurried, over-caffeinated and mind filled with details, she had forgotten that entry doors opened outward and had tried to shoulder it open. Instead, she shifted her shoulder bag and box of records she was carrying to her left side, grabbed the handle with three fingers of her right hand and she pulled the door open enough to jam her left foot in the gap, and then turning a half-circle, pushed the door open enough with her foot that she could slither through the opening.

Inside, she exhaled, dropped the shoulder bag with a thump, and kneeling, more gently placed the box next to it, trying not to spill the metal cup of coffee inside the box.

"If getting into the building was that hard, what's day going to be like?" she muttered.

She had taken two calls the first day. One from Calista Knox telling her that Leonard's store would be open all day and night as long as needed, and second from Mayor Jesus Ollivar, telling her to begin planning for the recovery.

She laughed sourly the day before when she had arrived at the bank for the first time. The place had no desks, just computer work-stations atop pedestals anchored to the floor. Alright, she told herself. Nothing will be easy. She had the pedestals ripped out and carpeted the floor with a sixty-four-square-foot tax-map version of downtown Ironton taped to the floor.

The bank manager had protested. "We had volunteered our lobby out of civic responsibility," he chirped, dancing around the room, following Lauren as she gave directions to her staff and the public works crew that were clearing out the space. He stepped in front of her and said, "I must protest. This is not what we agreed to."

Lauren, working on her third day of three hours of sleep a night, and more coffee than any one human could absorb, held up her right hand. She closed her eyes, took a calming breath, and then opened her left eye to a narrow, glaring slit.

"Mr. Jenkins, I thank you for the use of your space, but I'm the city planner and in this declared emergency I can do whatever the hell I want or need to do."

That was surprisingly calm.

She stepped around him, and he slid to stop her. His eyes blazed behind his little round glasses and his lips pulled his mustache over his mouth. "I must consider…"

The calmness deserted her. Lauren put a hand on his shoulder and steered him aside. "Buddy, I got about a minute of patience left and if you have a problem you can call the mayor. I'm sure with two smoking blocks of downtown piled up across the street, he'll be thrilled to hear from a whiny bank manager about how we have disrupted his precious office lobby." She turned to face him. "To which no one will be coming for a while, by the way."

"Well, I'll…" and he walked away.

"Hey, Mr. Civic Responsibility," Lauren called after him, "Drag a couple of those desks from the back offices and put them up against the wall." She smiled. "Thank you." She tipped her head to the right to indicate the spot. Jenkins huffed out a breath and turned to the back of the lobby. "Hey, Marty, give him a hand, huh?"

Failing to suppress a grin, Marty, a public works foreman, patted Jenkins on the back and said, "Mr. Jenkins, let's move some office furniture. Can you help me do that?" He looked back and winked at Lauren. "Don't mind her, she gets better by noon."

Lauren knelt down to one of the maps, markers in hand, bit the corner of her lip, and to herself said, "Ha!"

The stiff shuffling of paper and soft phone conversations took the edge off the silence of the high-ceilinged room with marble floors. The bank was built more than a hundred fifty years ago as a showplace to store the iron money that build Ironton. Its thick brick structure helped it survive a fire in 1883 that wiped out the blocks of wooden buildings on the eastern side of downtown; it was used in that fire as the last line of defense against the raging, advancing inferno. She had placed a brass plaque on the bank a few years ago to mark that event.

Wasn't there something funny about that fire? she asked herself, but then shook away the concern. *Not now.*

The tax maps had already been marked with four black crosses and dates, indicating a spot where a victim had been found.

What if this wasn't an accident, she thought. She shook her head, What are the odds?

Lauren knelt, leaned over the map, and scratched a green cross over a blue-outlined lot and block. Cleared. Then she ran a finger over a long row of papers taped next to the maps until she found the corresponding address and apartment. She marked another green cross.

She leaned back on her folded ankles and shook her head. *I don't get why they've only found four victims.*

"Hey, Marty, look at this list, will you, please?"

Marty pushed the desk he had moved against the side wall and rolled over a chair.

"Whatcha got, boss?"

"Don't call me boss," she said, laughing.

"Yes, Miss Fox, Ms. Fox, Ma'am, Madame planner…"

"Okay, wise guy, just look at this list. Anyone you know on it? Any name you recognize?"

Marty shrugged and scratched his salt-and-pepper beard. He ran a finger down the first page, flipped to the second page and flipped back to the first page. "I see some names of people I might know, but I don't know where they live. Why?"

Lauren screwed up her face and decided to keep her suspicions to herself. "Nothing. Thanks."

"You bet," he said as he turned away. "Boss."

"Ha!" She stared at the map again. "What don't I know?"

Two days after the explosion searchers found the first victim, an eighty-seven-year-old woman, Agnes Canfield. She lived on the second floor above the antique shop and died when the ceiling and roof fell on her.

Lauren examined the maps and nodded when she found the black marker with a date.

A day later, the second and third victims were found two buildings over. Their identities were being researched. Utility records said they were Marita and Juan Hernandez. But an identification card in a wallet in the apartment rubble said his last name was Morales. Their deaths had been recorded on the map, Lauren saw.

On the fourth day, the last victim was found, a twenty-five-year-old cook, Ethan Ricardo, who was called "Rickey," at the Cuban restaurant on the corner of Warren and Blackwell. The initial investigation said the explosion started in the basement of that shop. His death was so marked.

Lauren scanned the list of names and addresses that ran along side of the tax maps. The list held about fifty names: Parents, kids, singles.

"Something's wrong," she muttered as she grabbed a fistful of her brown hair and pulled it up and away from her head. She examined the split ends. "Man, I need a trim." She let her hair go and pushed it away from her face. "Something, something, something…" She stood and glanced through the window and then walked over and drummed the glass with three fingers, thinking. The debris pile loomed, dangerous and dark. She felt her tired body sway in rhythm with the long arm of a crane, a silent dance as the three-inch window glass dampened the sound. Rising, pausing, then slipping to the right, a pirouette to the left, a spin, up again, the jaws of the wide shovel opening then plunging into the pile to emerge with a mouthful of wood, steel, and dirt; then a slower turn and dip. The mouth opened; the debris fell.

She jumped as three knocks on the window grabbed her from the reverie.

Outside was the smiling face of Frank Nagler.

Lauren slapped at the window and smiled. "Scared me to death," she said, knowing he could only see her mouth move.

Inside the bank lobby Nagler wrapped an arm around her shoulder and kissed her hair. "What's all this?"

Lauren unwrapped herself and strode to the tax maps with her fists on her hips.

"This, my dear, is a puzzle and a problem. There's not enough dead people." She cast a side glance toward Nagler, pursed her lips and shook her head slowly. "Where'd they all go?"

"Won't they find them as they dig out the debris?" Nagler asked, wanting to joke about the statement, but pulled back because he saw how serious Lauren was. When she was that serious, he knew, she was right.

She waved her hand over the maps. "Seventeen storefronts, and thirty-four apartments. Okay, the storefronts ... most not open. Five a.m.. But the apartments. Nearly all were occupied, according to the preliminary lists." She turned to Nagler, her face a dark mask. "Where are the people, Frank?" She fell to her knees and ran a finger over the list. With each name she read her voice became darker. "Bob Storm, 13B Blackwell. Anita Fuentes and two kids, 17C Blackwell." A dry, grinding voice, then suddenly damp. "Daniel Castro. Olivia Rodriguez. Joseph Arreneto." She kneeled and placed her hands on the map and then leaned back and shook her hands in frustration, the possibility of her assumption becoming real. "There's no one in that pile, Frank. No one." She threw the marker across the room and covered her face and screamed, "Damn it."

The room fell to a hush as her staff stopped working, peeked over their shoulders, and then heads bent, returned to work.

"What are you saying?"

She rubbed her face with both hands to drive off the fatigue and anger. She stood and waved her hands over the tax maps. "Ghost tenants. Ghost apartment rentals. Empty spaces."

Nagler nodded. He got it.

"The fire chief said the real estate was just sold," he said. "A building filled with actual people is worth more at the sale than empty spaces. So, it's …"

"Fraud. God damn it, stupid fraud."

She laughed softly to dampen her anger. "Remember how we met, Frank?"

He just grinned back. "Old Howie Newton using his office as mayor to line his pockets." He shook his head and stared at the tax map. "All those buildings. Fire chief said that deal was a billion-dollar sale. Could that be right?"

"Jeez," she walked around staring at the tax maps. "I haven't done the math yet." Distracted, calculating: "The whole city has an estimated real estate value of four billion. The whole place, including the empty mills and buildings. Actually, not bad with all the economic ups and downs. But could maybe two blocks of downtown be worth a billion by themselves?"

She tipped her head to one side, closed her eyes, and sighed, playing out the work that was going to be needed to solve this mess. "Not likely. I wonder who owns the place?"

Nagler watched with soft eyes as she walked the perimeter of the maps. All that popped into his head was, "Beautiful." He told her, "You are the most beautiful smart woman I know. Or is it the smartest beautiful woman. I get them confused."

Lauren placed her hands in her hips and offered a weary smile. "Focus, Frank. Focus."

"Yeah, okay." He nodded at the maps, "Can I borrow your map a second?"

"It can't leave the room," she ordered, knowing it was taped to the floor.

"What? Right." Nagler stepped over to the map and asked, "Where's the corner of Warren and Blackwell?"

Lauren scanned the map and then pointed to the spot with her toe.

"There. Why?"

Nagler knelt.

"There was something Jimmy Dawson wrote today about the suspected origin of the blast. There. That's the corner restaurant, where a victim was found. How did the blast wipe out all the other buildings in a straight line?"

He unrolled the copy of the Register that had a blown-up drone photo of the scene with small colored labels over the spots where businesses were located or bodies had been found and held it over the tax maps. The photo was a square with Blackwell on the bottom and Warren to the right. Nagler had earlier turned the photo so that the intersection of the two streets formed a diamond and had made a dot where the two streets met and then drew two lines like foul lines on a baseball field.

"See? Somehow the force of the blast stayed between those two lines. Damage on the east side of Warren across from the blast – broken windows, external wall damage – was done by flying debris, the fire chief had said." He'd folded up the newspaper again. "I don't get it."

Lauren stood next to Nagler and ran her hand through his hair. She had seen this before: The squinched eyes, the focus, the mental probing, Frank withdrawing inside to some place he went when the lock tumblers began to fall into place.

"When do you see the police chief?" she asked. "You're ready, aren't you?"

He stood and embraced her. "I've been walking around this scene for three days, talking myself in and out of it. There's been moments when all that stuff that happened at Leonard's dedication comes back, and I feel shaky. But I see all the questions about something like this, Lauren. That never goes away."

****

On the fourth day after the explosion, the fire chief said as best as could be determined, the blast killed just four people.

Tony Spaso. Nagler felt his face flush. That was a Barry' cook.

His name did not appear as a victim. Barry still hadn't been able to find him, and his worried family didn't know where he was.

Nagler made the leap: And probably a suspect, since it might be determined that he was running. Was that the reason he had not been mentioned in any official report? Nagler pictured Tony at the grill, tapping his spatula, shoulders swaying, mumbling out tunes. "Naw."

He turned back to finish Dawson's story.

"It was like a bomb, man," said transit repair foreman Ralph Aniston, who said he was in the train yard four blocks away, preparing to shift cars for the morning commute. "Really loud. I looked back and the tops of the buildings just went whoosh, junk flying all over and they disappeared in a cloud of dust. I started running that way, you know, just in case I could help."

Like a bomb, huh? Nagler put down the paper. Junk flying everywhere. That yellow kitchen chair, flying through the air and landing upright. The force of the blast let loose up and out. He rubbed his forehead. Had to be more than just gas.

Nagler noted that no one had asked the question that Lauren Fox had asked: Where were all the people?

CHAPTER THREE

You have to get my father out of jail

"Good morning. We're gonna talk about lying. Which I just did because it's afternoon."

No one heard the joke. Detective Frank Nagler leaned back from the microphone snaking up from the podium, shook it once and tapped it a couple more times. It was dead. "Ach," he muttered. "I don't want to deal with this. Not today."

Then he grinned. The weight of uncertainty that had borne him down for the past months had been lifted that morning. This was to be his last academy class.

A month ago, the dead microphone would have soured his mood for the entire class and he would have mumbled through the lesson, slouching over the podium and glancing at his watch as if that would make the time move faster.

Instead, he toggled with switches on the power console and followed the cord to the wall where it was plugged in; know what? he said to himself, after today that is someone else's problem. He hadn't thought that going back to his old job, especially with a pile of downtown still being searched and sifted, would have felt so good.

He had been reassigned to active duty that morning after one last session with the chief and the rent-a-shrink from Ironton General Hospital.

With his balding forehead, thin face and goatee, the man could have been a stand-in for Freud, Nagler had thought. Dr. Phillips Ignatius sat ramrod straight in his chair peering over the top edge of the reports and interview transcripts he held. Chief John Hanson slouched behind his desk while Nagler leaned forward in his chair, elbows on the arms and his head tipped to the left, wondering who called their kid "Phillips?" They had been over this material numerous times. It all related to the day that ex-Ironton Police Commander Jerrold McCann shot four of Nagler's friends at the ceremony dedicating the square near Leonard's bookstore in his honor.

Three of them died, and Leonard was paralyzed by a bullet lodged in his back. It was all part of Tank Garrettson's crime spree that left financial and emotional wreckage across Ironton.

"Were you afraid that day, Detective?" Ignatius asked.

"I was afraid for my friends exposed on the speaking platform and for the innocent bystanders who could have been shot," Nagler replied.

"But were you personally afraid?"

"I can't afford to be afraid. Cautious? Yes. Suspicious? All the time. But not afraid. Fear is paralyzing and could get an officer killed."

"What did you do when the shooting began?"

"I ran toward the spot where the gunman was shooting from."

"You ran toward the gunman."

"That's my job."

"Hmmm," Ignatius replied. "Ah, but then later you were seen at the old swamp in tears and quite emotional."

Nagler recalled he had a different answer in mind, but said, "Friends of mine died. Am I not allowed to mourn? And in answer to your next question, yes, I went back to work, and we closed the case with the arrest of the criminals."

At that point Hanson stood up and thanked Ignatius for his assistance and turned to Nagler and said, "Teach your class this afternoon, Frank. Tomorrow you start looking for the bastard who blew up downtown."

Driving to the police academy after that session, Nagler had chuckled. *Already* looking.

In the days since the explosion, he had walked the perimeter of the site, staring at upper floor windows, climbing to roofs of buildings several blocks away looking for a vantage point, speaking with delivery drivers, the beat cops and even the drunks who lived in the shadow of the train station.

He even went back to the highway bridge and stared at the yellow backed metal kitchen chair still resting in the middle of the old theater roof.

What are you gonna tell me?

****

He squinted into the auditorium to see a couple dozen police academy students scattered across twenty rows of more than a two-hundred seats and, raising his voice, said, "Alright, you all need to move to the front rows cause this thing isn't working. There's twenty of you and more than enough seats in the first seven rows."

His voice had found again that authority. He stood erect on the platform, hands patiently behind his back. Like a teacher, he thought. Yes.

"Man, I just got settled," one student protested.

"Hey, Dempsey," Nagler yelled back. "This isn't junior high school and that wasn't a suggestion. You want to be a cop, you follow orders, even when you don't like them. So move down."

Dempsey laughed and gathered his backpack. "Just like you did, Detective Nagler? Followed all the orders, every one, exactly as they were given." A twittering chuckle drifted across the room as the students relocated.

Nagler smiled and shook his head and rapped on the mic again, just in case it sprang to life. "I earned my defections. And if you pass this class, you'll have the opportunity, too."

The shuffling ceased, and Nagler watched as the class pulled out notebook computers, pads of paper and pens, or stared up at him with blank, but earnest faces.

Ironton had stalled again, coughing and belching smoke like an old jalopy along the highway, the whine of the engine slowing, softly slowing, a clunk, then one more, a sputter, then silence, its heart and life departed in a gassy wheeze.

The Tank Garretson financial mess and murder spree a year ago. And now that downtown explosion. *Two years, I'll bet. The investigation, clean-up, the insurance, rebuilding, owners walking away. I'm supposed to tell these kids there is a future. Well, that's a lie. Probably a good place to start.*

He rapped on the podium to silence the room.

"So, lying. It's at the heart of everything you're going investigate. Here's the idea: That husband you discover standing over the dead body of his wife, in bloody pajamas holding a knife, when asked if he killed his wife, will say, "No."

"Then you notice that it's a kitchen carving knife and he's still holding it in his fist" –Nagler raised his right arm level with his head and balled up his hand – "like this, even though he called the cops an hour before, and it's not how a carving knife would be held and then you notice that the rips in her thin slip and the wounds, all centered on her shoulders and the center of her chest, seem to have been made with a downward stroke. And the husband, whose eyes have no warmth for his dead wife, is a good five inches taller than she is…"

Dempsey yelled out, "You see all that at once? I don't believe it"

That did sound implausible, Nagler knew. "You learn." He looked down the podium. Softly," You get used to it."

That'll never do.

He took a breath and tried a lighter tone. "Okay, look. That's a little unrealistic. He probably wasn't standing there for an hour. Try this. You've heard it before. Cop shows. The simple lie. I didn't kill my wife, officer, I was in Chicago. I don't own a gun. I was on the highway with a flat tire. Check with AAA. I called them; they'll have a record. Blah, blah, blah."

He waved his hand when they chuckled. *Better.*

"That's the difference between life and cop work. In life you can say anything, and most people will believe you. Your friends say, crying, 'Randy, it was horrible. We tried to reach you, but...' And Randy says, 'What a time for my cell phone battery to die...' In cop work, if a wife is killed in Ironton, and the husband is in Chicago, we think that is suspicious. Have to. Spouses make good suspects, often have motive. What's one of the first questions we ask?" He waved off the raised hands. "Did anyone else see you there? And suspicion is the start of the investigation."

Nagler listened as his voice became lighter, less strained. *Better.* He scanned the class and saw a few heads nodding, as if they figured something out, when they were really just guessing.

"And the thing you have to understand about this guy is that he keeps calling you, checking on the investigation and offering information that he thinks would help. Some of it we know and can't tell him we know. But a lot of it is information that we hadn't asked about. Strange visitors, a tip from a friend that his wife was seen with another man in a downtown restaurant and they were very friendly, whispered phone conversations that ended when he entered the room. He seems so eager to tell us this stuff, and it's the eagerness that becomes suspicion on our part."

A student from the back: "So, that trip to Chicago. He's got receipts, right? The airline, taxi, and hotel?"

Nagler nodded. "Right. It's a paper trail. Sure, on the face of it, a paper trail can look convincing. But you can fake a paper trail." *Just like a real estate deal.* Lauren Fox's worried face filled his mind. *Tax records revealed a string of odd deals for those destroyed properties. Not now...* "But then we ask questions and find that our lying husband was sitting in the hotel room alone, not mussing the bed, but buying porn on the in-house cable network, walking in the lobby, buying a drink at the bar, and visiting an ATM machine – all done just to be recorded somewhere – occupying time and space while the blood oozed from the stab wound in his wife's chest. And maybe he called home from the hotel and left a message that recalled the time they were in college and snuck into Wrigley Field to catch the last innings of a Cubs game. So, you lay it out before him and he says, 'See, I was in was in Chicago. I bought a new hat. Here's the receipt. You can see it on the ATM video. See, that's me.' You say, okay, show me the hat, and he says, 'Chicago, the Windy City … blew off and got run over by a cab.'"

Nagler smiled.

"And then you say, of course you were, sir, and then you prove that he killed his wife anyway." He shrugged.

Dempsey yelled out, "How?"

Nagler smiled. "You find the hat. It's a windy day, there is a crowd, a band playing…" He shut his eyes. His shoulders sank with a deep exhale. *That's not right.* "Okay, then you find the old friend who wore the hat to pay off a gambling debt to the guy with the dead wife. And he was walking along the far edge of the crowd. A red fedora." He could see the hat, dipping behind the faces and bodies, the police radio call: "Wrong hat." Nagler stared at the floor a second and coughed. "But that guy didn't know you were killing your wife, and he was into you for twenty grand with no way out, so he didn't ask a lot of questions. In the past it would take months to sort through all that. But today with video cameras everywhere, gets a little easier."

"How so?" Dempsey asked.

Nagler rolled his hand over. *The first company sells the property to the second company for a few thousand bucks. That company resells it. A couple months later, another company sells it. The paper never catches up. We never catch up.*

Dempsey asked again. "Detective? How so?'

Nagler blinked and wiped his forehead. *What the hell?* "Sorry, like this. United flies to Chicago from Newark. If you drove yourself, there's a parking receipt and video of you getting on the shuttle. If you took a cab, there's a video of you getting out of the cab at the gate, probably stiffing the cabbie. Then there's security check-in video and the general video of the concourse and the ticket counter and the flight gate. Man, you can't be in an airport unobserved. In the end, we add one and one a couple of times and say to the guy, you can't tell us you were never here."

He paused and watched a few heads nod. *None of those buildings had video cameras back then. That's why we didn't see the shooter. Until he shot.* "Then there's the weapon, and time of death. The guy will try something to disguise it, so he could claim he came back from his business trip, and lo and behold, his dear wife without a single enemy in the world, living in a gated housing development, inside a house with triple locks and an armed security system, had been murdered. Then Walter Mulligan, our medical examiner, will take her body to his secret lab and find that she died twenty-seven hours before the man claimed he was in Chicago, stabbed by a lefty using a thin-bladed Japanese kitchen knife whose entry was achieved with a slight right-hand twist. And you are, sir, a lefty, are you not?"

A young woman in the front row said, "But that's not the lie, is it? The paper trail is not the lie."

Nagler grimaced and nodded his head; he was sweating. *No, the lie is the lie, told again and again. Look there. No here. Where are you, Frank?* He gripped the podium so hard it began to shake. *Calista was at the podium. The first shot split the wood. I didn't see it, just heard it. Get this done.*

"What is the lie?" he asked her, briefly centered by her questions.

She squinted and screwed up her mouth.

"It's the way he tells it," she said. "His voice is too steady, the speech rehearsed, repeated without anguish. He doesn't pause, cough, or feel a catch his throat. He doesn't cry. He stands too erect or sits too still."

"Exactly," Nagler said. *Just like me.* "He's boiling inside. Squinting, shallow breaths. What's your name?"

"Mahala Dixon. I'm probationary in Boonton."

"Okay, Miss Dixon is right. It's not just the paper trail. That can be manufactured and the story rehearsed, and it's not to say that it is not a lie, but it can be dismantled with some work. In a personal murder such as this made-up case, it's the personal aspects that are the center of the lie. How many of you ever had a sibling, parent or close fiend die suddenly? Not killed, but died, heart attack, car crash, whatever. Think about how you felt. It ripped right through you. Did you try to hide the grief and sorrow? Try to be brave?" A few heads nodded. "But you sat hard, leaning against a wall or chair, or fell to the ground. Cried, screamed. Ran outside trying to get out of the way. Stared into the heavens." Nagler's voice caught, the words a dry scrape in his throat, and he felt the hollow in his soul open again. *Stop it! This is just a class, damn it.* But they are all there, always. And the gun shots, the running, the blood... And the never-ending sorrow that hangs on his heart. All the voices screaming at once. Shots fired! Get down! *Oh, no. Bobby, Leonard...*then running, terrified kids and mothers. Out of the way! The odor of gunpowder thick as flies in the narrow hallway, McCann's crumpled body, blood pooling on the floor, spattered on the wall...wanting to feel pity or relief, but just the boiling anger... Not even Lauren's warm hand in his as they stood over the clustered graves at Locust Street Cemetery could...Martha, Del and Dominick, the black hearse carrying Bobby's casket to the airport for the last trip home... the rustle of dry leaves blown along the driveway ... *This is all the stuff I buried, right from the start. From the moment I stood up from Martha's grave. That's the lie. My face to the world is the lie.*

"Detective? Detective Nagler?"

It was Mahala Dixon.

"Are you alright, sir? You stopped talking and stared into the distance..."

"Yes," he said. Then, a whisper, "No."

Nagler threw his shoulders back and blinked once or twice. He coughed. "Thanks. Class dismissed. Lieutenant Wilson is taking over on Tuesday."

Nagler leaned his elbows on the podium, covered his face and sighed into his hands.

The shuffling ceased; the room deadened in silence.

Nagler pushed away from the podium.

"Miss Dixon..."

"I know all about you, sir," she said. "Your career. Charlie Adams, the death of your wife, Martha. Tom Miller and Harriet Waddley-Jones, then the whole Tank Garrettson case. That's why I took this class. I wanted to learn from you."

Nagler squinted at her a moment with a puzzled look and felt the history of his career wash over head. *Should I be concerned?*

"I'm – I'm flattered, Miss Dixon, but I'm just a cop, doing a job." He blinked rapidly and rubbed his jaw, sweating. He felt himself pull back, spinning, disconnected, as if standing alone in a detached haze.

"It's more than that, sir," she said, standing her ground. "It's about helping people. I saw that, saw you do it." She hesitated. "It's about things like this," and she held out a folder wrapped in several elastics; the top right corner of the smudged folder was worn soft from repeated openings. "This is my father's case. He's been in jail since I was a baby for a crime he didn't commit. Fifteen years. Maybe you can help. His name is Carlton Dixon."

Her words rattled of his brain like bones. He wanted his feet to move, but they wouldn't. He shuffled up his notes and turned to leave. He held up one hand and pushed at the air, each movement quicker than the last, until he stopped. "Could we do this later?" His voice was weak and hollow; he needed the chorus in his head to stop shouting. "Please... later."

This always happens. A father, an uncle, brother, sister, wife... How to say no, politely.

"No. It's been fifteen years." She stepped forward. "I'm sorry. This might be a bad time, seeing that you might be sick, but I've had to take no for an answer for too long. Just read the file, please," Dixon demanded. Her face folded shut, eyes clenched, leaking tears, mouth, lipless, a line. "He's my father...sir."

Her insistence calmed him. He reached for the file, his voice a whisper: "Okay, no promises."

There was no relief in her eyes as she said, "Thanks." Just fire. She held his stare. A wrinkle of pain; then sorrow. "There is more here than meets the eye."

She turned and her heels slapped across the floor; the echo of the door banging shut slapped away the silence, then faded.

Don't close your eyes. He had said it a hundred times.

Don't close your eyes and the wooden podium on the stage in front of Leonard's store does not shatter. There is no screaming crowd. No running and diving. Bodies do not fall hurt and bleeding. The banner draped on the stage does not open with rips caused by bullets fired from a block away. Sirens do not wail, and hearts do not break, and people do not die.

If you don't close your eyes.

Nagler covered his mouth with his hands and sighed, then wrapped his arms around his chest to stop the shaking.

You're in a classroom at the police academy. Teaching. There are no shots, no blood. Just students.

****

"I'm okay," Nagler had told Police Chief John Hanson that morning during the meeting when he was reinstated. "Let me teach this last class, and I'll find the mad bomber." Nagler had laughed, and even the chief had smiled. "Counting on you, Frank. If it gets to be too much…"

"Hey, it's just the job. Ask questions, wait for the lies."

The last thing Dr. Phillips Ignatius said was, "When the memories return, call me."

CHAPTER FOUR

2006

Nagler pulled on the first rubber band wrapping the file.

It broke.

Half of it stuck to the paper and half peeled off in his hand.

He thumbed the pages, maybe thirty.

Lauren pushed into the kitchen, dropped her briefcase to the floor and slumped into a chair. "You need to save me from this. How could one small city create so much useless paperwork?" She reached for his beer and emptied it. "I called Danny Yang back in. I need him."

"Isn't he now a full professor at the university? Does he want to do this?"

Lauren laughed. "For what I'm paying him? Yeah, he'll do it. He asked me what took so long to call him. He said he had created some new forensic software that would speed up the data search. He was going to offer to let me use it, but I said," she took on a mock innocent voice, 'But Danny, computer software is so complicated.' So, he's coming in. He's still certified as a reserve officer. You know that?"

"Good for him." He learned back in the chair at smiled at Lauren. "How could he resist your charm?" The long hours had settled under her eyes and there seemed to be a developing crease across her forehead. "Get some sleep, kid."

She pushed away from the table and shook the empty beer bottle side to side. "Want another?"

He shook his head. "No. I just want to flip through this stuff and go to bed. Big day tomorrow. Back on duty."

"You ready. You sure?"

He reached for her with a distressed look, and she stepped to him and hugged his head. "Oh, Frank," she said, her voice with a worried edge.

"I think I'm ready, but today at class I sort of lost it, rambling about some phony case about a guy who stabbed his wife and goes to Chicago and something about TV cop shows..." He grabbed his head with both hands and sighed. "I just couldn't stop it."

She took his head in her hands, leaned her forehead on his and then stared into his eyes. "I need you to be Frank Nagler, Frank Nagler. I can do my part, but the chief wouldn't want you back unless he needed you. There is something really dirty about this mess. Even dirtier than we thought, something no one is talking about. So look, I've got your back. I need you to have mine."

He kissed her mouth like it was for the first time, sampling her freshness, inhaling her taste, tongues probing, giving, taking, until all that mattered was that shared moment, that shared breath.

She kissed his neck. "Oh, Franky. Remember where we left off." She winked and stood. "I have to be there at six." She flipped over the files on the table. "What this?"

"Some kid gave it to me, a student. A case about her father."

"You're not..."

"Made no promises."

"Right. How are you going to find the time?"

****

He pulled out the file and removed the paper clips. It was a collection of photographs, newspaper clippings from 2006, a couple letters and a dozen pages of what appeared to be copies of dingy police reports. They were stained as if water soaked at some point; some pages were fused at their dark corners, and he tried not to tear them apart as he folded them open.

He held up one of the loose pages to the kitchen light and said, "Man, this isn't going to work." He tried another page and found the same result: The old printing ink had faded into the yellowing pages, leaving smears of symbols between a few visible words.

All the copied pages in the file were in the same condition. He dropped them on the table, frustrated. The real paper files might be in storage in Newark. "But I thought we paid to have those old files digitized?" *Or maybe not. Or maybe they started with the most recent ones. I don't know. I don't want to drive to Newark.*

He retrieved a legal pad and a pen, and held each page up to the light and recorded the few words he could make out: Drug gang; Carlton; Blackwell; Sgt. Montgomery…; $1200(blur); Smith & Wesson; *Was that a number?* Injured; white Ford van; four dead.

Montgomery. Has to be Jeff Montgomery, Nagler guessed. Retired a few years back. *Wonder if he's still in Ironton? Probably in Florida.*

He circled Montgomery's name on the pad, and then tapped the point into the paper while he tried to remember Sergeant Jeff Montgomery. Was he drug task force? I know Chris Foley was, for a while. Montgomery? Nagler shrugged. "Could be."

He expelled a long breath. Foley. Nagler's first partner, now nearly thirty years ago. Sniveling, power-hungry little twerp. Still in jail and would be for the rest of his life. His murder convictions were upheld and for good measure they slapped on an additional ten years for conspiracy for his turn at revenge for using his cousin Tommy Miller to kill those college women, wreck Leonard's store and burn down the community center. All to get back at me.

How do I make such friends?

He turned back to the file and examined the photographs.

There were two mug shots: James Pursel, 17; Rachel Pursel, also 17; and a photo box with a question mark over the name Rodney McCarroll, no age. Why no photo of Carlton Dixon?

The Pursels, brother and sister? Twins?

McCarroll? Not a clue.

31

Many of the photos were from five newspaper accounts of police action. A fire, what appeared to be a car crash and several shots of people with their heads down and handcuffed being led from a factory or something, probably the arrest of the gang. The captions listed the names of those in the mug shots. One story was about a shooting, it seemed. The printing wasn't clear, and the three paragraphs of the story on that page didn't give names or an address but did say that four people had died. Maybe a warehouse? He guessed from the blurry photo.

He leaned back and folded his hands behind his head. Ain't much here. "That's not an accident," he muttered. "Where's the rest of it?"

The words "Dragon Alliance" had been circled in one story. He pawed through the other papers to see if that name had been repeated elsewhere. It hadn't. He wrote it on his legal pad with a question mark.

The four suspects were charged with possession and distribution of cocaine and heroin, speed, and marijuana. All the amounts listed were sufficient to kick the charges into a felony category.

He glanced again at the mug shots. Kids, really, all but McCarroll. Who ran the gang? Nagler knew enough stories about street kids who started selling at fourteen and fifteen, then moved up the food chain with their own crew of street sellers. That's probably the Pursels, who each were sentenced to five years. Carlton Dixon got 30 and McCarroll, life. Mahala Dixon said her father is in jail. So, who got killed in the shooting, and why?

That's a lot of dead people for only five newspaper stories, Nagler thought.

Even back then, before the Internet turned every sidewalk-spitting incident into a major news story, four drug-related deaths would have warranted a series of stories about the victims, the suspects, the drug trafficking. Coke, heroin, pot, speed. Stories with police officials and politicians decrying the increase in violence, drug use, oh, where has society failed, and so on.

But the file had only five stories.

Who wrote them?

Four were by Adam Kalinsky, somewhat of a local newspaper legend at the time.

And the fifth was by Jimmy Dawson, a newbie then, Nagler laughed, and now a legendary pain in my ass.

But at least he's alive.

Kalinsky, Nagler recalled, had been killed in a horrific traffic accident on the state highway. It was January; could not recall the year. Heavy snowstorm, icy roads, a gasoline truck ahead of Kalinsky trying to avoid a sedan that had snowplowed into the concrete median, bounced off, and careened in front of the truck. The truck rolled over as it jackknifed and Kalinsky's car, traveling right behind the truck, could not stop in time and plowed into the truck just as all three vehicles exploded.

As he recalled that accident, Nagler, who had not been assigned to it because he was finishing up something else, remembered he spoke casually with the investigators simply because of the horrific nature of the crash. He remembered that one of detectives thought there was something odd about it, details that didn't quite make sense for what seemed to be a bad, but sadly, somewhat common occurrence, a fatal car crash. Even more odd, he thought: The story didn't say what kind car Kalinsky was driving.

Nagler stared out the kitchen window into the darkness, then shook his head.

Oh, I don't know.

He wrote "Kalinsky crash" on his legal pad.

He slumped into his chair and draped his right arm over his head and yawned.

He gathered the papers, tapped them into order and placed them into the folder.

Then he stared at the folder with the stingy rubber band still embedded.

"Not enough."

****

The park glowed in sunset, the deep yellow sunlight hovering on the top floors of the west-facing homes across the road, the trees with golden crests, fading to red silhouettes and then black hollows against the gray of the warehouse beyond.

Late summer, Nagler thought, the last burst of warm light, the world all orange and yellow, fading too soon to a dull brown, then an icy crystal blue-white, the sky absent of birdsongs.

That's what's missing, he thought as he stepped into the gazebo shell. No kids screaming and yelling as they chased the ball around the park benches and trees. No mothers telling Juan to stop pushing. No bursts of music from a passing car.

The park, like the city itself after the explosion, had settled into a shocked silence, buried under the weight of loss.

He reached down to brush away a layer of dust on the bench, but it was more like a thin coating of mud. Even here, he thought. The park was eight blocks from the explosion site, but dust – cement, wall plaster, dirt, fine grains of wood, all the pieces of those buildings and lives – had been carried to the park where it had hardened after a morning dew or rain shower. He ran a fingernail across the coating and realized it wouldn't be removed easily. Instead, he leaned against one of the supports, and waited for Jimmy Dawson.

He smiled when as he scanned the park and focused for a moment on the playground equipment. "There's more here than meets the eye," Lauren Fox had said in her note before he realized she was speaking about the box with all the clues about the Howie Newton fraud case she had buried under the swing set.

That was something, he thought. Broke that case wide open.

But the words came back to him in a different voice. Mahala Dixon had said exactly that at the police academy when she forced her father's file into his hands.

"Guess we'll find out, won't we?"

Jimmy Dawson finally arrived. Nagler had said to meet at the gazebo in the park. They'd normally meet a Barry's downtown, but it was buried under a pile of rubble and Leonard's was too crowded now that

Barry had taken up the offer to operate out of there, cramming his diner crowd into the bookstore's tiny coffee shop.

The reporter slipped into the gazebo seat alongside Nagler, grinned an embarrassed smile and waved one hand in the air.

"Sorry, the cloud server we use for website back-up got hacked. Some ransomware thing. You know those? Pay thousands or you lose your data?"

Nagler's face was a blank.

"You don't know what I'm talking about, do you?" Dawson laughed. "That's alright. Until it happened I had never heard of it either."

"What did you do?"

"The company that owns the server farm shut down the attack. Lucky for us. Can you believe it? Three years ago, I had no idea how to operate a website, and here I am getting attacked over the Internet by some Russian secret agent."

Dawson watched the concern settle again into Nagler's face, saw the light in his eyes darken. That was his working face, Dawson knew. Bland, almost withdrawn, eyes dark and his teeth working on a corner of his lower lip; it seemed to Dawson the first time he saw that face, that Nagler was disinterested, not paying any attention, when it was actually a way to slow down the information in front of him, recording it, sifting it, storing it.

"So, look," Dawson began. "I went to the library to paw through the paper files for Carlton Dixon stuff and didn't find much. You were right. Seems awfully thin for what at the time was a big case."

"You covered the sentencing," Nagler said. "Your story was, shall we say, lacking in your usual detail. If I was running this case, I might think that someone was hiding something," Nagler said. "I'll bet the Pursels testified against Dixon and McCarroll and got a lighter sentence as a result. But I don't get the lack of coverage, or the weak statements made in your stories by the mayor and cops at the time. What'd I miss?"

"Better question," Dawson said. "What did we all miss, and why."

"Bigger question," Nagler said, "Where are the Pursels? Sentenced for five years. I'll bet they did three, and then what? Back to the drug life, or got the hell out of here?" He exhaled deeply. "Or dead. The department's files are a mess or missing. Someone was undercover, but I'm not sure who. Maybe McCarroll since there are no photos of him."

"I was thinking about that myself while searching the newspaper archives and library files," Dawson said. "Just not a lot there, and nothing to indicate why it was missing. I cross checked some listing, but just nothing. I was still sort of new to metro, remember. When I first met you I had just come over from sports. I know at that time the local owner had unloaded the paper to a corporation, big national chain with a reputation for cost-cutting. The corporation had changed general managers and editors, and we all were feeling a little shaky. I just remember trying to stay out of the line of fire. But you're right. It was like no one wanted to talk about that case."

Nagler nodded. "I remember that. The whole paper changed." He rolled his eyes. "Why didn't Adam Kalinsky cover the sentencing?"

Dawson rubbed his forehead and then brushed his hair back. "He skipped out for some reason. He did that all the time. He'd write three or four stories on a subject – big stories, top of page one Sunday stories, and then hand off his notes to someone like me, a relative rookie, and disappear. He was the star of the paper. We all were waiting for him to announce he was heading to The Times or the Wall Street Journal or was leaving to write a book. But none of that happened and we all began to think he was something of a phony."

Nagler wrinkled up his face.

"What?" Dawson asked.

"I'm just trying to figure out what to do with Mahala Dixon's file about her father. On paper it looks straightforward, but it doesn't feel that way," Nagler replied. "But it all happened so long ago … I don't know." He sighed. "I mostly get the feeling that someone doesn't want us to know."

"Yeah," Dawson said. "And that just pisses you off, doesn't it?"

Nagler stared at Dawson a moment with half-closed eyes. He nodded. "Yes. It does."

A silence fell over the park. The traffic at the corner signal stalled, the playground empty, the wind stilled.

Dawson hunched in his seat and held his head with his hands while he settled his elbows into his thighs. "You...?"

"I'm fine," Nagler said. "I'm gonna charge you a buck every time you ask."

"I, um, didn't ask."

Nagler closed his eyes, shook his head, and smiled. "You were gonna."

"Yeah." Dawson learned back. He glanced at Nagler. "I heard about the academy class. There's kind of a buzz about it. Haven't seen it, but I heard there was a shaky video on the Internet."

Nagler sat up, shook his head twice, then several more short, rapid shakes. "I'm sure there is. It was really nothing. I was trying to make up an odd and broad example of a case and it just got away from me. I'll bet old Dr. Phillips Ignatius has an opinion." He stared into the street. "I'm not like that when I'm working. I stay focused. All the bad stuff mixes with all the business and the good stuff and that seems normal. I hadn't been away from work that long in years. I just could not pull it back together once I lost control of the discussion. I could feel myself losing it." He bit his lip, stared first at the ground, and then at Dawson. "I'm not sure I had ever been that scared in a situation that was not life-threatening." He reached over and slapped Dawson's back. "So, Kaminsky. Died in that car crash."

Dawson looked back, tongue in cheek. "Yeah, okay, Frank. So, yeah, Kaminsky. A real mess," Dawson said. "He wasn't at the paper then. Left for some political PR job. And then left that," Dawson said. "Someone said he was researching a freelance piece on drug trafficking."

"Drinking?"

Dawson rolled his head back and forth. "Heard it might have been drugs. He didn't leave a lot of friends at the paper."

Nagler glanced at Dawson with one eye closed. "I know by reputation he worked stories hard. Maybe got too close? So, could he have been high that night he slammed into that gas truck? Might account for why the officer at the scene recorded that Kaminsky's car left no signs of braking in the snow. He probably would have fish-tailed or tried to turn and hit the truck sideways. Report said his car barreled straight into the side of the truck and got pinned. Think he was into something else?"

"He was no angel. But I know he had friends in the police department. Maybe they covered something up."

Nagler laughed. "In Ironton's police department? I'm shocked."

"Hard to believe, huh?" Dawson grinned. Then seriously, "Probably they were Kaminsky's sources, didn't want anyone to follow him back to them."

"Makes sense, Jimmy." Nagler closed his eyes. That thought just opened up the whole Mahala Dixon quest for truth about her father in a new direction. *Oh, man. Now I gotta do it.* "You hear from your army bomb experts yet?"

Dawson waved a hand and his face closed in. "Naw. Which means they know more than they will say in public. They're federal. They'll study the debris and in a year or so issue a report that no one will see. Unless they get pushed."

Nagler surveyed the park and the streets beyond. "That means they haven't been called into a possible criminal probe of this explosion. So, they're fact-finding. That sort of doesn't make any sense does it? They hang at the edges of every big case, sometimes force their way in. And now someone blew up a couple blocks of Ironton and they don't care?"

Dawson pursed his lips and rocked back and forth a couple times. "Time to push, huh, Frank."

"Hey, do me a favor," Nagler said, as Dawson stepped away. "If while you are investigating this mess, let me know if you come across the name Dragon Alliance."

"And why would I investigate that mess?"

"Why wouldn't you?"

CHAPTER FIVE

So, who'd want to blow up Ironton?

"I thought you'd have this solved by now."

Lieutenant Maria Ramirez pushed her chair back from the bank of four computer screens and swiveled to the voice.

"Well, if it ain't the great Frank Nagler," Ramirez laughed. "I didn't hear you and your calvary ride in. Where'd you tie up the horses?"

She leaned back in her chair and stared into Nagler's face like she had done a hundred times before. "You in there, Frank?"

He nodded a few times. "Yeah. I'm here. Whatcha got?"

She reached up and patted his cheek twice. "Strap in, pal. This one is a mess."

He touched his cheek. "I missed that, you know," he said.

"I'll bet you did. Who else is gonna be that good to you, well, besides Lauren?" She rolled her chair sideways and dragged over. "Sit. You're gonna want to see this."

As he sat Nagler asked, "Why didn't they make you a captain while I was gone? There was a slot open."

"We talkin' about the same city here, Frank? Ironton, New Jersey?" She shook her head and ran her hands over her short red hair. "Don't mean to sound bitter, but they gave it to Thomas Romano, their last white hope."

"Romano? He's an administrator. Never led a squad or an investigation that I can recall. Would it have helped if I'd been here?"

39

Maria shifted in her seat. "Not sure, but thanks. It's mostly that this department ain't ready for a Latina lesbian captain." She turned back to the computer bank. "Let me catch you up."

She jostled the mouse to call the screens back to life. Each screen had six separate camera feeds. "Look at this." She positioned the arrow over a screen and tapped the mouse. "Three, two, one. Bang."

The screen filled with a blast of black-and-white debris that flowed and swirled on the screen for three to four minutes, a solid grey blot until it lightened and became a gray cloud of dust.

Nagler had flinched at the initial blast, and then grinned. "You'd think I'd be used to watching files like that. Where was that camera?"

"A bank at the corner of Warren and Blackwell, across from the block that blew up. You should have seen it the first time we pulled up the footage. Twenty-four screens at once. Twenty-four separate cameras. We all jumped. Shit, Frank. You could feel the power of that blast just by watching. I have a tech sequencing the cameras by time stamp so that we might be able to watch the progress of the explosion."

"They all show as a much as that one?"

Ramirez waved her had a couple of times at the screen bank. "No. Some, the closest cameras, only caught a second or two before they were destroyed. Some like that one from the bank, have a couple minutes. It's mounted on the wall inside a screened box. It recorded until something smashed the screen. But we have some traffic cams from a block or so away that have the whole event, and there's one shot from a car dealer up on the highway that sort of has an overview." She leaned back in her chair a stretched her neck and sighed. "With all this, we still don't have a clear view of what happened."

"When will it be done?"

"Ramone says about a week."

Nagler stared at the screen running a loop of the explosion. An empty street, then a cloud of grey, dark flashes of things, splinters, stones, the lens overwhelmed, static; then an empty street, debris flying, static. He shook his head to break the entrancing spell of the action.

"Anything solid on the cause?" he asked.

Ramirez pushed out of her chair and crossed with a limp to a table covered with photos and maps. It was then that Nagler noticed she was wearing a walking boot.

"When'd that happen? And what it is?"

She glanced at her booted right foot. "Lovely, huh? Goes with my uni, matching gray," she huffed in disgust and then leaned over a table and lifted her foot to lessen the pressure. "High ankle sprain. Someone moved a flag on the pile, and I stepped in a hole."

"Accident, huh,. Those piles can be dangerous. Who was the commander?"

"Why?"

"Because you're the most careful cop I know. Even without a flag, you you'd never step in a hole. You'd see it first."

She leaned over the table and rested her chin in her hands. "Might have been just tired," she said, her voice wispy with fatigue. "Had been out there sixteen hours."

"Eh, still." Nagler passed his eyes over the series of photos laid across the table.

"It was Bernie Langdon."

He spun his head toward Ramirez. "Langdon? From the evidence division? What was …"

"It was all hands on deck, Frank."

"Yeah, but Langdon? Who put him in charge of a scene?"

"He's a captain. At that moment he was the highest-ranking officer on the block. I heard later that he flashed his badge at some volunteer fire brigade commander and pulled rank."

Langdon, Nagler thought. A few years back he had been nabbed for stealing drug money from the evidence safe, but someone pulled strings and he never lost rank, just the chance for promotion. When *was* that?

He pointed at the corner of Blackwell and Warren in one of the photos.

"This was where it started, right?"

Ramirez pushed herself up and hobbled to a corner of the table. "That's the theory. Gas. Then this blew up." She ran her finger across the photo that showed the rubble pile. "This is Barry's, right in the middle," she said pointing. "And this is the dress shop. One after the other."

"Ah, you don't believe that, do you?" He jabbed his finger at each of the spots that marked a store. "Here, then here, then here. They would all have to fill with gas in succession, wouldn't they? Did someone actually move from place to place, through I'm guessing, solid walls, to open a gas line in each of those cellars? There wouldn't be adjoining doors, right? And wouldn't that be more than a little dangerous?"

"There *is* a service alley." Ramirez ran a finger down a line on the photos. "About here. Back doors."

"Yeah, but Maria, did someone bust open all those doors? I read they are saying the explosion started in the Cuban restaurant at the corner of Blackwell and Warren, hmm?" He pointed. "Here." He shook his head and jammed his fists on his hips. "That's not right, but no one saying different, are they?"

"Hey, get me a chair." Nagler rolled one over, and Ramirez sat. "One little gas leak in one restaurant would not bring down a whole block. Tons upon tons of material. Had to be something else."

His face opened into a goofy smile. That was the Maria Ramirez he missed. Disruptive, questioning, not someone who puts up with a lot of bull shit. "Like what?"

"What are you smiling at? It's my foot, not my brain. Why not ammonium nitrate? Fertilizer. The Tim McVeigh special. It's cheap, plentiful, even with the federal restrictions in place after Oklahoma City. It's for sale in the county." She pushed aside a couple photos and pulled out a list which she handed to him.

"So, limpy, who would want to blow up Ironton?"

She stood. "That, my friend, is your department." She tapped his cheek twice. "Now get out of here and find out."

"In a minute. Any of the cameras catch someone at the scene prior to the explosion?"

"Not yet. The city traffic cams showed just regular middle-of-the night traffic, and the private security companies are giving us a hard time about footage stored from the previous week. It was 5 a.m. Most restaurant deliveries hadn't started yet."

Nagler frowned. "This doesn't seem like something the bomber would have done in one day, just that morning. Takes planning and equipment and, probably, help. Could have been setting this up for months."

"Whatdya mean?"

"We need to find out how long it would take a cellar space to fill with gas if say a line to a furnace was unhooked. Hours? Seems to me that everything else would have to be in place, and then you'd open the gas lines, maybe the night before. Wouldn't the residents smell gas and call us?"

"That's one more issue. We're having trouble find tenants."

"Yeah, so is Lauren."

"What?"

"Tell you later. Could you pull up the shots from the car dealer?"

Ramirez shifted the files on the screen. "Why this one?"

The camera stared into a static scene on a dark morning. Then it shook for more than a minute, the horizon blotted out by the rising smoke from the blast. As the scene cleared, Nagler realized the camera was not positioned to see the roof of the old theater and thus the yellow kitchen chair. "Damn."

"Now what?" Ramirez laughed.

"Got something to show you."

"Do I have a choice?"

****

The car lot security officer waved at Nagler to move on as he pulled into the lot.

"Can't be here, man. No one's supposed to come in," he yelled, and pointed at the lines of cars filling the lot. He was a kid, nineteen, twenty, long blond hair in a ponytail wearing an ill-fitting blue uniform with the name of the company, "Bob's Top Security" stitched into the shirt above the left pocket.

Nagler and Ramirez stepped from their patrol car and Nagler said, "Police business. Won't be a minute."

"I didn't do nothin' to the cars, man. They got all messed up by the blast. Fuckin' A, man."

"Were you here?" Ramirez asked.

"Naw. I start at like nine. I sort of direct traffic cause this lot's pretty small. When I got here there was chunks of shit everywhere. They hauled out, I don't know, maybe thirty cars all with windows and roofs smashed. Bricks, wood, glass. Fuckin' A."

"Was anyone here when the blast occurred?" she asked.

The kid opened his eyes wide and blew out a whistling breath. "Maybe Jack the head mechanic and a couple of his guys. They open up the repair bays early."

"They here now?" Nagler asked.

"No. The owner has another lot over in Rockaway. They shifted the repair work there. I'm just supposed keep an eye the cars while they wait for the insurance guys." He took off his fake police cap and ran and hand through his thick hair. "Think it's gonna be a while. But, hey, it's all OT, if ya know what I mean."

Nagler nodded. "Yeah, I know the place. Thanks. We'll be a minute. Come on over here, Maria."

"What?"

"Just across the street."

He crossed ahead of her and after one glance smiled. "Yup."

Maria leaned her knee into the guide rail to steady herself and to keep weight off her sore ankle. "What are you grinning about?"

Nagler pointed to the theater building. "Why is that chair there? That yellow kitchen chair."

"You dragged me up here to look at a damn chair?"

"I saw it the first day." He shook his head in response to the look of disgust on her face. "I know, but ask yourself how that chair got there? And when. Did it get blown out of an apartment, or did someone put it out there before the blast?"

Ramirez bit her lower lip and then smiled. "Should have known. That's what you wanted to see on that footage from the car shop..."

"Right," he said. "To see if there was any footage of that chair flying through the air. Might tell us what was used to set off the blast. If we can find it, that is. Otherwise, someone put it there on purpose and that could have been any time before the explosion. It's just a detail."

"Okay, We'll go through the footage. There's more coming, from a week to ten days ahead." She sat on the rail. "Nobody, Frank, nobody would even think of that."

He offered his arm as a brace so she could stand. "I know."

Nagler held her elbow as Ramirez hopped a couple times on her left foot before putting weight on her right ankle in the boot. "What is she doing?" he muttered.

"What, who?"

"Standing next to the car. Mahala Dixon." He called out to her. "Miss Dixon. Can I help you?"

"Hi, Detective. "They're supposed to be fixing my car." She nodded to the dealership garage. "But I'd guess they're not." She pushed the black hood off her head, her hair tight with braids.

"Rockaway. The security kid said the repair shop in Rockaway is open." This is wrong, he thought.

Ramirez asked, "Frank?"

"Mahala Dixon," she said and offered her hand. "You're Lieutenant Maria Ramirez."

"Yes..."

"You were the same cadet class as my father, Carlton Dixon. That's why it's important you reopen his case," Mahala Dixon said. "He'll get killed in jail. So far no one knows, I guess, because he's been safe." Her face tightened. "You *need* to do it, Detective Nagler," she said in a voice that gave no option.

"Wait a minute," Ramirez said. "What case?"

"You don't remember my father?" she asked in a scoffing, disdainful voice. "Don't you all track police involved cases like this? Maybe that's why he got lost in the system." Mahala stared at Ramirez with a grim face and hard eyes. "Maybe you should have paid more attention."

"Hey." Nagler stepped over to Mahala. "You ask for my help. That's no way to get it."

Ramirez touched his arm. "It's okay, Frank. Maybe she's right." She glared at Mahala. "Maybe she's just so mad at everyone, she needs someone to yell at. Maybe she doesn't know who her friends are."

Mahala glared back. "Maybe I grew up without a father and don't have time for friends. Maybe I feel as used as my father was." She kicked at the ground and turned away. "You don't understand."

Ramirez touched Mahala's shoulder. "I do. I grew up without a dad, too. My mom and four kids." Mahala shrugged the hand away. "You can drop the act, Mahala, the angry Black chick."

"You don't know how I was raised, Lieutenant Maria Ramirez. You have no idea. Just get him out of jail, Detective Nagler." And she turned and crossed the road to the stairs that descended to the street below.

After Mahala disappeared below the roadway, Ramirez turned to Nagler with a smirk. "Where'd you find her?"

Nagler unlocked the car doors with the remote. "She found me. At the academy, that day I had the meltdown. She didn't back off then, and she won't now."

Ramirez slipped into the car. "How long has her father been in jail and for what?"

"Fifteen years. Some messy drug case." He wiped his mouth with the palm of one hand and then closed the door. "The records aren't clear on his role."

"And you're surprised?"

"Maria, at this moment I believe that a yellow kitchen chair was a blown like magic from inside a building and landed half a block away in an upright position. So, I'm ready to believe anything."

"Do you also believe that girl is having her car fixed here?"

Nagler started the car and shifted it into gear but didn't drive off.

"No. Why would I believe that?"

****

"Hey, Nagler. What are you doing here? Find our bomber yet?"

"Not yet. I was waiting by the pay phone at the train station. Said he'd call."

Nagler ambled over to greet Chief John Hanson. The one thing that had healed in his time off was his damaged left foot; not standing for twelve hours a day seemed to have a positive effect.

"They still have a pay phone?" Hanson joked.

"Still waiting for Charlie Adams to call," Nagler said, smiling.

"Think he will?

"Not unless they let him out of solitary again. Heard he got a new lawyer."

Hanson returned the smile and shook Nagler's hand. "That case still hangs around, doesn't it, Frank? Come, sit."

Nagler shook his head and learned on the door. "There were so many pieces to that case. Stuff we probably never knew."

"Right," Hanson said., "But he's in jail for life, his lawyer's in jail, Chris Foley, your ex-partner is in jail, and old Mayor Howard Newton, who started it all, is dead." Hanson said. "Finito." He shifted in his chair and placed his elbows on the wide glass-topped desk. "So, whatcha got?"

"A Boonton kid in my investigative class, Mahala Dixon, asked me to look into her father's case, now maybe fifteen years old," Nagler said. "Lieutenant Ramirez told me yesterday she was in here last week asking about hearing of some type. Her father is Carlton Dixon, a cop. I looked at the file she gave me, and it seemed rather thin for what appears to have been a big-deal case. Four arrests, four dead, drugs…"

"You don't remember that case, do you?" Hanson asked, leaning on his elbows. He nodded for Nagler to close the office door.

Nagler complied but stood at the door. and said. "Not really. What was I doing?"

"Your job," Hanson said. "That was a messy case. We were part of it, but we didn't run it," Hanson said, his voice cold and distant, as if he didn't believe what he was about to say. "I was still a sergeant. but I told the chief then, Bill Jackson, that you should be assigned to it, but he said his hands were tied. They wanted unknowns. You were a little high profile. It was a joint county and state operation with a couple of feds along for the ride. New York drug gangs with Columbian connections were setting up shop on east side in some of the abandoned warehouses and factories. Dozens of dealers were working the region. But we started to turn a few, then got some undercovers, including Carlton Dixon, in the middle of the distribution network. Then it went south. To this day I don't know which of the three agencies screwed it up. Informants got identified – those were the four people killed – all kids, seventeen to twenty, I think, street kids. We pulled out the undercovers, and then the main warehouse in Elizabeth was burned down. I was working patrol then, heard bits and pieces. Later as I got stripes, I heard that there were some real estate types behind the scheme, laundering drug cash through buying and selling property. Never got proven."

"Just got dropped?"

"Fell through the cracks, more like it." Hanson screwed up his mouth and exhaled a long breath. "It disappeared into the tenant riots, boycotts and labor strikes that followed state and local budget cuts. There was also a big real estate deal that was going to tear down blocks of housing, bad housing, but housing nonetheless, and replace it with… something. But a lot of poor people were going to be on the street."

"I remember those riots. Lots of night standing at blockades facing kids tossing rocks and bottles. What a time. Any chance you recall the real estate company?"

Hanson shook his head and frowned. "No, sorry."

"So, what about Carlton Dixon?"

"Word was he got crossed up, half undercover, half informant. A cash flow issue."

"Not unusual. How'd he get thirty-plus years?"

"Someone put a gun in his hand."

"And…" Nagler interrupted. "And when he needed help, someone looked the other way."

Hanson just raised his eyebrows.

Nagler pulled open the door and spun to go, then stopped. "Meeting with the fire marshal later. Maybe we'll have a line on the cause."

Hanson shook his head with a sour look on his face. He held up a stack of paper that Nagler could see were the mayor's stationery. "Hope so, the mayor is shall we say, anxious. He's up for re-election and would like to run on our ability to solve this case."

Nagler laughed. "He sends you memos?"

Hanson let out a slow, "Yeah. He thinks the computer system has been hacked."

"Has it?"

"How the hell would I know? It's just an excuse to walk through the department and 'Take a look.' as he says." Hanson waved his hand. "Hey, get out of here."

Nagler turned to leave, then Hanson called him back. "Oh yeah. Ever heard of a Taylor Mangot II?"

"He's a real estate guy. Why?"

"Because he was at the front desk a day ago asking for Lauren Fox."

"Say why?"

"No. but she is the city planner."

Nagler shrugged it off. "Okay, makes sense. Maybe he wants to drop a few of his billions here."

****

The gray edge of dusk chased the sunlight across the grassy expanse of the Locust Street Cemetery, a burning streak of light between. Silence, windless, settled.

Frank Nagler knelt to adjust the flower vase at his wife's grave, his shoulders slumping in the renewed sorrow. He reached to brush imaginary dust from the top of her red granite stone, his hand seemingly powerless to move. Finally, he stood and touched the front of Del Williams' nearby marker. Peace, he thought, peace for both of you. He closed his eyes and felt again that last ambulance trip as the cancer claimed Martha, the pain that had edged her fine face finally gone. And Del, gunned down.

"All of this, here."

The flicker of an occasional eternal flame candle caught his eye, the tiniest lights in growing darkness. *Are they enough?*

He bowed his head and tried to still the turmoil.

When his left ankle cramped from standing, he turned to climb the hill back to the road. Parked behind his own car was a black SUV.

"Jerome," Nagler said to the smiling driver who held open the rear door.

"Frank." Jerome raised his eyebrows and grinned.

In the car, Sister Katherine adjusted the nose piece to her oxygen unit.

"Come sit, Frank. It's been too long."

It had been weeks since the announcement of her illness. She seemed smaller than usual, shrunken into withered, blue-veined skin. Light from the open window infused her thinning hair with a translucent glow. Nagler felt his heart clutch at her appearance. "Sister, I…"

"No, Francis, not yet. Not now." She reached for his hand. "I have arranged with Father Alonzo to hold a simple ceremony," she said, her voice thin. "I do not want the church leaders to stand before a congregation and praise my work when they schemed so hard to end or discredit it." She turned her head to gaze out the window and then looked back with a smile. "I would not want them to blaspheme."

"The work you did mattered to so many. I, well Martha and I…"

"No, Francis. I have watched you grow from a scrawny, poor worker's ghetto child into a man, a leader. I saw you and Martha face those challenges with love and bravery. That was my life. And now this is my life."

She reached to her side and handled Nagler a manila envelope.

"I understand you have crossed paths with Mahala Dixon. She is not what she seems, which you will see as you read this."

"How do you…?"

He had seen that smile before.

"I might have chosen a way outside the main flow of life, but I not totally separate. Besides, an old nun sitting at a table during a festival will not turn down the offer of a cup of tea and conversation." She coughed out a soft laugh. "It's something, I believe, about the garb. Anyway, I met Mahala and her mother Janelle during the time Carlton Dixon, Mahala's father, was involved in that case of which you have become familiar."

"She seems like an angry kid."

Sister Katherine nodded to the envelope. "It is more than anger. Read this." After a silence, she said. "This is not a place of just peace. And, no, I don't come here to examine which plot will be mine. It is already chosen, next to my sister. This is where we face the conflicts and trials, ask the hard questions of our lives. All these souls writhing, questions never answered. No, I don't come here to sample the supposed peace of life, but to confront again its inequities, its pains and injustices. My sister was murdered for greed and depravity. Del, much the same. I come here to battle for the lives who were tarnished, diminished, and forgotten. Before we pass, we must revisit the places of our horrors. Mine are here."

Nagler wanted to respond, but she cut him off.

"My horrors are here. Yours are not. Walk again the streets of the ghetto, the damaged, dirty streets of industry. Those are your places of sadness. That's where you are, Francis, where you have always been. Ask why. And as you ask, you may see why Mahala Dixon has done the things she has done."

She reached for his hand and kissed it with dry lips. "I must go."

From the roadside as the SUV pulled away, Nagler wondered if he might ever see the sister again. Before he could open the envelope, his phone rang. It was Mulligan, the medical examiner. "Got it, on my way."

****

When Nagler pushed into the medical examiner's office, he was greeted by Fire Marshal Dennis Duval's cry, "Man, that can't be right. It was over here."

Nagler watched as Duval then stabbed a black-and-white sketch of downtown Ironton with a red marker. "Had to be."

"Gentlemen," Nagler said as he approached the metal exam table which was covered with sketches and photos of the bomb scene. "What's all this?"

"Detective," Mulligan said.

Duval towered over Mulligan and his bulk shifted the medical examiner to the left edge of table, his puffy face bobbing over the material. Mulligan was not a small man, but his precision of action and speech made him appear thinner at times, near still.

Oh, shit, Nagler thought. He's wearing *that* look. Mulligan's eyes were hard dark balls peering into the world through narrow slits and his mouth puckered as if he was trying to suck his face into his head. The "don't challenge me" look. Mulligan, Nagler knew, liked clean cases – evidence, meet results – but he had never backed away or cut corners to get those results. Nagler was unsure whether the glare was related to the information Mulligan was holding, or the presence of Dennis Duval.

Nagler leaned over the table and spun one of the photos. "What's all this?"

"This," Mulligan said, "is the moment we were hoping to avoid, that instant when willful intuition, simple answers, and science part ways."

"We got a murder, Frank," Duval blurted, spilling his over-sized enthusiasm all over Mulligan's quiet precision.

"Don't we have *four* murders?" Nagler asked. Glancing at more photos. "The four bombing victims."

"Yes, and..." Mulligan began.

"This is *real* murder," Duval interrupted eagerly. "The guy in the..."

"Might I?" Mulligan picked up a stack of hard folders and slapped the edges on the metal desk. Duval stepped back, nodding and shrugging, chastised.

"As you are aware, four victims were discovered in the initial search of the scene," Milligan began. "And, as you are also aware, Miss Fox has raised concerns indicating that number of victims is insufficient related to the number of dwelling units and businesses in that zone."

"Yeah, we got that," Nagler said. "What's new, doc?"

Mulligan silenced him with a twist of his head and a raised eyebrow.

"It was speculated at first that all the victims had died due to injuries suffered in the blast and immediate fire. Subsequent examinations found that to be case in two of the victims, Marita and Juan Hernandez, who were crushed by a collapsing wall and ceiling. May I?" And he stepped toward the center of the table, forcing Duval to step farther back. "The Hernandezes lived here, reports said, in the rear, second floor apartment at 36 Warren Street, a three-story building." Mulligan touched the street sketch with a pencil tip.

"Yeah," Duval said, as he pushed back to the table. He pointed to the sketch. "This wall leaned in for a minute or so under the weight of the ceiling and roof above, which was being squashed by the weight of *this* roof next door, which was a fourth-floor roof. It wobbled for a while and then fell on top of those poor folks." He nodded, pleased with his summary. "They had been pinned by local debris anyway."

"Yes," Mulligan replied. "Judging by the dust and soot in their mouths and throats they were alive under the mass for mere moments before succumbing to their crushing injuries."

"That's awful," Nagler said. "Jeez. Who else?"

"Agnes Canfield…"

"The old lady?"

Mulligan paused. "Agnes Canfield lived in the front apartment at 12 Warren Street. Here." And he indicted the spot. "Her apartment was close, an estimated seventy to eighty diagonal feet from the suspected ignition point and as such sustained more damage than many others." He glanced up at Nagler with a pursed mouth. "She died of a heart attack prior to being buried under falling debris." He rushed his next words. "We know this because while her face was covered with dust, she had not inhaled any."

Nagler frowned and exhaled a fat-cheek breath.

"So, three murders and…"

Mulligan frowned. "It could be argued that the explosion and fire could have triggered Mrs. Canfield's heart attack."

Nagler nodded. "A contributing factor."

"Perhaps."

Nagler shifted closer to the table. "So that leaves the kid."

"Yes. Ethan Ricardo. He had been stabbed," Mulligan said.

Nagler stepped back from the table and raked his hair back as he pondered the implication of that information. Is this part of the bombing? *A separate crime? What do we know about this kid? Nothing. Who would want him dead? Don't need this.*

"Walk me through it."

Mulligan opened another folder containing photos and began, "There are two parts. "Mr. Ricardo was, we believe, 22, from Uruguay. There is something odd about his records. I'll leave that to you. As the photo shows he sustained three stab wounds. The one in the shoulder seems to have been the first, and judging by the bruise on his forehead – which was not debris related – may have occurred during an initial struggle. Judging by the curve of the cut and its lack of depth it might have even been accidental. The second wound was to his abdomen and led to significant bleeding, and the third was to his chest and heart, perhaps a lucky strike. He would have died immediately after the third knife wound. He was a dead before the explosion occurred."

"Yeah, okay. Time of death?" Nagler asked as he examined the series of photos. "Any more of these, you know, showing more of the room?"

Duval said, "Yup, over in my office."

"Get me copies."

"Mr. Ricardo died approximately seven hours prior to the explosion. Conditions of the room make that a crude estimate."

Nagler did the math in his head as stared at Mulligan. Explosion, 5 a.m., minus seven means 10 p.m. "So, this kid died the night before." Not news he needed to hear. "What the fuck," he muttered. "What was the weapon? Was it found?"

"Possibly an eight-inch serrated knife," Mulligan said and pointed out a ragged edge of one of the wounds.

"A bread knife. He could have been killed upstairs in the restaurant where he worked."

Mulligan nodded, and Duval interjected. "It wasn't at the scene."

Nagler flipped around another photo of the room. "You sure it didn't get shoveled into a bucket with the other debris?"

Duval leaned into his full height. "My officers are professionals. We were told to preserve everything at the scene. That's what we did," he added with satisfaction.

Nagler frowned and also leaned in. "In other words, you don't actually know."

Duval blushed as his jaw firmed. "My men are pros."

"So that's a yes."

Duval glanced at Mulligan for support, but the medical examiner's face was a stone. Then Duval turned back to Nagler. "It's a maybe."

Damn it. "Alright," Nagler said as he pondered trying to build a murder case in the death of Ethan Ricardo, "Get three of your professionals up to that debris pile at the high school and find me a serrated knife."

"There's tons of shit."

"Yeah, it's marked by location. "Find the pile for 8 Blackwell and start digging."

"But..."

"We have to find it. And, yeah, did any of your professionals report what seemed like a lot of, you know, blood in any of the debris in that room? You might have noticed, huh, maybe."

Mulligan stepped between the men. "Gentlemen, please take this elsewhere."

Duval palmed the photos and sketches into a pile, gathered them under one arm and stalked out.

"Make me copies," Nagler coldly called after him.

Mulligan reached to the table and gently placed his reports inside their individual folders and tipped his head to the door. "You need him, Frank."

"Yeah." A tired soft smile. "I know. I want it to be easy, and it never is. You poke and poke, lift the stuff on the floor, stare into empty rooms, empty faces, and the frustration boils up because the case is slipping away and that's when in my head I hear your voice from a million years ago saying, 'Just follow the evidence,' and I calm down." His face relaxed, eyes unfocused a moment, then sharpened. "Then there's guys like Dennis Duval..."

"Yes, Frank. But it wasn't a million years ago. It was probably last week."

Nagler shared a smile. *A Mulligan joke. Maybe one of three in my lifetime.*

Mulligan continued, "And there's always guys like Dennis Duval, as you say, but we both need to him to do his job. Catch him."

"Trust him?"

"In times like these, Detective, trust may be relative."

****

Nagler spotted Duval in the city hall parking lot in the middle of a hair-grabbing, arm-swinging, circling-like-a-dog phone call that ended with a fist smashed into the roof of his city vehicle. Even from the distance of thirty or so feet, Nagler heard his name twice and the phrase, "Don't fuckin' piss me off, John. Get three guys up there and don't come back without that fucking knife."

Nagler jogged over to make sure he caught Duval before he entered his car.

"I don't have your damn pictures, Nagler. I told you I'd get them to ya."

"I know. What were you and Mulligan talking about?"

Duval considered the question with a scowl, but then said, "Okay," and opened the car door and dropped inside all the papers except the sketch of the bomb scene, which he stretched out on the hood of the car.

"The working theory," he began as he tried to hold down the curling page. "Grab that corner, will ya. Thanks. The working theory is that a natural gas leak was ignited in this corner of the block, at Warren and Blackwell." He pointed to the spot.

"Right," Nagler said. "The Cuban place. Where the kid was found."

"Yeah. That seems to be all anyone can agree on."

"What do you mean?"

Duval, more than a foot taller than the car, leaned an elbow on the roof and faced Nagler. "Our collection of experts can't decide which of themselves might be right, and which might be incorrect," he said in a voice dripping with disdain.

Oh, crap, Nagler thought. "What's that mean?"

"The bomb guys thinks this all some big conspiracy. And the engineers think it's all about structural weakness of the buildings."

"Can't it be both?"

"Ya'd think so, considerin' that parts of two city blocks are lying in a pile at the high school about now. But these guys are looking at it from a thousand feet in the air" – he wrangled his hands in the air as if sorting items – "picking and choosing the parts that make them look smarter than the other guys. We ain't got copies of their report yet." He turned and leaned his back against the car, holding the sketch, and stretched. "They ain't listening to us guys on the street."

Nagler realized he was in deeper than he wanted to be, but asked, "What do the guys on the street think?"

Duval huffed and turned back to the car and spread out the sketch, nodding to Nagler to again hold down a corner.

"Alright," Duval pressed a fat finger into the spot of the Cuban restaurant. "These cellar walls go back to about 1890, cheap cement faces over field stone foundation. Weak stuff. A gas explosion of force could have blowed out this wall. Boom, then this wall, boom, and so on. Boom, boom, boom. Gas company has lots of busted lines in all these places, but in this one we found a chunk of cement with a line that seems to be disconnected, unscrewed, not cut or broken by force." He drew an imaginary line on the spot. "This cellar had a low ceiling, maybe seven feet, and was divided into two rooms by a flimsy plywood wall. In one room there was the furnace, about here, and a heavy old cooler, maybe four-by-four. It was pushed through the wall here, like a battering ram."

Nagler nodded. "So that could have..."

"Yeah, spread the gas." Duval shifted the sketch. "And here we found a mangled cot and a kerosene space heater."

"The kid was sleeping there. Gas leak, kerosene as an accelerant."

"Correct."

"I don't know. That's not going to bring down this whole thing." Nagler waved his hand over the entire sketch. "Could all of this have been an accident? Doesn't seem very professional."

Duval grinned like a wizard with all the secrets.

"Remember that fire, East side maybe six months ago? Garage and a small warehouse?"

Nagler squinted, then nodded. "Yeah, right, probable arson. Out of state owner engaging in a little instant urban renewal."

"Know what we found there but never made public? Gas cans and traces of fertilizer. Know what we found on Warren Street? Gas cans and traces of fertilizer."

"Those gas cans have fingerprints?"

"Dunno. They're in the evidence room. Knock yourself out."

Duval cracked his jaw and winked before pulling his bulk through the car door and driving away.

The car on bad springs bounced and scraped along the uneven curb as it left the parking lot.

Nagler stared after the car as it turned the corner, struck suddenly by the silence. For weeks downtown had been filled with the clanking, metallic crashing and thumping of heavy machinery and debris being moved and dumped, a clatter so persistent it left no space for other sounds, or silence.

And now all the noise was gone; the eerie quiet was not soothing, he thought, but dangerous.

Thick clouds draped the surrounding hills, announcing the arrival of the promised storm.

Fat drops opened craters of dust on empty sidewalks and a wash of water wiped across windows and walls, a crescendo of drumming rain that blurred the horizon.

Inside his car, Nagler swiped his hand across his head a couple times and shook off the wetness. The car vibrated with the pounding rain. He leaned back in the seat, glanced at the rear view mirror, and wondered why his eyes seemed so tired. He leaned his head back and closed his eyes, for a moment content to be inside the car in an empty parking lot, hoping the heavy rain would give him a few moments of peace.

That wish was dismissed by the ping of his phone, a text from Ramirez: "Where U? Must C this."

He exhaled deeply and glanced through the rain smeared side window before shouldering the door open and stepping into a face full of rain. Halfway across the lot his left foot slipped on a puddle and the pain doubled him over. "Oh, fuck," he gritted his teeth and limped to the rear door of the police department where he leaned against a wall and slowed his breathing to dispel the pain in his throbbing left foot. "One of these days," he shook his head and opened the inner door.

"Why are you limping" Ramirez asked Nagler without turning to face him. "Never mind, look at this."

On the center computer screen was a blurry image of a light-colored van.

"Two days before the explosion," she said.

"Where?"

"Bassett." She opened another screen. "Then here." She opened a third screen. "And here. Two days, A week before, two weeks before."

Nagler dragged over a chair and squinted at the images. They were recorded on cameras some distance from where the van was parked. "Any sign of a driver?"

Ramirez opened a new camera view of Blackwell, east of the explosion site. "Hold on. Here's the van again, about four o'clock, day before. Look at the side panel. That's where a company would have a name and logo. Seems to have been scraped off."

"What year you think that is?"

"Best guess, late 80s Ford Econoline."

Nagler chuckled. "So, one of several thousand."

"Ah, Frank. Such a pessimist. One of sixty-two in Morris County. I've sent out an alert including the photo."

"What does that tell us? One of the seventeen business in that strip got deliveries from a company with an old Ford van."

Ramirez patted Nagler's cheek twice.

"Tells us more than that." She reached for a file on the desk and pulled out a photograph of what appeared to be the same van parked on an alley near old industrial buildings.

"Six months ago, east side. Remember that fire?"

"Shit, yes. Duval was just telling me what they found there. Gas cans and fertilizer. What the hell."

In a mock seductive voice Ramirez said, "Oh my man, there is more."

She extracted two more photos of the van from the folder.

"Traffic was doing parking enforcement in that area – for the life of me I can't figure out why. Probably a cover operation for something else. It's mostly empty buildings – and saw this van at least twice more. "Guess who it is registered to?"

Nagler laughing. "Oh, come on. Why are you dragging this out?"

Ramirez shared the laugh. "What fun would it be if I just flat out told you? Then seriously, "Carlton Dixon."

"The cop, who's in jail."

"Yeah, look. Here's the reg."

He closed his eyes, scrunched up his forehead and shook his head.

"That was fifteen years ago, and he's been in jail that long. The files said they used empty warehouses as drug stashes and transfer sites. Didn't we close it down?"

"Loose ends, maybe?"

"That's some loose end. Who's driving it?"

Ramirez shrugged. "No clue. Doesn't his daughter live in Boonton? Maybe they've seen it."

"That's all we need." He stretched out his left foot to fight off a cramp and grimaced.

"What'd you do?" Ramirez asked.

"Slipped on the wet parking lot. Jammed my foot. Anyway, did those bomb scene cameras catch anything that looks like a driver of the van or a suspect, or is that asking too much?"

"We got a couple somebodies." Ramirez opened two new views on the screen. "This one is on Blackwell at the Cuban place. Night before. Skinny kid, probably that kid who was killed."

"You know he was murdered, right? Mulligan says stabbed." Nagler tapped the screen. "With a bread knife."

Ramirez scratched her forehead. "So, I need to be looking for someone else."

"I guess," Nagler said. "What time was that camera shot?"

Ramirez strained to read the time stamp. "Looks like nine-thirty, nine twenty."

"Mulligan said he was killed about ten. If the timing is right, he was walking into his death and the killer might have been waiting for him? Jesus. What else?"

"Sorry to add on, but there's this guy?" The screen displayed a figure of a hefty male leaving the alley. He was wearing ball cap and a shirt with wide vertical stripes. "Three a.m. the day of. On Bassett near the service alley." Ramirez opened another file. "So, the restaurant kid was killed at ten, the place blew up at five the next morning, and this guy is leaving at three."

"Can you print that out for me? Mulligan said the kid's body was moved after he was killed. We've got no one else to look at. Who the hell are you?"

When Ramirez handed Nagler the photo of the second person, he did a double take. "I know that shirt. God damn it."

"Who?"

"Tony. Barry's cook. He's been missing since the explosion."

CHAPTER SIX

The world returned

In the quiet times sitting alone near the front window, Leonard would see them in his mind – Bobby, Del Williams, Dominique – unpacking the boxes of used books, shaking off dust, laughing at the titles and the old, stylized drawings on the covers, occasionally finding a Braille text in a box from a school, and Dom asking him to teach the system to him. "I can learn this, boss. Be more use to you," Dom would say, his voice so full of enthusiasm and hope, Leonard could feel the boy's beaming smile. Leonard would run his fingers across the Braille text. Sometimes Shakespeare, sometimes a math text, once a Bible, and Leonard would call after Dom's retreating steps, "Don't call me boss."

Dom's laughing reply every time was, "Yes, boss."

And then they were gone. That day. Killed in the hail of bullets that also put Leonard in the hospital for surgeries that tried to save his mobility and his sense of feeling but did little to fill the hollow of isolation that surrounded him. There were days since when not even the friendly arrival of Frank Nagler's familiar tapping footsteps could pull Leonard from the darkness.

And now the clatter of dishes at Barry's diner counter in the far corner of the bookstore, the hum of voices, the fat aroma of bacon, fried potatoes, the sharp coffee smell, softly bitter, pushed Leonard deeper into his isolated opposite corner. The first time it happened, Leonard felt he was trapped inside a growing clear bubble that resisted his finger's soft touch, a sensation that had not faded even when Barry's steady, heavy footsteps would cross the wooden floor from the counter to Leonard's wheelchair bringing lunch or a beverage, or just conversation.

Why today? he wondered as he felt the bubble thicken, the voices soften to a blur of sound like an unfocused light on a white screen. Why today, of all days, had the gloom resettled?

There had been good news from Lauren Fox. Her office had secured approval from the governor for a grant and loan package. They could renovate the two empty warehouses he owned for housing and remodel the adjacent factory where his used book business was located into a street-level space for a new Barry's, an additional second-floor space for the used books and offices on the third floor.

Maybe it was the change in the weather. The summer had been cooler, but dry, and walking with Calista, even if he had to use the wheelchair, were days of freedom. September arrived wet and angry. Drenching storms followed by sluggish, gray days of northeast winds that often pinned him, like now, at a front window in that damned chair.

Sighing, he reached over and touched the glass, hoping to feel its smooth coolness, hoping, really, to feel anything.

The motorized wheelchair had been dragged out of storage and the battery replaced; he had hoped that after two years of walking and the loss of all that weight, he would never need it again.

Leonard shifted and wiggled his hips as the mesh of the chair's sides chafed against his fat and useless thighs. I want to move, he thought, to cross the park and find a cold seat on a bench and feel the wind and hear the pigeons cooing, to feel the brush of their wings as they rested briefly at my feet, pecking at broken peanut shells, to feel the rumble of truck traffic through the cement, the scolding of a jay, the scuffle of kids fresh from school, yelling to one another as they passed. To dwell again in the swirl of life.

He shifted away from the window and the view of the park and bitterly knew again that the space would never remind him of cheerful times. Each time he closed his eyes he would see the strike of the first bullet into the wooden podium, hear the shouted instructions to run and duck and above that, the urgent cry from Del. "Take my arm," and then the grunt as Del was struck by a bullet and the pain and blackness that followed as he, too, was struck; then falling. Then the silence.

The door near him swished open.

"Hey, Barry, gimme a lunch special, and coffee, black," the unseen customer yelled even before the front door closed. Then a firm hand on his arm, "Hey, Len. "How are ya?"

The touch and the voice, shocked Leonard from his reverie. "Good. I'm, I'm good. Thanks."

"No problem," said the happy voice. "Glad to see ya up and about."

Leonard smiled and blinked away a sudden tear.

That had been part of the adjustment, Leonard knew. His own customers were reserved, almost meek, in comparison to Barry's, who blustered into the shop, shouting life into the staid, dry air of the bookstore.

In that instant, through that voice, by that touch, the world returned.

****

Barry had weight, Leonard decided. Not physically, although the first time Barry crossed the store to sit with him Leonard imagined a large man with stained white kitchen shirt with one panel bulging untucked over this belt, an image he embellished until Calista told him when he asked that in fact Barry was a slim man of medium height, wore a multi-colored floral shirt that was never untucked, had slicked back salt-and-pepper hair, and wore a pair of half-bifocals on the bridge of his nose like a jeweler or a bookie.

Barry had weight, Leonard decided because of what he did and the authoritative, cheerful tone to his voice. It was, Leonard guessed, all those years of running a downtown coffee shop, the quick ins and outs, the hey, how are ya's to the regulars, slapping down the right coffee, to the right seat and with a raised eyebrow asking, "the usual?" only to chuckle when the customer said, sure, was thinking about it.

Barry's steps would draw a soft crack from the three wide stairs that divided the kitchen from the open books shelves, then shuffle through the narrower pathway near the checkout booth usually filled with customers, occasionally scraping an empty chair back under a table, dropping a gruff, "how are ya?" until he thumped into the padded chair near Leonard's post; until Leonard gently insisted he had been thanked enough, Barry's first greeting would be a heartfelt "thanks for giving me the chance after the explosion," followed by a meaty grab of Leonard's shoulder.

"This is better," Calista would say when she massaged Leonard's flabby, soft hands, trying to bring back feeling that had been stolen by the shooting. Some days, he'd believe her, on the days he could tap his fingers on the table and feel the wood push back. But then he'd recall the days after his discharge they had to pull out the mechanical wheelchair. He acted like a child, whining at his discomfort, and Calista would take his face in her hands and place her forehead against his and say, "Oh, my dear, we'll do it again," and he would accept her hope as his own.

****

"Ain't had a new spot before," Barry said, choking back tears. "Thanks, Len."

"We need a place to eat around here," Rafe jumped in as he re-moved the lunch dishes. Had to go five blocks to get Brazilian before. Maybe expand your menu, huh?"

"Rafe," Leonard replied. "Come on…"

"Not a bad idea, really," Barry said. We'll have more space, stor-age, seating. Wanna learn how to cook, Rafe?"

"Yah, maybe," the kid said. "Oh, we found a few books that you might find interesting, records from the Union Mining Company, seem like more than a hundred years old, and a couple journals."

Leonard brightened. "The historical society could be interested."

"Yeah, we were looking at the journals, me and David, you know, just to see. And there's some entries from a Nagler guy, the same name as Detective Nagler."

"Well, Frank would love to see them." Leonard turned to Barry. "It's not just me, you know. I can't work and just sit in this damn chair all day. It's Lauren Fox, she created the non-profit. And Calista, and Frank and all the kids."

Barry shook Leonard's shoulder. "Don't sell yourself short. I re-member you starting the bookstore, what twenty years ago when there was nothing on this block and how everyone thought it was gonna bust. But look at ya. Downtown's gonna be two years away, easy. City dies without guys like you. I'm glad to be here."

Barry pushed his chair back to leave when Calista arrived. They shared a cheek kiss. "Tell this guy he's a genius, will ya, kid?"

"Every day," she said as she slipped into the chair next to Leonard. "Beating up yourself again?"

Leonard turned to her voice. "There's just so much wrong."

"Well, maybe this will help things feel better." She unfolded a letter of very official heavy weight, watermarked stationery. "This came today. It's an offer from that real estate billionaire Taylor Mangot to make a donation to your nonprofit. Couple million."

"I've heard of him. Why is he interested in my little affair?"

"He says it here: 'Because of my family's long and historical connection to the City of Ironton.' What do you think he means?"

"Don't have a clue. Lauren did a lot of research to help me find this building. I don't recall any listing for a Mangot family, or company."

"Maybe they changed their name, or his surname is the result of a family marriage."

Leonard nodded. "Could be."

"But you're worried about something," Calista took his hand and kissed it. "What?"

"Let's talk to Lauren and Frank first. I'm just puzzled why a world celebrity like Taylor Mangot would want to help us, or how he even managed to hear about us."

****

Nagler resisted the urge to drive by the old East side arson site and took the left to Leonard's bookstore. While waiting at the traffic light, an old white Ford van approached and sidled to the intersection awaiting a left turn opposite Nagler; he strained his left shoulder against the door and knocked his head against the window trying to view the side of the van.

"Murray's Auto Parts," he laughed.

And then there was Tony, leaving the site before the explosion. Maybe Barry had been right, and Tony left after smelling gas. But why didn't he call the police? Ah, Tony, ya got a girlfriend there, buddy? Why has no one heard from you since?

The shadows of dusk settled over the neighborhood, still ghostly with brooding, empty shells of buildings, leafless trees, dark sentinels, guardians of gloom.

He parked his car across from the park. It had been filled that day, noisy shouting celebrations swirling through the streets, music echoing, clashing voices shouting life. The first shot came from a third-floor window and within a second shattered the podium from which Calista Knox had just stepped. Then the volley that ripped the banners and struck Del and Bobby and Dom and Leonard. The shrieking, scrambling crowd. Then Lauren, face torn and crying, then kneeling to Leonard.

He silently watched the sunlight fade and the park darken. This was what Sister Katherine meant. Visit the place of our horrors. *I'm visiting. Now what?*

The sound of a car door slamming broke the revery.

Mahala Dixon ran up to him from behind. "Detective!"

Nagler turned to her call. *What the hell?* He turned to face her, unsmiling.

"Miss Dixon. I don't know why you are here, but I'm glad you are. Do you own a white van?"

Mahala slowed but did not stop her advance.

"My father did, years ago. I heard that one like it was seen near the places that blew up."

"How do you even know that? I just learned about it a couple hours ago?"

Mahala smiled. "It's all over Boonton. You do know I'm provisional there. A white van somehow connected to my father's case now an item of interest in a bombing fifteen years later. Fascinating, isn't it?"

Nagler at first glared at her, but then softened his face, choosing to sidestep the call out. "I'd rather than you don't speak to anyone about it. It's part of an investigation and any further discussion could alter your status."

Her eyes flashed. "Is that a threat?"

"No, Miss Dixon. It is what professional police officers do. They don't discuss potential evidence with friends over coffee. But if you want to think that's a threat, so be it."

Mahala waved a hand at him. "You can't hurt me. I'm not in your department."

What the hell is all this about? "I don't want to hurt your career. I think you would be a hell of a cop. If you know something that I should know, tell me. But don't meddle. I've had an entire career of meddling. And I don't take it lightly."

Mahala turned and walked away. "Just get my father out of jail."

He watched as she drove slowly by and pulled a squealing left at the corner. A red Jetta, ten years old or so, black interior, a Boonton PD parking sticker on the right rear side of the trunk, and a spangly peace decal on the left rear window.

Nagler expelled two deep breaths and ran his hands through his hair. There's a leak. Gotta find it.

****

The bookstore was shuffling quiet when Nagler arrived, except for one of Barry's customers in a hoodie, oily jeans and a hardhat telling a story about making railroad track repairs in a Newark tunnel, "where the rats was the size of dogs and the water was green with oil scum and shit and wooden ties had been in the ground so long there were like preserved..."

Lauren Fox sat with Leonard, Calista, Barry, and Dan Yang at a corner table by the side window. The weariness in Lauren's face had become sadness.

"So, Yang," Nagler called out. "Why the beard?"

Dan Yang greeted Nagler with a handshake. "Without it, I look like a high school kid next to my students. And most of them are in their twenties. I thought it might add some authority."

Nagler laughed. "Yeah, okay. But you look like a high school kid with a beard. Whatever works." He leaned over to kiss Lauren. "Hey, kid." He dragged over a chair.

"Coffee, Frank," Barry asked.

"Be great, Yeah."

Barry waved at Rafe behind the counter, "Coffee, light."

Rafe arrived with the coffee. "Hey, Frank. Did they give you those books?"

"What books?" Nagler asked.

"Almost forgot," Leonard said and reached to a chair and produced three old books. "Thanks, Rafe. These are from the old Union Mine Company records, and this one is a journal of sorts. The writer is named Nagler."

Nagler accepted the books, inspecting each one. He ran a finger over the embossed leather, scrolling through the indented "UNION" across the top. He opened one of the books and saw the dates, January 1917 to December 1919. "My grandfather was a kid then, working in the Union mine," he said. "I wonder. Thanks."

Lauren took the books from Nagler and pensively flipped through the first pages of one of the ledgers.

"So, look, Frank," Dan Yang said. "Leonard asked me to research Taylor Mangot for him after he got this letter. You've seen it?"

Nagler took the letter from Yang, read it quickly and said, "No. Is this real?"

"Appears so," Leonard said. "But Calista and I wanted Lauren to look at it, and she referred it to Dan."

Lauren seized the letter. "Just a precaution. Leonard's foundation has limits about what and how much it can accept as support through private third-party payments," she said. "Trying to keep Leonard on the up and up." She passed the letter back to Yang.

"I'm familiar with Mangot and his organization," Yang said. "His Singapore operation is a case study in corporate malfeasance. He, shall we say, adopted some old and well-rehearsed habits in the gray areas where business and government intersect. That said, his U.S. operations are cleaner, though not totally clean. This country, too, has, gray areas, as you well know, Frank. That's where Howard Newton operated."

"Yeah, don't remind me," he said back. "How does this affect Leonard?"

"My advice would be to hold off just yet," Yang said. "The offer is open-ended. Let me poke around his finances and see what this guy is up to."

"You can do that?"

Lauren smiled. "That's what he's doing for us. We're trying to establish a paper trail of hundreds of transactions to determine the owners of the explosion site."

"How exactly?"

Yang cleared his throat and Lauren rested her head on her arms. "We're kind of hacking into the accounts," Yang smiled.

Lauren tipped her head to one aside and winked at Nagler.

"Do I really want to know?" Nagler asked.

"It's part of what I teach," Yang said. "We study the best hackers to learn their methods. The federal government hired some of these guys to point out the flaws in our defense computer networks, for example. Banks hire them." He stood. "Gotta run. I'll let you know."

"Welcome back." Nagler said, as Yang left.

"Great to be back. It's better than I imagined."

Calista scanned the Taylor Mangot offer again. "Can we trust him, Yang?"

Nagler shrugged. "We did before. Why?"

Calista's eyes darkened. "Too eager."

Lauren reached across the table and touched Calista's hand. "We've learned a lot. We are more careful than we have been. I've got this."

Barry nodded to Nagler. "Ain't heard from Tony yet."

"Glad you bought that up," Nagler said as he reached for his phone. "Does this look like Tony?"

Barry squinted at the photos and then offered a small, beaten smile. "Looks like his shirt. I'm carrying his wife and family. His kid's getting old enough to maybe work here. When was that taken?"

"Three a.m. Two hours before the explosion. Would he normally be there that early to open up?"

"Yeah, sometimes. Depended on the prep, deliveries."

"Just a heads up. I'm gonna have to release this photo, as a person of interest. No disrespect, Barry. Just my job."

Barry turned his head in response to a shout from the counter. "Yeah, comin'." He stood. "Not a problem, Frankie. He liked the horses some. The slots. Not heavy, but sometimes I had to tell him to screw his head on straight." He walked away.

Leonard said, "Sometimes Barry just sits at the counter, sort of muttering to himself. I don't hear all the words, but his voice is heavy and dark."

"Has he been getting more phone calls than usual?" Nagler asked.

Leonard and Calista shared a glance. "No," she said. "Why?"

"It's just odd that Tony has not reached out, that's all."

Lauren stood and leaned her head against Nagler's and then kissed his hair. "I'm going home. I need a long hot shower." She winked at Calista. "Make sure he gets home."

"I'm a big boy, you know," Nagler called after her.

"That's what I'm counting on."

CHAPTER SEVEN

Randy Jensen

Nagler found Lauren stretched out on their bed face down with her head wrapped in a white bath towel and second one draped across her hips.

He kissed the middle of her back.

Without looking at him over her shoulder she held up a jar of body cream.

"I need a lube job. That bank office is hot, dry, and dusty. By the end of the day, I feel like my skin is going to crack."

He removed the towel from her head, and she shook her hair before slipped her arms under a pillow for support.

He kneaded her shoulders and gently rubbed her back without cream on his hands. "Would madam prefer number one or a number two?"

"A number one, please," she laughed. "If I remember, a number two involved so much lotion I had to towel off after the rubdown. I need to be softened, not basted."

"Yes, madam," he laughed, and then kissed the middle of her back again, tracing a pattern along her spine to her hips. He pulled off the towel and slipped two figures moist with lotion inside her thighs.

"I don't recall that on the menu," she whispered.

"New menu."

****

"Hey, Frank, smile."

"What?" Nagler turned to the direction of Jimmy Dawson's voice and waved a hand at a video camera pointed at his head. "Christ, Dawson. What are you doing?"

Dawson lowered the camera and joined Nagler leaning on the new fence that had been erected on the shoulder of the bridge across from the car lot as part of new effort to secure the bomb scene.

"Recording history," Dawson said. "Been doing it for years. There is an extensive record of photographic history, but little if any video history. Been storing video tapes for years. Now it's digital. I can put it on my website."

"What are you shooting now?"

Dawson tipped his head toward the explosion site. "All that. Been doing it right from the start. I want to edit in footage from before, just to show what was lost."

A gust of wind threw dust in their eyes and brought with it a whiff of natural gas.

"I wonder how long it will take before people stop smelling gas, or think they are?" Nagler asked. He focused his gaze on the yellow kitchen chair. It seemed to be precisely when it had been the first time he saw it.

"Why is that still there?" he asked.

Dawson chuckled. "I have footage of some investigators on the roof from a couple days ago. They had tape measures and seemed to be finding the circumference of a circle around the chair, then the distance from the chair to the edge of the roof, even the height of the chair. Lotta work for a chair."

"It's a heroic chair, Jimmy," Nagler laughed. "What else you got?"

Dawson shifted the camera and leaned into the fence. "The Old Iron Bog, Smelly Flats, a few street protests, trains, coming and going, And, oh yeah, some video of your old neighborhood, the worker's ghetto, from a couple years ago before they tore down that block for the new public housing project. Seems they were swapping one type of poor man's housing for another."

Nagler felt himself withdraw at the mention of the ghetto. It had been years since he walked those streets. Maybe that was what Sister Katherine meant.

"Leonard's guys found an old diary from the mining days, written by a 'Nagler,' no first name." Nagler said. "I think it's written by my grandfather, who was kid at when the mines and factories were shutting down. You forget how much of a factory town Ironton was in those days. The company owned the housing, the stores, the land. The workers lived in their own ethnic enclaves and then there were the gangs, the enforcers for the bosses." He stared out over the broken streets. "Then it ended, Jimmy. The money went elsewhere, and the mess was left behind. Look how long it's taken us to try to fix it."

"Hey, no offense, Frank."

Nagler shook his head to chase out the uncertainty. "Don't worry about it. Mention of the ghetto made me think of Del Williams and how we used to run through the streets. We never thought of ourselves as poor, until someone would say, hey, there's goes those poor kids. Life's been a little different, calmer, without Del. Not sure that's an improvement."

"Wondering when you were coming back."

Nagler and Dawson turned to the voice, and Dawson gave Nagler a "what the hell" look.

It was the security guard from the car dealership. "Been a lot of people looking around that chair, you know." The kid grinned. "Gets a little slow. I grab a soda and lean over here to watch the construction. Been audacious."

"I'm sure," Nagler said. "But what about the chair?"

"Don't know really. But a couple days ago it looked like a couple women were there. Looking at it. Sittin' on it."

"You have any video of that, Jimmy?"

Dawson scoffed. "I'm not everywhere all the time."

"Why did you think they were women?"

The kid removed his ball cap and ran a hand through his long hair. "The way they moved. Not like guys. Seemed thinner, you know?"

"What were they wearing?"

"Hoodies. Gray, I think. Nothing stood out."

Nagler reached out his hand. "What's your name?"

"Randy. Randy Jensen."

"That's a good job, Randy. You'd make a good cop." Nagler said as he handed him a business card. "Anyone else visits that chair, you call me."

Randy Jensen beamed. "Yes, sir. You bet, Detective Nagling."

"It's Nagler."

"Yeah, sorry," the kid said as he retreated across the street.

Nagler turned back to examine the chair. "Now who would that be?"

"Let me go through the videos I shot in the last couple weeks," Dawson offered. "I'm not looking for anything investigative when I shoot the footage, just trying to capture the scene. But maybe there's something of more interest that just a city falling in on itself."

****

I wish I liked hats, Nagler thought, standing in the light rain at the corner of Blackwell and Warren. Most of the bomb site had been cleared of debris, leaving one-story tall pillars of brick or broken walls soot stained and windowless, voiceless ghosts in the mist.

How do we get you to tell us what really happened here?

Oh, he had read the reports from the experts – Dennis Duval was right – they were just lists of words, people talking to themselves, paragraphs of speculation the authors would read at some convention.

He traced an imaginary line from where he stood across the absent face of the block, up a floor, diagonally to another roof, then up again to a maybe fourth floor window blown out with such force that a yellow kitchen chair could have been launched to a point half-a-block away.

Ceiling voids, the reports said, gaps in walls, flowing natural gas, refrigerators kicking on, space heaters, explosion upon explosion. Burst to burst then finally… what? None of the reports said what caused an explosion so loud and forceful that his house a mile away shook from the concussion.

And before all that happened, Ethan Ricardo walked into his place of employment and was stabbed to death, his body then carried to the illegal room where he slept. The killer had hoped the explosion would cover his initial crime. Was this all done just to cover the murder of an immigrant kid?

Nagler wiped the water from his hair and sighed, not liking the thought that had just shown up. What if Ricardo's death and the gas fire in his room were *not* connected to the larger explosion, but just occurred at the same time?

"Oh, crap," Nagler said, trying to resist the hole that the new thought opened before him. *If Ricardo's death is not connected, then what about the white van?*

The rain picked up and he hurried across Warren toward the police station.

The sound of something being tossed against a stone wall slipped through the patter of the rain; through the thickening mist, Nagler saw a figure leaning against a wall a block away. Then it was gone. Nagler picked his way along the sidewalk still littered with odd bricks and boards, orange cones and ripped strings of yellow police tape. At the intersection where the figure had stood, the street was empty. He turned to the direction of a vehicle engine starting up and saw a white Econoline pull into Bassett and then take a left onto Sussex.

Nagler's eyes narrowed, and his lips compressed. Okay, he thought, now you've pissed me off.

****

He scrubbed a handful of paper towels across his head as he waited for the pot of coffee to brew. The office was empty. He hoped he had come early enough not to be interrupted while he spread out the files he had collected in an effort to make sense of what was just a big mess.

The phone rang before Nagler could sit.

"Jesus. How'd they know I was here?" he grumbled, startled as he glanced around the room. He tossed his jacket on the back of the chair, set his coffee on the side, and picked up the call on the fourth ring, thinking – hoping – damn, one more ring and they would have gone away. "Yeah, Nagler."

A voice he almost recognized growled on the phone.

"You still use that meeting spot out at the Old Iron Bog?"

"Yeah…"

"Still smell?"

Then it clicked. "Dancer?"

"Yeah. Say, two o'clock?"

"Sure."

A coughing reply. "Good."

Nagler stared at the receiver before he hung it up. *What's he doing back in town? Was he watching me?*

Detective Jeff Montgomery, whose nickname was not "Monty," but "Dancer" for reasons he would not explain.

He had retired and moved to Arizona maybe ten years ago after being diagnosed with lung cancer. The image of Montgomery in the old police building emerged. Hanging by the rear door, a brown fedora and oversized tweed jacket, right hand cupping a Marlboro with a paper cup of coffee in his left, his breath a shroud in the cold of the alley. He'd squint when he took a draw, his lungs probably killing him even then. That image fit the voice Nagler had heard on the phone. Maybe more surprising than Montgomery was in town, was that he was still alive.

Nagler took his usual circuitous route to the old bog on the north side of Ironton, and then parked a quarter mile away near the only street with houses. Too many times he had emerged from the hidden trail into the bog to find a strange vehicle parked along Mount Pleasant that drove off as he hit the pavement.

The rain had moved off; rainbows of oil residue smeared Mount Pleasant. Nagler picked up a broken branch from the roadside and used it as a crutch to maneuver down the path as his shoes slipped on the thick clay mud.

This time when he arrived, he found Jeff Montgomery leaning against a tree and smoking. He looked like hell. Skinny, no, boney, face the color of dried French mustard, eyes dark and burrowed into his head.

"Took a cab," Montgomery said in a heavy voice less harsh than the one Nagler had heard on the phone. "Some kid, told him I was meeting a Mob guy and gave him an extra twenty to keep his mouth shut. Told him if he told anyone he was here I'd know and it would be the last thing he ever told anyone." He hacked up a painful cough. "And it's Millis now."

Nagler laughed. "How long have you been waiting to use that one? And why's your voice different?"

"Probably since I left Jersey. Been a lot of places there ain't no cabs. Some of that voice thing is an act. If I sound like I'm sick as shit I can get away with a lot." He drew in another mouthful of smoke and tossed the cigarette into the brackish water. "Ain't gonna be long anyway."

Nagler pondered the statement, but let it be. "Wondered why you've been hard to find, Dancer. I had something drop on my lap and wanted to talk to you about it. Why the name change? It's Millis? And how's Arizona? If that's where you are."

"Yeah, Millis, for today at least. Been Robertson, Zaccaro, even Martinez, but I don't look Spanish. Fucking hot," Millis said and coughed. "But what do they say? It's a dry heat." A coughing laugh. "Who gives a shit how dry the heat is when it's a hundred and twenty at noon. Can't sit outside, can't use the pool, can't play golf. When I'm not working, just sit in front of the damn TV with the AC on. And smoke. And drink too much. Costs me a damn fortune. But the private work is profitable. You can't imagine how many hot, rich housewives think no one notices or how many Chamber of Commerce guys think the last hotel on the mule trail highway is a perfect spot to meet their musclebound gym instructor for a couple hours of private grunting and grinding. Ain't they never heard of GPS?"

Nagler took a breath and spit out the air. The smell of the old bog never faded. Dank, oily, stick-to-your-skin rotten. "Sorry about your health. But…"

Dancer's scratchy breath filled the hollow. "Somebody is watching you, Frank."

"Somebody is always watching, Dancer. I don't scare off. What can you tell me?"

A long silence.

"This ain't just watching. It's trailing, plotting. Your whole gang. Even that reporter."

"Dawson?"

"There's some weird shit going on here. They find me, they kill me. That's why I changed my name like five times. Worse than usual. Goes back further than you think."

"So, what about this Carlton Dixon thing scared you away? That was it this time, right?"

Another silence. The murmur of highway traffic pulsed across the cold, dark swamps, a sound worn into the stony outcrops and patches of weeds.

"Don't you think it's a bit odd that old case is back?"

Nagler frowned, a little confused. "It came back because Dixon's daughter…"

"Yeah, weepy-eyed, poor little me, my daddy's in jail because of these bad men. Came to you, just happened to have a file."

Nagler stared over the bog and scratched his neck. "Damn it. Sister Katherine said something about her the other day. Haven't had a chance to look at what she gave me."

"The old nun?" A hacking laugh. "She ain't dead?"

Nagler grinned. "She wasn't that day. You don't think…?

Dancer lit another cigarette. "Look, I'll tell you *what*. You'll have to figure out *who*. Been carrying this thing too long. Makes me cough, and then I want a cigarette, and then I cough some more. So, this Dixon thing. Dirty, Frank. Really dirty. Cops, druggies, businessmen, bankers, set-ups, traitors, money laundering, you name it. One big power grab. The Pursels were snitches, from inside the drug gang. All strung out, but effective. They're probably under a rock in the Catskills. Dixon was undercover."

Nagler interrupted. "Why is there no record of that?"

A scoffing cough. "There wouldn't be, would there? He gave us good intel. Go back about a year before the arrests. It's all there, case by case. He knew it was crashing. I was trying to pull him out, but…"

"Who blocked it?"

"Never found out. I thought it was from the cop side, but later I heard it was from the money side. Some said he was working both sides. Something in the real estate market, the stock market, some fucking trade deal in Australia… I don't know. But it ended, collapsed, and Dixon took the hit. There were a couple other players we never got a handle on. Background guys."

"Who was McCarroll? Couldn't find a picture anywhere."

"Enforcer. From the money side."

"He got life for the murders," Nagler said.

"Did you find him in jail, Frank? He ain't there. Did maybe a year. Sent to Europe for 'rest and rehabilitation.'" A garbled cough filled laugh. "He probably did the Pursels or ordered it. He's still on the payroll. I'd bet he's back in Ironton. He'll do Dixon when he gets out, or just before. And he'd do me if I was there when he stepped off that plane in Phoenix. But I ain't going back to Arizona. I'm thinking, maybe Nova Scotia, but I'm gonna have to learn to like fish. McCarroll, skinny, wiry balding. Looks like a gangster, talks like a revolutionary. But just a hood in the end, a hired gun. Ya dig deep enough into that explosion and you'll find him."

"How'd you hear about the explosion?"

A cough, then another. "Shit, Frank. Half a downtown blows up and it makes the news, ya know? So, look there's a file no one know about. That's why I called ya. It's in a janitor's closet in the girls' locker room at the high school."

"What?"

"Safest place. Who'd ever connect me with anything athletic? There's stuff in that file about me." He reached into his pocket for a key and gave it to Nagler, and then shook his hand. "Be seeing ya, Frank. You leave first."

"Need a lift?"

"Naw. I'll wait till dark. I'm crashing in an old warehouse couple blocks from here. Even the flea bag joints might not be safe. Stay the night. Got a rental lined up, then I'm gone."

Nagler stopped just shy of the pavement at the end of the trail. A broken street light half a mile away flickered on and off. He stepped back into the trail's brush cover as an old jacked-up Chevy turned onto Mount Pleasant from the right and slowly cruised past. The driver tossed a lit cigarette out the window, then hit the gas and the car peeled out, the screech of tires shattering the silence. *Been there, done that. Me and Martha late, jumping into our clothes, slamming the old Dodge up the bog road, onto the pavement, and then fishtailing the hell home. Maybe this is another of those places Sister Katherine spoke about. I've laughed here, loved here, screamed and cried here. Found bodies here. And now probably heard the confession of dead man.*

Nagler stepped up the empty road and scanned both directions. Dancer, still on the path, coughed into the darkness.

Shit, Nagler thought and began to quick step to his car. Watching. All of us. Lauren at the bank building on Blackwell. Street sounds and a white van.

CHAPTER EIGHT

Destiny

It was always gray, the ghetto was; dim, shadowed by the rocky face of Swedes Hill whose eastern ridge marked the spot in Ironton where the coal smoke from the stoveworks slammed into the eastern sunlight and then filtered down to coat the roofs of the workers' shacks, the dusty, cobbled streets, and the dreams of kids like Frank Nagler.

That was the life he saw as he examined the mural being painted by Destiny Wonder on the expansive wall that filled one side of the lobby of the new public housing complex.

Nagler's soft, "Wow" caught her attention, and she stopped painting.

"You're Frank, right?"

He turned to greet the voice. Destiny was a short, thin woman with blond hair spangled with streaks of blue and green. One strap of her black bib coveralls slipped from her bare, muscular shoulder.

"I'm Destiny. LT said you were coming."

"I'm supposed to meet Lauren and...LT?"

"Yeah, Maria. You know, Lieutenant Maria Ramirez. LT. I'm her partner."

Nagler tipped his head, trying not to be embarrassed. "I'm, I'm, sorry... all the time we have worked together... I never asked or even thought..."

"Hey, okay. She has to be cool about it. She wants to be chief, and this place ain't ready for a queer police chief." Destiny's voice took on a dismissive tone.

"Wait, that's not what I meant," Nagler said. "Maria should have been named captain while I was out. I'm going to take that up after we get this bombing settled. She's qualified. That's all that matters." His glance softened. "Do your job. That's all I care about."

A half smile. Destiny said, "She said you'd say that."

Nagler touched the mural.

"I grew up here." His voice was suddenly heavy and moist. He reached for a shadowed face, squared jawed with dark, brooding eyes. "That could be my grandfather. His face was always hard, except when he looked at my grandmother. Eyes between anger and sadness."

"It could be," Destiny said, as she tapped another face with the wooden bush handle. "This one's my grandfather, and this one his brother." She tapped another, incomplete face. "I'm basing the faces and scenes from family records and photos from the historical society."

"Why here?"

Destiny smiled. "That partner of yours, Lauren Fox, is one smart lady. She knew when this complex was proposed, she could not stop it for a bunch of governmental reasons, but she fought for some changes, more efficient heating and cooling systems, better sound proofing, a neighborhood playground, and this, to mark the history of the ghetto which was being plowed under. The developer was not pleased."

"Sounds like her. Who's the developer?"

"Over here." Destiny stepped over to a pencil drawing that looked like a dragon. "It's not done yet. I think I'll do it in red, for the dragon, and for the blood that was spilled by the workers that made the company all that money."

"Why a dragon?"

"That's the company's name, Dragon Associates. Why?"

Nagler squinted at the drawing and then at the floor. "I've heard that name before, or something like it." He waved hand at the mural. "Wonderful work. It'll come to me."

"You know what they will never figure out?" Destiny asked with a smirk. "How subversive this mural will be. Their corporate dragon logo is benign, almost cartoonish, symbolizing tradition and leadership. Mine will be angry, domineering with a trace of evil in its eyes. The company men will see it as a symbol of power, but the power I will draw will be in the faces of the workers. Their eyes will be both hard and yearning, fists clenched around tools, not symbols of progress, but of defiance, the torches they carry, not signs of safety, but of a rising."

Nagler smiled with appreciation. "That's a big goal."

"The trick," she said, "Is that on the face, it will seem to be a work celebrating the company that built this center, because we like simple stories and want to believe that all is good. But in detail it will be anti-establishment, celebrating not the masters, but those they thought they mastered." She stepped along the wall, brushing her fingers across painted faces and pencil sketches of others. "Celebrating not the end, because there is no end, but the struggle for what continues, for dignity, family, and love. It will celebrate you and your family and that of Del Williams..." she touched a dark face that Nagler recognized in that instant as that of his old friend. "And my family and Maria's, and everyone who came before to build this city and fill these unnumbered streets with life."

Destiny leaned her back against the wall, tipped her head back, her face composed. "And if they miss the point, which they will," she twirled and slapped her hand at a spot on the wall, "Right there will be me and Maria, arms enwrapped, lips pressed together, wearing brightest rainbow t-shirts I can create." She turned to face Nagler, her left shoulder pressed against the wall. "Because we all belong."

"Bravo!"

The cheering voices of Maria Ramirez and Lauren Fox echoed across the vacant space, their heels slapping on the bare concrete floor.

"She gave you the nickel tour, I guess," Ramirez said as she hugged Destiny. "Ain't she something?"

Lauren wrapped an arm around Nagler as he asked. "How did you pull this off?"

"The builder had a deadline to tap into a federal loan program. I had a choice. I could have dragged out the approval for months, which would have forced them to pull out of the development, or I could have handed them a list of, shall we say, needs, including this mural."

"Of course you did," he said. "Did they approve the artist?"

"I gave them no choice. I did offer a theme, 'the triumph of progress,' or some horseshit. I gave the project to Destiny and look what we got."

Nagler kissed her hair. "Yeah, but I don't think you wanted to meet me here for an art appreciation class."

"Yeah, we got a problem, Frank," Ramirez said, tipping her head toward a distant corner of the room. "That's why we're here. No prying eyes or ears."

Once there, Nagler said, "I know. We have a leak in the department. Remember that kid, Mahala Dixon? She said someone in Boonton was talking about that white van. I told her she needed to stop talking about it. How the hell would they know?"

The two women shared a look. "More than one, Frank," Lauren said.

"How…"

"We set a trap," Ramirez said, and pointed to Lauren to continue.

"After the flood five years ago, we got a federal grant to replace the computers in all city departments. We got new computers and a load of new software, especially for system security and intrusion defense. We announced that. What we didn't say is that we also installed in some of the most advanced anti-hacking software available from an unknown source as a pilot program. Stuff that was not available on the common marketplace. What no one knows is that our source upgrades the software constantly. A little trade-off."

"I never knew that," he said with appreciation. Then he chuckled. "I thought we didn't keep secrets."

Lauren patted his chest. "If I told you who gave it to use, I'd have to kill you." She smiled, teasing. "Actually, now that you know this, they may kill you anyway."

"Oh, good. I'll just go step in front of a truck to save them the trouble. Do we know who the spies are?"

"Not yet, and we might never know for sure," Maria said. "They've used multiple names and hotspots. "But we know that they are looking at the financial files that Lauren has gathered, and this is odd, the files from the old Carlton Dixon case, like photos of the white truck."

Nagler held up a hand to stop her. "This is beyond me. I can barely answer my phone, which you both know. "

Lauren shared a wink with Maria.

"Told you he'd say that," she said. "We're counting on our opponents also knowing that," she said to Nagler. "So, we set up a dummy Frank Nagler online."

"What's that mean?"

"In the real world not a thing," Ramirez said. "Virtually, online that is, and there is no way to say this politely, you are bait."

"That won't be hard," Nagler scoffed. "Maria, you remember Dancer, Jeff Montgomery?"

Ramirez screwed up her face. "Oh, yeah, blast from the past."

"I met with him this morning. He's Jeff Millis now."

"What?"

"He was just passing through. I'll just say that he is running, probably for his life."

"Who's this?" Lauren asked.

"Old detective," Maria said. "Grungy street cop, knew everybody, everything."

"Yeah," Nagler said. "Two things he said. First, we all are being followed and watched, and second, it all ties back to that Carlton Dixon case."

Ramirez narrowed her eyes. "What does?"

"Him, the bombing. And you'll like this – Mahala Dixon."

"Knew I didn't like her."

Lauren asked, "Who?"

"That kid. Remember that file I was looking at after the last academy class when I sort of blew up the world?" Nagler saw the recognition in Lauren's face. "That kid. Dancer said it was not an accident she gave me that file."

"Why do I hear a great sucking sound, Frank?" Ramirez asked. Then to Lauren. "And you, chickie, get a detail."

"Nooo…" Lauren protested. "I'm in that stupid bank on Blackwell almost all day."

"It's the 'almost' that worries me," Maria said.

"Lauren might be right," Nagler said. "We all start walking around with uniforms for an escort and we lose the advantage that we know they are watching. We just don't know who they are. Instead, text each other."

"Hi, Frank. At bakery. Want a doughnut?" Lauren laughed. "We'll have to develop code."

Nagler smiled and shook his head, "One last thing. Dancer said there was a file in the janitor's room in the girls' locker room at the high school. Let's presume there is a spy at the high school, so I can't just walk in."

"That's easy," Maria said. "Destiny and I play in a volleyball league once a week. I'll get it."

****

The envelope from Sister Katherine stared back from the middle of his desk like an accusation. He heard her voice rattling in his head like a voice of doom, knowing that when it sounded like that he was in deep shit.

He wasn't sure why he hadn't opened the file; maybe he just didn't want to know what Mahala Dixon has been up to just yet. Meanwhile on the other side of his head he heard Dancer's snarling warning about the young woman.

He pushed the nun's envelope aside. *In time.*

He reached for a legal pad upon which he had written a list of names.

The first name was Tony, Barry's cook.

Why hasn't he showed up? Go back to Colombia?

Next was Ethan Ricardo, and below it was Eduardo Tallem, the owner of the Cuban restaurant.

Tallem was at the bombing scene the first day, according to a police report filed by one of Ramirez's officers. Nagler tried to picture the man, but even after all the time Nagler had patronized the restaurant he could not recall a face, or a manner of dress, or a voice. Odd, he thought.

Tallem had also failed to attend any of the weekly sessions created by Lauren Fox to explain the recovery process – the available loans, permits and inspections required, and all that bureaucratic stuff that she was so good at.

There was pattern to disaster recovery, Nagler knew. A couple days of crying and helplessness, a couple more days of complaining to any reporter available that the government was not doing enough, pronouncements by mayors and officials like Lauren that programs had been established, deadlines set, and applications filed. All that was followed by the banality of recovery as shops reopened, customers returned, and drivers ran red lights with regularity.

The Cuban place was one of the more popular restaurants on Blackwell. So where was the owner?

And where, Nagler wondered, was Mayor Ollivar?

That was another routine that followed disasters: Politicians on street corners demanding attention, comforting residents and business owners or cutting ribbons at new housing developments or business openings.

Ollivar was seen huddling with the police chief and the fire marshal at the beginning but had since been suspiciously absent, considering he was running for re-election. Was he letting Lauren drive the recovery? She was capable of it, but it would be odd. Was he setting her up to take the blame should it all go sideways?

That would be more typical of an Ironton mayor, he knew. Maybe old Howard Newton left behind a playbook in a secret bottom drawer in the city hall desk of the mayor's office. It could have been called: How to Make a Mess and Blame Everyone Else.

Nagler leaned back in his chair and with his fingers laced behind his head, he stretched. The office was filling up; he closed the open files in his desk.

Ollivar had a commercial insurance agency, Nagler recalled. His clients financed his run for mayor.

Damn it.

With such a big event and so little information, it was easy to make everyone's actions and history suspect, he thought.

Still, Ollivar ran as a political outsider, a leader who would bring business sense and leadership to city hall.

So where was he?

Nagler started a third column on his legal pad, put the mayor's name at the top, and then added a heading: MIA. Missing in action.

"Hey, Nagler!"

Nagler glanced in the direction of the heavy, breathy voice to see Fire Marshal Dennis Duval barreling down the narrow space between desks.

"Got some photos for ya," Duval said as she leaned over Nagler's desk and dropped a folder. "We didn't find that fucking knife, but we found stuff you might be interested in."

Nagler gathered up the photos that had spilled from the folder. "So, yeah, thanks for looking, Dennis. What else did you find?"

Duval's face split with a toothy half-grin. "A chair that matches that yellow one you've been ratcheting on. The yellow one on the theater roof. And some beat up gas cans." He nodded to the folder. "There's pictures."

Nagler leaned back and closed his eyes, "Holy shit. Where was this stuff, I mean, before the building exploded?"

"Fourth floor, 42 Warren. At least that where the clean-up crew had shoveled the pile. It could be wrong, but I have no way of knowing. There was kitchen furniture. A stove, refrigerator, a busted wooden table, cabinets, all of it damaged and charred a bit. Know what was weird? No food. They saved everything, you know, for fingerprints and DNA, but no food containers. There was a few pizza boxes and some beer and whiskey bottles and couple wads of aluminum foil that had burn marks..."

"Crash pad," Nagler said.

"Exactly," Duval said. "But ask me if I think if some junkies blew up that block." He paused.

Nagler waited. "Well..."

"Shit, no. The gas cans were found one building over and one floor below the place with the busted kitchen. And them cans was blown up, exploded."

"So..."

"So, right. They was once filled with gasoline. Ya could smell the leftover, even in that trash pile. That's a midpoint between the spot of the first explosion on Warren and Blackwell and the top floor apartment on the last building a block away."

Nagler held up a hand to slow down Duval. "What are you getting at?"

"This wasn't one big explosion, Frank. But a series of explosions. Some were natural gas leaks, others were fires of combustible materials, still others were gasoline and space heaters. It was a plan, a series. Break up the walls and floors, weaken the structures, fire and natural gas leaks through 'em, then at spots encourage the fire with gasoline." Duval wiped his forehead. "And don't worry about them gas cans and some other stuff. I've got a van in a, shall we say, unknown location. I contacted a company I trust to run tests, and I'll get the results to you when they're done."

Nagler chuckled; Duval was so serious, and yet, absolutely right. "You don't trust our evidence department and Captain Bernie Langdon?"

Duval screwed up his face. "Why would I? He loses stuff." He turned away, and then back. "And if ya ain't figured it out, Frank. Somebody took down that block on purpose. Thought I'd just say that."

Nagler put on a solid face so he wouldn't laugh. "Absolutely, Dennis. Good work." He paused. "Question, though. Why would they set a series of explosions and not just set one big one and take down the whole place? And if it was a series instead of one giant one, and why did I feel the earth shake at my house, maybe a mile away?"

Duval leaned back against the partition across from Nagler's desk, a pensive look on his jowly face.

"Well, not to get technical on you, Frank, but that crash you heard was the result of all those little explosions, like blowing up the pillars of a building in a planned detonation. Eventually the weight is too much and the building collapses. Bang! Think of it this way. A single house can be blown to smithereens by a single gas leak because while it's heavy. It only weighs a few tons. A city block weighs thousands of tons, so it's harder to move. On the other hand, military grade explosives in a specific amount would have blowed that block into the next county, technically speaking."

"But no one…"

"That's right, Frank. No one reported any military grade explosives, so that leaves us with a controlled demolition."

"Something to think about…"

"And if ya also hadn't guessed, someone put that yellow chair on the theater roof to watch something. It didn't get blowed out a window." Then he left.

Nagler watched the large man waddle along, silently impressed. In the back of his head, he heard Mulligan's voice saying that Duval would be useful one day. And today he was.

Nagler flipped through the pile of photos that showed the damage to the block.

No knife, he thought. No murder weapon.

Probably means the killer took it with him.

Also means that whoever killed the kid, might have blown up the block.

So, Ethan Ricardo, wrong place, wrong time?

Or an accomplice who became a loose end.

Nagler closed his eyes and bit his lower lip.

Why a bread knife?

CHAPTER NINE

Drone shots

The drone camera soundlessly captured the sweep of downtown Ironton: The dome of a blue-gray sky, the rail station and the arrival of a west-bound commuter train, the flow of bodies from the open doors, the rush to the parking lots and sidewalks, the mass splitting into pairs, threes, then singles. Lines of cars and trucks at intersections, stalled, then bursting forward, walkers dodging, then a mass, then one stepping quickly and waving before the lead car edged into the street as the light changed. Pigeons like darts.

The voice on the video is Jimmy Dawson.

"We wonder why they build and rebuild, replace the fallen with new. It's because they need some place to store their money in plain sight. This block was burned to the ground in 1883 when a hay-filled barn attached to a wooden railroad hotel burst into flames that consumed the storefronts until… Hey! What the fuck!"

At that point the video showed the effect of the drone jolting to the left, then twisting and plummeting to the ground, the captured scene a swirl of sky, street, buildings, sky, then a skittering shot of car tires, metal posts, bricks and weeds; then a final view of the sky and shadows of bodies stopping and staring; finally just one backlit shadow and the shape of a foot growing larger and static on the screen. Dawson yelling, "Hey!"

"That's it," Dawson said to Frank Nagler as he folded up the case for the tablet. Dawson pointed to the hill behind the car dealership which was across the road from where Dawson had launched the drone. "The shots came from behind me to the right. One took out the drone. I thought it had been struck by a bird until another shot hit the guardrail next to me." Dawson turned back to the guardrail and wiped a shaky hand through his sweaty hair. "Had to be warning shot. I mean I was right in the open. How could they miss me unless they wanted to? I dove across the railing. I mean, what the fuck?!"

Ramirez on Nagler's radio: "Secured the drone. Hell of a shot, smashed a propeller."

"Any sign of a projectile, bullet?"

"No, Frank. We're walking the parking lot but wish us luck."

"Hey, send a couple officers to the south roof of the stoveworks. Dawson said the shots came from that general direction and that's the only spot high enough."

As he spoke Nagler scanned the tree line. In the summer with the trees in full bloom the shot would have been impossible. But now the trees were bare, and the thicket of cold branches provided both cover and a clear sight-line. Flat surface, with a scope. "Had to have scouted the area," he muttered. He reached over and grabbed Dawson's shoulder. "Take a breath. How many shots do you think?"

The reporter leaned on a car hood, hunched over, elbows stiff, staring at the ground his face open and eyes wide in shock. When Nagler touched his shoulder, his face hardened.

"Hard to say. I was focused on the drone. Little bit of traffic. I didn't really hear anything." Dawson rubbed his face, paused, and rubbed it again, harder each time. "Damn it. Can't let them get away with this, Frank."

"Don't intend to, Jimmy."

"I don't mean you." Dawson pushed off the hood of the car and walked toward his equipment strewn on the side of the road. "I'll send Ramirez a copy of that drone footage." Dawson loaded the equipment into his car, settled behind the wheel and pulled a U-turn back towards Nagler. "You'll know it when you see it." Then he drove away.

Nagler walked to the guardrail and scanned the overview. The yellow chair was still there, unmoved it seemed. It had become an Internet sensation with its own YouTube page. Dawson's website was even running a contest asking readers to guess when it would be removed. It's almost heroic, Nagler thought with a chuckle. Our brave little chair. But it's also a symbol of our inability to solve this case. He leaned on the aluminum frame at the top of stairs that led to the streets below. He had examined that scene twenty times since the first day. He witnessed the search, the clean-up, watched as engineers tested the remaining structures, saw in his mind the shadows of the bodies that had been seen in ghostly videos, the wisp of the white van. All meaning something; all meaning nothing. He kicked at the ground. We need a new way. Waiting's not working.

He took a few steps down the walkway, looking back to the point where Dawson had been standing when the shots were fired. Dawson was right – they'd missed on purpose. An officer had found the mashed bullet on the ground under a joint where two beams were attached with one-inch bolts to a metal pillar, in all about three-quarters of an inch of steel. *Why were they shooting at his knees?* Nagler raised his eyes to gain a new angle on the possible shooting platform. The stoveworks roof was too high, but not the roof of the car dealership.

"Come with me," he shouted to one of the officers.

In the parking lot Nagler found Randy Jensen, the security guard.

"How do you get to the roof?" Nagler yelled.

"What? Fucking-A." Jensen turned a full circle as Nagler rushed by.

"Stairs, inside," he yelled back. "And a locked ladder on the backside."

Nagler turned back. "A what?"

"A ladder," Jensen said as he ran his hand through his long hair. "You know, a service ladder. Been here for years. For repair guys."

"Show me."

On the backside the building, they found the ladder with a broken lock.

"Randy, get me the manager," Nagler ordered.

****

"The place opens at seven," Nagler said as he handed a flash drive containing the video surveillance from the car dealership to Ramirez. "Service crews arrive about six. This is video from about the last week. The manager is getting us six months' worth."

"Do we need that much? You plan on moving in?" she asked with a shake of her head. "Okay, let's see. What day is this? Good, five days ago. I'll fast forward…"

"No, don't. The shooter had to scout the site during the day, but I'll bet he cut that lock at night. The manager said the last time anyone was on the roof was last spring to replace an AC unit."

"So, we want someone pretending to look at cars but is actually trying to find a shooter's nest. Don't ask for much, do you, Frank?" Ramirez chuckled and shook her head. "Okay, let's see."

The cameras were set atop light poles at the opposite ends of the parking lot showing the span of the building. The dealership had been opened before the state widened the bridge and highway and took some of the property leaving the lot and one-story building wedged between a flat-faced, steep cliff above which was the stoveworks, and the road. The video was numbing. Cars passing, shoppers in and out of vehicles, salesmen, kids, more cars.

"Why Dawson?' Ramirez asked.

Nagler inhaled deeply and shook his head. "Sorry, I'm brain dead. Dancer said he was a target. He's a reporter. He knew Kalinsky, that reporter on the old Dixon case, and if you look at his website, he has that drone in the air almost every day."

Ramirez paused the video. "That has to be it. They think he captured something. Dawson doesn't even know it." She turned back to the screen. "I'm gonna run this backwards till we see Dawson. We know the shooter was there, maybe we can see him leave."

Nagler rubbed his eyes. "When they do this backward stuff in movies it's funny … wait, there's Dawson."

On the screen the reporter had parked his car and removed a drone, which he placed on the roof of the car, then a computer and halter, which he looped over his shoulders. He fiddled with the computer and launched the drone, which quickly flew out of camera range.

"Why didn't he shoot him then?" Nagler asked. "He would have had the drone and the computer."

"Wait, there's the shots," Ramirez interrupted.

Dawson looked over his shoulder and covered his eyes with one hand.

"The west side camera scans the building," Ramirez said and switched camera views. "Let me sync times, give me a minute, there he is."

The quality of the video was dark and grainy, but on the roof of the garage, a man holding a long gun with a scope knelt against a brace of some sort and fired into the air.

"That had to be the shot that got the drone," Nagler said. "Look at the angle."

"Look at the recoil," Ramirez said. "He fired more than once at the drone." Slowly. "One, two, three shots."

The shooter then adjusted his position and angle, and on the side screen that showed Dawson, the reporter dove to the ground.

"Hey, what's that?" Nagler pointed at the screen. "There's another guy."

"I see him."

Ramirez stopped the video from the eastside camera and enlarged the video from the west side.

"Christ, that's Tony. Barry's cook. I recognize the shirt."

"What's he doing?"

Nagler laughed. "I didn't mean to laugh, but really? He's hitting the guy with a stick. Tony!"

They watched as the video recorded the brief scuffle: Tony waved a stick in the air, the shooter knelt, then rolled away before Tony struck his hand and the shooter dropped the rifle. The shooter kicked Tony backward and the man fell over an unseen object. The shooter scooped up the rifle and ran out of camera range. Tony stumbled after, then stopped and grabbed his back.

Ramirez paused the video. "Tony probably saved Dawson's life."

Nagler touched the screen and the wavy image of Tony in a familiar Hawaiian shirt. "There's a path behind that dealership to the stoveworks. The homeless use it to get to the river. That's where the shooter parked. And I'll bet that's where Tony has been these past weeks. I'm heading up there."

As Nagler turned to leave, Ramirez asked, "Hey, Frank. How did the shooter know Dawson would be on the bridge with the drone?"

Nagler was glued to the door by the question. Eyes wide, furrowed brow: "He told me a couple weeks ago that his website had been hacked. Has to be it."

****

"Exciting shit, huh, Detective Nadling?" Car dealership security guard Randy Jensen rattled the cover to the outside ladder. "This is a temporary lock. Owner said he's gonna take this thing down." He pursed his lips and nodded. "I don't think it's gonna hold, myself."

Nagler had been scanning the hill behind the dealership. The trail to the stoveworks was easily visible without the seasonal leaf cover. Distracted, "Oh, yeah, yeah, that's good. You're sure you didn't see anyone back here?"

"No, no, sir. They put honkin' huge cement blocks and a fence at the ends because of the drop off. It's like twenty, thirty feet, straight down. I think somebody did a Thelma and Louise once. I don't check it."

Distracted still. "Okay, really," Nagler muttered, "They would have known that." He spun and kicked at a rock and sent it flying into the gully. "Know what, Randy, they know too much. They know it before we do."

Randy's worried face stared back at Nagler. "I'm with ya. Who's they?"

Nagler glanced at Randy, the gully, the ladder, narrowed his eyes and offered a wry smile as he reached for his phone "I think we'll find out. Hey, Maria, can we, I don't even know the word, link up with the car dealership's video system, you know, tap it, or is that just a movie thing?"

Nagler's phone was filled with a long breath and the sounds of Ramirez hemming and hawing. "That's a wiretap, Frank. We'd need a court order."

Nagler waved at the air. "I know … that's not really what I meant."

"Tell me what you have in mind. You're not about to do something really weird, are you? I thought you were going to the stoveworks."

"Change of plans. Look, call the guy and ask him to send over the video his cameras record beginning in ten minutes, okay?'

"Will I like this?"

"I think so. And after you reach the guy, wait another ten minutes and show up at the bridge in a patrol car, lights and sirens. Bring a couple patrolmen if you want."

"Frank!"

"Thanks, kid, Love ya."

****

At the edge of the front parking lot, behind a panel truck, Nagler wrenched his tie to one side, pulled out one side of his shirt and let it hang below his jacket, and practiced a stumbling walk. After a couple of trips, he shambled across the street to the guard rail and began waving his arms and pacing.

He moved his mouth as if speaking, but then decided he should actually say words to make it seem more authentic.

He turned his back partway to the road and looked over the damaged blocks.

"So, ya blew up my town, ya bastards," he yelled. "One more thing you have done that has damaged my hometown, hurt the people of Ironton and made you richer." He slowly rotated in a swirling pattern as he stepped unsteadily along the guardrail. "And here I am, trying to catch you. Me, old, damaged Frank Nagler. Crazy cop who blew up a class with stories of murders in Chicago and nonsense about hats. Had 'em worried, I did. They stood there with wide eyes and open mouths, wondering if they should call the funny farm." He stopped walking and leaned over the railing while pointing to his head. "It's all up here, all jumbled up into a big thing. A really big thing. All the stuff that hurts, all the memories of my dead friends and wife, all the baggage I carry around. And it's all your fault. You guys, you have been fucking with the city forever, taking what you want…"

He held out his arms and turned in a series of circles until he was dizzy and stumbled to sit on the rail. *Oh, boy.*

A car slowed in the road and the driver opened the window. "You okay, buddy? Can I call someone?"

Nagler rolled his head to his right shoulder, on his face a twisted smile. "I'm good." As the car drove off, he heard distant police sirens.

He stood and waved at the damaged downtown. "This," he yelled. "This is my place of horrors in which I must dwell, Sister Katherine. This city and all its stinking, rotting streets. Its families with sad, defeated faces, black futures." He turned and kneeled, facing the street. "I carry it all, every day. I see your weeping eyes and hear your worn voices and feel my eyes weep and my voice rip and tear." He ripped off his jacket and grabbed both sides of his head and began to shake it as Ramirez arrived with two patrol cars. "Someone take it from me. Someone take all this weight, all this living. I want to be free of it. I want to be light."

"Frank," Ramirez said. "We're here. Officers help him to my car."

The officers helped Nagler stand and pulled his jacket back on.

As Maria slipped behind the steering wheel and shook her head, he looked over and winked.

CHAPTER TEN

McCarroll

"Of all the…" Police Chief Hanson closed the video. "I'll hand it to you, Frank. It better work."

"I think it has," Nagler said, leaning on the office door frame. "When I was on Blackwell, a lady stopped me, patted my shoulder and said, 'I hope you'll be feeling better soon.'" He pushed off the door frame and smiled. "If I'm not, I'll be visiting Dr. Phillips Ignatius for some serious therapy."

"This will get their attention, huh?" Hanson asked.

"Some of their known associates have hit Dawson's website. Their network is big and hidden. We brought over Dan Yang, who's been helping Lauren with the financials."

"Yeah, alright," Hanson said, peering over his bifocals. "Anything else?"

"Our shooter left behind a couple casings and one bullet after Tony whacked him. They're being tested. Who woulda thought, old Tony?"

"Find him yet?"

Nagler shook his head. "Patrol did a drive-by at the stoveworks but just scared the homeless guys. I'm gonna do a solo walk through."

"That wise? They're looking for you."

"They're always looking for me, chief."

Hanson leaned back. "No more stunts."

****

Nagler parked in the power company lot, a half-mile from the stoveworks, his car tucked behind a couple rusted tanks. He thought about the chief's comment about no more stunts.

Can't promise anything.

A thousand workers filled these buildings, back then, he thought as he edged his way toward the main stoveworks building. The yard was littered with industrial detritus, and he skulked from broken rusted trucks to piles of stone and brick to stoves and doors and stovepipes dumped and crushed, all the while scanning the road, the rail line, and the empty buildings for any signs that he was not alone. His father's last job was shifting glowing metal parts hooked to chains and pulleys from the molding room to the cooling line; his father's face had a permanent tan from the heat and his arms were laced with small burn scars and his clothes had a dozen burned-edged holes. All that work, Nagler thought, all those hours and it barely kept the house warm. It hollowed him out, just like these building shells. These places once glowed with a holy fire of commerce, men and metal the fuel for the progress that seemed always one dim corner ahead. A hundred years of work left in cold, stark silence.

The afternoon sun shimmered in the west-facing windows of the two buildings that had been repaired years before awaiting occupancy that never arrived, while the rest shuddered in a long, shadowed canyon formed by the three-story stoveworks plant that lined both sides of the narrowing road.

A commuter train rattled by sweeping sound with it through the last turn before downtown leaving a windy silence and a scattering of dry leaves.

Nagler stepped through the hole in the battered chain link fence, the metal signs that glared in scarred red paint CAUTION and NO TRESPASSING rattling like empty laughter.

Inside the fence, he paused and swept around in a full circle to sense the areas of shadow and light. So many places to hide.

The homeless camp was at the southern end of the cavernous, hollow complex. Nagler stopped his careful sole-sliding walk and strained to hear any voices, but he was too far away. A few more steps, another stop. There was only the vague echoed drip of unseen water and the metallic creaking of ancient iron beams.

A flutter of pigeons above his head captured his attention; a faint rattle, maybe a can, echoed. A place so still, he could hear his own breathing.

Del and I knew this place, he thought. As kids they'd scrambled in and under the parked train cars, crawled over the piles of discards, and got yelled at by guards. It made sense later that Del in the throes of his addictions and poverty came here. Abandoned buildings, abandoned people.

In the dimness Nagler saw a worn pathway, the dust kicked aside by countless shoes.

Would they follow me here?

He varied his pace, at once quick, then slow with long strides. He slapped his leather soles on the cement floor in rhythm. Sometimes deliberately hard, then a sudden stop. *Was that echo my step or someone behind that wall ahead?*

Then, outside, the sound of a motor idling. But there was a wall without windows. Nagler quick-stepped to a partition near a window smeared with greasy dust, but it gave him no clear view of the road. He closed his eyes to concentrate: The engine sputtered to his distant right, the sound like smoke funneled through the concrete canyon. A slight grumble of acceleration, then silence.

He reached for his phone to call dispatch to send a patrol car along the highway looking for a white van but held off. *Jesus, Frank. If they were here. They would have already shot you.*

A voice shattered the silence. "Hey man, whatchu want?"

The sound caused Nagler to break into a cold sweat.

"Hey, Bennie, it's me, Frank Nagler." His throat was dry, and his voice creaked like a broken hinge.

"Oh, man, Brother Nagler. Don't be sneakin'."

Bennie was bearded giant, his bulk swollen by layers of sweater and jackets. He had become leader of the homeless clan since Del's death a year before.

"Wasn't sneaking, Bennie." Nagler coughed as the enormity of Bennie's stink filled the space. "Was there a van at your end a few minutes ago?"

"Yah. The county health folks. Somethin' about checkups, but shit, Frank, every time they want to check us, one of us ends up in lockup. So, we sorta politely decline, get it?"

Nagler pulled out Tony's photo and held it at arms' length. "Seen this guy?"

Bennie tipped the photo to the light, then nodded. "Off and on, last couple weeks. Said someone is looking for him."

"That would be me."

"Naw. Couple other guys. Here a week ago. Some Hispanic kid trying to act tough in his black hoodie over his head and reaching into his pants like he was packin'. The guy in charge was this old, shrunken Irish, black leather, scarred face. Tough guy, no bullshit. Said they was cash involved."

McCarroll. Damn it. Dancer was right. Wonder if he left town.

"Anyone tell him anything?"

Bennie wiped a smile on his face. "Naw. We hang together. You know that. We told Tony and he split."

Nagler pulled out a twenty. "Pass the word. Tell Tony I'll be at the Old Iron Bog. Two days. He'll know where."

****

"Damn it!"

Heads in the bank lobby rose and then quickly fell eyes nailed to the floor as Lauren Fox chose not to kick the piles of paper at her feet across the room.

Instead, she fell to her knees, grabbed her head, and muttered, "Fuck."

Not a fuck of anger, not a fuck of disappointment or defeat. But a fuck of tired recognition.

106

It had been there all along, the trail. The money, the properties, the players, one by one, year by year, deal by deal.

"And we couldn't connect it."

She scooped up a handful of papers, stood, and crossed to the white board at the rear of the office. *Until now.*

Just as she began, Frank Nagler entered the office and she nodded him to wait off to the side.

On the board she wrote DRAGON.

"This is them, guys." She tapped the board. "And this is also them."

She began to write: DRAG.ON, DRAG, DRAG-ON, DRAGN, D.RAGON, D.R.AGON, DRA-GOON, DGN, DRA.N, and then a dozen more.

"Then add associates, institute, company, corporation, LLC, any version of a corporate name. Danny, run a program to determine how many anagrams can be made from Dragon. Then we search. They are in those boxes of paper files, in hidden corners of electronic files, on agendas, resolutions, bank statements. They've been coming before the city with plans for decades. Let's find them."

"Who are they?" Danny asked.

"The owners of the block that went blooey," Lauren replied.

"I thought they were called Leviton, Inc.," Danny said. "That what tax record indicated."

"That's right. Leviton. Leviathan. Dragon," Lauren said. "They own nearly twenty percent of Ironton right now, a lot of the vacant industrial sites, and over the years have owned almost sixty percent of the real estate in this city through dummy corporations. We have corporate names, but not human names. We need 'em. They're clever, so we need to be."

"So, someone targeted their holdings," Danny said.

"No." Lauren took a breath and shook her head several times. "They did it to themselves. What we don't know is why." She turned to face her staff. "It's a desperate act to blow up your own property. We need to find out how desperate so we can anticipate what they will do next. Let's go."

Nagler greeted her with a smile. "Impressive. So why?"

Lauren used her foot to pull out a chair from under the adjacent desk, sat and dropped the papers in a messy pile. "Pick one: Taxes, bad investments, loss of tenants, death of a company principal. Those would be normal. But this is fraud, just like we thought. Remember all those empty apartments? It has taken tremendous skill and luck to hold all this together. Did their luck run out? It might not have always been a scam. But it is now. What changed? Stuff you wouldn't have to worry about now that you're a YouTube star."

"You saw it?"

"Hard to avoid."

"Convincing enough?"

Lauren just smiled.

"Anyway," Nagler said, "I remember you on your hands and knees yelling at a map of downtown Ironton."

"Well, it's worse than that," she said. "I ran into Jack Williams, a gas company VP. He was on a commission a few years back that set up new rules for apartment inspections and occupancy. Each vacancy triggered an inspection. Jack said there had been a lot of paperwork filed for new tenants in those buildings in the past couple years, so a lot of inspections."

"Would the new tenants be there?"

"No. Just the property owner or a representative."

"I get it. They can fake their way through it. Inside job?"

She chuckled. "Gee, Frank, what makes you think that? Another thing on the list. But who's paying the taxes, and if the apartments are empty where does the money come from? That's what we don't know. But worse? I don't know who among all these fine people will tip them off. You recall our conversation about leaks. Well, I'm just waiting,"

"I know. Me, too When you get a name, call me." He stared at the white board with all the DRAGON names. "Hey, isn't the owner of that worker's ghetto housing complex called Dragon Associates, Dragon something?"

She laid back in the chair and propped her feet on the desk and rolled her head back to stare at the ceiling. "Yeah, now that you mention it. God, I'll have to find that paperwork. One more thing. We'll figure it out, Frank. What brings you here? Unless you're wondering why I'm stretched out like this before you."

They shared a long, deep stare.

"We've answered that question before," he said, and then smiled. "Been looking for Tony, the cook, and stopped by to tell you that McCarroll is in town."

Lauren slipped her feet to the floor and rocked forward. "And he's…?"

"The hit man from that old Carlton Dixon case. If he didn't take those shots at Dawson, he knows who did, same for the explosion. I think Tony disappeared because he saw the bomber. I've got to find him and get him safe. And you, don't run around town without an escort, and text where you are. McCarroll is ruthless."

"So, this *is* all connected."

"Seems to be." Nagler scanned the room. "Where's Dan Yang? Had a question for him."

Lauren stepped over and leaned her head in his chest. "He went back to the college for a couple of days. Said he had to set up the new semester." She frowned comically, but her eyes held the worry. "So okay, I'll become friends with my babysitter. Can I ask a favor? One of the young guys, a workout freak who looks like a young Brad Pitt would be cool. Can you arrange that?" She reached up and touched his face, grinning. "Never mind. You'll do."

"We'll discuss that later," he laughed. His phone buzzed: Ramirez.

"You do know where to find me, don't you?"

"Yup. And I'll bring the body lotion." He kissed her hair. "Gotta run."

"Hey, you. Wouldn't McCarroll be after you, too?"

He wanted to reassure her, to say it would be okay. Instead, "Probably."

****

Ramirez greeted Nagler with a hard face, flat mouth, and dark eyes, like she was channeling Sister Katherine when the old nun taught Nagler in third grade and he didn't do his math homework.

What'd I do now? he wondered.

"You know what this case needs?" she asked.

"A resolution?"

"Fewer criminals."

"Now what?"

"Our shooter. Not who you were hoping it was."

Nagler reached for a chair and spun it before he sat down. "I didn't really think it would be McCarroll. Dawson would be dead."

Ramirez leaned over. "But you were counting on it. Our lead gangster. Possibly a trained sniper. Would tie all this up in a neat bow."

"I know, but Tony would never have snuck up on him. Tony's not that quick and I suspect that McCarroll's not that dumb." Nagler shook his head. Then again. "So, who?"

Ramirez turned back to the computer screen and called up a file. "Eduardo Tallem. Also known as Miquel Rodriguez and Donald Jackson. His prints are on the casings and bullet recovered on the car dealership roof. And he's in the system."

"The owner of the Cuban restaurant," Nagler said, musing. "The owner of the Cuban restaurant, who is rarely seen in his establishment. So, how much trouble is he in that he needed to shoot a drone out of the sky and take a shot at old Dawson? Who owns his ass?"

"He's got a history, Frank, and not just in Jersey."

"I'll bet," he said. "Let's think about that morning. A bombing, Tony and Ethan Ricardo in the building, and … is Tallem there?"

"Wait a minute," Ramirez said, catching on.

"Yeah. That's it. The owner of the space where the first explosion took place and one of his employees was murdered." Nagler leaned back and squinted at the ceiling. "So Tallem rigs up a little explosion thinking he'll get out from under the whatever the debt is, and then Ethan Ricardo, in early to open the restaurant, finds the set up and his boss, who then grabs a bread knife and stabs the kid, hauls his body downstairs, opens a gas line, waits a minute until he can really smell the gas and leaves." He popped to a sitting position facing Ramirez. "In the service alley, he runs into Tony, there to open Barry's. They greet each other, something they've been doing for years. But then what?"

Ramirez stared at the photo on the computer screen. "Tallem says something to Tony," Nagler said.

"It couldn't be a threat," Ramirez said, turning away from the computer. "Even Tony would have understood a threat. And that would have surprised him, since he and Tallem are, we suppose, friends, or at least friendly competitors."

Nagler slapped the desk. "Tony would have asked about Ethan. That's who he would have expected to see in the alley that early. 'Hey, Eddie. Where's Ethan? Ah, he's sick. Sleeping in the cellar. Flu or something'."

"Right, Tallem leaves." Ramirez squinted at the opposite wall. "How many figures on video did we see leaving that place? Damn it, I don't recall."

"But we saw Tony. I know there's no view of the alley, so what did he do before he took off?"

Ramirez nodded. "Smelled the gas, went to wake up Ethan, to get him out of there. Found him dead and ran?"

"And since then, he's been hiding from Tallem *and* tracking him." Nagler laughed. "Who knew Tony was so sneaky?"

Ramirez nodded with a little satisfaction, So little has made sense for so long, so why not this? "Wonderful tale. All we have to do now is prove it."

"I'm supposed to meet Tony tomorrow. Sent him a message through the stoveworks homeless crew. McCarroll was there… Shit, McCarroll. McCarroll and Tallem. Dancer said McCarroll was in town for the explosion. Did you pick up the file Dancer left at the high school?"

She reached behind her computer for a torn manila file wrapped in rubber bands. "Here."

"You look at it?"

"Haven't had the time to take off fifty rubber bands."

"What's this with rubber bands? Mahala Dixon's file had maybe a dozen. What was Tallem's name fifteen years ago? Did he become Tallem to open the restaurant?"

"What are you thinking?"

"At its heart, the Carlton Dixon case was about drugs. McCarroll, Tallem, Dancer, Dixon. Drugs and money laundering. What do we know about Mr. Eduardo Tallem?"

Ramirez smiled and punched open the computer. "Let's see." She flipped through a couple screens. "Born, here, U.S., Miami. Father, Colombian, mother, Cuban. Doesn't look like he graduated from high school. Minor scrapes with the law, here and Florida, car thefts, okay, drug possessions, did eighteen months, Florida corrections… well, under different name, Eduardo Castelleon. Picture's the same."

"When was that?"

"Um… twenty years, but look, Newark, fifteen years ago, Donald Jackson, shit! Let me see, Oh, man, Frank. Caught with a van filled with marijuana." She laughed, "A white van. A white Ford Econoline." She slapped the side of the computer. "Look at that." Ramirez reached over and patted Nagler's cheek twice.

He grinned back. "When'd he learn to shoot a rifle? And why was he using Dawson for target practice?"

"Guess we'll find out" she said. "Didn't you say he was planning something. Hope it's not something dangerous and dumb. Oh, and speaking of Dawson." Ramirez opened a new file on her computer showing the last moments of Dawson's drone, when it was smashed by a shoe. "Size 13E. Italian."

"How do you know it's Italian?"

Ramirez enlarged the image and drew a square around a few marks on the sole. The image sharpened to revel the words, "Naples, Italy."

"We think they are a pair of Paolo Scafora shoes, but the rest of imprint is too shadowy to be clear. Couple grand a pair. Handmade."

Nagler ran a hand through his hair. "Wow. And our guy used his fancy, handmade Italian shoe to smash a flying camera. Not sure what that says about his sense of value." He stared at the image. "He ain't local, is he? No one I've arrested in this town wears $2,000 shoes."

"He's also about six-foot-five," Ramirez said, pulling up another image. Another mouse click and a series of lines appeared over the fuzzy image.

Nagler just smiled. The way things were going he sort of wished the drone smasher was just some anti-technology conspiracy nut, but he knew better.

"So, whoever this is, was working with Eduardo Tallem and knows about the bombing and Ethan Ricardo and whatever Dawson caught in that drone …"

"And probably about the truck filled with weed, and a certain white van…"

Nagler leaned over the desk and stared at the ghostly, grainy image on the screen. "Why are you back now?"

CHAPTER ELEVEN

"What are you trying to tell us, Dancer?"

Dancer's files turned out to be seven pages of single-spaced chicken scratch interspersed with numbers, symbols, initials and maybe acronyms, some of the marks faded into the paper, some circled, others underlined. It appeared in a first read to be the kind of notes a detective might take while examining a crime scene. But there was an order to such notes, chaotic as they might seem: Date, place, time, victim description, names of neighbors – even "Mrs. S." – other first impressions. Window open, broken glass near desk, clothes torn, struggle, no struggle, bloody handprint on the wall.

But this, Nagler thought. "What are you trying to tell us, Dancer?" he asked aloud to the empty room.

"You look happy," Lauren Fox said joking as she kicked open the outside door to the kitchen. "Give me hand, please."

Nagler stepped to the door and took the files and folders from her arms and piled them on the table.

"What's all this?"

"What it ever is, Frank. A dusty trail to another stone wall."

She flipped over the papers on the table that Nagler had been examining.

"How can you read this? This handwriting is worse than yours."

"I know. It's Dancer's file," he said, sitting again. "He was hot for me to read it, but for the life of me … It's like code."

Lauren wrinkled her face and shifted the pages in the light.

"It's a diary, Frank. All these notations, odd phrases. Some probably dates." She handed him back the pages. "But you were never a teenaged girl."

"Not that I recall."

"So, you never had to hide secrets from your parents, dreamed about some hunk of a football player or wondered what it would be like to kiss your best girlfriend."

"What?" He laughed. "Come on."

"Didn't you and Del have some secret language, or you and Martha, like when you were heading to the bog to screw and not going to the library?"

"This is different, cop work."

She swigged his open beer, squinted, and shook her head. "Not much. The thing about diaries is that the diary writer hides the ideas in code but leaves enough hints that someone else reading it could think it's about them."

Nagler's eyes widened as he digested this bit of wisdom. "Who did he leave it for? Is it a confession or a warning? We barely knew each other back then." Nagler finished the beer. "If he wanted a cop to find it, he could have stashed it in the evidence room under some obscure case number for which there was no associated paperwork. There's dozens of boxes of cold case evidence back there that no one will ever look at."

"Where'd he leave it?"

Nagler leaned back and stared at Lauren before his face cracked a small smile.

"In the janitor's locker in the girls' locker room at the high school. Ha. I wonder who the janitor was at the time?"

"Wasn't Dancer narcotics?"

"Yeah."

"High school sting?"

"But what's that got to do with McCarroll and all that?"

She reached over a mussed up his hair. "You're the cop. I'm just a city planner."

He reached for her, but she spun away to the refrigerator and pulled out two beers.

"Remember what Calista said to you in the middle for the Tank Garretson case? Stop thinking like a cop. Think like a victim, raised by victims, taught by victims. Maybe that applies now. Maybe it's time to think like a conspirator."

He accepted the beer and drained half the bottle. "If you think like hammer, everything is a nail." He laced his fingers in front of his face and closed his eyes. "But we always have to be right."

"No, Frank. You only have to be right in the end." She scooped up the files. "Didn't you say Dancer told you that there was information about himself in this file, suggesting that he might have been involved or maybe undercover? What'd he say exactly."

"Just that I'd find information about him in this file." He flipped Dancer's seven pages of notes through his fingers. "He did say that he was trying to pull Carlton Dixon out, so maybe he was Dixon's handler."

She leaned over a kissed him. "That wasn't so hard, was it."

"But how do I find it?"

"Dancer's a nickname, right? Look for a symbol or letters that indicate a type of dancer. McCarroll's Irish,. How about "mick" or "MK." The Pursels were twins. Might be as simple as "T1" and "T2." Start there."

"Of course. I feel like a dummy."

"Ah, don't. I've been staring at Dragon acronyms all day. Pretty soon everything is a symbol or an acronym."

He touched her face and saw the lines around her dark eyes, eyes that had seemed lately to be darker, more worried and angrier than he recalled. He ran a finger along her jaw line, and she turned her head and pulled it into her mouth and sucked on it with a wink. Suddenly Dancer's diary didn't seem so important.

She pulled the wet finger out of her mouth and said, "Later."

"Was that an acronym?" he asked smiling.

"No, I'd say that was a pretty solid clue." She laughed and turned toward the door to the hallway.

"Ever thought of using your bank?"

"It has three eight-foot-tall windows facing the busiest street in Ironton."

"How about at midnight."

"At midnight we can do it here." Lauren stepped back to the table and tapped the diary. "Focus. You got a couple hours."

He laughed. "How come you so good at deciphering this kind of stuff?"

"Because I spend all day talking to politicians." Then she frowned and shook her head. "Speaking of which, Mayor Ollivar plans on announcing new development for the bombing site. Yes, it's a bad idea."

Nagler flopped back in his chair. "Come on, we don't even know…"

"He said it was time to move on."

Nagler crossed his fingers on top of his head and closed his eyes. "Of course he did."

"You better wake me up there, fella," she said as she left the room.

Incentive, he thought.

Then with the house still, he listened as Lauren shuffled to the bedroom and commanded "stay," as she dumped the folders on a night-stand and, he imagined, watched them begin to slip to the floor and she slapped a hand on the top of the pile; then one soft tap on the floor, then another as she kicked off her shoes, and a "do it tomorrow" as she draped her clothes over a chair and slipped naked into the bed.

He knew he'd find her later asleep propped on a pillow, a folder or file stretched across her chest.

He shook away the urge to join her and turned his attention to the scraps of paper piled in front of him.

He held up his notes from his review of the file that Mahala Dixon had given him and in the other hand, Dancer's diary. *If I could match up some old this stuff dates, names…*

Then somewhere in the daze of words, he found the start: A high school drug bust. Something so simple it was easy to ignore. Seven lines in a story by Adam Kalinsky. No names of suspects because they were kids, underage. Investigating officers, Jeff Montgomery – Dancer – and Bernie Langdon.

"Ha!" So simple. That's why Dancer was back in Ironton. "Cleaning up a mess you left behind. How's Nova Scotia, pal?"

****

Lauren had fallen asleep with her face planted on the page of an open binder. He tried to gently pull away the binder, but the page was stuck. Instead, he kissed her ear, and she lifted her head with a sleepy, sexy smile.

"Where have you been?" she asked in a softly grumbling flowing voice and rolled to her back, the paper loose, and fell again to sleep.

"I figured it out."

Her eyes popped open, and she smiled. "Of course you did. Now get over here."

"I have to get a message to them."

Lauren closed her eyes, leaned against the pillow, and rolled her neck to work out the kinks. "Get my computer."

Nagler dropped his pants to the floor and retrieved the computer from the dresser.

"Your video is on YouTube?"

"Yup."

"Okay, try this. She typed: "Crazy man cop on display. Old Bog, 2 p.m."

****

119

Nagler had sealed the last of the clear plastic envelopes when Maria Ramirez walked in.

"What's all this?" she asked.

Nagler swiveled in his chair.

"Originals, copies, my notes, and old newspaper stories from the past I found on the Internet. Dancer was right. The background was right out in public. It started with a high school drug bust."

Ramirez smiled in appreciation. "I don't know that to believe. That you did an Internet search or that a minor drug bust fifteen years ago led to a bombing of downtown Ironton."

Ramirez reached for a separate set of papers. "What's this?"

The smile faded. "Trouble," Nagler said. "Sister Katherine's file on Mahala Dixon. Finally read it. She had a juvie record. We need to find out how it fits into all this because I think it does."

"Okay."

"How old do you think she is?"

"She's at the academy right? Probationary. Early twenties."

Nagler reached for the nun's file. "Older. Late twenties."

"So…"

"She knew, hell, she ran with the Pursels."

Ramirez said, "Oh, Gawd. The Pursels from Carlton Dixon, drug bust and he's in jail and they're probably dead, Pursels."

"Right."

"Well, that's a bucket of shit, isn't it? What'd the sister say?"

"A note attached to Mahala's juvie file said that the girl's mother confided in Sister Katherine that her daughter was in bad company, skipping school, maybe selling, but certainly using. The official file is light on details, I'll bet because her father muscled into the case. She got probation. Possession, not selling."

"Selling what, pills, mostly likely. Easy to get into a school. Small bags of weed." Ramirez leaned over the desk. "So, she's running for the

Pursels, and they're running for McCarroll, who is the link to the bigger guys. Why'd she give you that file?"

Nagler scanned the report on Mahala's Dixon hearing. "Guilt? Daddy jumped in to keep his daughter out of juvie jail, Daddy gets caught on the wrong side of it all and ends up in jail after apparently killing four people in a drug raid that he was supposed to be planning as an undercover cop? Tell me that makes no sense. It's like this explosion. Pieces of stuff, trails running off in nine directions. No key suspects and what appears to be a series of smaller events that made a big event. Think that's deliberate?"

"I'm glad it makes sense to you, Frank," Ramirez said. "Something's not right. This is too all over the place."

Nagler leaned back into the chair and let out a long slow breath. "Because they thought no one would ever put it together." He popped out of the seat. "Or they were told no one would put it together because no one was trying to connect it all. That's why the cop files make no sense. They're not supposed to. What the hell is going on?"

"Why's Carlton Dixon been so quiet?"

"Because he's keeping someone's secrets, or he knows if he talks his daughter's in danger."

"Frank, we need to get someone inside to talk to him."

"But it can't be a cop. Mahala said that would put *him* in danger, and she's probably right." He stuck his tongue in his cheek, then nodded. "Calista."

Ramirez grinned. "Perfect." She reached over and patted his cheek twice.

Nagler gathered the papers. "Oh, other nugget. That reporter, Adam Kalinsky? The crash was not an accident. Dancer had a note. There's a smudge before it, but this … 'did AK brake job.' Sounds like murder to me. Was Kalinsky exposing the scheme, or part of it?"

Before Ramirez could, reply her phone chimed out a text. One word: "Black."

"Damn it. We gotta go."

"What?"

"Destiny."

As Ramirez barreled through traffic, she explained that she and Destiny set up a series of code words in case of emergencies. "Black" was the worst.

She and Nagler found the front door to the ghetto housing project open and heard the echoing, pain-filled cry of Destiny calling out: "Maria! In the back. Maria!"

"You go," Nagler said. "I'll call rescue and backup and check the building."

Ramirez gasped when she found Destiny leaning against a pillar, naked to her waist and pressing a white t-shirt over a bleeding wound to her side.

"Frank." Ramirez yelled. "How soon on rescue?" She turned to Destiny and cradled her head in her hands. "Oh, Sweetie. Let me look." She pulled off the shirt and flinched when she saw a long, but shallow gash. She pressed the shirt back over the wound.

"I'm cold, Maria," Destiny said in a hollow voice. "He kicked me a couple times before he stabbed me."

"Here," Ramirez said as she draped her coat over Destiny's torso. "Don't move. Sit as still as you can."

Destiny nodded.

"He messed up the mural. Wrote…" a gasp, "Threw cans of paint. That's when I caught him." She smiled weakly. "I jumped, him, Maria. How fucked up is that?" She tried to laugh but instead winced and sucked in air. "He rolled me off him and I pushed him away. Then he ran at me and when I fell, stabbed me. I was reaching for a can of paint when he slashed me." She winced again.

"Okay, kid, I hear rescue outside. You're good." Ramirez glanced over her right shoulder to see three EMTs running across the room. "They're here," and she kissed Destiny's forehead. "What happened to the attacker?" she asked before letting an EMT take over.

"Against the mural… knocked him out. He ain't moved. I wonder if I killed the little prick." She grimaced. "Maria…"

The kneeling EMT said, "I've got you, miss. You're good."

Ramirez tapped the EMT on the shoulder and mouthed, "Thanks."

She joined Nagler and they watched a pair of EMTs lift the unconscious man to a gurney. "He's breathing," one of the EMTs said.

"Destiny said she whacked him with a full can of paint," Ramirez said.

Nagler jerked his head back. "Jesus. Concussed, I'll bet. He's a kid. Can't be older than twenty."

"Who do you guess hired him?" Ramirez asked.

"Did you read the mural?"

"Kill Queer Cops." Her face hardened and she stared at the floor. "You know we're not a secret, Frank, me and Destiny."

He wrapped an arm over her shoulder. "I know, but there are hate groups…"

"But this is not them. This is the Dragon, whoever the hell they are. Queer cops is a distraction." Ramirez tapped his chest. "I'm heading to the hospital."

****

The overnight ice storm draped a glittering sheen across the Old Iron Bog, rainbowed as the afternoon sunlight pushed through the gray cover. Brittle branches shed their icy coating when pushed aside and the slick path coated by crystal ice cracked underfoot.

The silence of the bog, sinister on even the sunniest of days, hung like a threat.

Maybe I'm just projecting, Nagler thought. *I want to be out front of this, but I'm not. First Dawson, now Destiny.* Ramirez had called to say that the kid clocked by Destiny's paint can had come to but refused to talk. No car had been found near the project and since the kid wore gloves there were no prints on the recovered knife.

So, yeah, he thought, not an angry queer basher, but something bordering on professional. But like the shooter who tried to take out Dawson, the professional edge was missing. Pros don't miss a clean shot from a couple hundred yards and would not get hit in the head with a paint can when the advantage of stealth was so weighed in their favor. Density said she was blasting Melissa Etheridge in her earbuds and didn't hear the kid approach. But what if the shooter missed Dawson on purpose?

Nagler slipped to the bog before the announced time and prowled the area. No cars seemed to be parked in odd places and no fresh footsteps marred the icy, muddy ground.

Nagler was sure Bennie passed his message to Tony. That twenty was good for something. But Bennie was not Del Williams, whose life was always a step toward redemption, a path cut short when he took a bullet intended for Leonard a year ago. Bennie, Nagler knew, would have also gone back to McCarroll, if that was who the old Irishman was, and demanded fifty for the new information.

When does it all go away, the stings fade? There is not one place in this city that I can go and not recall some horror.

"Mister Noiglar, ya don't look crazy to me." The voice arrived at the same instant the ice in the muddy trail betrayed the entrance of Rodney McCarroll. Somewhere in the voice was a soft Irish lilt worn hard by smokes and too many years of American English.

Nagler turned. "McCarroll. Maybe you're not looking hard enough. How much did Bennie soak *you* for?" He saw the Internet message, Nagler thought, pleased. One more channel to follow.

A coughing, laughing reply. "Another twenty. Talk is cheap. Mister Noiglar."

McCarroll was five-six or five-seven, Nagler guessed. He was shrunken inside a leather coat he had apparently been wearing for years, judging by the worn seams and shiny edges to the collar and tail. Nagler wondered where his weapon was. It was hard to assess his age, Nagler thought. His face was scarred over and under his left eye and his cheeks were sunken. That leather coat was softer than his skin. Was this a man used up or one so hardened by the world the rough ways deflected all distractions? This man was not the gang leader, the brains, Nagler realized, but carried out orders. That's somewhat disappointing. but in its own way, useful. A thug for hire.

Nagler smiled. "You do realize my twenty to Bennie was to get you here, not someone you might be chasing."

McCarroll's face was still a mask but his right eye jittered.

Yup, Nagler thought.

"Oi, Mr. Noiglar, we do understand this situation, then."

"What situation is that, McCarroll? That one of your thugs tried to kill a friend of mine, two in fact, and that someone you know tried to blow up…"

"That blast was not mine, sir. If it was, nothing would be standin'. If it was me after that reporter fella, his brains would be in the roadway. But that queer girl was defacing property of the organization, so it had to stop."

That was sort of weak, Nagler thought.

"Well, your messenger failed. He's the hospital with a paint-can sized headache."

"Ah, Mr. Noiglar, he'll be soon gone."

"He's under guard."

"And so he is, but who's to say who is guarding him?"

Nagler steeled himself so not to react.

"What's your point, McCarroll? That the organization is untouchable? Am I supposed to be afraid? Nothing scares me, you know, not a threatening Irishmen and certainly not a faceless organization."

"We are not faceless, Mr. Noiglar. The Dragony is large and as old as your oldest memories. You've dealt with it before. It's in plain sight and yet hidden in the deepest shadows." McCarroll's face took on a sneering hardness. "If ya ever had the chance to crawl through them old mine shafts, you'd find our symbols scratched in the walls and beams. You'd find it tapped into the iron rails ribboned across the landscape and stenciled on the steel beams that raise buildings to the sky. It's carved into the main beam of a canal boat and the stones that channeled the water, in the bank notes that paid for it all, one rolling and unstoppable many tentacled being, inescapable as procreation and as necessary as breathin' with members so proud we gladly wear its mark."

McCarroll pulled back his coat collar to display what was probably a tattoo, but to Nagler some feet away appeared to be an old bruise.

Nagler tensed as McCarroll fiddled in his jacket pocket.

But he pulled out a pack of cigarettes and a lighter and looked around the clearing for a place to sit. Finding none, he leaned against a dead tree. "Now you also been tying me to that old Dixon case, father and daughter. Believing I killed all those folks and took the money."

Money?

"Well, did you? Weren't you sentenced to jail?" Nagler asked, losing patience. "We have a couple current murders. I could arrest you on suspicion."

McCarroll sucked in a deep draught and exhaled. The ripeness of burned tobacco cut through the chill and moistness of the bog. "Ya got nothing on me, Mr. Noiglar. Nothing from then. Nothing now. I don't kill people."

Nagler exhaled a breathy cough. "Oh, well, pardon me. You're just around when people die. Is that why you haven't shot me yet?"

McCarroll's face cracked into a sad grin. "Ah, I ain't carryin'. What good would it do us to have me shootin' the most famous copper in this dingy burg. The Dragony endures because it does not engage in the petty day-to-day, but strings events together over time."

"That makes no sense, you know. What are you doing here, besides following me around and threatening people I know? What good is this great Dragony if it can't be seen in the light of day but must hide in shadows. For whose benefit does it act, other than its own?"

"Ah, Mr. Noiglar, we are acquiring. That's what the Dragony does, acquires, absorbs, and then settles, digests if you will, until another opportunity arises."

"If Ironton is such a dingy burg, what do you want it for? What value has it? Or does it have no value, and that's why you want it, the almighty Dragony." He spit out the name, tired of the drama.

McCarroll settled back into his tree, "Your granddaddy knew, Mr. Noiglar. Back in the day. Jock Newton and he battled for the soul of the mining crew. It was a draw in the end. Old Newton vanished, dumped in a sealed shaft, hauled away in a pile of slag and buried, it was said. Your granddad went to other employment. Some say your old granddad did him in when the fight got too hot. But, me? No. Not the case. Your grandad and Old Newton, like you and me now, were foot soldiers in this great arc of time. This everlasting everlasting."

Nagler covered his mouth and stared at the ground to hide the mild shock of hearing the name Newton. Maybe an uncle of the old mayor, Howard Newton, maybe grandfather?

"Ah, the Newtons. Proud family, that." Nagler was covering, trying to find a way in. "Left this city in ruins more than once." He shifted one step forward, a test. This is the challenge, Nagler thought, as McCarroll scrubbed out his cigarette on the tree. This little bragging man fronting for someone of greater power and danger. If I locked him up, the trail might go cold.

"So, look, McCarroll, got anything else? If not, leave my friends alone. They have nothing you need."

"Ah, Mr. Noiglar, my presence here today *is* the message. What does it say that I can draw you to this stinking swamp for little more than a few dollars? It says we know you, know your life and its aches. So, it gets ya thinking, what else might we do? That is the Dragony. Besides. I was never here. I am just a rumor."

McCarroll nodded, pulled his collar tighter and left, crunching up the path to the road.

Finally, in the silence, Nagler shivered.

The face of the faceless enemy. But then he smiled. McCarroll was not wearing Italian shoes, and clearly, was not six-five. "You're not a rumor to Jeff Montgomery. So, who's your tall partner, there, pal?"

Nagler stood as a still as he could on the melting, shifting mud, straining to hear. No vehicle cruised down frozen Mount Pleasant indicating that maybe McCarroll walked to the meeting. It nettled Nagler that he had not earlier discovered a vehicle, because it could mean that McCarroll was not alone, and that maybe on Howard Avenue two blocks away or tangled in the warren of narrow alleys in the warehouse district there was a hidden…

"Hey, Frank, found the van."

It was Maria Ramirez whispering in an earpiece.

Nagler tapped his ear. "Do you get the whole thing?"

Ramirez laughed. "Oh, yeah. This is the Dragony," she said in a deep, mocking voice.

"Where was the van? Get it marked?"

"In an old garage. We dropped a couple of wireless nanny cams in there and a tracker on the van. The warrant was easy. The judge saw the connection between fifteen years ago and today. I don't get is why they haven't burned the damn thing."

"Maria, hey. Someone's coming."

Nagler stepped to the side of the opening behind a couple fallen trees and listened to the crunching, slipping steps.

"Hey, Franky, why didn't you just plug the bastard?"

In the clearing, trying to find solid footing, were Dancer and a haggard Tony, the cook.

Nagler took his hand off his holstered weapon.

"I guess you didn't like the fish in Nova Scotia, huh?" *Of course, he never left town. Jesus, Dancer.* "What are you doing her right now?"

"Been keeping an eye on you and McCarroll, just in case." Dancer coughed, spit out a gob, and then coughed again. "The fish'll wait." A strangled voice. "Cabbie who gave me a ride was working for McCarroll. Shoulda guessed. Told ya they was watching. And then I found old Tony here. The homeless crew at the stoveworks told a couple of bad dudes were looking for him. You need to protect him, Frank."

Nagler wiped his forehead, closed an eye, and stared at Dancer. "Do I need to protect you?"

"Protect yourself, Frank. They ain't going away."

Tony groaned and leaned on a tree with one hand, grabbing to hold his place. His other hand held up his pants by the belt. He had lost at least twenty pounds, Nagler guessed. "Jesus, Tony. Where the hell have you been, other that saving Dawson's neck?" He reached out and grabbed the man's sagging shoulder.

"I'm sorry, Frank," Tony whispered, each word a burden.

"Nothing to be sorry about," Nagler said. "Let's get you out of here."

On the street, Nagler told Ramirez. "Maria, need a car. Got Tony."

The reply in his ear: "On the way."

Dancer began to walk away, then turned back. "Hey, Frank, and Tony, I'm not here. Far as you know I'm in Nova Scotia eating codfish."

"Where are you going?" Nagler asked. *Great. No one's here. Not McCarroll. Not Dancer. A city filled with ghosts.*

"Got business." Dancer lit a cigarette and started walking away.

"Do I need to know what your business is? You know you're an ex-cop, right?" Nagler yelled. "Don't do anything stupid like getting yourself killed."

Dancer turned. "Franky, did you read my report? If ya did, then you know my business."

"Did. When's the English translation due out?"

"Funny man. Figure out who 'BL' is?"

Nagler wrinkled his face. *There was a "BL" in there?*

CHAPTER TWELVE

The glass tower

"They all gone?" Jimmy Dawson asked before he sat at the desk in the empty bank lobby that was Lauren's Fox's emergency office. Gathered were Lauren, Frank Nagler and Maria Ramirez.

Lauren nodded and smiled, "Just us conspirators."

Dawson opened the computer screen with the press of a key, and a photo of the wreck of the former silk mill emerged and the sound of Dawson's voice leaked from the tiny speaker.

"I completed a three-day walking tour of Ironton's industrial wrecks. Some were intact with FOR SALE signs nailed to their sides like a stack of used car doors at a junk yard. Others were dark, lined with wired windows lacking glass, doors canvases for layers of graffiti. Still others were like the silk mill: wreckage, hollowed by a decades-old fire, draped in scars of black soot, enclosed by rusted chain link fences.

"But if you live in Ironton, you know that. You drive by or walk past these relics daily, and sometimes think about what they mean. Still, we wear our past like a torn untucked shirt. Two buttons are missing, and the ones we find are too large for the holes. But we wear the shirt with pride because it holds all the sweat of our labors. I want to know who owns them. Here is part of what I found."

A newspaper headline filled the computer screen.

"The silk mill burned in 1987. The building had been vacant for twenty years. No electric power, no heat, water, or sewer service. A shell filled with trash. Someone blamed a homeless guy they found drunk under a cardboard box. Police said an accelerant was used, but the guy had no gasoline or matches. He went away, and the blame went away.

And when the city found the owner it was a company with a made-up name, a post office box in Kansas City and a phone number that was out of order. D-Rain Corp. exists only on paper."

The screen then filled with a photo of a single sheet of paper, with all but two lines blurred out. At the top of the page: "D-Rain Corporation." And at the bottom of the page an abstract signature and the typed name, "Taylor Mangot I."

"That is the paper. It took thirteen separate transfers before the old silk mill property ended up in Kansas City. On paper, that is. No photograph was found for Taylor Mangot the first."

A series of photos of warehouses, strip malls, vacant lots and finally, restaurants, flashed on the screen.

"One thing we love in Ironton is our food," Dawson's voiceover continued. "We have Greek food, Italian food in endless variety, Brazilian, Cuban, Chinese, steaks, subs, chow Mein, empanadas, fried chicken, Irish stew, hot dogs fancy and plain, and what about the pizza? So, what makes Pete's Pizza so special? Not the name, for sure. Maybe it's the location, on the state highway across from the middle school. Kids eat a lot of pizza. But four times as much pizza as a larger place a half-mile away?

"That's what bank records show. Sizable deposits twice a week, then smaller withdrawals the following week – makes it look like cash flow, payroll, supplies, taxes, things regular businesses pay. One name stood out. Dragon Wholesalers. Supposed to be a grocery supply outfit, except none of the larger companies that make or import restaurant supplies – flour, oil, olives, pepperoni, cheese, pizza boxes – have any record of selling anything to Dragon Wholesalers."

Three photos overlaid filled the computer screen.

"These buildings, according to tax records, are owned by Dragon Wholesalers. The corporation is licensed in Delaware. The address is a law office where no one answers the phone. According to the records of incorporation, the owner is one Taylor Mangot I. They're empty."

A new photo entered the screen. It was a gray, old newspaper photo showing a brick building with a crowd of people in front. Four of them, three men and a woman, were in handcuffs.

"This is one of the Dragon Wholesalers buildings, the one on Dubin Place. It was in the news fifteen years ago because authorities made four arrests there. Inside, it was said, was a drug processing operation, which police determined was selling millions of dollars of drugs across the region. Police also found four bodies in the warehouse."

A photo of several newspaper headlines filled the screen.

"Eventually state and federal cops tracked down the suppliers in two states and overseas. Fifty arrests were made, including a few customs inspectors and cops. One person who escaped apprehension was the building owner, Taylor Mangot I. Some police even wondered if he existed. Anyone can create a signature, right?"

Then a series of photos of buildings flowed across the screen.

"These are the properties of a series of companies that share some version of the name Dragon. They are scattered throughout Ironton and North Jersey. A few, like these three small offices building in Morristown, have rent-paying tenants.

"A few other, somewhat larger warehouses, have a single tenant occupying a tiny office. Many – *many* – others are vacant, yet income has been reported for each of them.

"All of those buildings matter because of this."

Four new photos filled the screen. The first was the block on Warren Street that housed apartments and businesses. Next was the same block collapsed into a dusty and burning pile of rubble. Then there was the same block stripped back to naked walls, some supported by a series of wooden cross beams. The last photo was the same block hidden behind a large billboard draped with a black plastic sheet.

"Twelve weeks ago, this city block blew up and the Ironton community was worried about the fates of perhaps a hundred people who it was thought lived there. That's according to city and utility company records which indicated the upper floors of those four buildings were fully occupied. Actually, only three apartments were filled. Records listed the names of tenants for all the thirty-five apartments. They were ghosts. Yet company records, the company being one of those entities with a Dragon name, showed rental income for all the units.

"That only matters because in a couple, days, Ironton Mayor Jesus Ollivar will announce a huge tax break for the owner of the site, Dragon Associates, to build a new giant glass-faced complex on the site of the explosion and neighboring properties that will be suddenly deemed in need of redevelopment. A plan on file with the city planning department indicates that every building from Warren Street to the old theater will be demolished. The theater is a registered historic site, and apparently the developers are in too much of a hurry to try to change that."

A new video filled the screen. Mayor Ollivar and a tall man in black suit and dark glasses walked along the edge of the site, stopping at the billboard. They turned, apparently in response to a voice, and then took up positions at the side of the billboard and smiled.

"The person behind this plan is Taylor Mangot II, the gentlemen on the right. At least, he seems to exist. Are these plans real? Is Ironton destined to be home to a towering glass finger, stunning though may be, a symbol of renaissance or just another pretty, but empty facade?"

Dawson struck a key and froze that photo on the screen.

"So that's the Dragon," he said.

"Can you enlarge his shoes?" Nagler asked.

"Sure, why?" Dawson asked.

"I wonder if they're Italian."

****

"When are you going to post that?" Lauren Fox asked.

"Day before the mayor makes the big announcement," Dawson replied.

"Is he right?" Ramirez asked.

Lauren put hands in her hips, exhaled and nodded. "Basically. We've been tracking the Dragony, as you said McCarroll called it, since the explosion. We were getting nowhere until someone found that reference from Delaware. We need to find the people who actually signed the documents."

"This thing is really gonna happen, isn't it?" Dawson asked. "Is there a way to stop it?"

Lauren scraped a chair out from under the neighboring desk and sat with a frown. "I can slow it down, and I should because there are about fifty zoning violations in the basic application. Then there's the question about the financing." She stared at the desk and shook her head. "The mayor wants this, and word is that he will do anything to get it approved. I must tread a fine line. He could fire me in a minute." Her face was drawn and serious. Then she grinned. "Fuck it. Been here before. This is so corrupt it has to be stopped. I can question the finances, and I know someone at the state preservation office who could challenge the application because of its proximity to the old theater. Might be able to get someone from the federal historic registry office to write a letter of concern. The developer could probably win, but all the filings would slow it down until we can expose the financial fraud."

"That's hardly dramatic," Nagler said. "I'd rather pin the killing of Ethan Ricardo on one of them."

"We could do both," Lauren said, with a snarky grin on her face. "Overseers of a park in Morristown held up a development for a couple of years because the building would cast a shadow on their park. You never know. Maybe give you time."

"Remember the last time an Ironton mayor put up a big billboard boasting about a development plan?" Dawson asked.

Nagler glanced at Lauren and sighed. "Yeah. Gabriel Richman and the transportation center on the Old Iron Bog. I ended up slogging through the muck looking for the body parts of a young girl. Richman, the old Mayor, Howie Newton and Chris Foley, my old partner, went to jail and Lauren left town."

"Where was I?" Ramirez wondered.

"They tried to pin the financial mess on me, "Lauren said, "But I left town with the records."

Nagler laughed. "You actually hid them under the playground at the city park. I'll never forget Richman's face when I had the park department dig them up."

"I told you there was more than meets the eye," Lauren said, and winked.

"Hey, didn't McCarroll say something about a Newton and the Dragony?" Ramirez asked.

Dawson was scrolling through the photos on the computer screen. "Wait, who's this guy? Is that who I think it is?" He expanded one portion of the photo to better show a man standing next to Taylor Mangot II. The new figure was perhaps a foot shorter than Mangot, thin and bearded.

"That's Yang," Lauren said., "Damn, Dan Yang. My hired financial gun," she sneered. "Bastard."

"What's he doing…" Nagler began.

"Doesn't matter," Lauren said, her voice now cold. Her face settled into a hard mask and her eyes blazed. "I know how we'll get to their finances."

CHAPTER THIRTEEN

Tony

"Boonton Police Department. Captain Dan Thomson."

"Captain, hello. Frank Nagler from Ironton. Have a question about your cadet Mahala Dixon. How'd she get approved with her juvie record?"

A long silence.

"A favor," Thomson said.

Figures. "Her father?"

"Hey, Nagler, don't get me wrong. Mahala has a mind for this. She's sharp and inquisitive."

Thomson sounded nervous, Nagler thought.

"But she also was caught selling drugs in school. How'd you make that go away?"

"Christ, Nagler, did someone a favor. Happens all the time."

"Except this favor was one step in a series that led to a major crime and Mahala's father in jail."

"That's not how…" Voice a cross between anger and panic. "Why are you asking about it now?"

What's that phrase we always use? Nagler thought. Oh yeah. "Came up as part of a new larger investigation. Don't you have any records on this?"

The receiver filled with a long breath and a soft, "Fuck. It was undercover," Thomson said. "You know that. No one wrote anything down back then. If anybody did, Langdon wrote it down. Hell, it was his show." Said with irritation. "Bernie Langdon and what's his name, Montgomery. Okay, Carlton Dixon caught his daughter with a stash in her bedroom. She was working with Ricardo, so-and-so-Ethan Ricardo.

"The kid who died in the explosion. Working with Mahala. His records said he was twenty."

"And you believe that? Come on, Nagler. Know how easy it is to get a forged passport when your boss is the forger?

"His boss, Tallem, the restaurant owner."

"No, some other guy." A hesitation. "Some Irish punk."

"McSally," Nagler said. McSally was a name in Dancer's notes. Worth a try.

"Yeah, yeah," Thomson said. "McSally. Big guy, mustache, face looked like it met a wall or two close up."

This is interesting. "So, is there a photo of this McSally in the records you don't have?" Nagler asked.

"What are you fishing for?"

"First time that name, McSally, came up," Nagler said. "Know what, heard there was a lot of cash in that warehouse when it was raided. Vanished, apparently."

"Really? I heard the feds took it. Anything else, Nagler?"

"Naw, just pulling strings, trying to solve that bombing, you know."

Thomson chuckled into the phone. "Good luck with that. Better you than me."

"Yeah, well, thanks, Captain." Nagler said. "Oh, last thing. We sent out bulletin on a '89 white Ford van. Might be in your town."

"Got it."

Nagler hung up the phone and rolled his eyes at Maria Ramirez.

"What was that?" she asked. "Isn't that Irish hood named McCarroll?"

Nagler grinned. "Why, yes he is. And he's a short, skinny beat-up looking guy. So, who's McSally? Also interesting, that was the second time someone mentioned there was a lot of cash in that warehouse, the first being McCarroll. There's no record of it. I wonder in whose basement wall it's hiding?"

"Why that Boonton cop?"

He nodded to her computer. "Pull up that video Dawson made. Go to the old photo of the drug bust. There, upper right. That's Boonton Sergeant Dan Thomson, BDT in Dancer's notes."

"What's a Boonton cop doing on an Ironton bust?"

"Normally I'd think task force, undercover. But this time, I'm thinking of something else." He grinned. "The Dragony, she be a many tentacled thing. Wonder how fast he calls Bernie Langdon?"

Ramirez laughed. "You're a sick man, Nagler."

"Let's see if we can put Thomson, Langdon and even Montgomery together."

****

The bombing ruins looked like a fake Stonehenge as light of the full moon was framed by the window squares in the standing brick wall.

I hope he shows, Nagler thought. He told Tony to meet him at the ruins at 3 a.m., hoping the darkness and the quiet of the night would help him recall details he had yet to explain. That was the time Tony said he had seen Eduardo Tallem before the place blew up. *I hope the moonlight doesn't throw him off.*

Nagler leaned against the rough, cool brick wall and closed his eyes. I'm tired of everything being broken, he thought. Broken, then glued back together, thrown against the wall to see what sticks, until it falls again. Then someone like Taylor Mangot II says he has a vision that will fix everything forever, But it's not a vision. It's a thing, his thing. Just a thing. So, it stands for a while, this new, empty thing. Until it breaks.

Nagler sighed. "And so here we are."

139

The mayor had unveiled Taylor Mangot II's tall glassy vision for the bombing site a couple days before. The future, Nagler decided after studying a scale model, was too shiny and too pointy; you could shatter it with a rock.

A shuffle sifted from around the corner two doors down, the walker trying to be quiet as if they were uncertain of their destination.

Tony.

"Over here," Nagler said, his voice a ripple in the dark.

"Oh, man, Frankie. I was, you know, wonderin'."

"Tony, we're good. Thanks for coming. Let's get this done."

Nagler lifted the yellow police tape that stretched across the service alley and the pair walked halfway down. Tony paused after a few steps, his breathing heavy. "Better if you just do it," Nagler said.

"This is the door to Barry's," Tony said and ran a hand over the familiar rough opening in the standing wall. "I get here about now, and Freddy from Antonio's bakery has already delivered. The alley smells like warm bread, all yeasty, ya know? So, I take it in and begin banging things around, setting up."

"Did you smell anything other than the bread?"

"Not really. You know that old kitchen, there's always smells, even a little gas smell from the pilot lights from overnight. I make some coffee and I'm about to light up the stoves when I hear voices in the alley and some moving around, but I think it's Satelli from the meat shop in Wharton. He's three days a week."

Tony paused and looked up and down the alley, trying to place himself in the foggy recall.

"I guess that's when I see Eddie, you know, Tallem. He goes into his place, and I hear some noises, like voices, I ain't really sure because it's muffled. Then Eddie sees me, and we talk about Ethan and then both go back inside our places."

"Voices? See anyone besides Tallem?"

"Na, nobody. I'm thinkin' he's yelling at Ethan. Sometimes that kid oversleeps, but Eddie says he is sick that day. So, I go back into our place and the gas smell is stronger. Now I'm worried. I don't touch nothing, not even to shut off the coffee maker. Because, you know, all it takes is a spark."

He pointed down the alley toward Blackwell and the Cuban restaurant.

"I'm in the alley, going to Eddie's place maybe to ask him if he smells gas, when he comes out, not even lookin', on his phone, waving his arm. So, he gets to Blackwell. And I hear him say, 'So you're in place, right?' And he's walking into the street looking up, kinda walking in a circle. Then he comes back into the alley. I go into the door frame, so he don't see me. And he says, 'Not yet, he's not here. I'm going across the street. When he comes, I'll call ya. Then wait for the light and blow it.'"

Tony leaned his back on the wall and wrapped his arms, shaking.

"Fuckin' scary, Frankie. Just fuckin' scary."

"So much for our bomb experts," Nagler said. "What'd you do next?"

"I run. The gas is stronger. I'm half thinkin' about Ethan, but I run."

"Where'd you go?"

"As far as I could away from the gas, ran out the back to Bassett, up the hill to the highway, then wham the place blows and I jump to the ground, cover my head and thinkin' I'm gonna die."

"Yeah, okay." Nagler grabbed Tony's shoulder. "Good." Did you see Tallem?"

"No. But I'm thinking he saw me, so I can't go home, and the streets are all filled with junk that's on fire, and the cop shop is on the other side…"

"Where'd you go?"

"Car lot. There's a busted hearse in the back, four rows deep, no windows." He grinned. "Quiet as hell."

Nagler laughed. His first good laugh in days. *Of course he did.* "That's where you were when you saw Tallem and the rifle?"

"I was heading up to the stoveworks. I helped those guys with food, and they let me eat with 'em. I saw a guy heading to the roof with the gun and just jumped him. Didn't think about it. So, look. I gotta go, set up, you know."

"A guy? Not Tallem?"

"Naw. Skinnier, a little taller."

Who the hell was that? Why'd I think it was Tallem?

Nagler shook away the confusion for the moment. "Yeah, thanks. Good job, Tony. Tell Barry I'll be in later."

Nagler in the alley listened to Tony's footsteps tap up Bassett, across Sussex and, fading, down Richman toward Leonard's. He took a sharp breath when the sound of screeching tires pierced the silence. But it was from the wrong direction, and the vehicle was heading away from downtown.

He followed the route that Tony said Tallem took before the explosion: Out the alley onto Blackwell, back and forth on the sidewalk and then into the intersection of Blackwell and Warren where he could see the upper floors of surrounding buildings.

The rooflines were similar: A flat façade that extended about three feet above a hidden roof that provided an unobstructed view of the intersection and the storefronts along Warren. Who were they waiting for? Who was *they* for Chrissakes? There were four deaths in the building, three it seemed were just tenants. And then Ethan Ricardo, who was killed before the explosion. *This wasn't about him.*

The walk-around didn't help. Maybe in daylight, he thought. Instead, he took a several-blocks long indirect route back to his car, parked two blocks west in the shadow of the furniture store, and waited.

Then he saw it, parked opposite, across Blackwell on the curve of the train station service road. A white Ford van.

"Hey, it's Nagler," he said to the dispatch officer. "Got a suspicious white Ford van on the service road, engine running. Got two cars nearby? Good. Lights and sirens. Opposite directions. Box it in."

Nagler pulled up behind the second patrol car. "Plates are old, and the reg is at least five years out of date," the officer said. "You know the driver."

"What?" Nagler asked.

"She said to call you." He handed Nagler a New Jersey driver's license.

Mahala Dixon.

At the van's driver's window, Nagler started, "What…"

"Here's your van, your stupid white Ford van," Mahala said. "The tracker is back at the warehouse."

Maybe because it was three in the morning, or maybe it was the thousand questions pounding through his head and why did she even know where the van was and why didn't someone check the video from the nanny cams to see her at the warehouse and where is McCarroll? Or maybe it was just the smirk.

"Read Miss Dixon her rights and take her to lock up. Charge her with possession of a stolen vehicle."

****

This place is too quiet, Mahala thought as she hunched her back against the wall of her cell. Where are the guards? They could get me here; don't they know that?

"In you go," the officer had said, and slammed the metal door behind her.

"Where's Nagler?" she asked agitated, and when there was no reply, she rattled the door and shouted, "He's supposed to be watching out for me. Where is fucking Nagler?"

"Not here," the officer replied dead-eyed before he left.

Five steps to the door, a buzzer, a door opening, then slipping shut. A second buzzer, then silence.

****

She heard her name.

Mahala shook her head. *Did I sleep?*

She opened her eyes to see a slim woman with bleached hair and purple streaks leaning against the cell door and offering a paper cup.

"Coffee?" asked Calista Knox.

"I only drink tea," Mahala said, squinting at the woman. "I know you, Calista, what, Calista Knox. You're friends with the cripple who runs that bookstore."

Calista turned from the cell and with a backward glance, dropped the cup of coffee into the trash can.

"Hey!"

"Sorry, the machine only had coffee." Calista said. "And you should show more respect. Leonard, that cripple, paid your bail." She turned back to the cell and slammed the bars. "And he's crippled because he took a bullet that was meant for me. What have you done for anyone lately, except play at this spy girl drug runner?" She stepped back and leaned on the empty desk across the from the cell.

"Yeah, alright," Mahala said. "I didn't know. And I'm not a drug runner."

"Really? What were you selling in high school? Chewing gum? There's a lot you don't know, missy, I'm mad at the world because my father's in jail because he caught me selling drugs in high school and took the fall for me."

Mahala glared back. "You don't know … I had no choice."

"You always have a choice, Mahala." Calista's face hardened and she spit out the words. "You, with your self-made agony, think you know me. I was raped by my father and escaped sexual slavery. I watched my brother step in front of a semi to end the pain and that would have been me if not for Leonard and Frank Nagler. And I watch Frank every day with that sadness in his eyes knowing he still carries that weight. And yet he takes you on. The city's on fire and he takes on your pitiful tale of woe because that's who he is. But you need to know, Mahala. He can walk away and leave you to the people you fear…."

144

"Bullshit. He won't walk after he talks to me."

"You think so? If I walk out of here the bail money goes with me. And Sergeant Hanrahan might forget what friendly guard he assigned to the door. And your preliminary hearing might get lost on the court calendar… the people you're working with."

"Ain't working with anybody."

Calista eyed Mahala as the she pushed back from the cell door and thumped on the bed, eyes dark with both anger and worry.

"You're in so deep you don't even know it. You're on a video from the warehouse before you took the van. Didn't you even think?" Calista said. "You and McCarroll. What are you doing with him? He helped put your father in jail. So, he's gonna get him out? Frank was right. You do need someone to keep an eye on you."

Mahala jumped to the door. "He had no right."

"You gave him that right when you handed him that file on your father. What's it been? Fifteen years? Come on, kid. It's time."

****

Calista pushed her way into the Leonard's and smiled when she saw Frank Nagler, Leonard, and Lauren Fox at a corner table.

"Done," she said, as she joined them and kissed Leonard's cheek before sitting. In the background Tony was singing off-key to Stevie Wonder.

"She bought it, huh?" Nagler asked.

"Her eyes were a little wide when I mentioned you had video of her meeting with McCarroll."

"Thought they would be. Thanks, Calista."

"Wait a minute," Lauren said. "That video of her and McCarroll is real?"

Nagler winked at Calista. "Might be."

"That's not fair," Lauren said. "She's a kid, right?"

"A kid who was in this thing from the start," Nagler said and shrugged. "If she's nervous, she'll talk."

"Alright," Lauren said, "One down." She pulled a form out of the envelope she had brought. "Leonard, this is the response to the offer by Taylor Mangot II. It's as we discussed. You express concerns about his non-profit, citing a 2010 filing with the State of New Jersey that indicated the treasury department had questions about the foundation's reserves." She smiled at Calista. "And yes, unlike the video of McCarroll and Mahala Dixon, this report does exist."

"He's not going to like that response, I take it," Leonard said.

"Oh, no," Lauren said. "He'll complain that the report is old, the information is inaccurate, and besides, it has all been corrected in the past decade. Mostly, he will be furious that anyone, let alone you and Calista, are challenging his supposed ability and authority."

"What's the risk to Leonard?" Nagler asked.

"Very little. We structured Leonard's foundation to be separate from his businesses, so if one failed, the other would survive."

"You're good with this, Leonard?" Nagler asked.

Leonard smiled. "We've done risky business before, my friend. Let's see if we can ensure they leave the guns at home this time."

Nagler reached over and touched Leonard's hand. "Right." He smiled at Lauren. Her face was soft, and her eyes weren't as dark as they had been lately, but still fierce. He had seen that look before, usually when the plan she has been concocting begins to roll out. "So, what did the state question about Mangot's foundation?"

Lauren winked. "The source of his funding."

CHAPTER FOURTEEN

There's someone in Ironton who scares you.

"It was a little pot to start," Mahala Dixon said. "Do you have to record this? I'm not a criminal."

Maria Ramirez offered a friendly nod, but her voice was cold. "Because if we like what you tell us, because if it helps us, we can help you. You like being probationary in Boonton?"

"You wouldn't. You can't. That charge was dropped, because the van was registered to my dad, and you know, not actually stolen." Mahala took off her hoodie and threw it on the table where she Ramirez and Frank Nagler sat opposite one another. "Why's it so damn hot in here?"

"Because the heat's on," Nagler said.

Mahala scoffed. "I get it. 'The heat's on' as in you're putting the heat on me to tell you stuff."

"No, Mahala. It's because the heat is actually on," Nagler said. "The thermostats in this room never worked."

"Cop tricks."

Ramirez leaned in. "No, kid, we can and we will. The van was registered to your father five years ago. Cop tricks are keeping you safe for the past couple months after that bomb went off. This," she glanced at Nagler, "Is not cop tricks. Didn't you notice that you had a shadow? You seem to have something that certain people want. That idea is what's keeping your father alive in jail, isn't it?"

Mahala leaned back, her face open and her eyes pained. "Met the shadow. Calista, right? My dad's alive because he's a cop, and you don't kill a cop in jail."

"Mahala, the lifers in the state prison don't care he's a cop," Nagler said. "They'd kill him if the order came down because it was Tuesday. I think it's more like this. You and your father have shared knowledge about someone and something. A pact. If he died in prison, you'd spill it. And if you died, he'd tell. Is it worth it?"

Mahala huffed a breath and shook her head, her eyes dark with anger. "It was clever to send in Calista. She almost got to me. And you think you're gonna get to me with this back and forth, fast questions, change the subject shit."

"Hey, who are you kidding?" Ramirez said, "Calista did get to you because here you are. You came to us. You've been living large, protected, but now there's someone in Ironton who scares you. They got Ethan Ricardo, and you know they can get you."

"Ethan died in that gas explosion, right?"

"No, Mahala. He was a killed the night before, stabbed," Nagler said.

Mahala kicked her chair back to the wall and sat on the floor in the corner. "Jesus, it is happening."

"What is *it*?" Ramirez asked, rolling her eyes at Nagler.

"Oh, man." Mahala wore a twisted smile. "It. The big thing. Happening now. Didn't you read that file I gave you? It's in there. I thought, you being so smart and all, that you'd get it right away. But you didn't and maybe it's too late. Wait till you see the size of it."

"Right, just tell us how it started," Nagler asked. "No bull."

"It was just me and Ethan. Nickel bags of weed. A little meth, some X, speed. Never carried enough to make the principal worry if we got caught. Did once. Had a nickel bag, convinced her that I was just smoking in the girl's room, you know, to ease the stress of being a black American high school kid, on account of my parents." She grinned.

"Oh, you poor dear," Ramirez said. "I'm guessing it got out of hand."

Mahala laughed. "Shit, yeah. Our dealer got popped by some Colombian in Brooklyn. We didn't even know the Colombians were involved. We thought it was, you know, just Miquel, some local dude. That's how dumb we were."

"Or that protected," Nagler said.

Mahala waved a dismissive hand.

"Hey, kid, you're not the first teen-age drug dealer we've ever seen," Ramirez said. "I'd stop thinking you're so special."

Mahala rolled her eyes and sighed. "Okay. I get it now. I just wish *you* would. Anyway, they threatened us, we carried more. So, my dad stepped in. He told me he had planned to bust it all up, but then he found out who the players were, and he had to deal. Say nothing, and I'd be clear.

"Why…?

"Because the players were all cops. You read those newspaper stories. But they only tell half the story, the half that the public would buy. It wasn't just drugs and money, though that was all very profitable. It was about putting something in place, a structure and organization that would last."

Nagler stared at the girl on the floor and wondered how much of a game her story actually was.

"Why would we believe you?" he asked.

"Because I still have what they want." She stood and moved back to the table. "And so do you. It's in the files that I gave you, and in the notes Montgomery gave you. Dig for it. But you need to let me out of here. I can cover for the van with a white lie. They're in play, but so am I."

Ramirez formed a tiny smile. "Remember when your tire got slashed a couple weeks ago? Who'd you call?"

"Captain Thomson, my academy sponsor."

"Why do you think he was your sponsor?"

"He's been a family friend for years. Took care of us when my dad went to jail."

Nagler nodded. "You know he was one of those players, as you call them."

"No…"

"Maria, show her that photo, the one of the line-up at the drug bust on Dubin Place."

Ramirez opened her tablet and pulled up the photo then nodded to Mahala. "Upper right."

Mahala squinted at the screen, and then poked the photo. "That bastard."

"Yeah," Nagler said. "If you know what this is, help us."

"Okay, but in my own way. I have things…"

"I get it, but we don't want to you end up like Ethan."

"Any idea who wanted him dead?" Ramirez asked, "or why, all these years later?"

"I have an idea but can't tell you yet. They'd guess it came from me. Please, I've been playing this out for a long time. I'm careful."

Ramirez and Nagler shared a glance and both nodded. "Okay, you do have a shadow."

"Take him off."

"No," he said. "You didn't even know he was there."

"We'll see."

Mahala leaned back and linked her fingers behind her head. "Detective, do you remember that lesson you were teaching the day you had that meltdown?"

He chuckled. "The lesson about lying and how if you found out who sold the guy his hat you'd discover he was not in Chicago the night his wife was stabbed to death?"

"Right," Mahala said. "It was about how people try to make themselves appear to be in a place they had never actually been, make themselves appear to be someone or something they're not. Maybe there's some lesson that could be applied to this case, Maybe, Detective Nagler? Don't blow my cover."

Mahala collected her hoodie and left the room.

"'My cover?' My ass," Ramirez said. "Chick's got some issues."

"We'll sort that out. Just keep her talking, Meanwhile, one more of our new acquaintances is not who they say they are."

Ramirez laughed. "Damn, there's a surprise." A pause. "So tell me, Frank, how much of what Mahala said is the truth? What's she up to?"

A crooked smile. "Depends on whether you believe she was in Chicago buying a hat." He stared at the door that Mahala let close behind her. "That's one scared kid, talking big."

****

Nagler flattened the pages in front of him and ran a finger over the lines of type seeking a certain word. Now I'll figure out what that symbol means.

"SOL," though in places where the ink had faded it appeared to be "SCL." And sometimes it seemed to be "8OL" or "8CL."

About the only letter he was certain of was the "L."

Maybe it's the context, he thought and began again the search.

He found the letters on the third page and had just circled them when his phone rang. He stared at the word and then glanced at the phone.

"What now?" Into the phone, "Yeah, Nagler."

"Frank, it's Maria. Dubin Place, now."

"The warehouse…"

"Right. The tracker that Mahala took off the Ford van just pinged at that location."

Nagler laughed. "So, Mahala stuck it…"

"Seems so."

Dubin Place was in the middle of an empty industrial section of Ironton, a place of lightless narrow lanes designed for mule carts, not eighteen-wheelers, with wrecked roofs and windows thick with generations of dust.

The only light came from the high beams on Ramirez' cruisier that blocked the road at the far end and a flashlight she was shining on a modern white garage door with a broken windowpane.

"Pretty fancy for 1890," she said. "The tracker signal is coming from here. I could make out the taillights of a vehicle in the back and then that." She handed the flashlight to Nagler and told him to scan to the left. "Who puts a new door on an old building?"

Through the dusty air, the soft orb of light outlined the rounded end of an industrial propane tank. That might have been usual in a place like this, he thought, but the glint of the light off something reflective attached to the feeder pipe was not usual.

"That tank in wired. Damn it." he said. "Don't touch the door. We need the bomb squad," he said and nodded toward his car parked twenty feet away down the alley.

"On their way," she said, closing her phone. "Thirty minutes."

"Modern automatic garage doors have a sensor that will stop the door from opening or closing if the light beam is disrupted," he said, as they kneeled behind his car. "The door sensor could be wired to the trigger on the tank, so if the door was opened the beam might be broken and boom."

"But there's no power here," she said.

"Batteries of some sort? But even automatic doors can be opened manually in an emergency with a key."

Ramirez stared at the door for several seconds. "So, if someone with a key raised the door, or someone like me had reached in and opened it, that tank could have gone off." She covered her mouth, eyes wide. "Damn it, Frank."

He let out a breath. "Right." Then he, too, stared at the door. "But if you're part of the gang you probably know the door is automatic – think about it – you drive up, have a door opener or a key…"

"And one of your buddies blows you up. What the hell is going on here, Frank?"

He scanned the door with his light and noticed the reflective glint from the road. "Once we know that, we'll know why there is glass on the ground outside the door."

****

Lieutenant Adam Wagner approached Nagler and Ramirez, who were leaning on his car.

"All clear," Wagner said. "You were lucky, Lieutenant. Whoever installed that rig crossed a set of wires."

"So, I could have set it off by jostling the door?" Ramirez asked, her face slack.

"Should have," Wagner said. "There was a motion detector aimed at the door. I'll show you." Near the door, now jammed open, Winston pointed to wooden pillar about five feet away. "The sensor was here, aimed here, about waist high. If that door had been lifted even a few inches, it would have set off the trigger. But here's the thing. It's hard to blow up a liquid propane tank. It can be done, but it would take more flash-bang than that little rig would have provided." He pointed to another, higher, beam and a wooden frame beyond that. "So, this was either was a fake, or an amateur. It looks real, but it's all wrong."

"What do you mean?" Nagler asked.

Wagner illuminated wires that ran across the beams to the tank. "First they didn't use a professional motion detector, but one of those backyard units that trips every time a squirrel jumps in front of it. The motion is supposed to trigger a light. Then whoever set this up ran the second line to the trigger on the gas tank, made couple splices, but the wires are so small they mis-wired it. No signal."

Nagler said. "And they didn't test it, I guess."

"How would they?" Wagner asked.

Nagler shrugged. *Of course.* "Well, good for us. Probably get prints off those units?"

"All bagged up. Odd, though, whoever wired the door was not the person who installed all the pencil cameras. That was a professional install."

"What the hell?"

"Right. This place was being monitored remotely."

"We can trace that," Ramirez said. "There has to be a transmitter."

Wagner grinned. "I just do bombs, Lieutenant. Oh, yeah. There's a Chevy in the back. Place is clear. All yours."

"So, Maria," Nagler said as they walked over to the propane tank. Nagler rapped it with his knuckle and gauged the dull echo. With appreciation: "Full." He traced the path of the wires and glanced into the dark spaces to the rear of the room which held the Chevy. "Could it be that the Dragony is spying on itself?"

"Yeah. But why here, and why now?" she said, then stopped, reached one hand to the tank, closed her eyes, and took a few deep breaths. "Thank God for small favors, Frank. I was about to reach through that broken window and jiggle the door handle. "If it hadn't been operator error…"

"Not your time, kid," he said. "Not your time."

He flashed the light around the dark space and shook his head.

"Something not right. The cameras, I'll buy that. But the door thing? If Wagner's right, too amateurish to be real. Look at this place."

"What?"

He flashed the floor.

"There's no tire tracks. All the dirt on the floor was disturbed by the bomb squad. And look at the car." He shined the light on the trunk. "It's got a half-inch of dust and dirt. What is it anyway?"

"An old Impala," Maria said. "Eighties something. A box on wheels. My old man had one, drove me and my brothers and half the neighborhood kids to Atlantic City. He'd drop us on the beach and hit the slots. It was what he was driving the last time I saw him."

"Wh..?"

"It's okay, Frank. I'm a big girl."

"No. I mean, why did they send us here? Somebody brought that tracker here. What did they want us to find? That is a set up for something."

"What's in that back corner?" Ramirez asked.

Nagler stepped around the car that was wedged into a narrow, wooden walled enclosure. He scanned the wall and saw what appeared to be an old opening now sealed. Makes sense, he thought. This place might have been a machine shop, with multiple entrances. He ran the light around the frame of the opening, saw it was loose, and then stepping over, pushed on the wall, which shifted.

"Hey, Maria. This wall moved."

"Where's it go?"

Nagler leaned his shoulder on the door, expecting more resistance, but it popped open with the first bump.

A shower of dust blew into his face as he lighted the small space.

"Oh, shit."

"What's that?" Maria asked as she added her flashlight to the search and landed the light on a misshapen object duct taped into a sheet of plastic. Resting on top was the missing tracker and a bread knife.

"Nice touch," Nagler said.

Dancer, Nagler suddenly thought. Said he had business. Everyone is trying to play us. He looked around the room and absorbed the dusty silence. And so far they are winning.

****

Medical Examiner Walter Mulligan said Eduardo Tallem had been dead for about twenty-four hours before being wrapped in plastic, and indeed, had been stabbed with the bread knife, which was smeared with traces of his blood.

"And before you ask," Mulligan said, "I cannot be sure this is the same knife that killed Ethan Ricardo. The wounds have the same dimension, but I would think all similar bread knives would. That the knife was found with the missing GPS tracker opens that possibility.

The autopsy may reveal more about Mr. Tallem's death that you need to know. The knife, while an obvious means, could prove *not* to be cause."

"But you're sure it's Tallem," Nagler said."

"Indeed. Mr. Tallem's identification was facilitated by comparison to his extensive police record."

"What do you make of his several aliases?"

"Somewhat typical criminal behavior, is it not?" Mulligan turned back to Tallem's body. "Now, if I might continue my work…"

"Perhaps our Dragony shed a tentacle."

"What?"

"Oh, that's from McCarroll, one of the gang members we are following. Called it the Dragony and said it is a many-tentacled thing."

"Dragony? Then you should see this," Milligan said as he pointed to a mark on the Tallem's neck.

"Look at that," Nagler said. "A dragon tattoo."

****

Nagler found Maria Ramirez swearing at her computer.

"That '95 Impala doesn't help us much," she said. "The VIN is right, but the plate is for a '67 Plymouth Barracuda, so a stolen plate, but stolen years ago. Might be pre-computer, which means there's a paper file stored in Newark, if it was even reported missing."

"What's with all these old cars?" he asked. "An '85 Impala, an '89 Ford van and a '67 Barracuda. Seems like unfinished business. Find a last owner for the Impala? Any help?"

"Only if he was alive. Sol Rosen died in 2006. The Impala is registered to him."

Nagler straddled a chair backwards and rested his head on his arms. "So, the Impala, and the stolen plates off the '67 'Cuda, and even Mr. Sol Rosen, all together fifteen years ago. Does that seem odd?" He held up his fingers as if he was holding a phone receiver. "Hi, Mrs. Rosen, this is the police. We found your husband's Impala. Yes, after all this time. No, he wasn't in it. Should he be?"

Ramirez tossed a wad of paper at him, laughing. "Christ, Frank." Then not laughing. "Wonder if there still *is* a Mrs. Rosen or little Rosens."

"How old was he when he died?"

"Just a second…fifty-two."

"Say how?"

"This is just an auto record. Why?"

"What's his old car doing in a warehouse owned by Taylor Mangot II fifteen years after he died, and what has it been up to? And why does it have the plates from a '67 Barracuda?" He snapped his head back and forth as if to dislodge that endless line of questions. "Have we heard from Mahala's shadow yet?"

"No. You think *she* moved the tracker to the warehouse?"

"She was pretty proud that she had left it at the other warehouse when we picked her up with the Ford van." He stood up and spun the chair with irritation.

"Wondering about things that seem completely random … What kind of car was that reporter, um, Kalinsky, Adam Kalinsky…what was he driving when he crashed?" Ramirez asked.

CHAPTER FIFTEEN

Dubin Place

What don't we know about this place? Nagler asked himself as he stood in the now emptied Dubin Place warehouse.

The Impala had been hauled to an out of county impoundment yard where, with the Ford van, a team of officers loyal to Maria Ramirez was tearing them apart.

"It's come to that," Nagler said as he strolled from post to post, running his fingers along old wooden edges, pushing on window frames and locked doors, feeling for, what? he laughed, a magic panel that would swing open? "Yeah," he said. It had come to that. Who to trust. "Where are the cracks that lead to the divisions in the department? What is the loyalty test, who needs to exploit it all?" Then he smiled. "That's what the Dragony is undergoing – some internal battle."

And just like, it all clicked. Nagler slapped at an old beam and laughed. He didn't know what their plan was, but knew they were in Ironton to execute it. He didn't even really know who they were but knew they would reveal themselves in full with just a little nudge. And he realized blowing up Warren Street was not the last act, but maybe the first. "It's beginning," Mahala Dixon had said. Maybe she was right.

Nagler waved at one of the tiny surveillance cameras hung from a corner beam. Nagler had ordered them left them all in place, trying to trace the encrypted, bouncing signal to its receiver.

And that was *why* he wanted them left in place. So he could wave at the Dragony. *Maybe they'll even worry about that.*

He walked the room again. Fifteen years ago, it had been the central transfer point. Drugs in from out of town, broken down into streets packs and then passed to dealers. No more than three or four operators at a time if past Ironton drug operations were a model. A dealer rep, a buyer rep and couple of muscle men to do the heavy lifting.

So why on that particular night were all the top brass of the Dragony in the same place? Had to be some really important deal. New suppliers? New product? What if it wasn't about drugs? Why does it all look the same?

And who, Nagler wondered as he stared into the tiny camera, was not there?

The one who called it in.

"I'm worried about you guys," he said to the camera, not knowing whether it recorded sound it not. *They can hire a lip reader.* "Y'all are apparently having some organizational troubles. Succession problems? You haven't all been in the same place for years, and now you can't figure out a seating arrangement for the board meeting? Is that why Eduardo Tallem is dead? Sat in the wrong chair? Forgot to bring the wine? Was it you he was talking on the phone with the night Warren Street blew up? Or was he talking *about* you?"

Or was it both? Nagler wondered. Was Tallem talking to an accomplice or a target? Or an accomplice who didn't know he was a target?

"So, look guys," he said to the camera. "You don't come out ahead in this. We know more about you than you think we do."

He stared into the camera a moment longer. He wanted to give them the finger but thought that would be remarkably immature, so he just smiled again.

Outside, leaning against the door of a hollowed-out shed was Jimmy Dawson.

"Running with a new crowd, Jimmy?" Nagler asked nodding to Dawson's green hoodie.

"Changed a few habits since they shot my drone out of the sky, and shot at me," Dawson said. "I look over my shoulder a lot. New clothes, new routes to work, walk more than drive." He started to cross the alley. "Just followed you. Haven't been here in fifteen years."

"Stay out of the doorway. It's wired with cameras," Nagler said.

Dawson stopped a few feet short of the doorway, leaned over side to side to peer into the dark space and then stepped back. "Wondered what they might be up to, but then you guys found Tallem dead inside."

"We never said it was Tallem."

Dawson grinned. "Just did. I was guessing."

"That's why I hate you, Dawson."

"I know, Frank. It's our secret." He stared at the ground and then up and down the alley. "But it's a hell of a secret, ain't it?"

Nagler pursed his lips and nodded. "That why you're here?"

"Naw. Been running through old drone footage, trying to see what I might have inadvertently recorded that made me a target." He pulled a flash drive from his hoodie pocket. "Home movies. I'm not sure what I'd be looking for, but you guys will know."

Nagler accepted the drive and nodded thanks.

"I've also been digging through the old newspaper archives and scanning reels of microfiche at the library. If you're right that this outfit has been around for decades, they left a trail. Don't know exactly what it would be, but I have a feeling it would jump off the screen." He shrugged. "I'll let you know." Then he pulled up his hood and turned to leave.

"What'd you say about Adam Kalinsky before?" Nagler asked.

Dawson stopped, squinted up the street, then back at Nagler. "Showboat, good reporter but at the end seemed shaky, preoccupied. Then he left and of course, died. Why?"

"We discovered that the plates from his Barracuda were on the old Chevy Impala we found here. You might say something about that."

"Why would I say it?"

"Because you find it interesting."

CHAPTER SIXTEEN

The story of us

History is a cruel mistress, Jimmy Dawson thought as he sorted the old newspaper clips and tried to read his hen-scratch notes.

1912: Three dead in housing riot, Sons of Liberty claim job.

1913: Food strike hits mine camp. Italians and Irish crews brawl.

1913: Mines close. Families out on the street. Looting gangs prowl.

And in '14, and '15. the Sons, the Sons. SOL, thugs for the companies, enforcers for the banks. *Ain't paid yer rent? Out you go. Ain't paid yer share? Don't be walkin' down dark alleys, now.*

1915: Shanty town burns. Where's the hosemen, families cry as home enflamed.

Dawson scratched his three-day beard.

Before him on his desk spread the lists he had culled from the old newspapers on microfiche the library and pulled from faded historic records in the county archive.

This is the story of this place, he thought. The story of us all.

We've all told the stories. The port arrivals after days at sea in stinking, dark holds, but the salt sea air smells like freedom. Here I will work, the ancestors said, I will work hard. I have always worked hard. I can make things with my hands. My wife can sew and weave. My children are strong. They can work.

Those were the stories *his* grandparents told, Dawson knew. The old men rocking on shaded porches, weaving the tales of *their* grandparents as if the stories were their own. Escaping famine, repression, sickness, hopelessness. Looking for a chance. So, into the mines because they knew the work. Digging a canal, forging tools, stacking bricks to make walls. Laying in a garden, selling the fruit raised from seeds carried hidden from the old world, loaves of ancient bread, working metal into jewelry, stone into statues, fabric into dresses, art from nothing.

Dawson held his head and smiled. Those were the stories, the good stories, the stories of progress and hope told without the bloody details of disappointment, doors slammed in an eager face – you're the wrong kind, the wrong color, speak the wrong language – the stories of ages we believe because we must.

Dawson had heard the stores, told by proud parents, tales of a grandfather ten feet tall and strong as a mountain, loved by a grandmother who could spin a dress from thin air, so pure of heart, the nuns were shamed by their piety.

But the histories before him said something different: What started as a unified force, working for a cause – blasting the modern world from the hard, cold ground, Nagler's grandfather wrote – soon cracked along the old lines.

Before him were stacked the payrolls, work rosters, lists of weddings, deaths, births, church memberships, school records, club records, tax records.

Pick a year, pick a town. Came for the jobs. Irish, Italians, Cornish, Germans, Swiss, Hungarians, Chinese, Russians. Jews, Catholics, Orthodox, Protestants. New Americans or wanting to be. But brought with them the old divides, the old differences. Stitched onto their backs, a voice in their ear: Remember. Lived side by side because that was the way the bosses built the shacks, but when the living is hard, there's scant time for learning or forgiving.

Moved to be with our own kind. Don't like the smell of their food, the way their women dress, the noisy kids; all the praying, at all hours – is that even the Bible? – that damned dog, the weird stringy music, the stomping they call dancing. Tried to borrow a smoke and the man stared at me like I was stupid, so I asked his kid and the kid stepped behind his old man's leg and said, not supposed to talk to strangers in some pidgin English. Took a swig of his jug and it tasted like pig piss, all the vines in the back yards, the festering pots of mash. And then there was the out-break, and we knew it was them that started it, them and their filthy ways.

Move to be with our own, Draw a line. Don't cross it. See that house, that tree? That's the border.

Irishtown, Germantown, Little Italy, Chinatown, Hibernia, Saint Mary's, Saint Sebastian, Sons of Italy, Sons of Erie, the Acadian Society, the Scandinavian Society, Germania Park, the Roman Hall, Mings. Friends of, Brothers of, Sisters of, Members only, passwords, hand-shakes, nods, winks.

Secret identities. Special identities.

Tattoos.

Dragons.

The Dragony.

Dawson learned what the records told him.

There were always gangs; skills learned on the streets. Newspaper filled with items: Rival bands clash at woods. Youths chased by thugs. Italians' tomato gardens ripped up. Bash up in Ironton worker's ghetto. Hungarian business burned, Storefront sign: Irish go home. No Catholics allowed.

Then the gangs found a common cause: Money. Alliances, part-nership, protection crews. Power. The moment all the living and swap-ping and distrust turned commercial. Became shadowy, underground. Working for the boss and the bankers and industrialists who told your grandparents that all they deserved was a leaky roof, two-bit shack. Old ways of intimidation and domination that never die, but just take on a new form.

Dawson wanted to laugh.

They never learn. They are still the bottom, waiting for scraps. When you wanted higher wages, they send in the army to break up the strikes. When you wanted better housing, they sent in the arsonists to burn them all down or had the bankers to sell the land. Get too uppity, and the mob shows up with ropes.

And now you work for them. Dawson issued a scoffing breath. We protect our own, you say. Draw the circle tighter. Live free or die. Us or them. The whole fucking world boiled down to a Saturday afternoon performance of "West Side Story."

"Is that *all* that this is about?" Dawson asked aloud. "Suspicions become hate; hate become action. And hate can be bought."

Out of the piles he pulled three documents: A roster of the Industrial Club from 1932, an undated photo of the Dragon Youth Club, and a story from the 1963 Register.

"The Dragon Youth Club meets in a converted warehouse on Dubin Place," the story began. "It is a spare place, the wooden walls unadorned, the worn floors still marked by the wheel tracks of laden carts. There is a desk in the corner, a few chairs, and a springy couch."

"When this reporter visited the club, I had to empty my pockets."

"Why?" I asked."

"Weapons," I was told by a fresh-faced youth known only as "Dancer."

"What is it you do here?"

"We meet. We talk. Plan."

"Why are you called the Dragon Youth Association?"

"Dancer laughed. "It's a scary name. We like to be scary."

"The apparent leader is Lew Newton. He does not state his age or address but appears to be about twenty."

"What do you plan?" I asked."

"I had spoken previously with Police Chief Richman, who had provided me a short list of encounters his officers had with the Dragon Youth Club."

"They're street runners," the chief said. "Petty thieves. They beat up immigrants, strangers. They've been known to paint slogans on the homes of, shall we say, a targeted minority. They're thugs. Paid thugs. Someone makes money from the chaos they sow."

166

"I kept that information to myself, as I questioned Lew Newton."

"Your uncle is Committeeman Howard Newton, correct?"

"Yeah, Uncle Howie pays the rent on this place and in return we help him out with his business."

"His fruit and vegetable business?"

"Yeah, right, that one." The kid laughed."

"No others?"

"The youth grinned."

"Uncle Howie got fingers in a lot of pies."

"I presented the next question with care."

"I must ask, because in discussions with the police they raised some concerns. Were any of your members attendant in the harassment of a family, the Nagler family, in the ghetto a week ago?"

"Lew Newton did not grin this time."

"That's an old beef. Goes back to the grandparents, opposites side of a question of money, I been told."

"And…"

"That's what it was last week. Uncle Howie sent some boys up there to collect, rent, I guess. Nagler didn't pay. It got outta hand. I went up to calm them boys down. Apologized and all."

Dawson laid the story back on his desk.

I'll bet he apologized, he thought. In between the threats.

He reached for a pen and the photo of the Dragon Club and circled a blurry face. Then he read the caption, found row two and counted in four names and circled it.

"So, there it is," he said. "All that way back. I'll be Frank doesn't even know it."

****

Nagler wrote the word *"Dragony"* at the top center of the white board.

So, who are you guys? Here's my list of your membership. What'd you forget to do? Or is the question what are you *planning* to do? As if blowing up downtown was not enough.

"McCarroll," Nagler wrote.

Said he was a member, acts like the boss, but I doubt it. Have to assume that all these guys are lying.

"Eduardo Tallem."

Who's he?

Depends on what state and year, records said.

Odd role; not at top of chain of command, but not a foot soldier. Facilitator. But of what?

Someone on the roofs of downtown. On the other end of Tallem's phone call.

Nagler wrote, *"Roof guy."*

Then, *"Ethan Ricardo."*

Street punk, drug dealer. Bread knife victim.

"Trainee," Nagler said.

Who was his boss who signed the fake passport?

Of course, Tallem was also a victim of a bread knife.

Does that make Tallem a traitor to the cause?

Well, he is dead.

"BLT," from Dancer's notes. Nagler wrote, *"Boonton Lieutenant Dan Thomson."*

Foot soldier, for sure.

How many are there?

"BL," from the notes.

No idea.

"T1 and T2." The Pursel twins. Added, *"James and Rachel."*

Drug stoolies in that raid fifteen years ago.

Everyone said they were dead. At least Dancer did.

"Taylor Mangot II."

From a distance. Ink stained, not blood stained.

Taylor Mangot I.

Nagler pondered. More blood than ink.

The four dead in that warehouse fifteen years ago.

Sacrificed. Fake IDs.

He stared at his list.

Incomplete.

"Dancer," he wrote.

Knows too much. Sudden reappearance, the scribbled notes recalled. Death and destruction.

Felt less bad about writing that name than he thought he would.

So, if Dancer, then, writing, *"Carlton Dixon."*

Maybe his taking the rap for the drug deal was not what it seemed.

But that one felt like a leap.

Still, if Carlton Dixon, then, writing, *"Mahala Dixon."*

Wannabe. Maybe.

Schemer. Scared for some reason.

Then, if Taylor Mangot I, then *"Jock Newton,"* old iron mine knock-around.

If Jock Newton, then *"Howard Newton."* Kept it in the family. Nagler added the name to the board.

Then added *"Gabriel Richman,"* and *"Chris Foley."* Howie Newton's sidekicks.

Really? Why not?

Who else? *"McSally,"* mentioned by Dan Thomson. Confused with McCarroll? Descriptions didn't match.

169

So, who's McSally?

Mastermind.

"Friend's list?" asked Maria Ramirez, as she leaned in the doorframe, then joined Nagler at the board.

"The Dragony. Anyone else?" he asked. "No one, it seems, would be a reach."

"That reporter, Adam Kalinsky," she said.

"Why?

"He drove a '67 Barracuda. Those were his plates on the Impala stashed at Dubin Place."

Nagler closed one eye, tipped his head, and let out a long, whistling breath. "Try anything. Okay."

He wrote, *"Adam Kalinsky."*

"And if Kalinsky, then Sol Rosen," Nagler said. "Why were they palling around?

Nagler added *"Sol Rosen"* to the list. Whoever he was.

****

The state highway has been re-engineered in the fifteen years since the winter crash that took Adam Kalinsky's life.

A '67 'Cuda. Classic muscle car. Fit what Frank Nagler knew about Kalinsky. Flashy guy. Flashy car.

With the dark street empty at two in the morning, Nagler straddled the center line and held up an enlarged photo of the old highway and stared over its top edge down the new road. A hump-shaped incline had been removed. In the photo the hump appeared quite sharp in its rise and fall, as if the builders didn't want to remove whatever had been under the ground at that point. Probably some old canal feature, he thought. Cheap engineering.

The rattle of a truck with a loud muffler that leaked from a side street caused Nagler to scan the area. The sound filtered away. *No one knows I'm here.*

He extended the photo again, and knelt down to imagine the conditions Kalinsky might have faced on a snowy night, highway lanes narrowed, headlights creating vortices of pinpoint snow, driving, squinting into the billow of white, a flowing snow wake caused by the tanker truck just ahead; concentrating on holding the center of the road, he might not have felt the quick rise, or the wheels slip across the crest, until out of the white mass there emerged the angled gray form of the jack-knifed tanker across the road.

Nagler stood. Police report said Kalinsky had no chance to brake or turn before his car struck the tanker and burst into flames.

The report also said a third vehicle had apparently stopped or slowed in the roadway in front of the tanker. Who reported that? Nagler wondered. The truck driver died in the wreck, and the official report said there were no witnesses.

After-accident photos of the scene seemed to show that any tires tracks had been filled in by the falling snow. Someone made an assumption, or made up the facts, he thought.

And what of Dancer's note: "…did AK brake job?"

Am I making something of nothing?

He scanned the road in both directions. It had been constructed over parts of the old canal path and many roadside buildings retained a flavor of that industrial past but were dressed now with neon signs and facades.

Where was Kalinsky going that night? Nagler read the top of the report. Three a.m. Kalinsky lived alone in Roxbury, the opposite direction of his travels and the newspaper office at the time was in another direction. So, deliberately going somewhere.

"Hey, Kalinsky," Nagler asked the empty street, "Where were you going? Was that what got you killed?"

****

Nagler tossed the photos into the front seat of his car and crossed Bergen Street to the city park. The playground equipment had been removed because it was out of date and unsafe, all metal and sharp edges.

What would they say today if they had found Lauren Fox's records of the Howard Newton financial scandal?

She had buried them in a metal box under the playground and passed to Nagler the hint that would lead to their discovery.

"There's more here than meets the eye," she had said.

We would have closed that case sooner if I hadn't been so dense, he thought. I almost lost case and almost lost her.

The park had always been the center of the city. In the iron days as the canal boats anchored loaded with goods, families rested, smoke rising above the canal basin, the center of Ironton as it was then. When the canal days ended the basin was transformed into a city park.

The world the monied folks let exist, he thought. It was what his grandfather had written in his diary. These towns existed because someone had to build them. And those who built, owned.

Conjure order from nothing, the money managers were told. So they did. Built houses for the workers. Created towns, and governments, stores, rules, thug gangs to enforce those rules; roads, then taxes to pay for the roads, then when the costs to maintain the entire hullabaloo exceeded their ability to extract more riches from the ground and the workers, they closed it all down, found something else to build, somewhere else.

And left holes in the ground filled with poisoned water, shacks for the former workers, now in the hands of the banks created by the moneymen, shacks with leaking roofs, newspaper windows, and towns with roads scraped from rocky hillsides, gifted now to governments with no means to operate them, because the governments had been constructed to extract wealth from the workers not the moneymen.

Left behind the brick shells that were now Ironton, empty of the shouts and hurrahs of workers, the clang and smash of iron and hammers, the meaning of what was done.

It, all of it, lives, fortunes, just a thing.

At the traffic light a pickup with a jacked-up frame and loud exhaust rocked back and forth waiting for the light to change, the engine roar rising and falling with each pulse until with a screeching side shimmy the truck filled the night with its rage. Then a shout from the open window and the sound of breaking glass on the sidewalk.

Kids, Nagler thought, and then, no, same truck. He leaned on a chipped wooden pillar of the gazebo, closed his eyes, and concentrated on the fading truck engine. It was not echoing, so the truck has crossed into that open block just before the new bridge that carried the road west. *Better move, just the same.*

As he crossed the park to his car, he recalled with fondness that the gazebo has been Lauren's project. She found the money, the volunteers, the worker's, all dedicated to adding something useful to the dying city park. It was, Nagler recognized, something that the moneymen had no part in, a thing they could not control.

So naturally when the gazebo was dedicated on that bright July day years ago, Mayor Gabriel Richman took all the credit, except that which he gave to his mentor, Mayor Howard Newton. The image flickered in Nagler's mind. Mayor Gabriel Richman and Mayor Howard Newton, who stood at Richman's elbow in his white Panama and dark shades, smiling like a snake.

Flags ringed the gazebo, police in dress blues saluted and a giant American flag suspended from the tallest fire truck ladder in the city filled the eastern horizon. The high school marching band played Sousa.

Lauren had already deserted Ironton, a move, Nagler learned later, was done for her safety.

Nagler smiled and slapped a light post. So clever she was. She had already planted under the playground the information that would send both Richman and Newton to jail. And there they were celebrating their stolen glory. All of them, even, Dan Yang ... "Damn it. Why didn't I remember that?"

Even Dan Yang. He had been instrumental in helping Lauren dig out all the money transfers, and so helpful in finding the suspected nuggets...

"Fuck. Because he had planted them." The cash flowing in and out of city accounts, the fake accounts with – "Why didn't we see that? – Lauren's name attached.

Dumbstruck, Nagler stumbled to his car.

"Fuck! Damn it. He fed it to us like ice cream."

And now Dan Yang is standing next to Taylor Mangot II, running the same scheme, but bigger with more moving parts, and if it works, more rewards.

More than meets the eye, indeed, my dear.

Before Nagler went home, he stopped by the office and added a line to his white board list of the Dragony.

"Dan Yang, cop, math professor."

If Howard Newton, Gabriel Richman, and Chris Foley, then Dan Yang.

Then and now. Nice disguise.

Outside, the air was coated with the odor of exhaust and from around some building corner leaked the rumble of a truck engine.

Nagler stepped from the lighted doorway into the shadow of a militarized utility van, nicknamed the Tank. The engine noise was the same. Big V-8 with a tricked-up exhaust. A slight pump of the gas raised the engine pitch. The truck was close, on Sussex maybe, past the front corner of city hall or that unlighted alley across the street that leads to a parking lot. *Why'd they touch the gas?* Nagler squinted into the dark alley trying to catch a reflection, the slightest smear of light, but saw none.

Try this. His own cruiser was four parking slots in from Sussex. He pulled his electronic key from his pocket and pushed the emergency button. The lights flashed and the siren filled the street.

The truck burst from the alley and jerked to a parallel stop in the city hall driveway. From his spot behind the van, Nagler saw the truck's dark, passenger side window open and a muzzle emerge. Three quick bursts of bullets shattered the windows of the four parked patrol cars. The truck squealed off as the lights and sirens of the damaged cars burst to life.

"I'm okay," Nagler yelled to the three officers running into the parking lot, weapons drawn. "Stand down. They're gone. Just shut 'em off."

He answered his ringing phone.

"Hoi, hoi, Mr. Noiglar. Just in case you had a thought you were beyond our reach."

McCarroll.

A photo text arrived: Lauren at her bank office.

****

The shower stopped and Lauren stood in the open doorway naked drying her hair with a towel. She shook her head and swiped the towel along her arms, then bent forward to dry her legs before wrapping herself at her waist.

"I don't give a fuck that they have a photo of me in that bank," she said. "It could have been taken weeks ago."

"But it wasn't," Nagler said. "You were wearing that red sweater. So, it was yesterday." He watched Lauren as she folded the towel on the bed and stretched, her sinuous torso extended and tight. She crossed her arms behind her head and rotated her shoulders as if working out a kink.

"Man, you are beautiful," he said and blew out a long breath.

She smiled. "You just noticed? That's why you're such a top detective. Keen perception."

"But it's also why I worry about you. You're not invincible. I don't want to lose…"

Lauren climbed on the bed and on her knees, legs open for balance, placed her hand on her hips, bent at her waist and thrust her chest out.

"I know. And you're not going to. We know more about them than they think we do. Waiting for the moment."

"Even Dan Yang?"

She wrinkled her nose and stuck out her tongue. "Even Dan Yang. We know this is about money. And as *you* know, once it's just about money it gets easier." She lay beside him. "Money crimes make people stupid, Frank. Besides, I've got Dan Yang exactly where I want him, you'll see."

"How does the Dragony get Mangot's cash?" Nagler asked.

Lauren leaned over and kissed him. "There is a price for that information," she whispered."

"Yeah, people are dying."

"Not in this room, they're not." Lauren kissed him again and scoured his surprised mouth with her tongue.

He laid his head back against the bed frame. "I'm sorry Lauren. This this is just eating me up. And you, too."

She wet her fingers and reached her hand under the blanket and stroked him.

"We can't fix that just yet," she said arranging herself at his knees. "But we can fix this." She rose and guided him inside her, sighing. "One thing at a time."

****

In the morning Lauren laid on the bed face down, towel draped across her hips, feet in the air and ankles crossed as she scrolled through files on her tablet.

"Sol Rosen, right?"

"Right. Heard of him?" Frank Nagler before he leaned over and kissed her lower spine.

Without taking her eyes off the screen, Lauren reached back and ran her fingers through his hair. "I'll tell you, but you have to promise me something."

"Really?"

"I'm an Old Iron Bog virgin, Frank. You need to fix that."

He rolled back and laughed. "What?"

"I know the stories."

"From whom?"

She wrinkled her nose at him. "You be surprised how much Leonard knows about you and Martha."

"Well, you and I christened the front porch of that old place, remember that?"

"Frank, you lived there. You and Martha didn't need to go out to the front porch. Besides her parents…Yup, here he is."

"What'd you find?"

Lauren rolled over and stuffed a pillow behind her back, focused on the screen.

"He was an accountant, um, here, Sol Rosen of Liberty Accounting Services of Ironton. Found him before."

Nagler leaned over and tried to read the screen. "Accountant." He thought of the 1985 Impala, bland, every day, unassuming. "Well, he drove an accountant's car."

"Mr. Rosen was not so straight and narrow. Liberty Accounting Services filed the financial docs for DRA Assets. That's one of those Mangot/Dragony enterprises. Remember I told you that the state denied Mangot's application for a non-profit? The entity that got denied was DRA Assets. The books were a little off."

"That little shyster. What year was that denial?"

"About '97 or '98. Why? I'll look it up."

"No that's good."

"Why?"

"Sol Rosen died in 2006,"

"So, you think…?

"Well, yeah." Nagler rolled off the opposite side of the bed and a grabbed his pants. "The crooked accountant who messed up your crooked books died after the crookedness was discovered. Cause and effect, right? I just need to prove it?"

Lauren stood and draped the towel over her shoulder. She scrolled through some screens on her tablet and then tossed it back on the bed.

"This might help." Lauren smiled and flipped the laptop on the bed. "Look at Dawson's news page."

"Big deal developer ran shady outfit," the headline screamed.

He read: "The shiny image of Mayor Jesus Ollivar's hand-picked developer, Taylor Mangot II, disguises a dark past of murky financial deals, Dawson News has learned. Newly uncovered financial statements call into question the history of the firm and its ability to fund the massive Warren Street redevelopment project, just announced. Ollivar is counting on the arrival of that project to cement his re-election chances next year."

"The mayor's gonna want your ass for that," he said.

Lauren leaned against the bathroom door and said, smiling. "Already taken. Besides, there's more to come and Ollivar not going to be in position to be on the attack."

Nagler leaned back and closed his eyes. Dawson's going to need a shadow, he thought, and I wonder if I can get Lauren's office shifted to a safer location. He stared at the ceiling. "I gotta protect Leonard."

He sat bolt upright. Liberty Accounting Services. SOL. Sons of Liberty.

He slapped the bed, and then slapped it again, laughing. "Son of bitch," he yelled.

CHAPTER SEVENTEEN

Sol Rosen's wife

Captain Bernie Langdon swiveled his chair away from the wall of filing cabinets and back to his desk facing Frank Nagler.

"When'd you grow the beard?" Nagler asked. Langdon did not have a face that was improved by hair; it was too thin, and the hairy addition seemed only to increase the depth of Langdon's sunken eyes and cheeks, adding to the overall wanted poster look.

"Ahh, was camping for a month. Forgot to shave and then said the hell wit' it." He shuffled the files he had extracted from the cabinets. "Don't see the one you're looking for, Detective. That little fire. Six months, you said?"

"That's the one. Fire Marshal Duval said you were holding some gas cans for evidence. Want to check them out."

"Oh, them," Langdon said. "No part of that fire. Duval knows that. They were just collected with a pile of stuff in that location. They got shifted to storage if they are even there now." He pushed the files aside. "No file here. But that was an electrical fire. Yah, somebody wired a string of lights off the old electrical box with fuses and it overheated." He stared silently at Nagler, trying to end the conversation. Then he sniffed and coughed.

"Damn," Nagler said with a hint of mild concern. "You know with the Warren Street bombing we're looking for anything that might be connected. I want to have those cans checked for prints and other possible evidence."

"Thought that was just a gas leak."

Nagler stood. "Might still be. There's some thought that some other accelerant was used, sort of a chain reaction thing. But I wasn't there you know, still on leave." Nagler tapped the chair he had been sitting in. "Heard you were there, though, helping with the search."

Langdon's eyes retracted. "Yeah, they needed help gettin' it set up. Pretty messy."

"Saw it after, quite a pile of stuff. Oh, Lieutenant Ramirez said thanks for helping her after she stepped in that hole. She was in that walking boot for a couple weeks."

"Bah," Langdon said. "She shouldn't have been there. Just got in the way."

Nagler dipped his head and wiped his mouth to hide his small grin. *Idiot.*

Ramirez in Nagler's earpiece. "Bastard."

Nagler turned to the door, then turned back. "Hey, Cap. Two more small things. When you were on the scene after the bombing, did you hear that someone was spotted running along a roofline maybe across Warren or on Blackwell?"

Leaning back in his chair, voice like water. "I was just there to set perimeters, Detective. Kinda focused on that."

"It was just a thing I heard."

"Anything else?"

"We found an old Chevy in that Dubin Place warehouse last week that belonged to an accountant who died in 2006. Weird, huh? Even weirder? It had the plates from the car that belongs to that reporter Kalinsky. Sol Rosen, that was his name. Think there's still a file on that?"

"No. Wasn't killed in Ironton."

"Killed, really. Didn't know that."

Langdon stood. "My brother, Jerry, he's a volunteer firefighter, he knew him. Canal Park in Boonton. Shot in the back of the head."

"Wow. So, like a hit."

A pause, a dry, vacant voice. "Yeah."

"Boonton, huh? Talked to a captain up there other the other day, Dan Thomson. Know him?"

Another long pause. "No."

In the street, Nagler hunched in a recessed doorway.

Electrical fire and no gas cans. Either Langdon or Duval was lying, maybe both.

Ramirez pulled up in her patrol car and Nagler folded into the vehicle and then grinned. "You should have just stayed out of his way, you know."

"He's the reason I'm not a captain, Frank." Her knuckles were white as she gripped the steering wheel. "Old Bernie said I would bring disgrace to the rank. Hispanic me and my dyke girlfriend." She sighed. "What's it gonna take, huh, buddy?"

"I'd say just time," he said as he squeezed her shoulder. "But in the meantime, let's make some room."

She nodded and patted his cheek twice. "So that's 'BL' from Dancer's notes?"

"Has to be. The question is, was Langdon the guy that Eduardo Tallem was calling that night, or was he the guy who was supposed to be on the roof?"

"Hey, he's making a call."

Nagler nodded. "McCarroll."

Then Langdon's voice leaked from Ramirez's computer. "Hey, Dancer. We gotta talk."

Nagler: "Gotcha."

Ramirez slapped the steering wheel. "Fuck 'em, all, Frank. Every one." Then she blinked and stared out the side window. When she turned back, she said, "We found Sol Rosen's wife."

"Yeah?"

"East Hanover. Got a nice Colonial."

****

The door opened and closed sweeping in a whisper of fluttering leaves, wordless shouts, and the scent of chilled fall air.

Leonard in his usual corner window seat, waited for the footfall to announce the entrance of a new visitor. But the expected call out to Barry for coffee, or from Barry – "Hey, Jack, special?" – did not follow. Whoever had entered paused, as if scanning the room; Leonard heard the crinkle of a leather coat being removed.

"Leonard, I'm Taylor Mangot II. So pleased to meet you."

Leonard forced a small smile but the ice of the voice crawled down his spine. The voice came from a point a foot or two above Leonard's head. Leonard then recalled that Taylor Mangot II was six and half feet tall.

"Mr. Mangot, welcome. "Please sit. May I offer you a beverage?"

Mangot reached Leonard's table in eight precise, soft steps. A tap of leather soles. Catlike, Leonard thought; he would be on you before you knew he was there.

Leonard shifted his wheelchair to face the table as a chair opposite him scratched along the floor and he sensed the weight of the tall man sitting.

"Pardon my manners…"

"Sir, I understand," Mangot replied. "If I might, how long have you been blind?"

"Since childhood."

"And yet you own this block and parts of another. How did you accomplish that?"

Leonard took one small breath as the frigid insulting tone of Mangot's question stung. He had been expecting this visit for several weeks after he had initially rejected the partnership offer from Mangot's foundation.

"I am blind, Mr. Mangot, but I don't lack ambition or skills. I have many friends with skills as well. People who care about me and this city and are willing to set goals. I grew up on these streets. I hope to make life better for others."

"As do I." Mangot said.

Leonard heard the self-important smile.

"I have taken the ineffective tiny company my father left me and fine-tuned it. I change cities, Leonard, not just blocks. I enrich, not just improve."

Leonard shifted in his chair. "I am impressed, your reputation precedes you." He added an edge to his voice, up to that moment, soft and welcoming. "But I find it interesting that you would come here and insult a prospective partner."

"You misunderstand. I don't have partners. I acquire."

Leonard heard Mangot shift in his seat and place his elbows on the table.

"If this were mine, I would transform it, while you desire to fix it." A scoffing tone. "These blocks cannot be fixed. They have the stench of age, the aroma of labor that would always remain if they were not demolished. Just like the block on Warren that was destroyed. For the better I might add. This city looks backward, preserving the old, dirt red brick as if it is an act of mercy, as if somehow the cries and sweat of the ancient workers are more meaningful than the efforts of the men who paid the wages, who took what the ground held and transformed it into vision of wealth and comfort. I will bring new people to Ironton, people with money and class. My father catered to the past, as do you. There is little room for you in a new Ironton."

Leonard listened as Mangot leaned back. He imagined his hard, cold, self-satisfied face.

"Ah, sir, the smell of old Ironton," Leonard said. "I walk these streets, you know, feel the rough edges of bricks formed one by one with hands of skill and intelligence. I feel that knowledge and know that each brick fed a family I might have known, a family who helped me when I was a child. I understand that knowledge was transformed into skill that engineered railroads and streets and the buildings you despise. They meant something, mean something. Besides, sir, is not glass but sand harvested, processed, and transformed? Who will do that for you? You see glass as money. But is that why they chased you out of San Francisco, and that your plans in Singapore were denied. Is that why your foundation has been suspended in this state? I am not a thing to be bought, sir."

Leonard let that sink in, then continued.

"I sit at this window, gazing often at the square where three of my friends were murdered by a man I imagine to be much like you. Dom, Del, and Bobby will be remembered by a giant brass plaque I will install in the lobby of that refurbished mill. It will be a place filled with music and lively chat and the aromas of a dozen foods. What will your glass tower be filled with, Mr. Mangot?"

"Ah, Mr. Mangot, I'm glad you are here," Calista Knox said as she took a seat next to Leonard. "I'm Calista Knox, Leonard's partner."

"Yes, Miss Knox. The prostitute, correct?" Mangot pushed away from the table and gathered his leather coat. "Those reports you mentioned are false, Leonard. Bad reporting. I am seeking legal redress against Mr. Dawson."

Calista stood and handed Mangot an envelope. "I've been called worse. Nice shoes. Italian?"

Mangot scoffed. "Not that you could afford them."

"Prefer Spanish, myself. Soft leather caresses the foot. Anyway, while you are pursuing that action, read this. It's our formal rejection of your offer. You will note, I'm sure, our attorney's concerns about your sources of income."

Mangot folded the envelope into a pocket and turned to leave. He stopped at the door. "Our organization is larger and more extensive than you know. I would urge caution. And, of course, I take this as a mere step in negotiations. No offense taken."

Calista watched Mangot's movements on the street. He made a quick call, ruffled his collar, and then entered a black, dark-windowed Mercedes that glided to the curb, then pulled away.

"Nice speech," she said, reaching to touch Leonard's face.

He smiled and kissed her fingers. "I wanted him to hear his own voice, the emptiness of his tone. I don't think Mr. Mangot believes he speaks to anyone his equal. He wants to sound like a visionary, but really sounds like a conman. To a room filled with bankers who are counting dollars in their heads, he sounds like a prophet. To someone like me who grew up on the streets, he's the guy hawking junk cars on a corner lot for cash."

"If he's building million-dollar condos in Dubai, why is he in Ironton?" she asked. "He's in trouble, somehow." She paused, "And he called me a prostitute."

"I wonder where Frank is," Leonard said.

Calista laughed. "Probably trying to figure what that yellow kitchen chair has to do with all this. Why?"

"The way Mangot casually mentioned the Warren Street explosion was curious. Dropped it into a sentence with no change of tone or hint of remorse or concern. Spoken as if it was a transaction. I think he was involved."

****

"Lotta house for a single widow and no kids," Nagler said as he and Ramirez parked at the edge of the circular driveway near the fountain.

Three stories disguised to look like two, fenced back yard with a pool, two rows of manicured shade trees, four plots of dormant varied flowers, dotted with evergreen shrubs.

"Four bedroom?" he asked.

"Probably five," Ramirez aid. "This is a trade-off house. Town gets to build four of these for every smaller other-side-of-track house for poor folks."

"What?"

"State law to expand the supply of homes for regular folks," she said, chuckling, and nodded to the grey, nearly silver house. "My sister lived in one of the smaller homes. Need to make the rich folks feel safe and included when you want to do something for the less fortunate."

The door was opened with a small suck of air by a slim, striking blond woman in a flower patterned dress and high heels.

"I'm …" Nagler began.

"Detective Nagler and Lieutenant Ramirez. Please come in. I'm Adele Rosen. May I serve you a beverage?"

She directed the pair to an extensive, sunny room overlooking the back yard through wide, latticed, double-paned windows and left them to retrieve their drinks.

"Seems young," Nagler said. "Husband killed in '06? Silk dress?"

"Mid-forties," Ramirez said. "Works out. Looks like, hardly off the rack."

"How…"

She laughed., "That's my future, if I don't gain thirty pounds first."

Adele Rosen returned.

"Lovely home…" Nagler said.

"Yeah, thanks, but let's get down to it," she replied as she placed the tray with a silver coffee service and porcelain cups and saucers on the low, mahogany table with a ceramic inlay, and then sat. "You want to know why my Solly was shot to death, right?" She waved at the coffee tray, "help yourself," and then filled a cup of her own.

Nagler shared a glance with Ramirez. "Well, yes," he said and poured a cup of coffee for Ramirez and another for himself.

Adele Rosen took a sip, then placed her cup on the table and leaned back in the chair, crossing her legs.

There was something just off in her presentation, Nagler thought: Her dress, clearly expensive, her furniture, the coffee service set, the home, but her face had an edge that didn't come from directing land-scapers about garden arrangements or chiding decorators about their choice of curtain fabric; the edge was earned elsewhere, probably the same places her eyes had acquired a dark look that was not hidden by her neatly styled hair and light touch of makeup. Inside that package of suburban sweetness burned an anger, and maybe a fear.

"No bullshit," she said. "He was a mob accountant. Ain't no nice way to say it."

Nagler nearly spilled his coffee but managed to land the cup on the table and glance at the floor. *There it is.*

"So that's why he was killed?" Ramirez asked.

"In part," Adele said. "Here's the story. Sol's fa-tha Abraham was a bookkeeper for truckin' companies, trash haulers, restaurants. All the business and cash flowed together. Abe's job was to make it look legit, keep the tax guys and inspectors happy."

"Happy how?" Nagler asked.

"How ya think? Ever see a part-time town councilman with a brand new Mercedes? Guy who makes fifty-five grand, four kids, driving a couple hunnered thousand-dollar car? Anyway, Abe taught Sol some things."

"Like what?" Nagler asked.

"Ya gotta understand, detectives. About money. Abe's job was to keep it moving among the businesses. That and leave enough of it in his bosses' accounts. He didn't ever want them askin' why a personal account didn't seem to have as many zeroes on the end as it did last year. You know, but not enough to attract the attention of the tax men. The trick? Maintain about the same balance every year and ship the rest offshore. It's all that switching, the ins and outs, that snags the attention. Makes 'em nervous, know what I mean?"

"Money laundering?" Ramirez asked.

"Bookkeeping," Adele Rosen said with a snap, and then shook her head. "Detective Nagler. I know you've seen this before. Inside guy, money moving from one account to another. Money from apparently nowhere just showin' up and then disappearing. That's how Abe worked, how Solly worked, and how these guys today work. There's just more of it, more sources of shall we say, income. Then Sol got a conscience, bless his soul."

"That's what got him killed," Nagler said.

"That, and four or five million," Adele said.

"He stole from them?" Ramirez asked, eyes wide.

Adele Rosen stared into the back yard, her eyes narrow and her face for a moment serene. Then her eyes closed, and she smiled the slightest smile.

"My Solly, he knew. The market crashed in '87 and never really recovered. Not even as Bush declared war in Iraq. The guy before Sol made bad choices. Got the money tied up in things that had lost their value and he started screwing the books to cover it. He went swimming off Atlantic City and never came back, if ya know what I mean. When Sol took over he saw that it was too complicated. How hard it is to protect a business owner, take bets, move untaxed cigarettes, skim a little off the top when you haul a load of computers? There was always enough, always enough to keep everyone in line. So Solly straightened it out. They made their money, everybody was happy."

"So, what happened?" Nagler asked.

"This house didn't drop from the sky, detectives. My Solly, he was older than me. I was just a kid, a secretary in his office, barely passed high school. But Sol taught me, he took care of me, and then took care of them, if you know what I mean."

Nagler glanced at Ramirez, and then at Adele Rosen. "That's why his car is still around. There's something… but our guys took it apart."

"Look, Sol was cleava. Left it somewhere no one would think to look, even if they asked. A couple numbers, look like auto part numbers."

"Numbers to what?" Ramirez asked. "Accounts, safe deposit boxes?"

"You'll know when you see them."

"Thanks for that, Mrs. Rosen," Nagler said.

"Adele, please."

"Did you husband know a newspaper reporter named Adam Kalinsky. I ask because the plates to Kalinsky's car were found on your husband's Impala."

A dreamy smile. "Adam was just kid, a sweet boy, had lot to learn but was an eager student."

Nagler let *that* thought pass. "So, Kalinsky and your husband…"

"They had a plan, detectives, a long-term plan. The plates ain't an accident. But Adam got sloppy when he was on his own after Sol was killed. I had to tell him to stop coming here because if they found me, they'd know." She stood and stepped to the window. She tapped the glass with her right index finger. Once, then again, then a ripple of taps.

"It's time for you to act, detectives," her voice hard and cold. "It's all in place. They will act first if you don't."

"I've heard that before," Nagler said, standing. "They're in place…"

"In city halls, police departments, banks, corporate boards, non-profits, there, acting, connecting the pieces, doing small things, then bigger things, each act a step toward greater control."

"Then what?"

"Then it's done, Lieutenant Ramirez. The world wakes up changed, and they get away with killing my Solly."

"One last question, Adele," Nagler said. "When did you send Kalinsky away, as you said. Right after your husband was killed?"

"About fifteen years ago, detective. He came over in the middle of the night, and, yes, we made love, several times, even in this room in the moonlight. But he had to leave. He was troubled, haunted, and I didn't want to know the details because it would lead back to me. So, he left, in that jazzed up car. What is that song lyric? I used him and he used me?" She folded her hands before her face, chin resting on her thumbs. "But it was time."

"Last question," Ramirez said.

Adele Rosen turned from the window and nodded.

"How do you know they haven't found you?"

"Because I ain't dead yet."

CHAPTER EIGHTEEN

Dancer's blood

Ramirez pushed aside the papers scattered on her desk and pulled out the keyboard. The overhead lights flickered, flashed, then turned on. Christ, fix the damn things, she thought.

A few keystrokes later, she stared at a photo of the license plate left on Sol Rosen's Impala.

L104.7B389.

"Lotta numbers," Nagler said from over her shoulder. "Special order plate. Think there's a record of the application?"

"If her Solly was so smart, he didn't need one," Ramirez said. "Ordered it right from the plate shop in state prison."

"Sounds about right," Nagler said. "What's it mean? Coordinates? Address? L...lower something. B...backside?"

"Sorry to interrupt," Medical Examiner Walter Mulligan said as he entered. "I have... Is that a license plate?"

"Yeah," Ramirez said. "It's a plate that was found on the '85 Impala in that warehouse on Dubin Place, but it belongs to a '67 Barracuda. The Impala was registered to Sol Rosen, who died in 2006, and the 'Cuda was registered to Adam Kalinsky, who was killed in a car crash that year."

"Dubin Place, you said." Mulligan leaned into the examine the computer image. "Why would someone put a lot and block number on a license plate?"

"A what?" Nagler asked.

"You own a house, Detective. I'm surprised you didn't recognize the form."

"You lost me."

"Have you ever read your tax bill?"

"The bank pays the taxes." Nagler shook his head, embarrassed.

"Well," Mulligan began in that scolding voice that reminded Nagler of Sister Katherine in fourth grade when he didn't do his spelling assignment, "Your tax bill has two notations, your street address, and a designation that appears on the tax map of the city." He pointed to the screen. "It appears in this form, lot first, then block."

"That's a weird clue," Ramirez said.

"Clue for what?" Mulligan asked.

Ramirez leaned back and ran her fingers through her hair. "Sol Rosen was an accountant for our gangsters. Seems he stole some money, up to five million. His wife told us that he and Kalinsky cooked up some scheme, for what we don't know and left clues on Rosen's Impala and on this license plate. Rosen was murdered – unsolved – and Kalinsky died in a car crash, maybe suspicious."

"I remember the Kalinsky accident," Mulligan said. "Blunt force trauma from the crash."

"That all? Report said there was a big fire, truck filled with gasoline," Nagler said.

Mulligan squinted at Nagler's question. "Don't believe so, Frank. I recall I wondered why there were not extensive burns. I'll check. As for Mr. Cohen, I'll have to examine that file as well. Where was he killed?"

"Boonton. Description seemed like a hit."

"Indeed." Mulligan tapped the computer screen again. "You might consult Miss Fox about any real estate developments about the time of Mr. Cohen's death. Oh, and this was the reason I came to see you. We disassembled the bread knife found with Mr. Tallem, and under the handle discovered blood belonging to Ethan Ricardo and former Ironton Detective Jeffrey Montgomery." Here's the report. "I suspect this changes the trajectory of the case." He paused, as if waiting for a reply, but receiving none, left, sucking out all the air in the room with him.

Ramirez spun in her chair and Nagler deeply exhaled and grabbed a handful of his hair.

"Dancer," he said, as he stepped over to the white board listing the suspected members of the Dragony. He slapped the board and it rolled in a semi-circle, crunching into the wall. "Fucking Dancer."

****

The room seemed to sway, the walls separating. Nagler felt himself unhinged from the floor.

He stumbled from the room and left Maria Ramirez, stunned, furiously typing on her computer keyboard searching for anything about Jeff Montgomery. Nagler burst into the Sussex Street parking lot where sat the four cruisers that had been blasted a week before by the unknown occupant of a black Jeep Wrangler, mind racing as the case before them shattered into a million shards, fell from the side of the skyscraper, papers blowing which ways all at once beyond his grasping fingers, never to be assembled again; to hear in his mind Dancer and McCarroll guffawing, that mocking laugh, calling down the supposed power of the Dragony, the fearsome history of suspicion.

Dancer, damn it. Hey, Frank. I'm dying in the heat out here and ya gotta help me get this monkey off my back cause they're gonna kill me.

Know what, Dancer? They might anyway.

Go back inside, figure this out, Nagler scolded himself. Isn't the first time some cop or friend turned.

Mind boiling. Not yet. Not now.

A chill sleety wind descended

Outside, the city was cement footed, unmoved, unchanged, bland, uncolored, too quiet by half, disinterested.

Blind, uncaring, angered, afraid, hateful. Nagler felt a rage brewing.

What the fuck is the matter with you, he wanted to scream, but held it in. Had he been at the Old Iron Bog, he would have wakened the sleeping birds with his cry. Instead, he was at the corner of Sussex and Blackwell watching the gray-faced, bent-hatted crowd huddle along the sidewalks, collars tight against the sleet.

There is treachery in this city, thuggery, stealing your future, criminals! See them. They stand before you and lie. They will take all you own and erect a shining glass tower empty of all that you know and love. Stop them.

And still in his mind they walked, plowing forward, he reached out his arms and pushed back, but still they marched mechanically on.

Is this my fight alone? The silence said: Perhaps.

Or was it that they all seemed so weary of it all, stared unseeing at the newspaper headlines about theft and corruption and death and explosions and how it now it was so familiar and why didn't they end it, fix it, and left the paper folded on the empty seat when they marched dead-faced off the train so someone else could read about it and shrug; elbowed to their cars, to the barbershop, the grocery, stiffly to a bar and ordered the usual and gulped it down and waved for another; mechanically played catch with the son and prayed weakly for forgiveness over the plate of meatballs and pasta, then after the kids had gone to bed roughly pulled off the wife's sweater as she smiled and teased, and mashed his hands over her full breasts and laid her face down on the bed and yanked off her shorts. The rage of the routine. Then slipped his finger inside her as he licked the backs of her thighs, stood, dropped his pants and rolled her over, entered and humped her while his mind recalled some skinny girl in high school who offered blowjobs for math help knowing his moaning wife was thinking about the furnace repairman who had come that day and how he seems helpful and smiled and how he knew she wanted to have him bend her over the washing machine because he never trusted her all those years even after two kids and the trips to Europe and paying the mortgage so they could retire financially secure and die in their beds. All the mindless ordinary suspicions of life. We can't trust ourselves, so how can we trust the others?

A truck backfired. Nagler, awakened, coat open to the wind, was chilled by the sweat running down his spine. He hoped no one passing noticed how wide-eyed his face was, how wrenched into confusion; how he slowed his breathing, blinked, closed his eyes a moment. Calmed.

Briefly fading: the faces of Martha, Del, Dom, Bobby, the sadness in Leonard's face, the anger of Calista, the strength of Lauren and Ramirez, the wisdom of Sister Katherine. Then the deceit of Mahala Dixon, the dishonesty of Dancer and McCarroll.

If I this is mine, then so be it.

His feet began to shuffle, along with his mind.

Why did Sol Rosen drive a Chevy Impala? It was a fucking boat. But that's all they made back then, boats on wheels. He was making big bucks. So why not drive, I don't know, a Buick Riviera, a proper upper middle-class car? I know he didn't want his bosses to see him driving a Caddy, no sir. Too obvious.

So, they stashed it in a place they tried to blow up. Maybe we're too late and they figured out the code marked on that car part somewhere. Or maybe the unschooled bomber knew nothing about the Impala, but wanted something else, recognition, revenge. Would that make the bomber with poor wiring skills an unnamed foot soldier demanding command, or Mahala Dixon, the avenging daughter?

She did give us the white Ford van and had that GPS tracker we found at Dubin Street.

His phone chimed. Ramirez.

"Gonna love this, Frank," she said. "Arizona has no records of a Jeff Montgomery or any of his other names securing a private investigator's license. He had no address there and the phone he called you on is a burner. My guess is he's been in Ironton for months. The question? Is he working with McCarroll or against him?"

He heard himself say "Thanks. Good work."

He stopped under an awning and wiped the sleet from his face. "I don't think any of them know what's hidden on that Impala, or where," he said. "But someone long ago said 'keep it,' so they did."

Nagler turned right and walked toward the explosion site. The crowd ahead crossed at the light at Blackwell and Warren, even if they were continuing west on Blackwell, anything to avoid the fenced-off destruction. He scanned the corner: Anyone taking the right on Warren stared at the ground. So maybe they did know or were they ashamed of what that space represented.

When he arrived at the corner of Bassett across from the billboard announcing the new development, Nagler smiled, then laughed. Spreading over the photo of the tall glass Mangot Tower was a long and wide sloppy, painted in a hurry, rainbow.

Destiny.

Of such small things, revolutions are made.

****

Screeching tires grabbed his attention. A block away he saw that a driver had slammed on the brakes rather than run the traffic light and now the vehicle was boxed in, igniting a car horn symphony.

Was there a light in Lauren's bank lobby office, to the left of that intersection?

No. Long gone, he surmised.

He had surprised her with flowers the night before. They had been living like renters for the last few weeks, greeting each other passing in opposite directions, leaving notes about the mail, trash day.

She thumped into the kitchen loaded with a laptop and two files which she dropped on the table.

She wrinkled her brow and bit her lip. He could not recall the last time he had brought home flowers.

She softly brushed the petals of the sunflowers and inhaled the scent of the purple flowers, whatever they were – he was no good at flower names, just bought them because they looked pretty.

She fluffed the arrangement and shifted the vase to the center of the table. He reached for her hand and pulled her to his seat. She brushed hair from his forehead and kissed it, wordless thanks.

"Hey, Detective Nadling. Over here."

Nagler turned to see car lot security guard Randy Jensen, who had just turned the corner on Bassett at the old theater, hustling up the street and waving at him. The grinning kid, still wearing that blue Bob's Top Security uniform with "Randy" in red stitching inside a white oval.

"Randy," Nagler called out and pursed his lips. *What now?*

"How ya doin', Detective Nadderling? Been a while. Just wanted you to know I been watching that yellow chair, like you asked."

"That's a good job, Randy. Appreciate it." Nagler wanted to turn around but waited. "Anything interesting?"

"Well, first I just watched it from the highway, you know, across from the dealership. Sometimes there ain't a lot of traffic. I started this little notebook," and he reached into a back pocket to produce a palm sized, wire-rimmed notepad. "I started thinking about stuff going back a couple months. Fuckin' A, amazing what you can remember if ya think."

Nagler coughed so he would not laugh. "Like what?"

Randy flipped through a few pages.

"Like this, like three months ago. Couple dudes walking on the theater roof. They'd stop and point and walk around again." He flipped a few more pages. "Then this. Dudes on the theater roof again, this time with like a spyglass lookin' over at the buildings on Warren Street."

Nagler glanced up at the ruins. What they were looking at is probably gone, he thought. He pointed to a building to his left. "So, not the building that's right there, across the street, but the one on the corner that collapsed?" He pointed to his right to an empty lot.

Randy scanned his notes, and then the street scene. "The one that used to be here." He pointed to the right and straight up. "This one, this place. It was taller than the others. One guy said, something like, 'He has to be in that room,' or maybe on that roof.' What did I know?"

Nagler stepped into Bassett and peered toward the theater roof, then up the slope to the highway beyond. "How did you heard their voices?" he asked with greater appreciation for Randy's observation skills.

Randy shrugged. "Light at the end of the bridge musta been red. No traffic."

Nagler grabbed Randy's shoulder. "That's really good, Randy, really good. Anything else?"

"The chair showed up."

It took Nagler a second. "What?"

"Yeah. Fuckin' A." Randy showed Nagler the page with the note. "See. About three days before the explosion. Then here's the explosion." He displayed a page with an exploding cloud and the word "BOOM!!!"

Nagler closed one eye and frowned. "Then what?" *Damn it, we missed all of this. But why would we have looked at that time, before the explosion?*

Randy's face took on a flat, sheepish aspect. "I went up there a couple days before it all went blooey."

Of course he did. "How? Look, it's okay."

Randy exhaled and color returned to his face. "Fire escape on the theater. Fuckin' A. Old wobbly thing…" He extended his arms, spread his legs, and wiggled back and forth a little as a demonstration – "I got some rubber gloves from the mechanics when they change oil, and a pair of those blue booties from the paint shop, so, ya know I wouldn't leave no trace."

"See anything?"

"Guys, dudes, maybe three. Top floor windows of the place that ain't there anymore." He pointed up. "Moving around. I woulda thought they was painting, 'cept for seeing those same guys on the roof before. Did I screw up?"

Nagler laughed and slapped the boy's shoulder. "You've told us more about that yellow chair than we could have known. Well, fucking A. I hate to ask. Anything else?"

"They was back. Yesterday, I think." He turned and pointed at the building a block away on the corner of Warren and Blackwell. "I was restin' on the guard rail, suckin' down a Coke, lookin' at the chair, lookin' around. And they seemed like they're doin' a roof job."

Nagler followed Randy's pointing finger to the bank where Lauren Fox had her temporary office. A quick angry breath and a clenched fist. *Not gonna happen.*

****

That's a long way up, three stories or more, Nagler thought as he shook the rusted metal frame of the theater fire escape and winced when he saw a half dozen broken bolts rattle against the brick wall. *Oh, man, but gotta do it.* He took a couple breaths and climbed the frame, worrying as it groaned and scraped side to side under his weight and felt his sore ankle buckle on the uneven surfaces.

At the top, he pushed off with his left foot from the last wobbling platform and threw his right leg over the two-foot broken wooden rail that encircled the theater roof, and onto the graveled shingles. He winced when his foot sank into a soft spot and sharp pain shot up his leg.

With each step he tapped the roof with his shoe before adding his full weight.

The yellow kitchen chair faced Warren Street. Nagler leaned on the frame and when it didn't shift or drop, he sat and scanned the rooftops, puddles reflecting the fading sunlight, cave-like windows dark with glittering drips from the sleet that fell, hollow spaces all.

What'd Randy say? They had three or four men up here.

Why here? Why this roof, of all the roofs in downtown Ironton? What was there to see from here, other than co-conspirators and possible traitors?

He peered into the windows of the third floor of the building across from the bomb site and imagined Randy's "dudes" moving inside; the echo of the phrase "He must be in the room" from Eduardo Tallem's overheard phone call filled his head. Was that the same guy Tallem was looking for a couple hours before the place blew up, when Tony saw him in the alley? *Are you an accomplice taking that call, or the target?*

"Target," Nagler said.

Nagler mused. "Has" to be in that room. A command, part of a plan. "Has" to be there or the plan fails.

"Must" be in that room. An outcome. A scheme. A trap.

"Target," Nagler said again.

Then, with a sly smile. "Dancer."

He was a cop for three decades, He knows how crooks think, so he had scoped out the plot.

Nagler smiled to himself. "What'd he say at the bog, 'got some business to do.' Tallem was his business, then, who first? the mystery caller, then, McCarroll?"

He shook his head in disgust. "Gang war, a stupid, every-day gang war."

Nagler squeezed out a laugh, closed his eyes and made the sound that happens when someone knows they've been had. "Here we are thinking this is some end-of-the world conflict, some bigger-than-life event. Maybe we wanted it to be. Maybe we needed it to be, to justify to ourselves the immensity of the damage, to make the thing as large as our outrage."

He pushed out of the chair with a grunt, slide-stepped to the edge of the roof, and started into the gap where three buildings once stood.

"And here I am standing on a broken roof in a busted-up city…" he shrugged … "What am I doing? Chasing. Ghosts, rumors, laughing. *But something went sideways. That's why they blew up Warren Street.*

"So, it's not just a one-off, is it? Not some shoot-out in Ironton's OK Corral. Took all you guys way too long to get here. Too much planning, but it fell apart. What happened, and when?"

His head felt lighter when the thought emerged. "2006. That's why Sol Rosen got a bullet in the back of his head. Been going on forever. But why?"

He turned, then wobbling on his bad knee, grabbed the damaged railing before leaning away from the roof's edge.

Why was Dancer's blood on the bread knife? And under the handle, of all places, exposed only when the knife was taken apart?

"We'd expect to find Ethan Ricardo's blood," Nagler said to the sky, walking in a circle that spun quicker and quicker. "We know he was stabbed to death. And Eduardo Tallem's blood was on the blade because he too had been stabbed. But Dancer? *What did Mulligan say? This changes the trajectory of the case. He knew why it did and was just waiting for me to catch up.*

"Christ, he's so slick. Mulligan knew how difficult it would be to get blood under a sealed knife handle, even in a severe attack, yet there it was. But does he tell me that? No. He says one thing, the obvious thing, leaves out the other option, presuming I'll get there sooner or later. He does that to me all the time."

Nagler wanted to kick at the chair, but knew how much it would hurt, and then he'd fall, look ridiculous and maybe not get up. Instead, he walked a widening circle, glancing back at the chair and at the changed view from the roof: The cornice of the bank at Warren and Blackwell, the gray tower of the Congregational church with its accusing finger pointing skyward, and beyond, the flatiron brick shell of the fabric shop, its windows coal smeared from a century of smoke from passing trains. Then Prospect hill, the path rich men took home in the evening, where they lived above the oily gray air their factories belched, the dust that settled into Ironton's valley bowl, then leaked through the windows and walls of their worker's' home and settled on beds and tables and the faces of a thousand children.

He reached into his jacket pocket and extracted two pages that Jimmy Dawson slipped him the other day. A map and a photo.

The old map was a copy of a developer's plan for what became known as the worker's ghetto. Three hundred lots crammed together, lots only big enough for a three-room house with walls so thin, kids said "bless you" when their neighbor sneezed. Streets of mud, yards of slop, homes of huddled poverty. Air so dank and odorous it seemed to change color. Home.

Dawson had outlined three lots: Nagler's grandparents' house, Nagler's own house where he and his parents lived, and a third with a note, "See photo."

The photo had been copied from an undated newspaper. The Dragon Youth Club. Circled was a face Nagler knew well as an adult. The name was underlined: James Howard Newton.

Nagler laughed out loud and ran a couple limping circles around the chair. "Ha!" he yelled as he threw his head back. "Ha!"

Then he knew, and he squinted and examined as well as he could the roof lines and poles that surrounded the theater roof.

"They're watching, or at least recording. They've been watching all along." He closed his smile. *Somewhere on a roof or a pole nearby there is a camera, maybe more than one, surveilling this spot. Been there all along, the signal somehow screened from detection.*

He read the name again. James Howard Newton. Not a coincidence. Howard Newton was the corrupt old Ironton mayor Nagler had sent to jail.

The face. Round and youthful, but even in a copy of a photo, the eyes were dark and threatening. Howard Newton's eyes; runs in the family. The face now sunken and gray, and the voice a coughing hack. Dancer.

Of course, Nagler thought. His grandfather battled the Newtons in the mining days and Nagler's father had cautioned his son about them.

"And here we are," he said. "That's why you were Montgomery and not Newton when you joined the force. Old Uncle Howie." *And everybody knew it.* "Ironton's proud tradition: Taking care of family."

And just like that, Nagler thought, relieved, we're ahead of the game.

"Just like that."

He steadied himself on the yellow kitchen chair and gave it a kick. He slipped, and it tipped over. *Not effective enough.* He pretended to struggle to his feet, rested one hand on the chair's seat and waved his other hand on the air, mouthed a silent curse, then with a little more acting than necessary, stood and kicked at the chair again and fell on his ass. *Does that make me look crazy enough? It hurt enough.*

He elbowed to a sitting position, scraping his shoes along the roof, his back and knees screaming, *What the fuck, Frank?* "Are we gonna find you stuffed in a warehouse somewhere, there, Dancer? Or are you sipping whiskey in a bar watching me, laughing?"

Teeth clenched against the pain, Nagler dug out his phone, held it up and began to record. "I think we'll ask the boys."

"Hey, guys, you Dragony fellas. Here I am with your yellow kitchen chair. Been told you were all here before, plotting. So tell me, which of you were on the roof scoping out the kill shot? And which of you was in that fourth-floor apartment with the gas cans and detonators waiting to be shot? You know who you are, so I'm thinking you figured out you were the target and never showed up again, right? I'd be looking over my shoulder if I were you, any of you. All of you. You can't trust each other. We have the bread knife, and it had the blood of three of your guys on it. How many are left? I've been thinking that you all just trying to make peace long enough to pull off your great big, giant scheme." He smiled brightly, obnoxiously, into the phone. "Seems I'm wrong. You're here. We'll find you."

He saved the recording just as his phone buzzed. Lauren Fox.

"Guess where I am," he said.

"You're on the theater roof, sitting in the famous yellow kitchen chair."

He pushed out of the chair. "What? How…"

"Look up the hill, the car dealership."

Nagler turned, squinted into the mist that had begun to fall again, and waved.

"What are you doing up there?"

She laughed in his ear. "Watching some crazy local cop put on a play. Think they saw it?"

"I recorded it so we can post it on the Fake Frank site. But I think they have a camera trained on this place."

"That would make sense." A breathy silence. "Look, Frank I'm heading out of town for a couple days."

"What…?" His voice like a torn cloth.

"Nothing like that, Frank. This is work. There's going to be a big news story about me in the Register tomorrow, about how I stole money from the city."

Nagler spun, lost, then waved both hands in the air toward the car dealership.

"Frank," Lauren softened her voice. "It's not true. I planted the files with a tracker so Dan Yang would find it."

"So, hacking the hacker." To himself, after a headshake, "Man, that's good."

"Yes. Thank you very much. I passed the info to my friends in the state treasury office, so if Yang accessed it, they have him. So, look, I'm taking my mother on a short trip to Niagara Falls. She's got a brother up there. No hotels. Pay cash. Driving her car. I'll be back in four days. I'll hold a press conference and nail that little fucker and the mayor to the wall."

"The mayor?"

She laughed in his ear. "You surprised?"

"They'll ask me. What should I say?"

"Yeah. The mayor's going to want a chat, even make a threat. Tell him it's a surprise to you, and you will pursue this crime with all the vigor of your past efforts, play no favorites," a laughing breath, "or something like that."

"Better yet, I'll tell him that I demanded the case be assigned to someone else, because of our relationship."

"Oh, we *have* a relationship?" Laughing. "But look Frank, in the time I'm gone you have to connect the Dragony guys to Mangot. I left something with Maria. Time to wrap this all up and stand in front of City Hall and declare victory."

A silence filled the phone.

"I'm walking to the car now. Look, four days."

"Okay. No calls. Anything to say or ask, message Destiny, like from a burner phone, and she'll get it to Ramirez."

"One last thing."

"Now what?"

"You're going to hear that Calista is missing. She's not."

"Do I want to know?"

Nagler could hear Lauren whisper/chuckle into the phone.

"What's the one thing Calista does better than anyone you know?"

"Pretend to be someone else."

"Got it. Four days, my dear."

CHAPTER NINETEEN

Walking worker's ghetto

The empty, dark house weighted, wisps of Lauren's presence hanging. Jeans clinging to a chair arm, a wadded towel still moist with her rose-scented body wash, hints of lavender shampoo, piles of musty, water-stained tan paper files, pages of reports open and underlined, a cup half filled with white skimmed coffee; in the kitchen sink a vase holding the flowers he brought her, the purple buds now brown, the sagging sunflowers. *"Don't worry," she says. "I've got this." And I have to believe that she does.* He leaned backside against the sink and surveyed the room: haphazard paper piles, the empty beer bottles on the table, her coat slung across the counter, a plastic bag left from Chinese takeout, three forgotten fortune cookies and a menu nestled in the bottom. This is us, Frank Nagler thought, the trail of us, the perfect imperfection, the chaos of two lives running in nine directions, pressed by all these things dark and light closing in, unable to even fill a flower vase with water to keep them alive, yet knowing just the same how delicately their scent drifted in to the dry air, how the frail petals slipped against her fingers, how she smiled, one moment in this unspoken, tangled thing.

He turned and stared into the darkness beyond the window, his face a wavy outline, a smear of light.

The moment is rising, he thought. We have no choice, but to stand.

Pushed from the house to escape its answerless questions, Nagler walked.

The day's mist, now cleared and frozen, drips made temporary stalactites frozen on the tips of dark branches, sidewalks sheen slick, streets still, shining as a glitter of light trapped in ice. Lights fuzzy with icy patina.

He had walked this route a hundred times, back through the years of his life, down streets that grew darker where the streetlights failed, along narrowing broken sidewalks to the darkened dirt paths, places memories deepened.

Past three-story, white homes with wide porches and picket fences, past the pretty parks to warrens of broken trees, weeds curled like snakes around stunted trunks; then descending along alleys lined with single story unpainted dull wooden garages and sheds with uneven doors and cardboard windows, dying grass at the corners.

Finally, to the bottom, the center: The empty lot where his grandparents had lived. The old man would sway in his chair, hands bent and gnarled gripped the rails, feet locked to the floor, eyes pinned to the past, a face like iron.

"They meant well," he told his grandson from that chair one day before he died. "But they had no idea what they were doing. No means to govern other men. So, they stopped trying. Governed for themselves. Greed gets easy. The cheap houses they built, the company stores, wages gleaned, and when the troubles started, hired the thugs to maintain order, the friendlies, the sons, the cousins, brothers, nephews. Hired their own kind, all else be damned."

Nagler remembered the old man leaned forward, elbows on the chair rails and growled, "It will go on till someone stops it, Frankie, someone from these dreary streets, someone who knows…" His grandfather had collapsed back into the chair, weary. "Knows what, Grandpa?" Frank asked. "Our life, Frank boy. Knows our life."

When Nagler told Martha that story years later, as teens sitting on the front porch of her parents' comfortable home under the soft light of a summer day, she turned his face to hers and said, "That wasn't a curse, Frank," before she kissed him. "Feels like one," he had replied. "No, no, no, Frankie." She wrapped her arms around his neck. "It was his blessing."

****

Clouds filtered in, blocking what light the half-moon had offered.

He pulled out Dawson's map and shined his phone light.

Two blocks.

The old homes, the mining houses, were still clustered empty along the winding, cluttered alley, roofs crushed by trees, darkness leering from broken windows.

Not even worth tearing down.

Mangot's housing project was ten blocks to the east, on the fringe between the worker's ghetto and the middle-class neighborhood. A better place, Nagler knew, to soothe the bankers' concerns about housing poor people. The puzzle: What contaminates this piece of the ghetto? We were all poor.

He kicked at the leaning gate, expecting to hear the rusted cry of a hinge; instead, the gate and the attached fence leaned even more.

The door was ajar, as if he was expected, but he looked again. The top hinge had pulled away from the door jamb.

Announcing himself, Nagler kicked the door open.

"Hey, Dancer." His soft voice filled the cold space like fog, the dark space thick with the aroma of musty rot.

Nearly a whisper. "Back here."

Nagler stepped lightly across the cluttered, creaking floor toward a dim glow coming from the room to his right.

Dancer was seated on the floor leaning against the wall supported by a couple couch pillows.

"Thought you'd be here," Nagler said as he rested a shoulder on the door frame.

"We all go home in the end, Frank." Dancer's voice was more like a wheeze than a breath, air exiting after being sucked through an unseen opening. He tried to take a deep breath and winced in pain.

Nagler waved his phone light across the room. The front of Dancer's shirt was darkly stained: Blood.

"Want help?" Nagler asked.

"Naw. What's the point? I'm already dead, The lungs, cancer. Was no joke when I told you I had six months." He coughed, closed his eyes, and squeezed out a breath. "Probably less." He nodded to his bloody shirt. "This thing has festered. Knife missed my heart but seems to have got something else important. It bleeds when I cough hard."

"So who and when?"

"McCarroll. After you guys found Dubin Place. He's Mangot's guy, back to the old man."

"Tallem?"

"That's me. Pissed me off because he did that kid, Ethan, whatshis-name…"

"Ricardo. Why?"

"Wrong place, wrong time. Kid was supposed to stay with friends that night. Feds were about to nail Tallem for back taxes. He panicked, wanted to gas his own place. He's a petty thief, not a bomber."

"A waste."

A coughing growl. "More than that."

"Why blow up Warren Street?"

Dancer leaned his head back trying to clear his throat. "That's Mangot. Can't build a glass monument to yourself if the city won't tear down the old buildings. Mayor needed some persuasion." He pointed at Nagler with a waving finger. "Not that hard to find, Frank. Mangot needs place to bury his cash."

Dancer seemed to shrink inside his clothes, fading; his faced calmed.

"Sure you don't want help?"

"Man with a conscience would want help, Frank. I got no conscience, no regrets." He grabbed his chest and forced out a bloody mess from his throat. "We was kids, Frank. Parents gave us the keys to the hotrod. It went way back with all of us. Grandpas, uncles, fourth cousins. Shaking down immigrants, stealing trucks filled with cigarettes, booze, refrigerators. We stole bananas, for chrissakes. Got in good with the waterfront gangs. A big game. But it's like gambling. Addictive. So ya never quit, just look for a bigger pot."

He fell silent. Seemed to stop breathing.

"Hey, Dancer."

He smiled. "Still here."

"Why Dancer?"

"Don't make me laugh. Hurts too much. Cause I could dance, man. James Edward Newton? A shopkeeper. But Dancer? That's how I got laid. Skinny kid like me. Still can. I'd show ya, but I can't stand up." He leaned back with a groan. "Uncle Howie, Frank. He told me to use a different name so it won't get back to him, as if that woulda mattered. Man, he pulled so much shit, stuff you'll never find. That accountant, Sol…Sol…"

"Rosen…"

"Yeah. He guessed right, I was told. About to sell the info, him and that Kalinsky. Keep 'em both outta jail. Easy knockoffs."

"You do Rosen?"

Head shake. "I was off doin' some other gig in '06. Probably truck heists. Rosen was supposed to have buried all these records in the woods somewhere. Wouldn't say, gets plugged."

"By whom?"

Dancer waved a hand. "Not from me." Short breath. "No. I think you already know."

"Kalinsky?"

"In those notes I gave ya. Big hero reporter. Gonna expose all this."

Dancer waved a hand. "Clueless. A nuisance."

Nagler recalled the smeared line…a mark, then "did Kalinsky brake job."

"Why's the Impala still around?"

A wheezing laugh. "That fucking car … was supposed to be a rolling clue. I think we looked once, like the trunk, the wheel well, but moved on. Somebody shoulda torched it. What the fuck, huh?"

"Last question. Why a bread knife?"

"Style, Frankie. Actually, Tallem used it on a whim. Playing with ya. Came back to bite me, though."

Nagler squinted at Dancer and turned on his phone. *I should call. No one deserves this.*

"Hey, Frank, get outta here. I don't deserve your pity or scorn. I made my life, fuck it. I'd ask ya for a smoke, but I know you don't carry."

"Camels, right, unfiltered." Nagler closed his phone and pulled a pack of Camels from his pocket along with a lighter. He shook out a cigarette and placed it on Dancer's cracked lips and lit it. Dancer's face found peace with a long draw as the smoke filled his lungs.

Nagler shifted away from the door. "Little short on pity, Dancer. And I'm way past scorn." He turned away, turned back. "Guess you're not getting to Nova Scotia."

"I hate fish, Frankie."

Nagler dropped the Camels and the lighter on Dancer's lap. The lit cigarette clung to Dancer's lips. His eyes were closed, his face soft and silent.

"Yeah," Nagler said, and left.

****

Nagler pulled the car alongside a clearing between two stands of mature forest. A chain strung from two bent metal posts laid on the ground between the scrub and tall grass that hid what used to be a road into the property. Nagler guessed the poles were about four feet tall, enough, if standing, to block a vehicle.

"You're sure?" he asked Maria Ramirez who was in the passenger's seat staring at her tablet.

"This is the address Lauren left me for Lot 104.7, Block 389, the number on Sol Rosen's license plate." She got out of the car and shielded her eyes with one hand and waved the other at the open land. "It was a subdivision plan filed in the Sixties, four hundred houses and a small shopping center."

Nagler turned in a circle and scanned the empty, ragged place before he shut the car door. No place else in Ironton was this desolate, not even the Old Iron Bog. The air was still enough that their footsteps on loose gravel seemed loud; the grinding swish of traffic on the Interstate, a mile away, filtered in, a soft motorized buzz.

"So, what did old Solly know?" Nagler asked himself. The site had been cleared once, he could see, used for something. Clumps of trees roughly the same height, but shorter than the surrounding forest, dotted the lot, and brown, dry grasses wandered through the landscape like curving streets. "Why didn't they build it?"

"Water," Ramirez said. "Lauren's note said the water table was polluted with military and industrial waste, oils, chemicals, and the rear, where that hill rises, maybe a half-mile in, to the left, was used years ago as a target range. It's filled with thousands of lead bullets."

Nagler kicked at one of the posts in the ground and moved it off center. "Someone has been here, but not recently." He kneeled and lifted the pipe section. It had been sawn from a section anchored to cement in the ground. The cut was old, the pipe rusted. "Who wanted to build here?"

"Taylor Mangot I, under the name of DRG Builders."

Nagler stood. "Of course he did. Couldn't bribe someone into letting him build? That's a miracle." He wiped his hand through his hair and turned to open the trunk of their patrol car. "Hey Maria, give me a hand, please."

"What?"

"Just come here."

Ramirez stepped to the open truck.

"Pretend to be looking for something," Nagler said. "We have company."

"Where?"

"Straight ahead, couple hundred yards, backed inside the tree line. If I'm not mistaken, that looks like the black Jeep someone was driving that night they took a shot at me."

"How the hell…"

Before Nagler could answer, the dirt across the road exploded with the impact of five rifle shots.

"Get down!" she yelled.

They both ducked behind the open trunk and waited for another round of shots. "They're back for seconds," Nagler said, peering through the gap at the rear of the open truck through the car toward the Jeep. He shook his head. "Can't see much."

"Neither can they," Ramirez said. "We can get into the tree line before they spot us."

"Think they moved?" he asked.

Ramirez crab walked to the side of the car facing the open road and peered toward the Jeep with a pocket monocular.

"Not really clear, but it seems someone is leaning on the hood. The rifle is on the hood," she said when she returned. "Don't think they sent their best marksman."

She pulled a shovel, a black cloth bag and a metal detector from trunk.

"You dig up what's in the woods. I'll get our would-be assassin."

"No. We both…"

"Frank, you and your bad ankle aren't going to be running through the woods." She patted his cheek twice. "You get the box. I'll get Jeep-boy."

Ramirez stood, took a quick glance, and darted down the path to the cover of trees. Nagler followed carrying the tools. He knelt at the bottom of the slope after the shovel banged against a rock and the empty air rang with the metallic sound.

He had to have heard that, he thought. He strained to detect any sound but heard none.

Ramirez stopped after about a hundred yards and checked the map she held. She pulled the long grass off a cement marker that said "389. "This is it."

214

"Dancer said Rosen buried 'it' in the woods," Nagler said. "I guess this would do."

Ramirez scanned the tops of the trees. "Thick enough for good cover, but not too dense so I can't see." Ramirez pointed to an opening through the trees. "There's my path. You dig, make some noise, and wiggle a few trees. If he comes after you, he'll have to come through me. I'll get our boy."

"You sure?"

"He's dumb enough to park where we can see him, and even dumber to shoot and miss, Frank, so, yeah."

Nagler watched as Ramirez slipped into the trees, looked at Lot 389 and let out a long breath. "Subdivision in the sixties? Half-acre, maybe. I need an earthmover." He dropped the shovel and strapped on the metal detector. He inserted only one earpiece; he wanted to be able to hear any sound Ramirez or the shooter made.

He waved the detector and listened as it hummed and buzzed. He shook a tree or two for effect as he learned how to maneuver the wand though the grass and brush. He yelled out an occasional "Damn it!" or "That's my bad ankle" for effect. The military base was about a mile north at the bottom of the ridge that ran to the New York State line. Steams that flowed through and under the base were among the most polluted streams in the area. The wand signaled something solid. Nagler thought of the shooting range. *Could be a stray bullet.* He laid down the wand to mark the spot and took up the shovel.

He stopped to listen. That he heard nothing but the wind was not calming.

He poked gingerly at the ground, thinking, if Sol Rosen was burying records here, what else did they bury? He wasn't the only one who knew about this place.

He shook a load of dirt on the shovel and after digging with his fingers, pulled out a silver dollar. He flipped it in his hand and with his thumb brushed away the dirt. 1974.

"You'd except to find a quarter, dime, maybe."

He put the coin in his jacket pocket and jabbed the ground again, and finding nothing, picked up the wand. Three feet away, another hit, and another silver dollar. 1974. He backtracked toward the front of the lot and within another few feet found another coin. It was a trail of silver dollars, all minted in 1974. "What the hell does that mean?" There were gaps in the trail of coins. Perhaps the coins had been covered by growing trees, he thought.

He stopped and listened again. No sound. Then, was that a shout?

"Take me all day to dig this place up one coin at a time."

He had more or less learned the sound the wand emitted when it found a coin, so Nagler followed that trail.

About fifty feet in, next to the trunk of a hollowed-out maple, the wand emitted a louder, more solid shriek.

"That," he said, "is not a silver dollar."

After a few minutes digging in soft soil, he found a two-foot square metal box with a combination lock, wrapped in plastic.

"If this is what we are looking for, it makes even less sense," he muttered. "Too easy." The plastic seemed, from what they had learned about him, to be a perfect, practical Sol Rosen thing.

Nagler stood, eyes closed to find a hint of motion. Nothing. That was not soothing. Then, a muffled voice and a car door slammed.

As he lumbered with a limp toward the street with his tools and the box, he could see someone in the back of the cruiser. Ramirez was on her phone.

"I need you to take it out of county and tell no one but me where is it, got it?"

Nagler dropped the box and the tools in the trunk. "You okay?"

Ramirez nodded and grinned.

"Who's our friend?" Nagler asked.

"He has no name, and the Jeep has stolen plates, and this." From behind her back, she produced a semi-automatic rifle. "I'll bet the bullets match the ones we took out of your car. I've got a crime scene team on the way to search the area. She handed Nagler the kid's phone and nodded to the box. "That it?"

"Hope so," he said.

The kid's phone rang and Nagler smiled before he answered.

"Mr. McCarroll. How nice of you to call. Yes, We're fine. Thanks for asking. You need better help, just sayin'."

"Ah, Mr. Noiglar, you just keep getting in deeper, dontcha? There ain't nothing in that box. Sol Rosen never had the goods."

"And how would you know that, McCarroll, unless old man Mangot sent you after him? You sound nervous. Did you screw up there, pal? Because if I was an accountant for a crooked boss, I think I'd have more than one copy of the records, and when the boss wanted them, I'd make sure he got the wrong set. That about right?"

McCarroll scoffed into the phone. "Them records is long gone, Mr. Noiglar. Long gone. And that kid don't know nothin'."

"Not sure that matters. That box wasn't empty, and you wouldn't be calling me if it was. But look, we gotta go. We got your kid here and the Jeep and his weapon, and we're gonna hang on to him for a while, and your department guys won't be able to get him out. And, oh, you should send flowers. Dancer's dead." He hung up.

Nagler shook his head to quiet the question on Ramirez's face. She tipped her head to draw Nagler away from the car. They turned toward the lot.

"The EMT's picked up Dancer right after you called. He's in Hunterdon County somewhere, right?"

"Yeah. No one needs to know that, especially McCarroll. I suspect he believed he killed Dancer. I also suspect that he's surprised that we know Dancer's condition. We should let him ponder that."

****

"His name is Robert Jamieson," Ramirez said as she scrolled through files on her tablet as they drove back into downtown. "Records say he's twenty-five, though he doesn't look a day over seventeen." She turned and looked over her shoulder at the man shackled in the backseat of the cruiser. "You twenty-five, kid? Don't answer that. You don't have a lawyer."

"Don't need a lawyer," Robert Jamieson snarled back and kicked Nagler's seatback. "I got friends."

"Hey, Frank, he has friends. When was the last time we heard that?" She turned back to Jamieson. "Try yesterday. The guy's friends didn't show, and he's sitting in county."

Jamieson laughed. "You could send me to county. I got friends in county, brothers. All in for the cause. You could send me to state. I got brothers there, too. The boss of us is in state, running things. We got cops. We got C.O.s and lawyers. Got 'em all. And you got nothin'."

"You really should stop…"

Nagler tapped the console to get Ramirez's attention and then flapped his fingers against his thumb, including she should let Jamieson talk.

"You haven't got a brotherhood," Nagler said. "You're just some half-assed gang."

"We're believers. All of us. Protectors."

Ramirez, with a mocking sourness, "What are you protecting and from whom?"

"Ha. We're protecting our families, our way of life and our beliefs from you and your types."

"And what type am I?" Ramirez asked, eyes flashing. "I'm a woman and a police officer."

Jamieson shook his shackled hands. "Naw, you're queer and dark. You don't belong."

Ramirez winced. She had heard all that before, too many times. She stared out the side window.

Nagler jumped in. "God you're a jerk, Jamieson. The only saving grace is that when you get to your new home in prison – and you *are* going – you'll spout that bullshit to the wrong guy and your brotherhood won't be able to get there fast enough. You guys, you little crooks, punks. Think you're all special, but in jail, my friend, you're just a toy."

"You ain't my friend. You're the enemy. We'll beat your ass, all of you."

Nagler glanced at Jamieson through the rear-view mirror. "Well, I'm just frightened. Aren't you, Lieutenant Ramirez? Aren't you frightened? Does this little punk scare you?"

"Absolutely, Detective. So afraid. This warrior was so clever that he parked his black Jeep in the one sunny clearing in that whole forest. And was so attentive that he didn't hear me walk up to his door because he had his earbuds on so high I could hear the rhythm from outside the car even with the windows up. That and your squeaky singing. Man, you didn't even know I was there. Easiest collar ever."

Nagler winked at Ramirez. "So, look, son. This has puzzled me for a long time. Why blow up downtown? What did that protect?"

"Protected us from them. Place was crawling with them. Outsiders, moochers, queers. Better off without them. Heard more than thirty of them died. Better off now."

"More than thirty? I'm impressed. Who told you that?" Ramirez asked with a smirk. "What was the official count, Detective?"

"I believe the count was four, Lieutenant. Three old people and that kid, Ethan…"

"Right, right," Ramirez jumped in. "Ethan Ricardo. He was one of yours, wasn't he, Jamieson?"

Jamieson sat back, deflated, face hollow. "Ethan ain't dead."

"Oh, afraid so. Seen him lately?" Nagler said. "Killed by one your gang bosses. Stabbed. I'd pay attention. That's what's in store for you."

Jamieson turned his head toward the window. His lower lip quivered. "They'd never do that. I'm protected."

Ramirez glanced at Nagler and shook her head. "That's what Ethan thought, too, kid. You're better off talking to us."

Jamieson kick the car seat again. "Hey, cop, get over it. When our leader gets back in the department, you'll be history."

"And when that supposed to happen?" Nagler asked as pulled the car into the city hall lot and Ramirez radioed for a prisoner escort.

"Any day, man. Everything changes then. Everything. This has just been a warmup."

"Out," Ramirez ordered, and reached for Jamieson's arm.

Jamieson pulled away and the escort grabbed his other arm. "Don't touch me, queenie, unless you want something you ain't had in a while." He wiggled free from the offers' grasp and ran toward Ramirez, who spun him to the car and jammed her arm across his lower throat. "You stupid dyke cunt cop!" He spat in her face. Ramirez applied more arm pressure and called for the other officers, who dragged him away. "Brotherhood forever! The Dragony lives!"

Ramirez wiped her face with her sleeve. "The Dragony lives, my ass."

Nagler dampen his handkerchief with water from a bottle from the front of the car and handed it to Ramirez.

"Welcome to my world, Frank. Everyday."

"Hey. I'm sorry, Maria."

"It's the world we live in. No one can be different, or smarter, or have other ideas. We spend the whole day primping into our cell phones, aren't we so cute. That's our world. Us. Me." She kicked at the sidewalk. "Fuck 'em, Frank. All of them."

Nagler watched as Ramirez marched ahead. *It's not just that kid. It's something else.*

"What else, Maria?"

She stopped, sunk her head, and turned.

"Destiny's being followed. Came home the other night, said there was a man – it was dark and he was half a block away, so she had nothing else. She slipped through a couple back lots, but he was still there. He knows where we live."

Inside her office, Ramirez sat and slammed the side of her computer, once, then again. "Let's end this thing, Frank."

"There's one more big thing that's gonna happen. I can feel it," Nagler said. "It's like they're waiting for a signal."

"What'd that kid Jamieson say, the boss is coming?" Ramirez asked. "That'd be a signal, right?"

"I'd say so. Who's the boss?"

Nagler peeled off the plastic wrapper and spun the lock dial on the box they had retrieved. The box was just dirty with a little rust. Didn't seem like it had been buried for more than twenty years. No scratches, no pry marks where someone might have used a screwdriver to open the lid. And it would not have been hard, he thought. Cheap metal box. *Something's not right.*

"Isn't there a pry bar in the bottom drawer of that desk?"

Ramirez sent a file to the printer. "Don't think we need it. Didn't Adele Rosen say her husband scratched something on that Impala, like a part number? Ron from the body shop sent me this. Said he found this on a rear spring. Look. "L36. R15. L21. R12. A combination. Try it."

Nagler held up the paper and spun the dial. "You have to go past zero once, right?" The lock failed to open.

"No, you have to pass the first number once, then to the next number. Let me try."

After two tries Ramirez opened the box. Inside were four plastic wrapped packages about two inches thick, and a leatherbound ledger, also wrapped in thick, industrial plastic. None appeared to have been tampered with, but could have been expertly rewrapped, Nagler thought.

"Where do we start?" Ramirez asked.

The packages had no marking to indicate what each contained.

"The ledger," Nagler said. "Might be a summary of some type." He flipped the book in his hands, looking for the starting edge of the plastic wrap, but put down. "Better idea. Someone's after these. Let's make sure they find them."

****

Sol Rosen had neat handwriting.

Page after page of the ledger, all in capital letters, written precisely inside the lines: Judges, cops, mayors, councilmen, bankers, attorneys, and a list humorously called "associates."

Dates, places, amounts. Years' worth.

Information that Sol Rosen was not supposed to have recorded.

Information that got Sol Rosen killed.

Armed with a few borrowed reams of paper and manila envelopes, Nagler Ramirez and Destiny had moved into the back office at Leonard's store to copy the contents of the packages inside the metal box.

"He started this as soon as he became the lead accountant," Nagler said with appreciation. "But the dates show he was going back into the organization's history as if he was trying to create permanent financial record. Is that just me, or does that seem obsessive? He had to know…"

Destiny stopped shuffling paper and asked, "Know what?"

Ramirez smiled at her companion's innocence. "If somebody found this material, he was dead. And he is."

As he perused the pages of the ledger, Nagler asked, "How'd he hide the cash he used to set up his wife? What'd she say, five million? That's a lot of flowers." He shook his head. "A lot of these people are still alive, out of office, but alive. Rosen was killed in 2006. A lot of these marks were probably in their twenties, thirties, just getting started, Families, kids, mortgages, careers just beginning, maybe college debt for law school, medical school, their MBAs or doctorates. The system was already in place. They just took a seat on the bus."

"So, a little extra kept the roof over the family, paid for that trip to Hawaii, a few fancy dinners, private schools," Ramirez said.

"Yeah. This was the eighties and nineties. No one was flush."

"What if 'flowers' was a code for pot, marijuana?" Ramirez said. "Not original but look at these receipts. That Dubin Place bust was mostly pot, right. Easy business to be in. Look." She peeled off several receipts. "Flowers, flowers, flowers, floral arrangement, bouquet. I mean, he was paying for a judge here or there to legitimately buy flowers for his wife's birthday, but he was also slipping his wife's, shall we say, inheritance, out the door in the same fashion."

Nagler picked up two fistfuls of the receipts. "I don't know. He wouldn't write *that* down, would he? Either way, Adele Rosen was right. There was so much money floating around no one paid attention."

"It was more than that," Destiny said. She thumbed a pile of maybe three dozen receipts. "I'm not a cop, but these are gambling debts. Look, 'Cash. AC.' Atlantic City. See. 50K, 25K, 10K. Consecutive days, a weekend, I'll bet. Someone went to Atlantic City and lost their shirt."

"More than their shirt. Frank, look at this notation. "TM2"

"Hello," Nagler said, mouth open, tongue in cheek.

"Right. Look 250K, 500K. Seems Taylor Mangot II has a gambling problem."

Nagler tipped his head to the side and shook it back and forth six or seven times, thinking. "There has to be someone else. It had to be personal for Sol Rosen. Mother, brother, girlfriend, Uncle Ernie in the old country. Somebody." He leaned over the table that held the piles of paper. "What'd Adele Rosen say about Sol Rosen's father, just keep the bosses happy? These records weren't kept for the bosses. Sol Rosen was working for someone else. That's what got him killed. It's in that ledger somewhere."

"Think the wife knows?" Ramirez asked.

Nagler huffed out a small breath and stared at Ramirez. "Think she'll tell us?"

Nagler leaned his head against the wall and laughed.

"She doesn't have to. Lauren did it for us."

"What?"

"Follow this. She said she planted files in the city computer indicating that she stole money. You heard the mayor's comments, right? Dawson asked him directly if the city was prepared to release details of those files to expose the extent of the theft. What'd Mayor Ollivar say?"

"Um, they can't be made public because they could be part of a criminal investigation."

"Right, standard BS. But he also said this: The manner in which Lauren's files were attached to other city hall accounts had not been determined."

Ramirez laughed and covered her mouth.

"What, Maria?" Destiny asked.

"They can't decode it," Ramirez said. "They can't separate her files from their original files without exposing themselves. That's brilliant. Where'd she learn that?"

"From the guy who set her up the first time when Howie Newman was mayor," Nagler said. "Dan Yang. That's why she brought him in. She's known about this all along. Sal Rosen set this in motion, and Lauren picked up the trail. But there's someone in between. We find that person, we find the Dragony connection and our downtown bomber."

CHAPTER TWENTY

As dark as a bad idea

The buzz of the emergency call on his phone nearly knocked Nagler out of the kitchen chair where he had leaned back, hands laced behind his head, asleep.

"What the…Jesus, three a.m."

He rocked forward to the table, elbows landing on the pile of photos, receipts, and Sol Rosen's ledger. Eyes wide, an exaggerated yawn as the phone buzzed again.

"Dubin Place. Fire."

"Oh, fuck."

He rammed the car down the dark, empty streets, pounding the steering wheel with an open palm. "So, this is what you're gonna do? Erase the trail one place at a time?"

The closest he could get to the fire was two blocks away and he jammed his car into the wrecked loading dock of an old shoe factory. Sirens flowed in from all directions, the sound of grinding fire trucks echoed down the narrow streets as the windows in ancient building shells trembled. The sky roared red.

A block in, Nagler spotted Fire Chief Damien Green.

"Damien," he yelled. "Damien, what the hell."

"Gasoline, Frank. Soaked the place with it. Plus, a five-hundred-dred-gallon propane tank wired to explode once it got hot enough, but the charge just punched a hole in the tank. Wasn't a sufficient charge."

"Like two weeks ago."

Green stared into the raging fire. "This time they did it right. Only difference I can see is that tank wasn't full and our guys got here on time. Otherwise, we'd be standing a half-mile away. The side door was wired with a small explosive device and that's what got the victim."

"ID?" Nagler asked.

Green shrugged.

"Damn it. Duval was supposed to have sealed this building and had that tank removed," Nagler said.

"Guess he didn't," Green said before turning to leave. "Ramirez is inside the building across the street where they found the body."

Nagler ducked behind a wall just as an aerial truck unleashed a flood. Radios barked out commands and squawks of fire horns and shouts of unseen firefighters rattled though the tight space.

The wall of the building facing the fire scene was missing, replaced by a pile of bricks and glass covering a Dodge sedan.

Nagler found Ramirez with Medical Examiner Walter Mulligan.

"Who?" he asked.

"Captain Bernard Langdon. Let me get him out of here," Mulligan said before walking away and grabbing the arm of an officer with a gurney.

"Langdon," Nagler said squinting at Ramirez whose head was framed by a spotlight shining from outside the building. "Son of a bitch. Langdon."

Ramirez stared at the fallen officer. "He had it in for me, Frank. But I never thought…"

"He's in Sol Rosen's ledger, Maria. Maybe a dozen times, starting in 1990. Hell, he was still a patrolman then. He hated that you are gay and could lead the department, but the reason he didn't want you to be a captain was just about money, thousands."

"So, he walked into the same trap that we did," she said. "Why didn't he know about it? Why didn't he know the trap had been reset?"

With a hollow voice: "Don't know. And that's damn scary."

"Who else is on that list, Frank?"

"Dancer, for one, going back years before '06. I asked him if he killed Rosen and he said, 'No. I was just a kid.'" He kicked at the dirt. "He's no kid. He's eighteen, twenty years older than I am, past sixty. Langdon was fifty-four. That Boonton Captain Dan Thomson is fifty-two. Duval is forty-seven. It's like they were the young guns."

"Duval?"

"Yeah. He was supposed to have removed that propane tank and sealed this building."

"Find him in that ledger?"

"No, But I will."

"Frank, I hate to ask this, but since Sol Rosen was killed in 2006, who took over as the accountant? And who's making the payments now?"

Nagler turned to her, raised his eyebrows, and let out a fat-cheeked breath in admittance of his ignorance.

****

"This time they wired it correctly," said bomb squad Lieutenant Adam Wagner. "Signal off the electronic door opener, and as a backup a laser beam across the opening. Explosive on the tank. Break it, explosion." He waved at the damage inside the building shell. "This was better, but not a professional job. A pro would have just blown the damn place up."

"But the tank ruptured," Nagler said.

"Propane is a liquid, but burns as a gas," Winston said. "If the tank had been full it would flattened this place. The best I can say is they wanted enough propane in the tank that when it was breached by the explosion, the burning gas would ignite the gasoline spilled on the floor and start the fire, not blow up the building. There's natural gas lines all over down here and I'll bet we find they had been cut. They wanted this place to burn. They just didn't plan on the FD getting here so quickly."

Nagler pondered and stared at the bent, burned Dodge across the street.

"Langdon?"

Wagner wiped his mouth and sighed. "Um, yeah. We didn't find a door opener in the car yet, or in the area search. Still looking."

"So, he opened the door with a key, if it was locked."

Nagler mimed the action of stepping out a passenger's side car door, stepping to the garage door and lifting, and then looked across the street. "That's why they found him twenty feet away. He didn't know."

"Seems about right."

"Fire marshal Duval was supposed to have sealed this building. Any signs that he did so?"

Winston, with a nonchalant shrug and disinterested shake of his head, "No."

****

The Old Iron Bog was as dark as a bad idea when Frank Nagler arrived; the swirling water sucked the color from the thick clouds that closed off the tops of the Ironton hills.

This place was made for conspiracies, he thought, watching a smear of an early October dawn shimmer along, like a hint, a murmur of suspicion, around the dimensions of shaded rocks, past leaning trees, tops dipped in the murk until sucked underwater in a whirlpool. You follow it, all of it, he knew. Had no choice. Dark corners of hidden depth, all the hints, the signals, all the lies, the pieces of stories washed ashore like oil traced to an old car wreck, the rumors of lovers in Room 316, kisses stolen, passion's cries and tears; payments in dark alleys; winks across a crowded room, deals made with no more than the point of a finger; layers and layers, scratched clues on a door frame. It's a marvel, he understood – all of this, all of them, like two people in love who won't admit it just to maintain the distance because if they shared that glance with meaning in the company of others, everyone would know.

And now Dancer stabbed, Langdon dead, Dan Thomson missing. And what to make of Dennis Duval? Foot soldiers, all. Each doing a job, laying one stone of the foundation.

Dragony Rising

****

About four that morning Nagler had finally made sense of Sol Rosen's ledger, the descent through fifty years of land deals, payoffs, crooked cops, lawsuits dismissed with a wink, handshakes, hookers, drinks all around, making room for our kind, pushing out the others, good old Mom-and-Pop success.

The sleep-deprived hours of checking, circling, cross checking this paper to that page, a date, a photo, a line of numbers to an address, a face, a name; deeper as the sourness in his stomach rose, deeper as the trail through gleeful greed descended to poisonous cynicism: A deal. That was fun, let's do it again, but bigger this time.

The knowledge drove him from the silent, desolate house to the orange-tinged streets of Ironton, past Dubin Place, where hot spots and simmering piles of wreckage flared, streets held together by dark, huddled crowds gathered as if their weight would stop it all, pointing, blaming, the glow of cigarettes rising and falling, bursting into red dots with one last puff before dying to black on the ground. Brick walls scorched and cracked, leaked heat like suspicion.

Nagler parked on a lightless, street strewn with boxes and boards and bricks blown from the shattered, burned building. The air was ash, stinging, wet with soot that clung to the hairs of his nostrils, settled on his neck, the sky open and wounded where once there was a wall.

"This!" he shouted; a pain released. "This is what you do, the great Dragony? Kill your own? How much more can you burn? What will satisfy your lust, your hate?"

He recalled the kid they had arrested with the rifle, Robert Jamieson. The vicious rant against Ramirez, and then this. It's all the same, from the same place. All the mistrust, the hate; voices, like flames, incendiary.

He stared into the glowing hulk of the warehouse, a circle of destruction lit by towering spotlights; smoke and steam rose like ghosts.

Is this the place, Sister Katherine? The place of our horrors? Or is this scene, these wretched, broken streets, this hollow, damaged town just the stage for their ancient war, and we the audience made victims? Their crimes leave wreckage and blood and grow greater by their repe-

tition as we assign them meaning they don't deserve. Such small things. What would we say to our friends and lovers lost, what would we say if we only stood in fear? I see your faces, Martha, Bobby, Del, and Dom. The glorious pieces of my life. I must rise to deserve you.

Nagler pushed away from the damaged streets, too crowded with dread and death, and had fled to the Old Iron Bog.

But, yes, he knew. He had read that ledger. This *was* what they did, Dubin Place, one more deal. Who benefits from this? Which of the mayor's friends, relatives? Whose bank? If Warren Street was Mangot's game, then whose was this one? McCarroll? They busted you and your gang fifteen years ago. Dancer, Langdon, Thomson, all there as arresting officers, grim-faced in the photos as the drug gang was hauled away. Grim faces that hid the smiles because the fix was in. Even the beat cops brought in for show got a C-note.

That group shot, that championship photo, he thought bitterly. Celebration all.

But one face was missing. Carlton Dixon. He was there, they all said – his daughter said – he was there. But why was he not photographed, handcuffed, head down like the rest of the gang arrested that day?

But neither was Carlton Dixon in Sol Rosen's ledger, an absence even more puzzling than one name found there – McSherry. The full name. No code, abbreviations, or nicknames. McSherry. Two mentions, and it only stood out because Boonton Captain Dan Thomson had mentioned it before.

First light; birds in the bog begin to talk, chipping away the silence.

Dawn would burn the sky yellow.

****

Nagler rolled the white board with the Dragony roster from the corner of the office.

He found *"BL"* on the list, changed it to *"Bernie Langdon"* and drew a line through it.

He added *"Dennis Duval."*

"Frank, the box is on the move," Maria Ramirez said as she entered the office with her tablet. "Look. About three minutes ago." She held up the tablet displaying a tracking map.

"Where's it going?"

"West end."

"What's in the west end? Train service yard…"

"Bus station," Maria said. "Look. It stopped."

"Lockers," Nagler said.

"Want back-up?"

"No," he said as he slipped behind the wheel of a cruiser. "I'll drop you off at that vacant lot across the street, the old gas plant, and I'll park in Maxie's repair yard on the back side."

"Think they could have been using the lockers as a drop box?"

Nagler nodded. "Makes sense. Would explain why there was so little chatter that we could trace. Okay, here we are. See you inside."

"The box hasn't moved, so they either left it, or someone's inside. Who we gonna find Frank?"

He glanced over and raised his eyebrows with a grin. "Duval."

"Duval?"

"Yeah, I'll tell you later."

In the side mirror as he drove away, Nagler watched Ramirez sidle up to a row of parked buses and peer through the large glass front of the station. The crowd was mid-day thin and the parking lot a clutter of idling diesel buses grumbling in place, coughing out black fumes.

"You're right," she told him through her radio. "Duval. Just sitting there."

"Waiting for someone?" he replied.

"That's my guess. Crowd is sparse. We can see him, but he could spot us."

"Let's not wait. I'm in Maxie's lot. Two minutes, we go in."

"Wait, he's talking to someone. A woman. Okay, she moved. I can't see the box."

"Stay with her. I've got Duval."

Nagler pushed through an exiting crowd heading to their bus. The lobby bristled with nasal announcements of bus arrivals and departures broadcast through cheap speakers and interrupted the tinny music.

Nagler slipped along the back wall looking for any familiar face in the terminal. Duval sat, shoulders slumped, face to the floor. *What is he waiting for?*

Nagler used a circle of teenagers wearing earbuds and staring at cell phones as cover and crossed the room to Duval. The box sat open and empty at his feet.

"Who's your friend, Dennis?"

Nagler stood toes at the box, leaning over the seated Duval. Nagler noticed the pistol in Duval's hands.

"You're not gonna do anything with that gun, Dennis. Not here. I'm going to take it now. Besides the safety is on."

Duval offered no resistance as Nagler recovered the weapon and slipped in his jacket pocket.

"They set me up, Frank. Said they needed that box."

Nagler reached for Duval's arm, to stand him up. "No, they didn't Dennis. That's want they wanted you to think. They were making you part of their team. Fed your ambition to be fire chief with pipe dreams." Nagler pulled again on Duval's arm, to get him out of the chair. "Stand up, Dennis, and grab the box. Don't make me embarrass you here."

Duval clutched the box and stood.

"They wanted a favor, didn't they?" Nagler asked.

"Yeah, they kept askin'," Duval said, his voice watery, hollow as a tin can. "How'd you know?"

Nagler sighed. "They're always asking, Dennis. Always."

"How'd you figure it was me?"

Nagler nudged Duval to walk. "You left your fingerprints every-where. Haven't you heard of gloves? Come on. Besides, I showed your photo to a couple witnesses. You're all not as sneaky as you think you are."

Duval turned to face Nagler. "This is not the end of it. You do know that?"

Nagler nodded toward the exit. "That's what you're going to tell us, Dennis."

Outside, Ramirez and Duval's contact leaned on the hood of the cruiser.

Ramirez held up the pages of blank paper. "Just so you know. This was in the box."

Duval spit and shook his head.

"Yeah, Nagler said, "We set you up." Then he stared at the woman who had taken the files. The face was familiar, younger in the photos he had seen, but harshly beautiful, eyes hard in a way that he knew they would never be soft again, eyes hardened years before. He was puzzled. There was something familiar about her face not related to the photos. "I thought you were dead."

****

Rachel Pursel reached for the photos on the table before her with her left hand. Her right arm hung loosely as if detached from her body at the scar that ran from behind her ear, across her shoulder and down beyond her collarbone.

Nagler guessed that she rarely in public took off the paisley scarf that was tied at her left shoulder but draped across the right side to hide that scar, which added meaning to the story she pulled out of the faded newspaper photos.

She reached for a new folder of photos and struggled to open it.

"I'm sorry. After I was attacked and left for dead, my right arm is occasionally useless and my left has occasional spasms. The nerve and muscle damage could not be repaired. I believe they had intended to sever my arm but failed."

"I'd like to be sorry," Nagler said, "But I've learned in this case there's no one to be sorry for."

Rachel Pursel tipped her head back and a grim smile crossed her lips.

And in that instant Nagler knew who she was.

"Adele Rosen is your mother," he said with a huff. "And I'm guessing Sol Rosen was your father. She didn't mention you when we spoke, and there were no photos of you in her home."

"There wouldn't be, would there."

Nagler smiled, caught. "Yeah, because you're dead. And any photo of you there would be a giveaway." He gazed at her with half-closed eyes. There it was. The same rough edge to her face that her mother's had, that edge that all the finery and posing could not hide for good. "So, Rachel Pursel, who actually are you?"

The door opened and Maria Ramirez joined them and took a seat at the table.

"Duval settled?" Nagler asked.

Ramirez nodded. "Yeah, not doing good, but better. Sergeant Hanrahan set up suicide watch."

"Ah, Mr. Duval," Rachel Pursel said. "But every great endeavor has it casualties."

Ramirez leaned back in astonishment. "So, who the hell are you? And why are you messing with Duval of all people."

Nagler waved a hand between the two women. "Lieutenant, I'd like you to meet the previously suspected to be dead Rachel Pursel, the daughter of Sol and Adele Rosen."

"Son of a bitch. Can this get any weirder?"

"Maybe," Rachel Pursel said. "What do you know about Dubin Place?"

Nagler tipped his head to Ramirez.

"Drug house, owned by the Mangots through one of their affiliates," Ramirez said. "Raided, four dead, four arrests including you and your brother, who I'm guessing now was not your brother, McCarroll and Carlton Davis. All go to jail, Carlton Davis in still in, McCarroll and you and your brother released. Then you're dead. We know now the raid was run by dirty cops."

"Well done," Rachel Pursel said. "You've memorized your homework."

"So, what really happened?" Nagler asked.

"The Mangots had a falling out. The old man was suffering from dementia and cancer, the kid was a junked-up gambling mess. We could have bought Rhode Island with the money he lost."

"Who was the target?" Nagler asked.

"Taylor. The kid. McCarroll's plan. He's an old thug, Irish gun runner, waterfront hood, connected. Beck and call for the old man. The idea: Kill off the kid, clean up his mess, buy off his cops and the rest, and put the mayor in charge."

"Wait a minute," Nagler said. "Newman? Howard Newman?"

"No, no, the young guy."

"Richman?" Nagler stood up and walked a circle around the table. "He was an idiot. He also wasn't mayor at that time."

"Worse than just an idiot," Rachel Pursel said. "Lecherous, greedy… you know, some people just can't follow directions." She leaned back and sighed. "He was being groomed."

"But something went wrong," Nagler said. "That night, with that raid. What?"

Ramirez waved a hand in the air. "Wait a minute. You were part of that gang. We know that." To Nagler: "Why are we talking to her?"

Rachel Pursel smiled, tight, satisfied, a touch of evil.

"Who do you think was doing the books, Lieutenant. I am after all an accountant's daughter. Sol taught me, and Taylor thought it was cute, his girlfriend, the accountant."

"Shit, Frank. Didn't I ask you that question the other day?"

"But you never imagined that I would be the answer to that question, did you?"

"But you were, what seventeen?" Ramirez said, glaring. "Come on."

"No, but I was young enough to look seventeen. Oh my God!" Rachel Pursel laughed. "A few short skirts, no panties, no bras, flowing summer dresses, long blond hair, swig a few beers, do a few lines of coke, bend over, flash my tits, and that whole police department stood at attention. Ah, men. Besides, I was Taylor's, and no one crossed Taylor."

"Again, I ask," Ramirez said. "Why are we talking to her and not putting her in a cell?"

"Until that night." Nagler said.

"Right," Rachel Pursel said. "Taylor was tipped off, didn't show. The drug deal, which was real, went south. Someone stated shooting…" She shrugged.

"But you went to jail," Ramirez said, standing, then twirling back to slap both hands on the table. "This is fucked, Frank. None of this sounds right. First, a drug deal, then a hit. What else are they gonna tell us it was?"

Calmly, Rachel Pursel said, "It's not supposed to make sense, Lieutenant. The cops made up a story. This is, if you'll pardon the phrase, a criminal organization. We lie all the time. Did you ever find a record of my incarceration?"

"Bah," Ramirez said. "So, are you still Taylor's plaything? All this time?"

That hardness returned to Rachel Pursel's face. "I am no one's plaything, Lieutenant."

Ramirez stared back, licked her lower lip, and offered a tiny smile. "Neither am I." She glanced at Nagler and then back at Rachel Pursel.

Nagler stepped back and eyed the two women. Their voices had a teasing sharpness; he was not in the middle of a territorial dispute, but a flirtation.

"So why is Carlton Dixon in jail?" he asked.

"Ask his daughter."

Nagler let that answer hang in the air.

"What's the end game?" he asked. "You didn't come back to Ironton to bust old Dennis Duval."

"You're right." She reached onto her bag and produced a flash drive.

"This contains the records since my father was killed, but not in code. Names, dates, amounts, places. Lauren has a copy as does that reporter, Jimmy Dawson."

"Lauren?"

"Yes, she was not in Buffalo for the last few days. We were finalizing all this data. She'd be a great, cop, Detective."

"Well, she's a planner," Nagler said. "She looks…"

"…At the holes in development applications," Rachel Pursel said. "All the ways a builder and the banks and authorities try to cheat the system. She found me months ago, right after the explosion."

Rachel Pursel reached for Nagler's hand as his face drained of all color.

"She had to keep it a secret. Any leak would have gotten her killed, and me killed, again. Didn't you assign an officer to her for protection? You knew."

"What now?" he asked.

"Your Mayor Ollivar. Watch what he tries to do over the next week or so. It's the last act in a plan that has been decades in forming. The details are on that flash drive. As they once said, follow the money."

"Ollivar? Another lightweight."

"But a malleable lightweight. This goes all the way back to the beginning. You know that. You feel it. The Mangots and the Newtons and whatever Ollivar's family was called back then. They're the middlemen. Goods in, goods out, Money in, not so much money out. My mother told you that. Too much cash to actually know how much cash there is. Cash buys influence and power, and they've been buying it for years."

"Why now?" Nagler asked.

"Betrayals," Rachel Pursel said. "Betrayals on betrayals. Little slights festering over years grow to plots. There's only so much room on that glory platform so someone must be pushed off. The pushing is now. But the stakes grow, the money gets more real than in the past. Someone sees a way to claim it all." She paused and smiled. "Then, of course, there is revenge, that anger distilled, never forgotten. They did kill my father, after all, and took a knife to my throat. And Detective, you should ask Lauren about how payback feels."

"What happens to you when we stop this, which we will?" Ramirez asked.

"Me?" Rachel Pursel asked. "I'm already dead and would prefer to remain so." She winked.

Nagler was neither soothed nor amused by the wink.

CHAPTER TWENTY-ONE

No one heard the shot.

The storm never came.

The promise of the storm had arrived.

Muscular clouds pressed gloom below the hilltops.

Trickster winds flipped the fall's last leaves from wet grass to the shoulder of a passing mourner, only to stick them to the darkened glass of the Cadillac hearse from Madison's Funeral Home.

A taste of ice, a few crystalline snowflakes.

But the storm had not come.

A silence, deep, the lines of shuffled feet settled. Rows of solemn faces.

Shoulders shivered as the long blue line of Ironton police officers held their places with white-gloved salutes as the casket of Captain Bernard Langdon was lowered into the ground.

Then Taps, the bugled mourning, warbling in the wind.

No one heard the shot.

No one saw Mayor Jesus Ollivar lean forward against the podium or fall to the ground.

They all heard the scream and turned.

Detective Frank Nagler, positioned away from the line of officers, traced a possible line of sight up the hill past the War Memorial to the dark trees.

He thought he saw movement.

CHAPTER TWENTY-TWO

Is it all true?

"Here."

Nagler stood at the edge of the tree line and followed the sloping winter-brown lawn to the naked oak where Ollivar had delivered his remarks.

"Tape all this off," he ordered.

Below, graveside, Ramirez was quizzing each of the one hundred officers present. Some crushed their dress hats in troubled hands. Some pointed.

No one had heard the sound of a shot.

Ollivar had been struck in the center of his forehead. One shot. One expert shot. Nagler ordered a search of the tree stand, looking for the shell casing in the leaves and dry grass. It would not be there. This was an expert shot.

But even experts make mistakes.

Nagler watched as Medical Examiner Walter Mulligan supervised the removal of the mayor's body from the site. Mulligan had yet to report on the cause of Langdon's death.

The rumble of a dozen police car engines seeped into the air, the snap of branches breaking under foot; finally, the squawk and chatter of radios pushed the silence aside.

"Detective Nagler, over here."

Nagler turned to the voice of an officer on the backside of the tree stand, near an iron fence that marked the edge of the Locust Hill cemetery.

"Looks like cloth, caught here on this point. Pants maybe."

"You're right, good," Nagler said.

"And look, on the other side. Maybe a handprint? Like someone tried to climb or jump the fence, caught their clothes, and fell forward," the officer said.

"Right. But, here," Nagler said, kneeling. "Is that blood? Our shooter might have stumbled, maybe on those wet, loose stones back there, and caught something on one of the iron spikes and fell. Look at the soil there, like one foot hopping in a circle like trying to get unhooked. Misjudged how quickly the slope dropped." He stood, the shock of the moment, and the gloom that followed, lifting. There is no such thing as a perfect crime, he thought, buoyed by the sight of torn cloth on an iron fence. "Okay, Officer…"

"Cooper, sir, Duane Cooper."

"Good, thanks. You stay here. Don't let anyone touch any of this fence, ground, trees, anything. I'll get a team up here to photograph the place and take samples."

So, McCarroll. Didn't trust this to any of your young guns, Nagler thought, walking away, stepping around jagged field stones and exposed roots. Don't blame you, given their lack of skill of late. Came yourself. But those old spindly legs and cranky knees betrayed you. Thirty years ago, you would have vaulted that fence like a track star. But not today. You're an old man in a young man's game.

"And that will be your undoing."

At the cemetery entrance, Nagler found Sergeant Hanrahan pushing back a crowd of neighbors, reporters, and busybodies.

"I got ten guys walking the neighborhood, Frank," Hanrahan said. "Asking about strangers, odd vehicles, hear anything, you know, the usual."

"Good, Tell the officers to look for a blood trail. It's possible the shooter snagged himself on the fence and might have bled. We'll add officers as soon as Ramirez clears them."

"Hospitals?" Hanrahan asked.

"Naw, our guy ain't going to a hospital."

"Who's your early favorite?"

"McCarroll."

Nagler turned away.

"Watch your back, Frankie," Hanrahan said, before telling the pushing crowd to quit shoving.

****

Nagler met Chief John Hanson halfway down the hill, and for a moment neither spoke.

Hanson finally sighed. "A mess, Frank. A fucking mess. Dawson's story didn't help. Have you seen him?"

"Wasn't really looking, but I didn't see him in that scrum," Nagler said nodding to the crowd. "A little surprised if he's not here."

Hanson's face soured. "Gotta say something to them." He turned up the hill, then stopped. "Is all that true, in Dawson's story. About the money, the bribes, all those deals?"

Nagler kicked at the ground and said, "Yes. All of it. Years of it." He exhaled; the storm was only building. "Hey, Chief. Advice. Just say you knew the mayor as a good leader, a good family man and we are all shocked by the allegations just released. His death … you know. Beat up Dawson a little. He can take it."

"Yeah," Hanson squeezed his face into an official posture and stepped toward the howling crowd.

Finally, Ramirez.

"Damn it, Frank. There aren't too many of them left. When do they come after us?"

"There's more than we think. Dawson printed a hundred of their names in the paper today."

"The chief told the whole department out get out of their blues and into gear," she said.

"That's good," he said, "But I wonder given what we know, how many of those street cops are sympathetic to the cause of the Dragony? We didn't get here – cops dying, the mayor shot – in a vacuum."

Ramirez turned to leave. "See you at HQ, Frank."

Nagler stared up then hill, didn't respond. Then, "Yeah, right. Maria, does Destiny have family out of town?"

"What?" Ramirez eyes widened as she accepted the meaning of the question. "Yeah. Yes, she does."

Nagler nodded. "A few days."

As Nagler watched Ramirez make a call, he wondered if Lauren had come back to Ironton. She said four days, and this was day four. He, too, placed a call. It went to voicemail but the mailbox was full. He wanted to hear her voice but knew that she had one of those answering services with the detached mechanical voice that did not use her name. It had been his idea. He closed the call.

The cemetery had emptied, its peace shattered. He squinted into the settling gloom and scanned the wan landscape, the darkening rim of trees, branches outlined against the lowering clouds, finally releasing their spit of cold rain.

He placed one more call.

"Dawson. Call me."

CHAPTER TWENTY-THREE

Something, not much

"Thank God for camera phones," Nagler said as he watched Maria Ramirez at her computer scan through some of the dozens of videos that had been posted online.

She had sequenced them by time and location and produced a running commentary from bystanders after the mayor's shooting. Most were selfies so they showed little of the actual street scene at Locust Street Cemetery they were describing, but there was some consistency.

Ramirez posted four videos across the screen. "Watch, Frank. They are all recording the ceremony, which from that distance makes no sense, but what the hell. But look. They all turned the same direction at the same moment, and on this one" – she enlarged one video and raised the computer's volume – "You can hear a muffled bang, probably the shot."

She posted four more videos, all taken while the phones' owners jostled down the street, all capturing what appeared to be a man scrambling out of the trees into the road, falling once, then crawling/jumping into the open door of a green SUV that was rolling slowly away from the cemetery.

"He had an audience," Nagler said. "He didn't count on that."

Ramirez paused one video. "You can see he was carrying something, even used it as a cane at one point, but the quality of the shot is poor, blurry from the running, so from this we can't say it was a rifle. Still…"

Nagler huffed out a scoffing laugh. "I'm not sure what it says about all these people, but when they heard what could have been a gunshot, they didn't duck, run the opposite direction, scream, or panic. They ran toward the shot holding up their cell phones."

Ramirez posted another series of videos. "They want to sell the video to cable news. Anyway, look at this. This is the SUV. Then, here five blocks away, speeding. Here, twelve blocks away where Locust meets the highway, and then here, taking the right turn north at the car dealership." She enlarged one scene. "Got a partial plate number here, but it's blurry. One thing? It's not Jersey. Might be New York. I sent out an alert with a description of the SUV and possible plate to all states. We can be sure it'll come back stolen."

****

"Doctor Mulligan," Nagler said as he entered the examination room, only to find the room empty. Lights shined on the metal exam tables, rolling carts with instruments nearby; the antiseptic air scrubbed of all taste or odor held a hum of refrigerators.

"Doc?"

Nagler found the medical examiner in the side office at his desk, head bent, hands clasped on his neck. Mulligan left out a long sigh when Nagler entered.

In front of him on his desk were open four folders thick with charts, photos, and pages of script. It was an uneven pile, pages folded open, folders overlapping, photos floating between one folder or another, unattached.

Nagler paused at the door, surprised by the messy display, especially from a man so precise and organized as Mulligan, a man who had never failed to find exactitude in the spillage of blood, the breaks of bones and skulls, to find in all the wreckage that can be inflicted on a human body, meaning and closure.

But this was not closure, Nagler knew.

"You alright, doc?" he asked.

Mulligan's head jerked up, and he glared, suspicious of Nagler's presence; he closed his eyes and leaned back in the chair. "Weary, detective. I am weary." He waved toward a chair, "Please, sit." His voice was scratchy, a sound dragged up from a place he had kept hidden until now.

Nagler sidled to the chair, concerned. Mulligan had never been weary.

"Are you well?" Nagler asked.

"Quite well, Frank." Mulligan smiled softly. "Thank you for asking. I am not sick. I am weary of all this," and he waved at the material on his desk. "I am tired of the layers, of the repetition, of the callous disregard evidenced in these reports, how meaningless to some is human life."

"Is this about the mayor?"

Mulligan's face hardened, as did his voice. "It's about Mayor Ollivar, and Captain Langdon, whatever their roles, and the four who were killed in the explosion, and the displaced, and how Miss Fox must again run to be safe. And it's about Mr. Kalinsky and Sol Rosen, and those powerful enough to believe that only their interests prevail, that everyone else can be tossed aside, trampled beneath, used and forgotten."

"It's all connected," Nagler said. "We thought—"

"This is connected to this," Mulligan said, spilling out his anger as he picked up and dropped photos. "And this is connected to this," as he shuffled files and reports. "And this, the years of this, the deaths, the thefts, the plotting, can all be connected to a single .22 caliber rifle. It was used to kill Kalinsky, to kill Rosen, and yesterday to kill Mayor Ollivar. Find the owner, and this house of cards, this reign of terror, ends."

Mulligan leaned back, emptied, but unfulfilled.

"Kalinsky—"

"No." Mulligan stopped Nagler mid sentence. "All the records were falsified, Frank. All."

Nagler scratched his furrowed brow. "So that would mean that the note in the files Dancer – Jeff Montgomery – gave us about someone tampering with the brakes on Kalinsky's car, was also false. They were lying to their own gang members."

"Did you find Kalinsky's car?" Mulligan asked, somewhat amused.

"We found the plates on Sol Rosen's Impala, but no '67 Barracuda."

"I suspect you won't," Mulligan said. He had calmed and was focused as usual. "I had done a little detective work. There was a fiery crash of a gasoline truck on the highway on the night mentioned. But Kalinsky was not there, and neither was his car."

"I saw that report," Nagler said. "Walked the route in the middle of the night." He sighed. "I thought something was wrong, but it got lost in the…" He shrugged. "Just got lost. And it was more than a decade old. Jesus. How did they hold all this together? So, they just made him disappear."

"As they did others. We cannot leave the conclusion of this in their hands, Frank." Mulligan peered over the rims of his glasses. "You must end it," then added, "Of course I mean we all must end it. Did anything come of the search of the tree stand?"

"We have a blood type, and sample of everyday blue jeans," Nagler said. "Something, but not much."

CHAPTER TWENTY-FOUR

The night of fires

The first attack rumbled through the train station parking lot. A mob of screaming men smashed car windows, pulled down signs, tipped over trash cans and set fire to the contents.

Masked, jack-booted, wearing spiked gloves and helmets, in pairs, threes and fours, they surrounded commuters, tore dresses from the backs of women, punched and pummeled the men who came to their defense, only to end gleefully howling in the middle of the train tracks.

As if signaled, they burst through the gathering crowd, pushing and punching, screaming a constant roar as sirens echoed in side streets, and the gang met with another smashing their way down Blackwell, till another mob joined from Bassett. What had been twenty was then sixty, then eighty. A hundred.

As soon as it started it was over. Police in patrol cars with the help of firefighters in fire trucks blocked the side street exits while battle-geared officers drove the gang to the city hall parking lot, where outnumbered, the gang, grinning and glassy-eyed, surrendered.

In the parking lot, Nagler shook his head in disbelief.

"What was the point of all that?" he asked Maria Ramirez.

"No point," she said, then "Hey, I know that kid. Officer, just a minute."

Nagler and Ramirez approached an officer holding Robert Jamieson, the kid who had shot at them while they dug up Sol Rosen's box of records.

"How'd you get out?" Ramirez asked.

Jamieson tipped his head and winked. He wore a lazy smile. "Got friends, told ya."

"Whatever, kid," Nagler said. "What was this about?"

Jamieson laughed, "Attention, man. Distraction. Someone finally paying attention to guys like me. You didn't believe me. The Dragony rises. There ain't enough of you."

The officer dragged the struggling Jamieson away. "Dragony rising, man. You can't stop it."

****

So began the night of the fires. A dozen or more, across the city. Vacant sheds, open dry fields, broken rail cars at the end of the storage yard, dumpsters filled with construction debris near Leonard's bookstore, derelict vehicles at a car lot on the highway; fires rising so fast the crews could not respond in time, fires so random they defied logic.

Nagler climbed the fire escape to the theater roof where the yellow kitchen chair stood sentinel and listened as the night screamed and sirens rained down the Ironton hills to settle into the smoke-filled valley.

Smudges of orange-brown smoke filtered against hazy streetlights. Sirens blurred into one long angry song. His radio crackled with a dozen anxious voices at once, a city crying.

"What did we do to deserve this?" he asked, staring hard-eyed, knowing there was no answer.

As he turned to leave the theater perch, Nagler saw flames erupt on the roof of the bank where Lauren had once placed her office following the explosion. The fire ran along the roof line fueled by old oily tiles and whatever the arsonists had used as an igniter.

"Dispatch," he yelled. "New fire, Blackwell and Warren. The old bank."

As he watched, four figures danced before the flames, arms waving, circling, celebrating.

"Frank, we're on it. A truck is at the explosion site, a block away."

"Great, dispatch. Four suspects dancing on the roof."

"Got 'em. Hey, Frank, the ghetto is burning."

Hurried, angry, Nagler banged down the waving, creaking fire escape, and when a couple of rusted bolts snapped he jumped over the last few steps and crumpled in eye-watering pain as his ankle folded.

CHAPTER TWENTY-FIVE

McCarroll

Nagler squirmed his back against a wall and under his breath muttered "fuck" about twenty times. He held his head in his hands, filled his cheeks with air, then with gritted teeth sucked in and expelled a series of grumbling breaths to dispel the pain.

"Dispatch." Two short breaths. "What's burning in the ghetto?"

"That new community center housing building."

"That's not even finished." Holy crap, Nagler thought. What the…

"Yeah, how weird is that?"

Nagler took a few more deep breaths and banged his head against the wall.

"You don't sound so good, Frank. Need help?"

"Thanks, but not tonight. You got other things to worry about. Hey, any deaths reported?"

"No. That's the other weird thing. Lots of empty places. You know, if I was a betting man, I'd put my money on someone trying to reduce their inventory."

Nagler pushed to his feet. "Probably right. With Duval in jail, who's running point?"

"County guy, um, Ingles, Winston Ingles, assistant prosecutor. He's at the community center. Looking for you. He said to look for the white hard hat."

Nagler winced, leaned, limped. "Why a country guy? Where's our fire chief Dennis Green?"

"Not sure, Frank. I'm just passing the info along."

"Right. On my way."

In the narrow alley, Nagler sucked in the foul air, reached an arm out to a wall for support and closed his eyes against what he knew would be a painful walk. His foot dragged, the scratchy sound trailing. Then his knee bent as his body recalled motion; at times he braced himself against both walls and shuffled along, finally limping without support into a dark street.

It was oddly quiet, he thought, the distant sirens, the radio chatter, gone. Is it over?

He squinted into the darkness to bring to focus a familiar figure outlined in the smoke, arced by soft light.

"McCarroll," he yelled. "What the hell are you doing? Celebrating? You couldn't blow up the city, so this is your plan?"

Nagler shifted unsteadily on his bad ankle and waited for McCarroll to notice and possibly advance.

McCarroll instead leaned his shoulder against a pole.

"Mr. Noiglar. Fire purifies, does it not?" McCarroll said in a voice far too cheery. "We'll purify Ironton and rebuild. I've lived through the fires. My parents hid in the Underground when Hitler flattened London. And I ran the streets in Belfast when they burned and stood in the dusty cauldron of Manhattan when the towers fell. It's how we come out clean."

"So, you'll add Ironton to your photo gallery?" Nagler huffed, hopping twice to shift the pain. "McCarroll, you are a lunatic, and a criminal."

"No, Mr. Noiglar you cannot attach my name to these fires. I gave no orders, put no lighters or gasoline in the hands of anyone. But you'll soon learn who did. I tell them to defend themselves. The Dragony learned years ago that one must push out those who don't belong."

McCarroll shouldered off the pole and took two steps toward Nagler, who shifted his feet to maintain an uncertain balance, bracing for a swift charge from McCarroll.

"You and your fucking Dragony. A joke you are. And who decides who belongs?" The bitterness of his voice muffled by pain; he winced and stumbled when the ankle collapsed. He righted himself, prepared again that McCarroll might move forward even more.

"You can't mock us, sir. The Dragony choses. We rebuild for ourselves." McCarroll stood straight up and laughed. "Ah, Mr. Noiglar, you are a damaged man, and this is a damaged city. I can only fix one."

"So, you turned those kids loose…Who asked you to fix anything?"

"Those kids are not all the Dragony, Sir. The Dragony sits at home and worries that all they worked for will be taken from them, that their children's dreams die abornin'."

"So, you burn it down? How many homes of the Dragony are lost in the fires, McCarroll? You wreck what you claim to protect. What do you get out of this? A pure heart? What does Mangot get? You act for personal gain, as criminals do, soaring rhetoric aside. All you know how to do is terrorize and destroy."

Silence between them; sounds from afar leaking in.

"So *you* judge. Fear brings pain, my friend. Pain destroys hope. It must be seared away. You must burn away your own pain, Mr. Noiglar. Let this city burn. Only then does your future begin."

"You don't believe that. You, in fact, believe in nothing." Nagler locked his ankle and stood tall.

"Ah," McCarroll said with scorn. "What ya believe about it don't matter when it's happenin' right in front of ya."

McCarroll turned, his frame dimmer in the haze as he slipped away.

"Damn it," Nagler hissed. His face closed up as he knew that he had to let McCarroll go. He could never catch him on his bad ankle, and even if he did, McCarroll could easily shake him off, or worse. He stared into the direction McCarroll had walked and registered the notion that the man curiously was not limping. The mayor's assassin, after failing to clear the iron fence, was limping in the street videos. *So, who?*

"Hey, dispatch, any free units downtown?"

"Frank. Maybe one. What's up?"

He hopped to a wall and leaned his head back. "Never mind. Thought I saw someone, but it was a shadow."

"If ya say so. Oh, yeah, that county guy called back. Sounds a little nudgy."

****

A county guy?

Nagler pondered the question while winding through streets jammed with residents, fire vehicles and debris, and trying to keep his ankle from rolling over in pain.

"Why would a county assistant prosecutor be in charge at a local scene?" he asked himself. He had called Green's phone before driving but got no answer. "Could be there's so many fires he's at HQ directing the effort." He stopped at an intersection while a fire truck backed into a K-turn and left. "Why am I talking to myself?"

None of this makes sense, hadn't from the beginning, he thought. City blows up and they leave it to local guys like me and Dennis Green. Except now. What changed?

He eased out of his car with a wince as his ankle adjusted to carrying weight as he turned into a scene of dark, swirling mist and smoke, air shivering with sound as a row of fire trucks and tankers grumbled curbside and shouted commands slipped around building corners, through cracks between vehicles and found ears.

The dense air shimmied with light as it absorbed the red and blues from trucks and the yellow of dusty spotlights; Nagler squinted searching for white hard hat.

Then a voice: "You're Nagler, right?"

He turned to see walking toward him a short man in a white hard hat carrying a clipboard. "Over here," the man shouted, pointing to the rear of an emergency command van.

Winston Ingles wore clear plastic protective goggles over his horn-rims. A mic was pinned to his official county emergency management jacket, which he wore over a white shirt and tie.

Who wears a tie to a crime scene in the middle of the night, other than Mulligan? Nagler wondered.

"Just a minute," he said to Nagler. "Ronnie, I don't care what's an issue. Find a pair of officers and secure that scene." He turned back to Nagler. "Sorry." He glanced into the street.

A scolding voice brittle with authority. "How could you let it get to this point, Detective?"

"Let *what* get to *what* point?" Nagler spit out the reply. He was not going to be bullied by a county guy in a white hard hat and horn rim glasses. He nodded to the wide bumper of the truck. "I'm gonna sit because my ankle is killing me." He slumped as the pain receded.

"If you must." Ingles rolled his eyes and piously shook his head. "A mayor shot, murdered at a funeral of a decorated police captain. Have you suspects? A bomb explosion, fires, gangs running the streets." He pointed to the community center. "And now this? But, of course, you're the officer who cracked up at a training session, aren't you? What would be expected from you? And then there is that famous Internet harangue. Why didn't they retire you? I would have."

Nagler let the comment slide but wondered why and how Winston Ingles would have seen that staged street event. *He sure is enjoying himself.*

"Then there those two other deaths.," Ingles said, voice rising. "Un...ac...ceptable," as he turned the word into three syllables.

"Two deaths?"

"Yes." Ingles fingered in a pocket to produce a slip of paper.

He brought notes?

Nagler pinned his eyes to the ground so he would not laugh.

"Let's see. Eduardo Tallem, a restaurant owner, and, um, Montgomery, Jeff Montgomery, a former Ironton police officer."

Dancer? He's not dead. The only person who thinks so is McCarroll because I told him, which was a lie. So, how'd this jerk find out?

"How'd you hear about Montgomery? Thought he left town," Nagler said, lying. "I found Tallem."

Ingles fumbled as he folded the paper back into his pocket. "It was in," he waved a hand, "Some report."

"Not a report I wrote."

Scolding. "Others wrote reports, Detective."

"Ah, you're right, McWilliams probably filed it. In another division."

"McWilliams. Sounds right."

Except there is no McWilliams. There is only McCarroll, and you're his sacrificial lamb. He probably doesn't even know your name.

Ingles' mic squawked. "Excuse me," and he stepped away, a little downslope of the truck.

Nagler clenched his fist to dispel the nerves.

So, there it was. Belief and disbelief, all at once. It was not *who* was in place, this Winston Ingles, this little government nebbish wielding a clipboard as his shield of authority with his notes and plastic goggles and fancy communication equipment, it was simply that he *was* in place. Nagler closed his eyes and felt the shiver along his spine as the understanding of that knowledge sank in. What had Adele Rosen said? One day you wake up and the world has changed.

This is the world changed, Nagler realized. This night, this string of nights.

Nagler watched as Ingles twirled in a little circle barking orders at whomever was on the end of that conversation. Ingles pushed up his jacket sleeves. "That's final," Nagler heard him yell.

Not if I have anything to say about it. I'll not be taken down by this twit.

Ingles returned, but stood a few feet away from the truck, leaving his head at Nagler's eye level. "So, Nagler, we're taking over. I'll have a team here in the morning. Your department is clearly over its head."

"On whose authority?"

"The county has the authority, Nagler. You have no sitting mayor, the fire marshal is in jail, and your planning director is under investigation for theft of money and city property."

Nagler's lips quivered but he buried the smile. They found the files that Lauren had planted, but unlike Mayor Ollivar, Winston Ingles did not realize the significance of what they thought they found.

"I wondered why she left town," Nagler said, his voice light and mocking. "I haven't seen it all, but it was pretty deep and long term."

"That's what I heard, too."

Nagler coughed to cover his disgust. It was no secret that he and Lauren were a couple, that was, except to Winston Ingles.

"How are you going to prove that records and funds were stolen?" Nagler asked with fake concern.

A casual, self-important shrug. "Standard investigation. Follow the file trail, look for the money."

Nagler nodded in agreement. "Oh, *good* plan. A tip? I heard those files were faked, which is why we were proceeding slowly. Someone planted them to trip up someone else. That something you heard?"

There it was. The wrinkle of doubt that crept across Ingles' forehead. *That's not in your notes, is it?*

"Yeah, we heard it was about something the mayor and that financial guy, Temple Mangot..." Nagler said, his voice deepening with dark sourness.

"Taylor," Ingles interrupted. "Mr. Taylor Mangot."

"Oh, right. Names, what are you gonna do?" A harsh laugh. "Hey, doesn't Taylor, right? Taylor Mangot, own this place? How'd the fire start?" Making up his own answer, Nagler said, "Word on the street is that someone is burning down their own buildings, part of some financial scam, not a street riot."

Ingles fiddled with his mic, glanced his clipboard, and dropped it to his side.

"This was a trash fire, set in a dumpster near the rear of the building," he said.

"So, arson," Nagler said, "That's something. Suspects? Have you heard about that gang of cops that was operating in Ironton? Maybe this is them."

"Cops aren't burning down this town," Ingles said. "This is just…" He pursed his lips and sighed. "There's no gang of cops. You are mis-informed."

Nagler stood, towering over the shorter man as he grabbed Ingles' arm so the man could not cover up the dragon tattoo. "Then why do you have their tattoo on your left wrist? A little kids' club, there Wallace…"

Nagler closed his eyes steeling himself against the sharp pain.

"Winston."

"Right. Winston." Nagler swallowed his anger. No need to waste it on Winston Ingles. "Know what, Winston? Thing I can't figure out. Is your presence here – you're just a messenger, after all – a sign of their arrogance or their desperation? And before you answer that, you should know that we have lists. Lots of lists, lots of names, and while we weren't looking for a pissant like you, I'll bet we find you, and if we look hard enough, we'll find your father and grandfather. That's how you got your job, right? I mean that is how this works, this thing, this Dragony." Nagler paused, sizing up Winston Ingles, who seemed to shrink inside his official county jacket and his white shirt and tie. "So, what kind of a car do you drive, Winston, when you're not tooling around in one of the county's fancy machines? If it's anything other than a plain Ford sedan, we might have a few questions. How's your pension? Kids going to college?" He paused. "That could change."

Ingles shifted to find level ground and stared into the darkness. He looked as if he had a been run over by a truck he never saw coming, which, Nagler thought, was pretty much the truth.

"What do you want to know?" Ingles asked.

"Who shot the mayor?"

****

Firefighters were hosing down hot spots when Nagler approached the damaged building. The air stung with a wet charcoal aroma so thick it coated his throat as he breathed.

A few fire companies were preparing to leave.

At a Boonton truck, a firefighter with a heavy knee brace was storing hoses. "Jerry Langdon," Nagler called out.

Langdon turned to the voice with a scowl. "What?"

"Frank Nagler, Ironton."

Langdon's eyes shrunk. "Yuz got a mess on ya hands here."

Nagler stuck out his hand. "Sorry about your brother. Hell of thing at the funeral."

Langdon offered a weak handshake. "Yeah, thanks. Bernie deserved better."

"How's the knee?"

"Gettin' better. Floor caved at a fire scene last week."

"Too bad."

Limping back to his car, Nagler thought, McCarroll gave up the shooter too easily. And Jerry Langdon knows he's been outed.

The only question was this: What does McCarroll, and probably Taylor Mangot, want in return?

In his car, Nagler called McCarroll, and received a message that the number had been disconnected.

CHAPTER TWENTY-SIX

One more target

Nagler stared at the computer screen on Maria Ramirez's desk with disbelief.

"Jerry Langdon was an insurance salesman. Really?"

"Empire Insurance," Ramirez said. "Commercial insurance, buildings, liability, corporate stuff. But look," and she called up another file. "He was also a licensed private gun dealer. His house was empty when we got there with a search warrant. But there was steel cabinet that had a few rounds. We sent them to ballistics for testing."

"What caliber?"

"A few .38s, a couple shotgun shells and four .22s. What are the odds?"

Nagler waved at the screen. "Probably great. Probably a thousand percent. McCarroll handed him to us and told Langdon that he had done so. Damn it, even Bernie Langdon told us. He told me his brother knew Sol Rosen and knew he had been shot in Boonton's Canal Park. That wasn't in the files, so how did Bernie know it?"

"Because Jerry Langdon shot Sol Rosen and bragged about it to his brother," Ramirez said.

"Or because Bernie Langdon was there. Rosen was shot in the back of the head. Probably took two guys to do it."

Ramirez spun in her chair. "Is that why Bernie Langdon was killed?"

Nagler stepped over to the white board with the Dragony names on it and drew an angry line through *"Bernie Langdon"* even though the name was already marked.

Then he circled two others, repeating each circle three times.

"Something else happened at that warehouse on Dubin Place fifteen years ago, Maria, something that is not complete. All this destruction, all the killings, were set in place that night."

Maria joined him at the board.

"We have two versions of the events, one from the police and the other from Rachel Pursel," she said.

"And both of them have reasons to lie."

Nagler tapped one of the circled names. "We need to talk to this guy. Shouldn't be hard. He's in jail."

Ramirez smiled. "How odd would it be if all this came back to Mahala Dixon and her father. I'll have the warden arrange a private meeting. Possibly a medical excuse."

"Yeah, maybe Carlton Dixon needs to have a mild heart attack."

"We don't want to kill him, Frank."

"He maybe already be a dead man," Nagler said biting his lower lip. "This thing is not over. McCarroll has at least one more target."

****

Nagler found Randy Jensen leaning with a crutch against the side of the car dealer's building. When the kid responded to Nagler calling out his name, Nagler could see the bruises around his eyes.

"Who did it, Randy?"

"Not supposed…"

"Yeah, you are, so who?"

Randy pulled a chair closer. "Boss gave me this chair, so I'm gonna sit."

"Get off that leg. Broken?"

"Knee. Had a club. After I fell, they punched me a bunch of times, kicked my head. Said, you know, it was a warning."

"To keep your mouth shut."

Randy squinted into the street. "Yeah."

"What do you remember about them?"

"My age. One Hispanic kid, one white kid I sort of remember from school, but I don't know his name. Couple other guys, you know, just a blur. They kept yelling about the Dragon something."

"The Dragony."

"That's it. What it is?"

"A gang."

"Drugs? Cause I don't do drugs, Detective Nadler."

"It's hard to say."

"They have somethin' to do with all those fires?"

"Seems so."

"Fuckin' A." Not said in wonder, but anger.

Nagler smiled down at the kid. *A better kid than I thought.* "Need to know if you can recall anything else about what you saw from the theater roof."

Randy shifted on the chair and pulled out his notepad. "Had time, ya know, sittin' here. Remembered some details, then I saw that picture in the paper. You know about the new development, that glass tower thing? And I thought, fuckin' A, that was one of the guys in that apartment window I saw before the explosion. In the picture he was standing next to the mayor and smiling. Tall guy, really tall guy. I remember the suit, really sharp."

"Damn it, Taylor Mangot," Nagler muttered. "Why am I not surprised? Look at these," and he pulled out several photos. "I know it was from a distance, but recognize any of these people?"

Randy shuffled the photos and handed one back to Nagler.

"This guy. He was looking all around, so I saw his face. Had a stick or something kept putting it to his shoulder like he was shooting. Kneeled down at one point." Randy held out his arms like he was holding a long stick; he pulled an imaginary trigger and jerked his arms back in recoil.

Nagler stashed the photo of Jerry Langdon in his shirt pocket with a photo of Taylor Mangot II.

"The other ones I'm not so sure. But her, positive. Absolutely."

"Her?"

"Yeah, couldn't figure what she was doing there, but there she was, pretty friendly and all."

****

In his car, Nagler called Ramirez.

"Hey, Maria...what's that noise?"

"A winch. Get to the bog. We found Dawson's car."

A wheezy, "Damn. Find Dawson?"

Breathy air filled his ear. "No. Just his car."

Nagler, softly, resigned. "On my way."

He punched Dawson's phone number and let it ring till it reached voicemail and hung up; then he called it again.

The green slimed, dripping Toyota was hooked to a tow truck when Nagler arrived. Ramirez faced the lake with one hand shading her eyes.

"We're getting three boats in the water," she said, pointing to a rocky point to the right. "Some pilot taking photos of the interstate called it in."

"Pop the trunk?"

"Waiting for you," she said.

Nagler sighed. "Yeah. Guess so."

His shoulders slumped as he took the crowbar from the driver.

The lock cracked and the lid slowly rose to revel an empty trunk.

Nagler exhaled and offered a twisted smile. "Good news, I guess."

He peered through the windows and opened the driver's side door.

"Car's too clean, Maria. I've seen Dawson's car before, and rode in it once, unfortunately. The back seat was usually filled with newspapers and notebooks, food bags and other junk." He patted the roof. "If you were going to drown someone in their own car, would *you* clean it out?"

She chuckled. "Hardly. So, Dawson sank his own car?"

"Why not? What better way to tell someone who was after you to stop looking?" He wrinkled his brow and added, "Including us. I haven't seen him since he published the story on Rachel Pursel's list."

Ramirez circled the car and looked through the passenger side windows.

"What the hell? Frank, look." She reached into the car and from the key slot on the steering column, extracted a locker key.

At the bus station in locker 1436, they found an envelope containing a flash drive.

****

The video opened with Dawson, seated before a black background, face lighted by an off-screen source like he was making an old-style vampire film.

"Hey guys," Dawson began. "Got tired of being followed, so I ditched the car, which if you are watching this, you obviously found. I added some video I recorded with the drone. Stuff you've never seen, but it puts faces and situations to the names on that list I got from Rachel Pursel. You know, Frank, we thought Howard Newton and his gang had written the book on municipal corruption with the thefts and job placements, deals and open defiance. That was practice compared to this. This bunch is murderous, which I think you understand. But there are more deaths than you know or will discover. People eliminated quietly and replaced with a friend, so to speak. And they will hide in those background jobs until something needs to be done. You'll meet them and wonder who the hell they are. And they'll be so smug and confident you won't quite believe it. But this group is in for the long haul, but the whole deal is not in place yet. There's another move, but I don't know it. That little fire six months ago, and the scene at Dubin Place and even the explosion downtown were just distractions. This is not about buildings, but about holding the reins of power and making permanent change. Mayor Ollivar is the key to the next move."

Dawson wiped his face with both hands.

Winston Ingles, Nagler thought.

"Anyway, there's one person in the second video I've never seen before. Based on how he is pointing at the others, and the hard look on his face I'd say he's in charge. And he ain't happy. The other videos here are older, some of it you might have seen. The second video with the unknown man is about three weeks old. Hey, look, I'm not gone forever. I'm watching. Save me a seat when Barry's opens up again."

Ramirez closed that video and pulled up the menu, then paused.

"He made this before the mayor was killed," she said. "So, what's that mean?"

"That the mayor's murder was not the next thing," Nagler said. He pulled over a chair and sat. "It means the mayor became a liability. I wonder what he did?" Fidgety, he stood and pushed the chair out of the way. It crashed in the wall. "We've always known this was about money. That's what Lauren said right at the start. The Dragon companies. I'll bet that insurance company that Jerry Langdon worked for is one of them. Collecting and hoarding money, about protecting that money and shielding the access to it. How do they do that? Adele Rosen told us: Own the bankers and lawyers and accountants. But you need more than that. Money by itself can accumulate with the click of a computer mouse. But what did the Mangots do?"

"They owned land and real estate, buildings. That's how they washed the money," Ramirez said.

"Right, and to do that without a fuss you need to control government. Need a zoning change? Call your friendly on-the-payroll zoning board member. Need an ordinance change?"

"Call the mayor."

"Who's the next in line to be mayor now that Ollivar has been removed?"

Ramirez waved her hands and shrugged. "Don't know. Let's look." She stored Dawson's video and pulled up a file of Ironton officials. "Looks like council president in line to become acting mayor in the event of an emergency, but it has to be a public vote. In the meantime, the city administrator has emergency powers."

"That's more complicated than I thought it would be," Nagler said.

"For a reason. Take a public vote otherwise it looks like a coup."

"Right. So, who is council president, and why don't we know that?"

Maria opened a new file that contained a photo of a pudgy faced man wearing a phony, political smile, and a brief biography.

"Um, Bill Weston," she said. "Been in office since 2006. He's an accountant."

Nagler leaned over her shoulder. "Of course he is. The Dragony needs accountants. They keep killing them. I've never seen him. 2006, huh? Why does everything in this case begin in 2006?"

"What?"

"The mayor's office is still locked down, right?"

"Yes. Computer offline, the office locks changed. I also put an officer in the hallway with strict orders to report anyone who tried to talk their way into the office."

"When's that meeting scheduled, the one when they vote on the acting mayor?" Nagler covered his mouth and pinched his lips. "We need to get the mayor's computer down here. You do that and I'll rifle through his desk." He smiled. "I've always wanted to rifle through some official's desk."

"Ah, a career highlight. That meeting is next Monday."

"Good. We've got a couple days. I'm heading over there. After we get Ollivar's computer, you see if Bill Weston is on any of our lists. Maybe we can figure out why Mayor Ollivar was sacrificed for the good of the Dragony."

CHAPTER TWENTY-SEVEN

The photo on the wall

The air in Mayor Ollivar's office tasted like the sterile odor of a long-shuttered attic, the room lifeless, soundless, and dark. Dust had collected on the desktop and shelves, on the armchairs and the stack of reports; more important, Nagler thought, the office phone, cabinets and printer had grown a dusty, fuzzy layer of gray and strongly suggested that no one had been poking around.

A dozen photos lined the wall opposite the desk. Official things, ceremonies with Ollivar grinning and shaking hands, cutting ribbons, the spaces shared with a collection of equally happy faces, a few of which he recognized.

In ordinary times no one would give those photos a second look.

But these were not ordinary times, and Nagler knew that any number of the men and women in those photos could know why Ollivar was shot, or worse, participated in the planning. He made a mental note to have the photos delivered to Ramirez.

Three metal filing cabinets were largely empty.

Made sense. Most modern government work was done on a computer.

So much for rifling. Ramirez would be disappointed.

A mahogany desk dominated the space, easily three feet deep and from the centered chair, wider than arm's length in either direction.

Nagler sat. *Nice chair. It's good to be the mayor.* If there had been family photos, they had been removed. He was familiar with Ollivar's desk phone, an Ironton department standard for years. He picked up the receiver and was surprised the line was still connected.

The most recent messages were hang-ups, which made sense since they occurred after his death weeks before; then a series of short inquiries – "Mr. Mayor?" "Jesus?" "Where are you, pal?" Nagler didn't recognize any of those voices, all male, all official sounding.

While the messages played on, Nagler sorted through the trash can under Ollivar's desk. It seemed an odd place to keep a trash can. *Hiding it? Why?*

The police chief's voice leaked from the phone, details about Bernie Langdon's funeral. The chief wanted tighter security.

The trash can was filled with wadded printer paper. Some of the pages had a few lines, others seemed to be part of a longer continuous document, maybe a speech, a policy statement. A speech would make sense, he thought, maybe Langdon's eulogy. But you'd write and correct the draft on the computer, Nagler thought. And Ollivar would have had his staff write the eulogy.

Nagler unwadded and sorted the papers while the answering machine blurted out the messages. Occasionally a voice sounded familiar and Nagler replayed the message, then shrugged.

The printer was running out of ink while Ollivar was printing this document, Nagler decided. The pages at the top of the trash can were covered with lines of dots and dashes, like splashes of ink. He held a few pages up to the light to see if he could decipher any words.

Why keep printing?

He checked the printer, which had run out of paper.

No ink. No paper. *What the hell?*

He called Ramirez.

"Hey, Maria, did you break into the mayor's computer yet?"

She laughed. "We're not breaking in, Frank, not yet. As mayor he had higher levels of security on his machine. Twenty minutes."

"Okay, find the last document he created. He was printing it and ran out of ink and paper. Just odd."

"Got it."

A few sheets of paper later, some words began to appear like silhouettes.

"Have them do it over."

"Wrong," then, "remix."

A couple pages later: "Cement."

Some of these must be from email, Nagler thought, some back and forth with someone.

The hair on Nagler's neck stood up as McCarroll's voice came from the phone speaker. "Mr. Oll-e-var. You will pay for this. Betrayal has a cost."

How did Ollivar react to that word? Nagler wondered. Exposure has one meaning; betrayal a second.

Nagler set aside the papers as the messages ran through a few more hang-ups. These papers, whatever secret they hold in their dots, dashes, and sparse words, were Ollivar's betrayal.

Then a voice he didn't recognize: "Damn it, Jesus. What's gotten into you? I've told you. Everything will be fine. It'll not come back to you."

Nagler paused the messages.

That voice had to be Taylor Mangot.

Nagler rifled through the papers to see how they were connected to the phone messages. He replayed the last message and noted the time: "2:15 p.m. 10/17."

Then he replayed McCarroll's threatening message and noted the time: 4:43 p.m. 10/17.

McCarroll and Mangot were piling on the pressure.

Ollivar was killed at the funeral on Friday, the 19th.

Deeper onto the pile of paper in the trashcan, Nagler watched the ink grow darker until he found a page with nothing but a time stamp across the top. A faxed page.

"Oct 15. 2:05 p.m."

Ollivar was sending this message to someone at the same time his life was being threatened.

He restarted the messages.

The last two:

12:15 p.m. McCarroll: "Mr. Mayor, we are ready to close the loop, but we're runnin' outta time. Get back to me today."

11:32 a.m.: Taylor Mangot: "Jesus, this is Taylor. No one will know. You just have to act on the bill. I don't understand why you haven't. Time is of the essence."

Running out of time for what? Is it odd that Mangot identified himself in the message? Is that sloppy or desperate?

Ollivar's response was to fax something to another person.

What bill? Nagler wondered. A payment? No. These guys would deal in cash. What else does a mayor sign? He smiled. Ordinances, resolutions, legislation. Bills. He grabbed up the papers. What the hell did the city council pass that was so urgent to the leadership of the Dragony?

He scanned the photos on the wall before. All you guys, he thought. Why do I have a feeling that none of you are going to wish you were such good friends of the mayor?

He stopped as he glanced at the last photo at the top of the row closest to the door, just above the height of regular and casual line of sight. It was off center from the rest because its frame was slightly larger. "Huh," he said. "That's not an accident. You either put it there so no one would see it during the rush out of the office. Or you *wanted* someone to see it. What are telling us, Mr. Mayor?"

Nagler studied the photo. "No." Then, "Damn it." In the center of the second row was a face Nagler had heard described – "like it had met a cement wall close up a couple times" – but had never seen.

McSalley. Finally, the mysterious McSalley.

Nagler dropped his bundle of papers on the desk and turned to pull the photo off the wall.

The door latch ground open.

He stepped to the side so the open door would shield him. His plan, for what it was worth, would be to slam the door into the intruder; he placed his right palm on the center of the door as it opened. He held his breath.

What the hell? No one knows I'm here but Maria.

He almost laughed when he saw her.

"Lauren. What the…"

Lauren Fox turned and placed one finger on his lips.

She locked the door and turned off the lights.

He kissed her finger. "I know why…"

She pressed her finger back on his mouth. "Shush."

"Where…"

"Hush."

Her face was dark, her eyes softened with sadness and fear.

He brushed her hair from her forehead and kissed each eye.

"How…" He exhaled a relieved breath. "You're…"

She wrapped her arms around his neck and offered a gentle quivering kiss. She held his face, and said, "No," when he tried to speak. "Just this." She took his hands and leaned over and whispered in his ear.

A thin smile, and he led her to the wide mahogany desk.

****

"Well, lady, you've been busy, but you look beat up," Ramirez said when Nagler and Lauren entered her office with the stack of papers and the photo from Ollivar's office. She stood and embraced Lauren, holding her head with one hand, and whispered, "It's okay." She turned to Nagler. "What they do to you, kid?"

"Nothing, Maria," Lauren said, her voice scratchy and weary. "I just haven't slept much in two days." Her eyes met Nagler's with a brief sparkle. "I'm better now."

Ramirez grinned, knowing. "Found that miracle spark, did ya? You guys. Mayor's office that quiet, huh?"

"Let's say his desk will never be the same," Lauren said.

Nagler brought Lauren a coffee, stirred it and said, "Can't promise anything, but it is today's."

Lauren settled into a chair, grasped the cup with two hands and smelled the coffee, and smiling, sipped. She gagged a little and wrinkled her nose. "It's great. Thanks." She ran her hand through her hair. "I need a shower."

Nagler glanced at Ramirez and said, "We met Rachel Pursel, so we know that part. What else happened?"

"I was followed, two days. I didn't want to lead them to anyone else, so I drove. Took the highways and the interstate, hid when I could, then up into the Highlands, crossed the Delaware a couple times, but couldn't shake them. Finally at the truck stop near the Water Gap, I managed to park behind a couple of big rigs. I found the tracker. They were inside, a couple kids, having a midnight snack and yukking it up, full of themselves. I stuck the tracker on their Jeep and flattened all four tires and the spare."

"Should never cross you, huh?" Ramirez said.

Lauren, flatly, "No, they shouldn't." She stood and reached for the pile of papers. "Okay, I know why the mayor was killed. It's all in here, but this is a mess."

Nagler said, "We do, too. Something about the construction of the community center. I think that's why they burned it."

"That's right," Lauren said. "I have all the documents."

"Lauren, you're not a cop," Ramirez said.

"I had to gain his trust. Ollivar reached out to me after I planted the phony documents in his files. He thought they were real, and he knew he was screwed. He was going to give me everything and leave the country." She smiled. "And, oh, Ollivar turned in Dan Yang. You know. A gift."

"Why didn't you come to me?" Nagler asked.

"Because he wouldn't give them to you, and with all the Dragony cops in the department, he didn't trust you. They saw themselves reflected in everything. He saw *me* as a fellow traveler on the road to conspiracy. You have to understand, even after you arrest them all, what they did is still on the books. It'll take me and fifty lawyers to undo it."

"So, what about the community center?" Ramirez asked.

"Off-market materials, cement blocks imported from some third-world country, below grade mortar, aluminum wire. The whole place would have melted in a fire." She shook the papers. "What's supposed to be in the pile of papers you found, Frank, were the contracts and emails that set up the scheme." She shook her head. "What is it with you guys and technology?"

"Hey, I'm better," Frank said.

She smiled softly. "I guess. I gave him a flash drive and told him to store it all there and erase the computer. But he insisted on making paper copies and faxing it to me. That's what this is." She shook the papers and then tossed them on Ramirez's desk. "I finally met him in his office and copied the files. I was afraid I was going to lose it all."

She reached inside her shirt and pulled a small leather pouch and took out the flash drive.

"It's all there. The suppliers, contractors, bankers, and the code officer who signed the approvals."

"Why the community center?" Nagler asked.

Lauren crossed to Nagler and rested her head in his shoulder. "Some final fuck you to Ironton. One day it would fall apart, and the insurance would pay them off, after they laundered years of cash through it, just like they did downtown. Fake tenants, fake inspections, the whole works. I think Ollivar saw the light. When that building came down – and it would – his name would be on the dedication plaque in the lobby. He was coming in Frank, after Bernie Langdon's funeral."

"But they got him first," Ramirez said. "They knew."

"And they burned down the community center to hide the evidence because they had their friendly investigator on the scene who would cover for them," Nagler said. "That's why Winston Ingles was there."

Three quick nods, and Lauren bit her lower lip. "They knew about Ollivar because of me. I shouldn't have gone to his office. I should have known someone was watching. That's why they followed me. That's why they killed the mayor. That's why they tried to burn down the city." She turned back to Nagler's shoulder and sighed.

He kissed her hair. "Not your fault, kid. If we have learned anything about the Dragony it's that they open doors they know are traps. They do it to their own kind. So why wouldn't they do it to you?" He glanced at the photo he had removed from the mayor's wall. "Why don't we do it to them?"

****

Nagler spread the photos on the table: The one from Ollivar's office, a print of a shot from Dawson's video and the ones he had shown Randy Jensen.

Ramirez added a head shot of Jerry Langdon copied from the Boonton fire department website.

Nagler held up Dawson's print and checked off the faces: the Langdon brothers, Dancer, McCarroll, Ollivar, Eduardo Tallem, Taylor Mangot and two of particular interest – Mahala Dixon and the man identified only as McSherry.

"Why does he have his arm around her?" Lauren asked.

"Little creepy," Nagler said.

"Here's why," Maria, at her computer said, as she printed out another photo. "He's her father." She dropped a photo roster of a class from the police academy on the table. "Remember I told you he was in my academy class. There he is. Carlton Dixon."

"He's white," Nagler said. "Mahala is black. Why did we assume he was black? Damn it. Have we been looking at this all wrong?"

"Sorry, Frank," Maria said. "He was one of about fifty in that class. I just knew the name, not the man."

"That's not what I meant. I know about two officers from my class because they scattered to other departments. This is about what Mahala told you that day she found us looking at the yellow chair and you and she debated her credentials for acting like an angry black girl. What if she had a reason, and it's not just some social attitude?"

"Mixed-race kid in a town that is more than ninety percent white," Ramirez said.

"When was she in school?" Lauren asked as she sat at a computer.

"Maybe, fifteen years…" Maria said.

"2006," Nagler said. "Two-thousand fucking six. Everything in this case starts in 2006."

"Okay, here it is," Lauren said, reading from the screen. "Oh, man. They closed an old school for apparent safety reasons and refurbished a school on the other side of town. Kids had to walk across an active train line and a four-lane highway."

"Let me guess," Ramirez said. "Poor kids walking, probably black and Spanish kids, to a school on the white side of town."

Lauren called up more news stories. "'Bout right. Rallies, protests, marches, some vandalism, cars burned, and oh look, who's in the middle of it – Janelle and Mahala Dixon."

"Fits the Dragony mythology," Nagler said. "Outsiders, feeling oppressed, acting out. What do we know about her mother?" Nagler asked. Sister Katherine mentioned her once. Didn't Mahala say her father raised her alone? I had the impression that it was from a young age."

"No obit listed," Maria said, "or a divorce listing."

"She just leave?" Lauren asked.

"Oh, wait," Maria said. "How interesting. Guess who was considered a suspect in the firebombing of a bus garage at the old school?" She turned and pointed to the computer screen. "Mahala Dixon."

"Who buried that case?" Nagler asked.

"Dan Thomson," he and Ramirez said together.

"A gift from the Dragony," Nagler said. "See what you can find on it – insurance filing, fire department reports. "I'm gonna talk to our former fire inspector."

"Dennis Duval? He's in jail." Maria said.

"They set him up. I think we found his partner."

CHAPTER TWENTY-EIGHT

Be ready for honor

Dennis Duval alternately glared across the desk of the prison warden at Frank Nagler or stared at the opposite wall with heavy sorrowing eyes.

"I don't know, Frank. I'm not sure…"

"You don't have much choice. You can refuse and stay here where it appears the weight loss program has been beneficial, or you can make that call."

"You never liked me, did you, Frank? You thought I was a fat, dumb faker. But I solved stuff, you know." Duval patted the receiver of the desk phone, then pulled his hand back.

"There's a lot of guys I work with I don't like, and a lot of them don't like me," Nagler said. "But this is not junior high school, Dennis, it's the difference between you doing long hard time for the millions of dollars in damage your arsons caused, or some shorter time for the attempted arsons we could be willing to discuss."

Duval picked up the receiver and with a shaky hand put it to his ear. He didn't dial but pushed the hold button. "He said never call unless…"

"It's an emergency," Nagler said and removed Duval's finger from the button. "This qualifies, trust me."

"And you'll get me outta here?"

"Your ride is waiting." Nagler scraped the mild friendliness from his voice. "Call."

Duval took a breath and dialed, his eyes flashing around the room. "Carlton, it's Duval. I know. Look, they figured out your daughter helped me...Naw, I didn't say nothing. Some guard said he heard it from that queer chick lieutenant Ramirez...I told them I needed to call my lawyer, 'cause you know they been trying to turn me. Yeah, great, thanks. Me? I'm good. Yeah, I'll watch my back. We hang together in here. Waiting for what's next. No, wait. Didn't mean anything by that. Just waiting, you know for orders. I mean, just waiting. Just thought you should hear about your daughter."

Duval dropped the receiver like it was burning his hand. "Think he believes it?"

Nagler shook his head once. "No, but it doesn't matter. It's the doubt. They'll eventually figure something out because the guard who told you about Ramirez should pay you a visit tonight or tomorrow to thank you for your service to the Dragony, so to speak, and you won't be there. We gain some time. You know why he said to watch your back?"

Duval stared back with a defiantly vacant look on his face.

"It was a warning, Dennis, that a friend of his would be dropping by."

"You mean ... wait, there is no guard. You told me about..."

"Exactly. But a guard will visit your cell, and we'll have him. And now we also have Carlton Dixon's phone."

"Damn it, Frank. You're using me, too. You probably killed me." Duval exhaled, relieved. "When do I leave?"

"Now." Nagler stood and opened a door letting in two officers wearing matching gray suits. "Thanks. You gotta understand, Dennis. If you stayed, you'd be dead. They killed Langdon and Dancer."

"Langdon and Dancer? Jesus. Those guys were my recruiters. And leadership killed them?"

"Yes," Nagler said, even if it wasn't exactly true. "Who else did they recruit."

"If I give you names, would that help me?"

"Won't hurt," Nagler said as he offered Duval pen and paper.

Duval took the pen and stared at the paper for a moment before writing a dozen names. He stood and the officers flanked him. "Where am I going?"

Nagler shared a flickering smile with the two officers. "Somewhere."

****

"Duval said 'waiting for what's next.' So, what's next?" Nagler asked.

"This notice," Ramirez said. "I found it on the dark web."

"Tuesday, noon. City memorial. Proper dress required. Be ready for honor."

"That's the public service for Mayor Ollivar." Nagler said. "Proper dress? Riot gear? Armed?"

Ramirez frowned. "I'd say yes."

"Why did the chief agree to hold it?" Nagler asked as he read the notice on the computer screen.

"Because he had no choice," said Lauren Fox as she entered the room. "It's not a memorial, but a coronation."

"What?" Nagler asked.

She held out a notice." This was in my mailbox when I went back to my office. It's a copy of the ordinance the city council is expected to pass on Monday."

Ramirez read the title: "'An ordinance to reform the duties of the city council of Ironton, New Jersey.' Reform how?"

"By taking away their statutory rights to power and making them an advisory council," Lauren said, taking the papers from Ramirez. "Um, here, see?"

She read, "'The council shall with this act rescind all powers of appointment, financial oversight, and legislative authority; with such powers being transferred to the mayor, whose term limits are hereby suspended, per Article 256-2006.' That means that Bill Weston is about to become mayor for life."

"What about elections?" he asked.

"Suspended," Lauren said. "Let me see," and she shuffled the papers. "Here. "'Public elections may be suspended under the emergency powers granted under Article 256-2006.'"

"What emergency?" Ramirez asked.

"The assassination of the mayor," Nagler said. "Holy Mother of God."

"They put this in motion in 2006, Frank. That meeting was not a drug deal but a coup," Lauren said.

"Is that article even legal?" Nagler asked.

"I'd say no, but…," Lauren said with an uncertain shrug. "Best guess? It exists until some party of standing takes it to court."

"Who has standing?" Ramirez asked.

"A taxpayer, business owner," Lauren said.

Nagler smiled. "Leonard. Who's his attorney?"

Lauren smiled back. "Calista. You didn't notice all the law books at Leonard's? That's where she's been, completing her degree and taking the bar exam."

"I thought you said she was off, well, being Calista?" Nagler glanced at Ramirez? "Did you know?"

"We kept it quiet, Frank. With the tentacles of the Dragony reaching everywhere, we thought the fewer who knew the better," Ramirez said.

"Even me?" Nagler asked, "Come on!"

Lauren took his face in her hands and kissed him. "You were busy, Frank."

"Yeah, all right," he said. "Maria, is that fake Nagler site still up?"

"Never went down."

"Good. I have a message for the Dragony. Meantime, let's find out how many councilors are on the payroll."

****

Nagler kicked a stone along the Warren Street sidewalk. The sound would have once got lost in the shuffle of walkers and the grumble of trucks stalled in traffic and shouts of kids cutting the back alleys to the soccer field. No one would have heard it. It was just a stone, bouncing along a cracked sidewalk, kicked maybe by another foot, then another, maybe sliding between bars of a drainage grate, its splash unheard.

But in the dark street emptied by explosion, the stone cracked along the silent dusty path coming to rest at the left post holding the billboard announcement of the glass towers. The face of the sign had been painted and repainted three or four times, Nagler guessed, until the pointed glass towers emerged from a smear of colors produced when Destiny painted her rainbow over the original drawing of the development, followed by a black, slashed DRAGONY RISING, then another layer or two of bright rainbow colors until what remained was a semi-circle of pastel yellows, reds, oranges, blues, greens and purples, layered over darkened, blurred streaks of the word, DRAGON.

For the first time, with sunlight streaming over the tops of nearby buildings, Nagler appreciated how much of the city block had been destroyed. Nine buildings had been removed and including the alley a space more than sixty feet deep had been cleared.

He had come to the site to record one more challenge to the Dragony. Instead, he'd caught a glimpse of the yellow kitchen chair still on the roof of the theater.

He recalled the photos that he had shown Randy Jensen. The whole gang, he remembered thinking, the whole Dragony gang.

"Damn it, I'm stupid," he muttered, and slapped a nearby wall. That's what Duval had said: "We were all there." Including one tall man in a rich guy's suit: Taylor Mangot II.

Nagler turned back to the police station in a trot and called Ramirez. "Maria I figured it out. Mangot was the target the night of the explosion. Randy our rent-a-cop ID's Mangot in the apartment and in a way put Jerry Langdon on the roof with a rifle. We can figure that out later. Remember Tony said Eduardo Tallem was in Blackwell Street looking at the roofline and asking if someone was in place? That had to be Langdon. I think they are planning to take out Mangot at that ceremony on Tuesday.

"Makes sense," Ramirez said. "We just got word that Langdon bought some .22 shells in Maryland. Caught on an in-store camera. Maybe he'll pass through a traffic cam. Either way, that can wait. You need to see what we found on the mayor's computer."

****

"Whatcha got?" Nagler asked as he limped into Ramirez's office.

"You trip again?" she asked.

Nagler frowned and pulled up a chair.

Ramirez opened her computer screen to show the start of an old-style video.

"This looks like it was recorded on an older camera, possibly on tape and converted to a digital file. It's really dark, badly recorded. The visuals are uneven, and the sound drops out from time to time. I cleaned it up some. But… Frank … It's that meeting, from 2006 in Dubin Place."

The still image on the computer showed Ollivar, Dancer, Carlton Dixon, Tallem, Bernie Langdon, Dan Thomson, Taylor Mangot II and a blond woman at his side, her face turned from the camera, possibly Rachel Pursel. The backs of heads filled the front bottom of the shot.

Ramirez hit play and the video jerked to life.

Ollivar spoke.

"All right, to finish up, here's where we are. Ray…where's Ray? Okay, put your hand up. Good. Ray's in the planning department. All our applications will go through him, and the inspections. They'll be the cleanest fucking inspections you've ever seen." A general laugh. "Same in the fire department. Duval is working on a few "accidents." He'll inspect them, of course, and declare them solved in such a way that the insurance companies will have no questions. We have real estate and legal people who will handle property transfers once the settlements are complete. The properties will be consolidated under a variety of companies controlled by Mr. Mangot. That's the first step. The police have others. Dancer?"

Dancer stepped forward and nodded. "Yeah, look. There's some guys we're gonna have to deal with. So, if you're working with someone one day, and the next week he ain't there, don't worry and don't ask questions. If ya get asked about it, play dumb. 'Sol died? I din't know that. Sorry to hear.' We don't need heroes. Just do your job."

Ollivar shifted to the front of the crowd again. "Thanks, Dancer. Heed that warning. Do your job. This is not a frontal assault on Ironton. This is a takeover. Quietly. With stealth, not brawn. It will require patience. It's the model we will use to move forward, town by town. Now, you all have heard about Article 256-2006? It is an article that will consolidate the power of Ironton's government in one person. Councilman Bill Weston – Stand, please Bill, thanks. – Bill is our first player, newly elected. He has introduced Article 256. It did not get a second, and therefore no vote. But we planned for that. It will be reintroduced, and gain a second, but fail again. Then again, and add another vote, and again, until one glorious year, it is passed into law and signed by the mayor of our choice."

Scattered applause.

Ollivar: "Thanks. Our leader Carlton Dixon has a few words."

A shuffling of bodies. Handshakes. Embraces. Raised fists.

"Thank you, Jesus. People think revolutions take place on the streets, are loud, violent things. Crowds with torches and bricks and flags threatening overthrow. That is theater. Revolution are ideas, formed and refined in meetings like this, in meetings your ancestors held a century or more ago to take power back from the new folks who wanted it. Your ancestors stood up and said, no. No to the pollution of their lives. No to the slippery degradation of their beliefs. So, they rose up and took back the purity of their lives."

Dixon help up one hand to silence the murmured approval. "Society and its creation, government, at times rot. Such is that time. But society is a pile of rocks strapped together with the dreams of believers like you all. It is time to seek out the dreams that have putrefied. Pull out the loose rock, weaken its hold on the faulty structure. Pull one and it leans, makes a hole; pull another and it shivers, another, and it falls. Find your rock, that weak crumbling rock, brothers and sisters, and pull."

A cheer filled the room. Dixon smiled and gently motioned for the cheering to cease.

"You will not see me often, but you will know the time has come when you hear me referred to as 'McSalley.' Think of it as a code. There will be an event of destruction. It will be a distraction, and while they try to solve it, our work will go on. Also know this: When this gentleman reappears in Ironton, it has begun."

Dixon pointed to the far corner as out of the shadows stepped McCarroll.

A cheer and an uncertain, "Oohh." Then another sound.

Ramirez shut off the video; McCarroll's blurred face shimmered on the computer screen.

"Is it really that easy?" she asked in a tortured whisper.

"Maybe," Nagler said as he stood. "But it hasn't happened yet. Play that last part again. I thought I heard something."

"What?"

"A voice. A familiar voice."

On the screen Dixon again pointed to McCarroll.

Over the "oohh," a voice: "Enjoy it. Yuz all dead men."

Mouth open, Ramirez stared at Nagler, then smiled.

"Was that…?"

"Jerry Langdon." Nagler tapped the computer screen. "We have two days. How can we use this?"

Ramirez spun to face the computer and after a few keystrokes, turned back. "The Internet is a wonderful thing."

****

Bill Weston was nervous. This was not going according to plan.

It was only nine a.m. and he had sweated through his good dress shirt and suit. The ceremony was scheduled for noon. The streets were filled. *Good I told my family to stay home.*

The meeting the night before when the transfer of power had been planned went so badly the council only managed to appoint him as acting mayor. Article 256-2006 never was raised for a vote. McSalley said not to worry because as acting mayor Weston could declare by emergency decree that the article was in effect.

The small council room last night had vibrated with the loud anger of the crowd, Weston thought as he sat in the mayor's seat at the center of the dais alone in the council chambers. A day later he could still feel the rage. The shouting had started before the meeting was called to order and he could not stop it. This was the seat he had wanted all that time; craved it, lusted for it and the power that Article 256-2006 bestowed on him. On him, and him alone. He would choose his successor, purge the disloyal, exercise the absolute authority to make of Ironton what he wanted, no longer Bill Weston, faceless accountant, party loyalist, but Bill Weston deal maker, Bill Weston king maker.

Bill Weston, king.

It was all he had ever wanted.

But the crowd last night would not shut up. They roared at him. He pounded the gavel and they roared more loudly. The signs! Kill the Dragony. Fight for Ironton. And they chants: "No more Dragons! No more Dragons!"

Weston tried to clear to room, ordered the police to clear the room, but the crowd filled every seat and the aisles, and were god knows how many rows deep in the hallways; surrounded he was. Trapped. The police did not respond. They were ordered to respond, and they stood against the wall, hands folded at their waists glaring at him. Didn't Dixon hand pick them? Our guys, our cops? Clear the room, damn it. As acting mayor, I order you to clear the room. They turned their backs; some officers even walked away – to cheers!

Now sitting alone, the rising sounds of a gathering crowd in the streets outside city hall penetrated the walls, pushed aside the silence. Weston cursed that video that popped up on the Internet. *They called me traitor. "Kill the traitor," they yelled. "Traitor." "Traitor." "Traitor."*

It was that fucking video. There was Ollivar practically anointing me ruler of Ironton. My baby daughter asked me what it meant. But my teen-age son sat across the table this morning with those dark threatening eyes.

Weston sat back in the wide, thick chair, closed his eyes, and took several deep, settling breaths.

"Fuck 'em all," he said. "The brotherhood is with me. It will be rough at the start, but they will adjust. They have no choice. This is a new day. The Dragony rising."

He smiled against the sounds of chaos rising outside the chamber's thick windows.

****

From the post office steps, Frank Nagler scanned the gathering mob with slitted eyes and a knot in his stomach. *This ain't gonna end well.*

He nodded when he spotted Jimmy Dawson crouched at the far end of the platform. *Back for the end of the world, Jimmy?*

The surging, howling mass bludgeoned its way into the open square before city hall. Words lost; just sounds, cries of the aggrieved, voices ripped with anger, rage seeking those who invited the rage. Signs waving. Angry, threatening signs, Kill the Dragony. Death to Traitors. The crazed stamping of a thousand feet. There were shovels, the symbols used two years before during the economic rally led by ex-mayor Rashad Jackson, who declared, "We know how to rebuild Ironton. We have the shovels," before being sent to jail for fraud the next year. *Was Jackson a part of this? Why not? It goes back for years.*

"Where do you think Langdon is?" he asked Maria Ramirez. She had just scouted the perimeter of the crowd.

"I'd say a rooftop, but we have officers on every building surrounding the plaza," she said. "So the target is Mangot?"

"Well, if I trust our crack rent-a-cop Randy Jensen," Nagler chuckled, "Taylor Mangot was in that fourth-floor apartment the night before the bombing and an armed Jerry Langdon was on the theater roof with the yellow chair." He shielded his eyes and gazed toward the theater. With the bombed buildings removed there was a clean line of sight from the chair to the platform. "Damn it. Get someone with a rifle to the car dealership. It overlooks the theater, and you can easily see the platform from that damn chair."

"Why's he doing it?" she asked.

A shivered shrug. "Don't know. Turn coat. Disaffected Dragony. Traitor to the cause. Savior. May depend on you ask."

Nagler heard the shrill urgency in his own voice. He jammed his hands on his hips and stared at the ground. Slow down, he told himself. Don't let the moment get too big or you lose it. He followed the roof-lines of the buildings surrounding the plaza and spotted the tree-topped ridge of Baker Hill to the south.

"Maria, get someone up to Baker Hill. If he changes tactics and weapons he might want a longer-range shot."

"Got it. You all here, Frank?" She squinted at Nagler, then looked over the pulsing, growling crowd.

"What if it's not Langdon?" he asked. What if it's someone else and it's not about shooting someone, but using an explosion to wipe out the crowd? What if we're wrong?"

A fight broke out near the platform. A rush of sign holders jammed at a line of helmeted, vested men, the Dragony security, who swung clubs at the attackers.

Stones, sticks and debris were thrown at the stage as the leaders of the rally mounted the platform from the rear, surrounded by armed guards, as the air filled with screams.

Taylor Mangot, Bill Weston, and Carlton Dixon huddled at the rear of the platform surrounded by armed guards. The honor guard, Nagler thought sourly. Weston tapped the mic on the podium and said, "Hello?!" which set off a roar of "Traitor, Traitor, Traitor," the growing cry matched by the rhythmic pounding of feet and shovel handles and signposts on the ground and fists against walls, a wave of anger that drove Weston two staggered steps back from the podium with his head turning, seeking aid.

Nagler called Sergeant Hanrahan. "Bob, get your guys in there. We gotta get control of this."

From the alleys and side streets lines of police in riot gear with shields wedged into the melee, compressing the bodies even more as the police drove the screaming crowd away from the stage.

A second wave of protestors slipped through the police line and rushed the Dragony defense line, knocking some to the ground as a cheer went up. Two men jumped to the stage. One ran at Weston and received a rifle blow to the head. The second crashed into the podium, sending the mic to the platform casting a screeching electronic cry through the plaza, a shriek so loud and piercing the crowd as one shuddered.

Two guards on the stage grabbed the protester, who in the struggle pulled off the helmet of one of the officers, before being pummeled to the platform.

"It's Langdon. Maria, on the stage. Drawing his weapon."

"You go left. I'll go right," she yelled and jumped onto the crowd.

As she ran, Ramirez picked up a broken stick and at the foot of the platform smashed Langdon's legs, knocking him to his knees. After the blow, she tripped over a fallen body. "I know you, you fucking dyke," Langdon looking down yelled. "My brother hated you." Nagler tackled Langdon just as he fired. Ramirez fell back.

Nagler grabbed Langdon's hair and smashed his head against the wooden platform twice. "Bastard," Nagler yelled.

Langdon grinned. "Hey, Detective. Yuz got it wrong. I ain't the show today." He tipped his head to the left. "She is."

Nagler turned and saw Rachel Pursel pull off her helmet and step behind Taylor Mangot and with her left arm around his throat twice smack his head with the butt of her pistol, forcing him to his knees.

"Rachel, how the hell? Your arm?! No!"

"Sorry, Frank. Don't you know acting when you see it? This has to end."

Dixon burst through the bodies on the platform. Rachel Pursel calmly fired three shots into his knees and abdomen.

"Maybe you'll live," she spit at Dixon. "Just maybe."

Nagler crawled to his knees, his bad ankle screaming in pain. He tried to stand and stumbled to one knee. "Don't. We've got these guys. Rachel."

Mangot twisted to wrestle from her grip. "No, you don't Frank. Yeah, they'll go to jail, lose their money. Haven't you learned? The Dragony doesn't die but evolves. It's evolving right now." She pulled Mangot back upright by his hair. "But I'll never get the chance again to be an avenging angel. Besides, I'm already dead, remember?" She leaned toward Mangot. "This is how you did Sol, right?" And she shot Taylor Mangot II in the back of his head.

She aimed the pistol at the remaining guards on the stage, and they stood in place while Ironton police officers scrambled onto the platform shouting instructions.

Rachel Pursel turned back to Nagler, wearing a smile of triumph and dark sadness. "I'm done." And with a wink, she put the pistol in her mouth and pulled the trigger.

CODA: Anna

Six months later.

"This place doesn't smell so bad," Lauren Fox said, tracing the line of the muddy water rippling across the Old Iron Bog.

Frank Nagler laughed. "It's early, and we just had a couple days of rain." Wait till August and a week of ninety-degree days. The stink is so bad you can walk on it."

Lauren nodded in appreciation. "Think they'll come back? Is there anything left of the Dragony?"

Nagler leaned back.

"Bill Weston went to jail, along with Dennis Duval and Jerry Langdon. Dancer skipped town. Talked his way out of that hospital, and as far as I know, went to Nova Scotia where he can hate fish. Carlton Dixon's trial begins in a month. He's finally out of the jail hospital. Rachel Pursel really messed him up. He's a true believer. As they put him in the ambulance, he whispered to me. 'Revolution is messy.' He was smiling." Nagler shook his head.

"Any word on McCarroll?" she asked.

A guffaw. "No. He stepped back into the mist. But I expect somehow that one night I'll turn a corner and he'll be standing there saying, 'We need to talk, Mr. Noiglar.'"

"Any idea why Mayor Ollivar left that video on his computer? One last piece of the old Dragony, I guess."

"He didn't."

"What?" She turned.

"Mahala Dixon did. Got it from Jerry Langdon. Seems they were working together." He laughed. "She was right – she was 'undercover.' She sent the video to Ollivar and he left it on the computer, I don't know, just so soured by it all. He must have guessed we'd find it. Mahala turned on her old man in the end after starting this whole thing when she begged me to get him out of jail. She was the best actor of them all."

"They find her?"

"Traced her to Florida, then lost her. She hooked up with her mother, who was Argentinian. Probably left the country."

Lauren stood and wrapped the flannel blanket around her shoulders and wiggled her bare toes in the cool mud. She climbed back onto the hood of the car and ran a hand across his bare chest.

"Quite a year, Franky, I'd say."

"You would, would you?"

"Yes." She straddled his hips. "One time on the mayor's desk, a first, and now on the hood of a car in the Old Iron Bog. What could top that?"

****

"Are you done with your tea, Sister Katherine? They're expecting us."

"I know, Jerome," the old nun said as she turned her wheelchair away from the open window. "I was daydreaming, which is all that's left for this old woman. Thinking about my sister Sarah. I was so small when she left home, but I thought she was so beautiful. I was eternally grateful when Calista brought me those photos."

"Photos, ma'am?

"Yes, in that folder on my desk. Please bring that. I must sign those papers."

Jerome retrieved the folder and scanned the papers and photos. "She was beautiful, Sister. But so are you." He handed her one of the photos of two girls sitting on the bank of maybe a river or a pond. "Where was this taken?"

Sister Katherine brushed the faces in the photo with a finger. "This was a year before they took her," she said, her voice wet and halting. "It was Hurd Park along the pond that formed when the creeks merged. About this time of the year. She had come for a visit from Paterson where she worked in the mills." She tipped her head and closed her eyes. One aching sigh. "They killed her, Jerome. You know that? She brought them down, but it was not worth her life." She kissed the photo and offered the sign of the cross. "She would have been Anna's age."

Jerome collected the photo and the file from her hands. "Bless you, Sister,"

****

Destiny leaned across the end of the scaffold and looped the metal eye hole over the hook secured in the wall.

"Don't cover it up," Calista yelled from the sidewalk.

Destiny slipped her legs between the metal bars as she sat on the planking. "You know it's not done, just sketched and outlined in color. I need two more weeks. The idea is to reveal it when Barry's opens. That was your idea."

Calista chuckled. "I know, Leonard's just anxious. Right, Leonard?"

At her side, Leonard also laughed. "No more anxious than you."

Destiny climbed off the scaffolding. "What gave you the idea for this canopy?"

"When we talked to our architect about the renovation of the new building, she suggested we remove the old powerhouse in that alley and demolish the walkway that was attached to the buildings at the third floor to open up the space to sunlight and air. She suggested a metal archway frame to support a brick structure," Leonard said. "Barry can use the area for outside seating."

Destiny embraced Leonard. "I'm grateful for the chance, my friend. So proud to see you walking again. When will she be here?"

"Maybe ten minutes," Calista said. "If we do this right Sister Katherine will already be here."

"Paper's all signed?" Destiny asked.

"Yes!" Calista shouted, "Yes." She kissed Leonard. "We gained custody rights a week ago. You know this is why I became a lawyer. Just for this, to dig her out of a system that had lost track of her." She hugged Leonard's arm. "We found her again, Leonard. We found her."

"So glad," Destiny. "What's left?"

"Test results and more paperwork," Calista said. "Getting blood from my father proved difficult because he wanted to trade it for a reduced sentence. Randolph Garrettson, always a deal maker. It wasn't enough that he raped me. Feds said, no deal. In the end he backed off." She rolled her eyes to the sky and wiped away tears. "The past... so hard to put away."

Destiny surrounded Calista and Leonard in a hug. "That's what we're here for today. Hey. Sister's here."

They turned to the street as Jerome pulled the black SUV to the curb.

"Hey, Captain," Destiny yelled as Maria Ramirez slid from the front seat and opened the rear door to help Sister Katherine from the vehicle to her chair which Jerome had rolled up.

"That's a lovely piece of canvas, young lady," Sister Katherine said as she hugged Destiny. "Going abstract are we, Leonard?"

"Why wait?" Destiny said, as she crossed to the scaffold and pulled on the long rope, releasing the canvas.

"I thought..." Leonard began.

"One surprise at a time," Destiny said and waved her arm at the mural. An outline of a rainbow sky rose above a dozen sketched but incomplete faces. "It's not done," she said as she kneeled beside Sister Katherine. "Thanks for the photo. Sarah and you will be at the far right, and then there will be the workers and the women and the lovers and the builders, everyone who made Ironton, the celebration of us all. There's even a spot for the yellow kitchen chair."

Sister Katherine kissed Destiny's cheek.

Captain Maria Ramirez touched the sister's shoulder. "Destiny had started this piece at the community center. But it was demolished after the fire and Leonard suggested this site. It's perfect. And Barry's going to use the chair in the new diner."

A car horn at the curb had them all turning. Frank Nagler jumped out and waved as Lauren Fox and a girl stepped from the back seat.

Calista ran to the girl and touched her cheek and then embraced her. "Come."

She was tall, even in flat shoes, Thin, a face like white porcelain; her eyes, once dark and hollow, gleamed with life in the sunlight. She danced, stepped lightly; smiled, open to the world.

The girl kneeled beside Sister Katherine and bit her lower lip as she softly giggled out a tearful cry.

"You could be her, young lady," Sister Katherine said as she brushed a finger over the girl's eyes and cheek. "You could be Sarah."

The girl kissed the nun's cheek. "Nothing stays bad forever," she whispered.

Calista kneeled opposite the girl.

"This is my daughter, Sister. The girl you saved. This is Anna."

*****

Continue reading for a free preview of *The Red Hand*, the Frank Nagler origin story and the prequel to *The Swamps of Jersey*, the book that launched the Frank Nagler mysteries.

THE RED

A Frank Nagler Mystery

HAND

MICHAEL STEPHEN DAIGLE

The Red Hand

By

Michael Stephen Daigle

PART ONE

The long dry season

Of course they were red, the handprints. The color of blood, red; the color of life, dripping between the hollow cracks of the siding. Leaking, crimson, chosen carefully. I'm here, the killer said, bragging. Try to find me. — Jimmy Dawson.

CHAPTER ONE

Someone is experimenting in death

The first mark had appeared after the third death: A red handprint dripping paint slapped on a wall of the busted-up hotel where cab driver Felice Sanchez had been found dead. Underneath, "HAND OF DEATH" splotched in an awkward scrawl.

Is that a joke? Detective Frank Nagler thought when he saw the mark for the first time. Pretty crude, but you might be in a hurry to leave your calling card after you killed a woman. But he wondered: Where were the marks left after the deaths of Nancy Harmon and Jamie Wilson, the deaths that were now believed to be the first in this cycle?

Police Chief Robert Mallory had ordered the markings scrubbed from the wall, after the police work had been completed: Photos, samples, measurements, interviews; the victim's family, don't you know. Then he changed his mind: Who would know to place that mark at that exact spot? That made it a statement, a claim of ownership. Instead, the chief ordered the buildings with the marks to be included in daily foot patrols. "They'll fade in time," he had said. "The public will stop paying attention." Was that a taunt, a challenge to the killer? Nagler wondered, the chief in fact saying, *"We know you've been here. We will get you."*

Of course, the public did not forget, but turned two of the marks — at the hotel and the old train station — into instant shrines with bundles of flowers, photos of missing friends and family, and hand-made posters.

For Nagler, staring at the red mark on the hotel had been the door that had cracked open, exposing a dark and sinister place, but the call that a body had been found near the downtown train station was the moment that his new job became real.

307

He'd been a detective for a month following another round of police department layoffs. He had investigated a burglary or two, probed a potential arson that destroyed an empty house, broken up a few husband-wife fights, but he felt he was running just to keep up, slogging through the everyday stuff of what he didn't know, what he couldn't imagine, one hand outstretched to feel the fog.

And now, ready or not, he was learning the awful lessons of murder firsthand.

"Where is she?" he asked a patrolman standing sentry at the dark edge of the train station.

"Half-way down," the patrolman replied, his voice a drip in a tin can echo. He tipped his head to the left. "It's bad, Detective. Just sayin'."

"Thanks," Nagler replied, trying to sound confident. *How bad?*

Dispatch had said she was carried or dragged to the train station.

Nagler winced.

And then, if there wasn't enough for Nagler to absorb, Medical Examiner Walter Mulligan forcefully said this: "Someone is experimenting in death," while leaning over the body of the latest victim.

That's when Nagler felt the ground shift and a tiny hollow spot opened in his heart. We're supposed to be dispassionate, professional, he reminded himself. Try as he might, that hole never closed.

He ran a shaky hand through his sweat-soaked hair and squinted into a golden haze of a rooftop spotlight across the railroad tracks from where the body was found, and then nodded to Mulligan, trying to appear that he knew what that meant. *My first murder case, and it's an experiment in death. Oh, man.*

It wasn't the statement alone that startled Nagler. It was the chilling tone, an end-of-the-world whisper, a voice inside a dark cave. And the certainty. *How does he know that?*

Three women, murdered, apparently weeks, possibly months, apart, killed in different ways, in different parts of the city; different jobs, lives disconnected from each other.

And now a fourth.

THE IRONTON RIPPER, an out-of-town newspaper headline had screamed when the third death had been announced.

Nagler absorbed the scene: Dim lights from the train station platform, silhouetted cops, shadows shifting, lighted then gone; faint grinding of late night city noise, bugs buzzing, heat as thick as syrup.

And she lay dead, slashed, exposed, dragged, discarded.

Crap, Nagler thought, shaking off the pity, seeking resolve. Where is this going?

Any doubt Nagler had about what was ahead dissolved when he looked into Mulligan's face. He was wearing *that* face, the one experienced officers had warned about, a mix of resignation about the need for his services and a dark anger, a stay-out-of-my-way face.

"This death is related to the others," Mulligan pronounced after he pulled Nagler aside. "Examine her body closely."

"So that's the experiment?" Nagler asked, nodding at the detail that according to the reports he had read, had been present previously. "That makes him a serial killer?" he asked, barely aware of what that term meant.

"A technical term for academics," Mulligan said, as he shook his head in disgust, and then smiled, trying to encourage the new detective. "We have four deaths, Frank. Just follow the evidence. Don't worry about the meaning yet." He reached for Nagler's arm. "But this is a detail you should keep to yourself. Knowing it, and the time to release it, could be critical to catching our killer."

Nagler nodded and turned to speak with the first patrolman on the scene.

"Who found her?" Nagler asked.

The patrolman pointed to a man clinging to the side of a patrol car. "Our drunken friend."

Oh, great. Nagler approached the drunk. The man shifted, then leaned, then tipped back, arms folded, head nodding.

"Hey, thanks for calling us," Nagler said.

The man squeezed his face into a grimace and through squinting eyes, looked up at Nagler. "I didn't call. Just yelled. Your guy was driving past the train station and stopped. Hurray for me." He tipped his head to the right and closed his eyes. "I'm tired, man."

"Okay, where were you headed?" Nagler asked, admiring the man's existential gallantry.

"An old shed, down in the rail yard. Got a...got a sleeping bag there."

Nagler smiled. "Bet you do. Know what? We'll put you up for the night."

"Naa, that's okay. Someone will steal my bag, and my, um, stuff, if I don't... Maybe I can get a drink?" He leaned forward and nearly toppled.

"Ahh, no." Nagler pushed him upright.

The man wiped his nose on his filthy jacket sleeve and shook his head again. "Too bad."

"Yeah." Softly. "Yeah." Firmly: "Look at me."

"What?

"Look at me. Got a couple questions. Did you touch her?"

"Who? Nooooo. Never. She's dead, man. She was bleedin' and all. No. Shit, I didn't touch her." Shrugged. "Okay, kicked her shoe to see if she was, maybe... naw... dead." He jabbed out his right foot and nearly fell.

Nagler shook his head. "Maybe...if she had some money on her?"

The man shrugged then wiped his nose. "Maybe."

"Did you see anyone with her?"

The man closed his face as if the question was too hard.

He was fading, Nagler knew. Last chance. "Hey, buddy. Was anybody with her?"

The drunk grabbed a handful of his hair and yanked on it. Irritated. "I'm thinkin'." He glanced up at Nagler and then off to the left.

"A guy. Ran off that way." He waved in all directions. "'Hey,' I yelled. 'You left your friend.' Then I looked at her and she was pretty dead."

"Big guy? Fat? Short? Skinny?"

"Shit, man, I don't know. Little dude. Seemed so…" Voice fading. "Little dude…I…guess. But he was far away."

****

Nagler hunched along the dark street and parking lot following the blood trail back to the Chinese restaurant on Warren, apparently the original crime scene. A crime tech photographed the blood drops, exploding light into the darkness. "Lotta blood," the tech said. "Man."

Why carry her to the train yard?

At the restaurant, a shapeless pool of blood filled the sidewalk a few feet from the door to the China Song restaurant, and a smeared trail of blood leaked off toward Blackwell and the train station for a few yards and then stopped at a point the assailant must have picked her up. A blotch of blood was centered on the side window of the corner phone booth, as if the assailant had staggered for a moment under Chen's weight.

Pretty strong for a little guy, if our drunk friend was right, Nagler thought. But the victim was a small woman, so I guess anything is possible. It reminded Nagler of one of those nature specials where a lion kills a zebra and carries it off to be devoured later. A hunt, a kill. A trophy. *Of course. That's what Mulligan meant.*

The restaurant lights were still on and Nagler saw the face of a man peeking around a red pillar inside the second, inner door. A grocery bag of packaged food had been spilled on the sidewalk, and a purse leaned against the curb.

A bloody spot dotted the brick wall. A second medical officer took samples.

"Related?" Nagler asked.

"Seems so, from what the dishwasher told us," Patrol Sergeant Bob Hanrahan said. He had run from the City Hall police station a half-block away and secured the scene. "She apparently stepped out of the restaurant, carrying that shopping bag. The attacker rammed her into the wall. She was probably stunned by the blow to her head, staggered and then was stabbed."

Hanrahan nodded to Nagler. "It's your scene now."

Nagler examined the oversized purse and found a locked blue canvas overnight deposit bag containing what felt like two or three inches of bills. "Probably not a robbery." He found a wallet with a driver's license.

Joan Chen, thirty-one. Weston Street, Ironton.

Nagler felt his head spin, exploding with details almost faster than he could examine them.

"You alright, Frank?" Hanrahan asked.

"It's like I just took the plastic wrapper off my 'Crime 101' manual and the killer is on to volume two." He screwed up his face and glanced at Hanrahan and then at the ground. "I want to do this right."

Hanrahan grabbed Nagler's shoulder. "Slow it all down. We know some stuff. It'll come."

Nagler nodded.

Hanrahan said, as he shrugged toward the restaurant door, "That guy's the dishwasher, said he stays after closing to clean the place for the next day. She's the manager and was going to the bank to make a deposit. He was locking the doors when someone came out of the street, slammed her into the wall, and stabbed her. He said he ran back into the main part of the restaurant to grab the pistol they keep behind the bar, and when he came back, she was gone, as was the assailant. He said the attacker had his head covered, wore dark clothes, but the attack was fast."

"Did he say anything about the attacker's size?" Nagler asked. "Our witness at the train station, as drunk as he is, said it could be a small person."

Hanrahan shook his head. "He said it happened really fast."

"Any other witnesses?" Nagler asked. "Customers?"

"No. Place closed at nine-thirty, two hours ago. Dishwasher said Chen's habit was to eat a light supper, close out the daily receipts and hit the bank on her way home."

"Weston's on the other side of town. She must have a car parked somewhere," Nagler said as he scanned the street. "Bet she left at about the same time each night. Someone who knows that pattern..." He sighed. "This could be the first one of these that makes sense. She married?"

****

These, Nagler thought bitterly. How much more impersonal can I make murder?

He sat in the far table at Barry's diner the next morning and watched the morning crowd lean into their coffee and eggs, the hum of chatter swirling with the dense, sticky air. He had read the files on the other three deaths after his wife Martha had fallen asleep. He had brushed a stray hair from her cheek as she slept, and then shook away the worry.

He sipped his coffee. These deaths. Four dead women. Strangers? We're supposed to look for connections, patterns.

One is random, or an accident.

Two makes you wonder.

Three becomes heavy.

Four brings fear.

He mulled the details: Jamie Wilson, thirty-two, a secretary; Nancy Harmon, thirty-seven, a doctor; Felice Sanchez, thirty-five, a cab driver; and now Joan Chen, thirty-one, a restaurant manager.

The records showed all the women seemed to be approximately the same height—five-foot-four or five. Harmon and Wilson had been reduced to skeletons when they had been discovered, subject to predation and the unseasonable heat. Both Sanchez and Chen weighed between one-hundred-ten and one-hundred-twenty pounds. So, small, he thought. Smallish. He closed his eyes, trying to capture an image that might offer some comparison. No. He smiled. He had conjured the image of his wife Martha lying naked on their bed. Martha was five-six, and he never asked her weight.

He mulled that detail. Smallish. Could be overpowered with enough force and surprise by an equally small person.

How?

We have no clue about why.

Jamie Wilson had been found in the Old Iron Bog, and Nancy Harmon in an empty warehouse near her medical office. Felice Sanchez was found in the abandoned Wilson Hotel on North Sussex.

All three had been killed days or weeks before their bodies had been discovered.

And now Joyce Chen, attacked in the open at her restaurant, on a public street, and with a witness, then dragged to the train yard and discovered on the same night. That one was brazen. Why now, and why change the pattern? Getting bolder? Or a different killer?

Nancy Harmon had been declared missing after a colleague and several patients who found the office locked at the time of their appointment called the department, the report said. At first, her death had been considered a suicide.

Jamie Wilson's family had called after she missed a weekend family reunion. The cab company called the department after they found Felice Sanchez's cab on a back alley off Richman Avenue with the keys in the ignition.

To the public they were all random, isolated deaths.

And that's what they had remained. Nagler stopped reading and wondered how much the changes in the department had affected the investigation. Names on the reports were those of officers who had retired when the department downsized; each previous case had been assigned to a different officer.

He circled the officers' names on the various reports. He'd have to chase them down.

What tied them all together was the detail of their deaths the department would not reveal, something that was collectively decided only the killer would know. When do we use that? Nagler wondered.

They had discovered Joan Chen's white, late model Dodge in the ramshackle central parking lot along the river, the site of the old iron mill that had dominated the city for a hundred and fifty years. When it was torn down, the site became a shopping center with a drive-in movie theater, and when *that* was torn down it became a parking lot, trash trapped in a bent chain-link fence, potholes and crushed concrete steps, a symbol of Ironton's economic demise.

The parking lot was across Warren Street from the restaurant, so it made sense her car was there, probably in the same spot she used every working day. Her car had not been touched, nor had her home, half of a duplex in a neighborhood that was a buffer between the old workers ghetto where Nagler grew up and the nicer neighborhood where Nagler and his wife Martha now lived. Chen lived alone, her neighbors said.

Nagler stirred the cold coffee and stared at the newspaper headline.

"DEATH TOLL MOUNTS!!"

"Ironton police are at a loss to explain the recent deaths of four city women. The latest victim, Joan Chen, was found in the Ironton train station after she had been brutally attacked at her place of employment, the China Song restaurant, less than a block from the police station. Police had no comment on how Chen was taken to the station, or why.

Marion Demint, the owner of the Ironton Laundry around the corner from the murder scene, said she was scared.

"Why can't the police find this person? I don't feel safe."

"And the red handprints!" said commuter Ron Allen. "What's with the red handprints? It's a gang sign, I'll bet. City's going to hell."

Nagler dropped the paper on the table and nodded to Barry for a refill.

Hysteria much? he thought.

Who wrote the story?

Jimmy Dawson. Wasn't he in sports? What's he doing writing crime stories?

"Tough stuff, hey, Frankie?" Barry asked.

Barry's was the survivor in downtown Ironton, an eatery that had weathered all the ups and downs. It hadn't always been called Barry's, but no one, not even the current owner, whose name *was* Barry, knew when it got that name or who named it.

"Yeah, it is," Nagler replied. "I wish we knew more."

Barry leaned over. "Me, too. I see customers with guns under their jackets, talking about where they can buy more guns. I don't like it. Something's gonna happen."

He turned then stopped.

"Hey, Frank. If I find a red handprint on my front window does that means I'm next?"

Nagler smiled and shook his head.

"No, Barry, no one is coming after you for Tony's lunch special."

"Hey, Frank," Tony the cook yelled back. "I heard that."

But Nagler asked himself: What came first, the deaths or the handprints? Where they a warning or a sign of some declaration of victory?

*****

The Red Hand is available at the following retailers:
Amazon - Barnes & Noble - Kobo - Walmart
Buy your copy today!

ABOUT THE AUTHOR

Michael Stephen Daigle is a writer who lives in New Jersey with his family. He was born in Philadelphia, one of five "Navy brats" who lived in several Northeast U.S. states and is an award-winning journalist.

Other books in his Frank Nagler Mystery series are, "The Swamps of Jersey", "A Game Called Dead" and "The Weight of Living; with a fifth book already in progress.

Aside from this series he has also published an electronic collection of short stories, "The Resurrection of Leo," and a story about teenager Smitty, baseball and growing up, "The Summer of the Homerun."

Smitty is the hero of a work-in-progress, entitled, since these things must have titles, "Three Rivers."

Another work in progress is a generational novel called "That Time the World Visited Mount Jensen, Maine."

Samples of his work are available at

www.michaelstephendaigle.com

OTHER TITLES FROM IMZADI PUBLISHING

Gabriel's Wing

The Rain Song

Going to California

I Found My Heart in Prague

The Hedgerows of June

The Other Vietnam War

Vietnam Again

Staring Into the Blizzard

Who Shot the Smart Guy at the Blackboard?

My Pilot: A Story of War, Love, and ALS

Black Market Bones

Frank Nagler Mystery Series (Reading Order)

The Red Hand

The Swamps of Jersey

A Game Called Dead

The Weight of Living

Dragony Rising

www.imzadipublishing.com

A NOTE FROM IMZADI PUBLISHING

We hope you have enjoyed reading *Dragony Rising,* the 5th book in the award winning *Frank Nagler Mystery Series* by Michael Stephen Daigle, along with the preview of *The Red Hand;* Frank Nagler's origin story.

You, the reader, are the backbone of the publishing industry; without you our industry simply would not exist. As such, we depend upon you and your valuable feedback. Would you like more Frank Nagler mysteries?

If so, please take a few moments to leave this book a rating on Amazon and a few words telling us your thoughts on the book too. A review does not need to be long, just a few words will do and we appreciate and read every single one.

Happy reading!

Made in the USA
Middletown, DE
07 April 2024

52539230R00196